SMASH & GRAB

Also by Amy Christine Parker

Gated
Astray

SMASH & GRAB

Amy Christine Parker

Random House New York

Text copyright © 2016 by Amy Christine Parker
Jacket photo copyright © 2016 by Adrianna Williams/Corbis

All rights reserved. Published in the United States by Random House Children's Books, a division of Penguin Random House LLC, New York.

Random House and the colophon are registered trademarks of Penguin Random House LLC.

Visit us on the Web! randomhouseteens.com

Educators and librarians, for a variety of teaching tools, visit us at RHTeachersLibrarians.com

Library of Congress Cataloging-in-Publication Data is available upon request.
ISBN 978-0-553-53382-8 (trade) — ISBN 978-0-553-53383-5 (ebook)

Printed in the United States of America
10 9 8 7 6 5 4 3 2 1
First Edition

Random House Children's Books supports the
First Amendment and celebrates the right to read.

For my family, with all my love.

1

Lexi

I'm breathless by the time we reach the helipad on top of the US Bank Tower—exactly 1,018 feet above LA. The city sprawls out beneath us in all directions, a wide carpet of neon and white lights that dazzles me after the relative dark of the stairwell. It is heady stuff, seeing the world from this high, dizzying . . . and exactly what I need right now.

I laugh a little. My father was arrested this morning for a bank-fraud scheme that I still don't completely understand, and *I'm* the one preparing to jump off a building. I look over at my big brother, Quinn, and he's laughing, too—probably having the same thought I am—that this is crazy, but a strangely Lexi-appropriate way to cheer ourselves up. He wouldn't be up here if it weren't for me. He says yes to my schemes because he likes to think of himself as my protector. I'm glad he does. I wouldn't have nearly as much fun doing this on my own.

Our tight band of friends and fellow adrenaline junkies are gathered around Quinn and me—Oliver, Leo, and Elena. Five of us altogether. Elena's sister, Whitney, is the only one missing—if

1

you don't count Derek, that is, and I don't. Whitney had to distract the night guard while we sneaked into the stairwell, and she'll drive the car to pick us up after we've gone over the edge. Derek's not here, because I didn't invite him. After tonight he won't be part of our little group anymore. Not that he really was to begin with. Just because we've been dating doesn't earn him a permanent place with us. I feel a twinge of guilt about it and maybe something else, something more difficult to pinpoint, but I don't want to dwell on that now. Not here. All in all, the vibe is right for this jump. And somehow the number for our group is back to normal. It feels decidedly lucky. We all feel it, I can tell.

Everyone's eyes are bright, their cheeks flushed. The impending free fall has them revved, has *me* revved. I can feel my whole body humming with a high that comes only from doing something outrageous, a high that most of the ground dwellers below us never experience. Alcohol and drugs can't touch it. It's 100 percent pure adrenaline and it's amazing. Addictive. No matter what maneuver we have planned—this jump or the motorcycle race we pulled off in the spillway last month—the thrill never weakens. These moments are the only times I ever feel truly alive.

It's the same for all of us, even Quinn, though he won't usually admit it and complains whenever I come up with some new dare. It's probably the main reason why we're all friends in the first place. It's how we choose to deal with problems. We don't have to face them if we keep moving fast enough, if things are exciting enough. If we keep distracting ourselves.

Leo shuts the stairwell door, so we're stuck out here. The only exit now is jumping. The slam of the closing door makes me wince, reminding me of this morning and the way our front door banged against the foyer wall as the FBI agents invaded our house, one after another rushing in, hands on their guns, eyes scanning every inch of our home like our whole lives were suspect and not just my father's. My heart was thundering in my chest then, too, especially as they dragged my father out into the yard, morning stubble shadowing his chin, his skin an ashen, guilty shade. I hated the way it felt in that moment, like my heart might start contracting—charley-horsing—and never stop.

My father's in jail. Right now. Somewhere down there, in a cell. If he's convicted, he'll be in there until I'm his age, maybe longer.

I shake my head. I don't want to think about that anymore. That's why I'm up here. Quinn, too.

Keep moving; distract yourself and the hurt you feel will fade, I tell myself.

"The security cameras are still down, but we don't have much time," Quinn says, adjusting his gear one last time. My brother is a computer genius. He hacked the security from his laptop a week ago so that tonight's feed is of old footage. If they figure out we were up here, there won't be any recorded evidence. We are basically ghosts.

"This wind is ridiculous!" shouts Leo, my best friend in the whole world, his eyes squinted against it and steadily tearing up. His freckles are pronounced against his pale face.

3

"We need to get on one of the outcroppings over there to make sure we clear the building," I say, gesturing to the right.

Leo lifts the camera he's carrying and looks through the lens, adjusts it, then looks again and starts snapping pictures of us: first Quinn, looking like Jason Bourne in his all-black clothes, and then Oliver and Elena, who are on the edge of the helipad platform with their arms around each other. "Your turn," he says as he turns his camera on me.

I put my helmet under one arm and strike a pose. The rhinestones on my fingernails catch the light from the flash and look like twinkling stars for a second. I decided a while ago to embrace my inner bling monster—the Jimmy Choo–wearing, Prada bag–carrying creature my mother raised me to be. As much as rebelling against anything that makes her happy appeals to me, I actually love all that stuff. Shallow or not, I don't care. The girlie glamour is too enticing, the dress-up fun of it. When I was little, I was obsessed with the girls in James Bond movies— sexy and beautiful, but tough, too. Doing things like this jump makes me feel like one of them. Invincible.

"You're beautiful," Leo says, not a trace of lust evident in his voice. This makes the compliment that much more flattering because there's no agenda attached to it. Plus, it doesn't make me want to squirm the way it would if, say, Derek said it. *When* he said it.

"Good," I say, beaming.

"All right, enough pictures, let's go!" As usual, Oliver is amped, ready. This is especially true tonight, since his father's construction company just finished the renovation of this building. That's part of why we chose it. And because I'm a sucker for an architecturally distinct locale. It infuses the jump with a little extra finesse. Oliver has spent most of his life under the strict eye of his father, a man so rigid and physically abusive that he drove Oliver's mom back to her native Japan and powerful enough that he managed to maintain custody of his kids. By sneaking to the top of a building his father helped renovate, Oliver is defying him without actually having to do it to his face and risk his father's anger.

"Chill out. Rushing means mistakes," I say. I haven't pored over building plans, structural details, weather conditions, and city maps just to leap off the instant Oliver decides he's ready. "We do it as planned, and that means climbing down to the ledge and *then* flying."

Tonight's maneuver is my baby, my contribution to the BAM (short for *badass maneuvers*) book we keep, an adrenaline-soaked alternative to a slam book, where we record all our adventures— documented meticulously with Leo's photos and Elena's near-poetic descriptions of them. We started it to cheer up Oliver after his parents' divorce, a sort of joke that over the years became something bigger. Now we have more than twenty pages of capers, most of them directly related to crappy moments in one or all of our lives. Like my dad's arrest. Or Leo's mom's breakdown.

I put on my helmet and motion for everyone to follow me toward the far corner of the pad. We get on our stomachs and, one by one, lower ourselves to the narrow shelf below that borders the whole building, coming to points every so often so that from the sky it must look a bit like a starburst. The point nearest us is the one we need to use—far from the stairway flanking the opposite side of the building and the other obstructions. Landing on them would be deadly.

Together we climb onto the lip that separates the shelf from the open sky, arms out like tightrope walkers' poles, the wind prodding at our backs, threatening to unbalance us. The streets below are mostly quiet this late at night, but there are still cars here and there, slowly making their way toward the freeway, the drivers totally unaware that we are up here watching them. Seeing the rest of the world from this high is freeing because it's too far away to feel real.

"Say 'BAM,'" Leo says as he snaps another picture that includes, I'm sure, the giant billboard with an advertisement for Left Coast Construction, Oliver's dad's company, plainly visible in the distance. Oliver will probably be tempted to hang it up in his room. The flash is blinding and I sway a bit.

"Hey, cut it out, man," Oliver grumbles, struggling to balance. Elena latches on to his arm to keep from falling. He looks down at her and his expression softens. "How about a kiss, Lanie? For luck." He pulls her closer, leans in to nuzzle her neck. This thing developing between them is about a year old and more intimate than I think any of us expected. Watching them feels odd, wrong. I'm not sure I like it. If it goes bad, it'll mess up our group. Elena's not good at staying faithful, though I think with Oliver she's trying. Still, the odds are against them.

Elena rolls her eyes. "I guess if it's in the name of luck . . ." She tilts her head up and presses her lips to his as Leo takes another picture.

I look from Quinn to Leo to Oliver to Elena.

It's time.

When the moment is right, I can always feel it. I look over the edge, hold a hand in the air, and judge the wind. *Yep. Perfect.*

"Let's do this. I'm going first, okay?" I say.

"No. No deal. I go first. Or we don't go," Quinn says in his best big-brother-in-charge voice, all low and firm and businesslike.

I don't fight him. He's the one guy I let tell me what to do. He has my back no matter what. The only one in our family who does. My father sure doesn't. Even if I didn't already know that, today makes it glaringly obvious. And my mother is the poster girl for bad decision-making. She said as much when the FBI agents pulled my father outside this morning. "Marrying you was a mistake," she told Dad right up close, their noses nearly touching, her voice loud enough that all the neighbors gawking at the spectacle from the sidewalk could hear. Her face was pinched, her eyes streaming tears. "How could I have been so stupid?" The question isn't new. She asks it every time she and my father have a fight. It's meant to hurt him, but it hurts me, too. It makes me feel like maybe Quinn and I are part of what she regrets, extra ties to this man who she obviously doesn't love, who she maybe never loved. Sometimes when she says it, it makes me hate her. And sometimes it makes me hate my father for somehow tricking her into marrying him, but mostly it just makes me promise myself that I won't do what she did. I will never let some guy get so close that I get fooled into a destiny that I don't want.

"Okay. Fine. You go first. Steal my thunder. Rain on my parade," I tease, putting a hand on Quinn's shoulder and squeezing it. "See you on the ground, big brother." He leans his head to one side and rests it on my shoulder for a second, so unexpectedly tender that my throat feels thick and strangled, and I want to cry. He's the only guy I will ever depend on.

"Oh man, you got this!" Oliver hollers over a loud gust of wind. He's all riled up, jazzed like he's tempted to try to chest-bump the sky.

As nervous as I am for BASE jumps—and I am always nervous, because even with months of prep and practice, the risk is enormous—waiting for Quinn to land is always the worst part, that moment when I have an image of him falling fast, his chute not opening, then him hitting the ground. The picture in my mind is so sharp that I almost hear the heavy thud of his body's impact. It would be all my fault if he did. My idea. My jump. My risk. I have to fight the urge to tell him to sit this one out.

"Three, two, one." He looks back at me long enough to wink and then dives straight out, arms spread wide, embracing the night. His chute deploys, an explosion of fabric. It fans out, filling with air, and he disappears beneath it.

"Later, losers," Oliver says. He jumps without a countdown, saluting us with one hand as he steps out into the sky, his body already tilting forward into a stomach-down position.

Quinn's almost on the ground, arcing his way toward the street and the grassy area that's our landing spot. I breathe for the first time since he jumped.

"Beautiful up here," Leo says, taking it all in one last time. He grins at me, his helmet cam on, the red light a staring eye. He blows me a kiss and takes a swan dive, looking like one of Peter Pan's Lost Boys or something, flying without pixie dust.

"Here goes," Elena squeals, and then she's gone, too, screaming madly all the way down. I stand on the ledge a moment more. Alone. I wait, my hand going to the zippered pouch on my jacket where I keep my phone. I pull it out and unlock it, then look up the last few texts from Derek. I feel this need to read through them one more time. Up here it's easier to know what I want.

Where are you? Thought we were supposed to meet for coffee. UR late. WTF?

It's the *WTF* that bothers me most—angry and entitled, like I owe him something. There are more. Three more. The first one's angry, the last one concerned.

The news. God. Your dad. Call me.

And that's the one that did it. Put the nail in the coffin for me. I don't want to talk about my dad with him.

I finally leave a text of my own. *A cowardly one,* I think, but I don't let that stop me.

It's over. Sorry. I can't do this right now.

It's a weak breakup, but it's a relief to type it anyway. And besides, after the news covers Dad's arrest on every major television station tonight, Derek will thank me for letting him off the hook. He won't want to be mixed up with me. Our relationship is over. And I am happy about it.

I am.

I swear.

I close my eyes and listen to the wind whistling around the building, to the distant screech of tires on asphalt, to the faint echo of my friends calling to one another below. This is where I belong. I want to savor the high coursing through my blood for a moment or two longer, knowing that I got Quinn, Leo, Oliver, and Elena up here and then safely to the ground.

They could've died. The risk is there—real—or this wouldn't be illegal. One wrong pull on my lines and I crash into this building or one beside it. If the chute gets twisted coming out, there won't be time to right it. Less than a minute from here to the ground, and any mistakes mean that minute could be my last. Standing here now is like looking straight into the face of death and deciding to jump toward its gaping black mouth with the intention of steering away at the last minute . . . or not.

Things have been bad lately. More than bad. The arrest was almost a relief. There was all this awful tension building at home. It is at the very least an explanation for why my parents spend most nights yelling at each other, for why our house doesn't feel like a home. I'm not suicidal—really, I'm not . . . but I can't deny that sometimes I am curious about it. About how peaceful it might feel to let things end.

I let out a long, slow breath. Then I close my eyes and step into the air.

2

Christian

The van is cool. Well, not cool exactly, but the perfect getaway car for a heist. It's nondescript, dust-covered gray, with a lineup of cartoon-character people stuck to the tinted back window. A mom. A dad. Two kids. A dog. Man, I hate those stupid gringo decals. Like anyone really needs them to figure out whose ride this is. But as awesome as they are, the real kicker is the MARY KAY CONSULTANT sign stuck to the driver's side door. *Eddie's gonna love that.*

"This one," I say, smiling at the prospect of showing it to him. Getaway drivers—hell, *all* guys—like something sexier than this, but since he's not here . . .

I'm getting that slight tingle in my fingers. It's my gut's way of telling me the job's going to go right. I unzip my backpack, pull the tow kit and my gloves out from under a stack of college books, where I hid them. I tell the other guys the books are just props to make me look more like a student—out studying late for an exam, instead of a thief trying to steal a car—in case one of LA's finest happens to pull me over. But that's only partly true. I've actually read most of them. Plus, I like having them with me. They're my good-luck charms.

My cousin Benito—he goes by Benny—yawns and takes point at the back of the vehicle, eyes glued to the entrance to the apartment building's parking lot. I'd lay odds he's not watching the street, though. He's been staring at the sky on and off for the past hour, daydreaming. The LA skyline is pretty sweet, but not something he hasn't seen a million times before. We don't talk about it, but I know he dislikes this part of the job as much as I do. You'd think stealing cars wouldn't be nearly as big a deal as the bank jobs, but in some ways it's worse. More personal. This van belongs to someone—a woman with kids. We have to steal our getaway cars.

"I gotta get a Red Bull or something, dude. I'm dyin'. Hurry up already." Benny stretches and groans loudly, his arms coming up over his head, his back arching. He's nearly four inches shorter than me, twice as thick, and nothing but muscle. He reminds me of a boxer or something, all coiled-up energy. "You think the boys are still at the party?" Benny sounds wistful. We left the rest of our crew at Jeannette's house. We never take the whole team to lift a car. We'd attract too much attention. Last we saw of them, they were gathered in Jeannette's backyard scoping out the girls. "Maybe we could go back after we drop this bad boy off?" he asks, hopeful.

"Nah, man. It'll be over by now." I stick the wedge into the car door and pry it back enough to shove the air bladder into the gap. I start squeezing the hand pump, the bladder inflating in time with the pulse in my neck. Two seconds more and I've got the long metal rod in place, hovering over the unlock button. The car clicks. The lock disengages. The sound sends a tremor down my spine. I pull open the door. The cinnamon-apple scent of the car deodorizer makes my lungs squeeze shut in an instant. It's so bad that I consider breaking into a different car. But that'll just waste time, so I yank the air freshener out and throw it to the ground.

I drop into the driver's seat, check all the usual places for keys. It's nuts how many people leave a key inside their car. Stupid. Every time I find one, I want to leave a note that reads, "Doors have locks for a reason." Mom types are the worst about it. I mean, I get it. My sister's only three, so I know little kids'll make you stressed and forgetful and stuff, but this is LA. You can't let your guard down. Ever. Still, somehow they always do. Easy targets. I'd be a pendejo if I didn't go for their cars first.

The glove compartment is stuffed with insurance papers and not much else. There's nothing in the driver's side door, tucked into the visor, or under the floor mat except crumbs. But then, boom! There's a key tucked into the coin tray beneath a thin layer of sticky-looking pennies and a stash of baby wipes, diapers, and a box of Goldfish crackers. I grab the crackers, then slip the key into the ignition and start 'er up. Some god-awful kids' music fills the car, a dozen high-pitched voices singing about peanut butter and jelly. It's a song that my own mom would never be caught dead playing for my little sister. She'd rather play Maria some Plastilina Mosh or my dad's stuff from when he used to do covers around LA with his band. I start fiddling with the buttons until I find a station that doesn't make me want to rip out my eardrums.

"Let's roll," I say.

Benny slips into the passenger side. I put the car in drive, and we ease out of the garage. I'm in no particular hurry. It's quiet this time of night. Most people who live around here are asleep. I put on my turn signal and hang a left. There're maybe ten other cars on the street and then a stretch of empty road, but I don't speed up. The first rule of stealing is not to *look* like you're stealing. Speed hints at panic, and panic calls attention to itself.

"Wanna grab a burger or somethin'?" Benny yawns again, and suddenly it's contagious and I'm yawning myself. The brief jolt of adrenaline I had when we settled on this car is already fading away. There was a time when I would be jacked-up for hours, but now stealing cars is just too easy, that's all. Thinking about it makes my stomach sour. I don't want it to be easy. It means it's become my normal. *Not good.*

"Nah, I'm beat. We got church in the morning, remember?"

"Ha! It *is* morning, genius. Don't be such a tight-ass white boy. You might as well stay up all night now. So . . . burgers? Come on, you know you want one." Benny jabs me in the ribs, grinning. I hate it when he calls me white boy. Makes me feel like I'm not like him, that I don't totally belong. I try not to care. The boys tease Carlos for being fat all the time, and he doesn't complain—except it's not the same. Carlos can lose weight. I'll always have a white father. I give Benny the side eye and punch his shoulder.

"Ow, bro," he laughs, massaging his arm. I rub my eyes. They're squinty with fatigue. I won't even get four hours' crash time before I'm squished into a pew, listening to Father Diaz give the mass. I shovel a few Goldfish into my mouth and offer Benny the box.

"No burgers," I say. "I gotta help my mom fill an order for her company before church. It's gotta go out Monday first thing. I'm gonna be wrecked if I don't squeeze in an hour or two of sleep."

This is only partly true. I do have to help my mom tag and box over a hundred T-shirts for this hipster clothing store downtown—her first big order in a very long time—but I also want to read this book my English teacher recommended. Benny doesn't need to know that, though. He'll just start ribbing me again. It's better for both of us if he thinks I'm doing something nonintellectual. Benny and I are more than cousins—we're best friends—but this is one area of my life he doesn't get. None of my boys are all that interested in pleasure reading *Twenty Thousand Leagues Under the Sea* or *To Kill a Mockingbird*. You'd think they would be, because it's such an escape, but man, for them it's the opposite. Benny had issues learning to read in the first place, and getting called out of class to hang with the reading specialist embarrassed him big-time. The others would rather be shooting hoops or out picking up girls or whatever. Gabriel dropped out of school a while back, and Eddie and Carlos have started entertaining the idea of doing the same. It's just not that important to them. I get why. Hard to think about the future when you're trying to survive today. It just sucks when they get defensive every time I try to do something different.

It's a theory I have. The hole theory. Sometimes people who are stuck in a really deep hole don't see the point in trying to get out. The climb just feels too high. And when *you* want to escape, they get all freaked out because if you actually manage to *get out,* they're stuck in the hole alone. I think Benny's afraid that if I get too into books and stuff, we won't have anything in common. Or that I'll start seeing him differently. That won't happen, but I can't make him believe that, so I just don't talk about what book I'm into currently or acing my SATs or applying for college scholarships.

"Oh, bro, that sucks." But Benny doesn't look the least bit sorry about the prospect of my having to fold a bunch of lady shirts before mass. In fact, he's grinning like a freaking five-year-old who's just heard the world's best fart joke.

"So how come Eddie doesn't take this crap over for us? He's the driver—it should be him," I say, barely keeping the frustration out of my voice.

"'Cause Eddie's about as stealthy as an elephant. What, you don't like spendin' time with me, homes?" Benny pretends to be insulted.

"Not even a little bit," I say dryly. Dude practically lives at my house, we hang out so much.

He laughs, lowering the window and sticking his hand into the wind. He lets it ride the current, dipping and swooping. He's back to watching the sky. Again. His expression changes, goes all serious.

Probably he's thinking about the fact that none of us is completely in charge. If we were, we wouldn't be robbing banks in the first place. The question of who the real boss is is complicated. For us, it'd be Soldado, the leader of Florencia Heights, but he answers to dudes even higher up than him. We're just the final link in a very long chain.

After a bit he says, "You know you wouldn't seriously let Eddie do it anyway. You gotta have your fingers in the whole thing all the time."

He's not exactly wrong. I feel better when I have more control—even if it's just perceived control. Simple truth: we're the guys on the ground. If stuff goes sideways, we'll be going to jail. Not Soldado or whoever he reports to. When it comes to putting my butt on the line, as much as I love my crew—*my boys,* Eddie, Gabriel, Carlos, and Benny—they aren't all that careful about stuff. This is also part of my hole theory: If you're deep in the hole, you aren't scared of going deeper. But if you're halfway out, man, the fall is freaking terrifying.

I think it ticks Gabriel off that I want to control things—like I don't trust him or the other guys or something, but it isn't that, not exactly. I mean, they know all my secrets and have my back no matter what. And I got theirs. But I don't always trust their decision-making when it counts. Not for nothing, but Carlos gets sloppy sometimes. Like the bank we hit a few months back when he let out a string of curses in Spanish, handing the cops the biggest clue so far as to who we are. I mean, they don't know for sure we're Mexican—we could be Puerto Rican or Cuban—but given how many Mexicans there are in this city, it's the first conclusion they'll reach. I doubt they're going to think it's a bunch of white dudes dropping f-bombs en español just to screw with them. Every job leaves a trail, no matter how hard you try to muddy it up.

Eddie is the getaway man mainly because he lacks the kind of presence you need to have to go into the banks. He's maybe one hundred fifty pounds soaking wet, and even at a yell his voice is weak. Like someone socked him in the voice box or the balls or something.

Gabriel is the only cool head other than mine, but as good as he is at being in charge, too, I can never quite let him, not all the way, even if he is five years older. Mostly because the way he acts, sometimes I think he *expects* to end up in jail someday. Like he figures it's his birthright, since his dad's there. His mom has told him as much more than once after he's screwed up. And most of the time he doesn't seem to worry too much about the consequences of what we're doing.

The God's honest truth is that the guys rely on me to be the brains. And as the brains, I feel the need to oversee all the decisions these guys make when it comes to the jobs. We'll be okay. As long as we keep to the rules we came up with when we got roped into this whole thing:

1. Get in, get out.
2. Only shoot in self-defense.
3. Don't get greedy.
4. Don't get caught.
5. Only trust each other.

Simple enough. But I'm always surprised at how hard it actually is to follow them in the heat of the moment. We've managed so far—longer than any crew I know about, but that doesn't mean we aren't on borrowed time. We can't afford to screw up. I can't even begin to think about what it would do to my mom and Maria if we got caught. What it would do to all the people we love. I couldn't keep doing this if I thought about that too much, so no slipups.

The traffic light in front of us goes red, and I slow to a stop. We're at the heart of the financial district, near our next target. The bank's blinds are drawn this time of night, the windows dark. I stare anyway, waiting to see if the same rightness fizzes across my skin, like it did with the car. Nothing. I can't tell if this is a bad sign or nerves. I'm banking on nerves. Ha! *Banking.* I laugh even though it isn't all that funny.

Thonk!

Something's landed on the car.

I startle so bad that I accidentally step on the gas and the car jerks forward. A pair of boots attached to a long, thin pair of legs appear as a person scrambles across the front hood, tries to keep his balance, fails, then goes down to one knee, his hands darting out to steady him.

"What the—?" I manage to sputter before those boots are launching themselves off the edge of the hood. The dude's pant leg rides up on one side, and I get an up-close look at the tattoo on his moon-pale calf—a goldfish that looks as if it's preparing to dive straight into one boot. There's a little thud as first that boot and then the other connect with the blacktop. The person is smaller than I thought he was. Wait. Not a he. *A girl?* She has a black helmet on—is dressed head to toe in black, the outfit so tight that there's no question anymore that she's definitely female. There are cords attached to a pack on her back and a length of fabric trailing after her, blown sideways so that it landed on the road and not the car. It takes me a second to realize that it's a parachute.

"Ho-ly crap!" Benny laughs out loud, and the girl must hear him, because she half turns. I get a flash of pale white skin; full, slightly parted lips; and wisps of blond hair escaping the front of her helmet, glinting gold under the streetlights. She blinks, black lashes against a flushed cheek, before she's off and running, the chute swishing over the ground behind her like some kind of wedding dress train. I can't stop staring. My heart thuds hard in my chest. It's like watching some black-ops Cinderella make her getaway. She leaps onto the sidewalk across the street without looking back once. I watch the chute trail after, lifting into the wind a bit almost like it's waving at us, and then the girl and the chute disappear behind a building.

We're the only car at the intersection, so I put it in park and get out. Benny follows, both of us looking first at the building she went around and then up at the sky. I want to run after her, to catch her and turn her around so I can see her face. I need to know who she is. But I can't seem to make myself move.

"That was insane, bro!" Benny shakes his head and trots a little ways past the intersection, obviously trying to see where she went, and when he can't find her, he looks back up at the sky. "You see anyone else up there?" he calls.

I look up at the skyscrapers surrounding us, looming large and seeming to sway. There's no sign of anyone else, no shadowy silhouettes of other jumpers or whatever. It's like she just appeared 007-style. I half expect a guy with a scar running down one cheek and an Uzi in his hand to show up next, but instead there is the unmistakable whine of a police siren, faint, but getting louder quickly.

"Time to go," I say. Benny's already slipping back into the car. We might not be the only ones breaking the law tonight, but if we stick around, we'll be the only ones who get caught.

I pull out into the intersection and head south, toward home, the girl still imprinted on my brain. I'm not superstitious, but I can't help thinking that her landing on the car just as we were by our target bank is some kind of omen. Of what? I'm not sure yet.

3

Lexi

Fifteen. Fourteen. Thirteen.

I count down the seconds, wind rushing at me from all directions and a blur of lights and buildings speeding past, my whole body sinking like a lead weight, my stomach clenched tight against the pull of gravity, my eyes tearing up because I've forgotten to blink.

I deploy my parachute when I run out of seconds to spare, and the canopy spreads out behind me like a giant shadow, lifting me before I begin to float balloon-like toward the ground. I work my lines, maneuvering myself between the buildings to my right and left, trying to keep my wits about me. There's a car on the road, coming up fast. It's a minivan, idling at the traffic light. My last thought as I try to avoid it is *I hope this van doesn't contain sleeping babies.*

My legs buckle a bit when I hit the hood, and I go down hard on one knee. I put my hands out in front of me to keep from catapulting off the van and onto the asphalt headfirst. Picturing what I must look like and the shock on the face of whoever

23

is driving is enough to get me laughing hysterically, especially when the guy in the passenger seat starts hollering.

I turn enough to peer into the car. Two guys around my age are in the front seat, staring openmouthed at me. The driver leans forward like he wants to get a better look at me, his scruffy jawline getting closer to the steering wheel, his dark eyes coming into view.

Time to bolt.

I leap off the car and literally hit the ground running, my chute trailing behind me across the street, swishing on the asphalt. I can hear the van's car doors open and I turn. Yep, both guys are standing beside the car. I pick up speed and duck out of sight. I don't think they'll follow me, but you never know.

The key to any good maneuver is a quick getaway, so I run onto the sidewalk and immediately cross another street and then another, hoping like mad that my chute doesn't catch on something and tangle, effectively tethering me to one spot. I can hear police sirens now, faint but getting louder every second. I run down a side street to a line of bushes and a patch of shadows where a streetlight's gone out. I crouch in those shadows, safely tucked behind the bushes, and begin reeling in my chute, stuffing it into my pack as fast as I can, my breath loud in my ears, my hands shaking from the jump. I get the chute put away in seconds and rip the helmet from my head, stuffing it into the pack as well, and then start walking again, away from the sirens and toward the spot where Whitney's supposed to pick me up.

I shake out my hair, so blond that it's almost white under

the streetlights, and wrap the elastic around my wrist. My long-sleeved black shirt comes off next so that I'm in a sparkly gray tank top and jeans. I slip the necklaces I had stowed in my front pocket around my neck and then put on some bright red lipstick, dotting the color onto my lips with one finger so that it goes on right even though I can't look in a mirror.

My pack is a little too sporty to pass for a going-out-type bag, but that can't be helped. I'm relying instead on the fact that I'm blond and a willowy five eight—about as dangerous-looking as a bunny rabbit—as reason enough for any passing police to rule me out as one of the jumpers. Quinn and the others will have more trouble being inconspicuous. It's good they jumped first.

Two blocks of brisk walking and I can see Whitney's Escalade parked along the side of the road.

"Lex." Oliver pops up from somewhere behind me, bumps my shoulder with his own, and then drapes an arm around me. He has his lighter out—an old Sarome Japanese cigarette lighter that his mom gave him. It used to belong to his grandfather. He flicks the lighter on and off, on and off. I think it's comforting to him, like a security blanket.

"Oliver, carry this for me?" I push my pack into his chest and he grunts.

Quinn is already in the car with Whitney and Elena. "Hurry up, you two. Time to go."

"Leo?" I ask.

"Right here." He runs up behind us, his face flushed pink

from the wind, the jump, and the run. The police sirens are louder now.

Oliver throws my pack into the trunk with the others before crawling into the backseat. I go after him and then Leo squeezes in.

Whitney looks back at me, frowning, the mirror image of her twin sister, Elena—if you reverse their style sense. Her hair is smooth rather than curly, a dark black curtain falling against her neck. Her shirt is almost always unbuttoned low enough to give everyone a good glimpse of her lacy bra. Tonight she's dusted glittery powder all along her neck and cleavage, and it flashes every time it catches the light.

"You broke up with Derek?" She holds up her phone. *He told her? Ugh.* "With a text? Hon, that's so not cool."

Everyone looks at me and I shrug. "I just beat him to the punch. Who wants to date the daughter of an infamous criminal, anyway?"

"*Alleged* criminal," Quinn says quietly, hurt clear in his eyes. I immediately feel bad and mouth "Sorry" at him.

"You don't know that. Derek's a sweet guy." Whitney shakes her head as she pulls out and starts speeding down the road. "He deserved better." There is disappointment in her voice, not reproach. Even if I'm in the wrong, she supports me.

Derek did deserve better. He did. I know this. Breaking up with him by text was impulsive. I'm sorry about that, but not about the breakup itself. Even if this thing with my dad hadn't happened today, my days with Derek as a couple were numbered.

We'd been together three months. Long for me. Too long. He was starting to think we had a future.

"You okay?" Leo asks, the only person in the car who can figure me out just by looking at my face.

"Yeah, of course," I lie. "Why wouldn't I be?"

We look at each other, and it dawns on me how ridiculous this statement is, and we both crack up.

"He wasn't the right guy," Leo says.

"I don't think there is a right guy," I say.

Leo grins. "There is. You just haven't found him yet. God help him when you do, though." He thinks a minute. "Actually, God help *you*. Because you are going to fall *hard*, my friend."

"Never gonna happen," I tell him. "I'm not interested in becoming my mother."

"Apples and oranges," he says.

In the front seat Elena's fussing at Whitney to slow down. "Who are you, Danica Patrick all of a sudden?"

Whitney rolls her eyes. "I didn't get to jump. Let me speed," she says. "And relax. I've got skills."

The skills she's talking about developed after a few dates with a stunt-car driver her dad hired for one of the movies he coproduced last year. If he hadn't found out about those dates and told the guy just how young she really was, there probably would've been a few more. It shocks me that the guy didn't know she was seventeen. Of the twins, Elena is the one who looks much older than she is—which is weird because she and Whitney are identical. They have the same green eyes, dark brown

27

skin, and delicate frames, but everything about Whitney screams high school, from her sense of humor to her habit of crinkling up her nose when she flirts, whereas Elena radiates sophistication, from her dry way of talking to the gliding, confident way she walks. Maybe it's all on purpose, their way of distinguishing themselves from each other. It works. I never confuse them. No one does.

Elena and Whitney continue to bicker back and forth about what speed we should be going and whether Whitney does in fact have skills. I can imagine them having this very conversation when they are old and gray and rooming together in a posh nursing home somewhere—Whitney will be full throttle on an electric scooter. I half laugh at the thought and put my head on Leo's shoulder.

This is good. This is where I need to be.

I try to savor the moment. I don't need some boy to love. Or a normal family. All I need are the people in this car. They are enough.

4

Christian

I pass the stolen car keys off to Eddie in the church lobby as soon as we're inside. Hearing them jingle, I can't help thinking about the girl again, the one who landed on the hood last night. I actually dreamed about her once I finally fell asleep: I caught her in my arms before she landed on the car. Dream her was sexy. Made me regret not taking off after her. I don't even know what she looks like. Not really. Or where to begin trying to find her.

"What'd ya get me this time?" Eddie asks, holding up his fist and giving me dap, his hair still wet around the edges from the hurried shower he must've taken to get to mass on time. He reeks of cigarettes and Axe.

Carlos is next to him, his stomach folding over his pants, his shirt so tight across his giant arms that the seams look ready to burst. He's mostly muscle, but for the past year that's been changing. If homes doesn't start working out again, he's going to be a liability during the jobs. Too big and bulky to run away fast. Too easy to identify. I'll have to find a way to bring it up later on.

After the service, when he'll be at his most pious and forgiving for the week.

"Same old, same old," I say, my eyes roving the crowd of people, looking for Gabriel.

He hasn't been showing up to church for a while, breaking his routine. He's been partying and drinking a lot more. And he's been going to visit his old man in jail, too. I don't like anything out of the ordinary happening while we're doing these jobs. Anything that might suggest we've got some bad stuff going down. The less conspicuous we are, the more closely we keep to our usual habits, the better. It ticks me off that he doesn't get this. We always attend mass. It's expected. Period. You don't and people start to really worry, the tias light candles and pray for you. Last thing we need is extra eyeballs scrutinizing our every move. Even if they mean well.

"Why can't we ever go with something manly—a Hummer or somethin'? Why does it always gotta be the estrogen mobiles?" Eddie shakes his head at the keys dangling from a key chain with a plastic frame, some little baby's face grinning out of it, before tucking them in his pocket. Bet the lady who owns the car's realized it's gone by now. I shrug. It doesn't matter. What's done is done.

Benny snorts and tries to stifle a laugh as Eddie groans.

I don't answer. He already knows why. Between him and Gabriel, I'm starting to lose my patience. In their heads, they see us like we're in some kind of vigilante posse. Worst thing I ever did was show them the movie *Heat*. Now they think they're the teenage Sizemore and De Niro. Me? I don't get the glamour of going out in a hail of bullets. Robbers who get too cocky or start to glamorize the job have a bad end. I can't let that be us.

We head inside and find our families. Benny settles into a pew near the front and puts his arm around his mom. She leans her scarf-covered head on his shoulder. She started chemo a little while back, and now she's completely bald. Soldado worked it out with the Eme (the Mexican Mafia, otherwise known as rulers of the street, the Florencia Heights gang, the Pelican Bay State Prison, and everywhere in between) so that all her bills are taken care of. He's even been having some of his Florencia Heights homeboys drive her to chemo when Benny's in school and his sister's busy working. He's good like that. Always has been. None of us wanted to get jumped in to Florencia Heights, but he's still had our back ever since the first day we met.

Still, if Benny ever stopped doing the jobs, Soldado wouldn't be able to convince the Eme to keep helping. Benny'd have to drop out of school, and he and his sister, Rosie, would have to carry the family's expenses. No way his mom would stand a chance of getting better then. Rosie may be Soldado's girl, but the Eme isn't a charity and saying no to something they want you to do is suicide. High up as Soldado is, he wouldn't be able to protect Benny. It sucks, but the way they see it, if Benny really loves his family, he'll keep toeing the line. It's like that for all of us. Gabriel does the jobs and his dad stays protected at Pelican Bay. I do mine and my dad's gambling debts are canceled out.

31

Carlos and Eddie get enough dough together to put their sisters through college and get them out of the hood.

I make my way to my family's usual pew and drop down next to my mom as the organ grinds to life. The hypocrisy of us all being in a church after what we've done and what we're about to do tomorrow is not lost on me. Sometimes I break into a cold sweat over it, especially when the priest starts talking about damnation. I can't stop myself from expecting some white-hot God light to come down and fry me where I sit.

Even if I don't confess my sins to the priest, I do confess them silently to God from the pew, every single one, and I tithe some of my share from every take. So I hope the Big Man keeps giving me a pass, because this situation is strictly temporary. I've almost paid off my dad's debt. If Mom's business starts growing the way she thinks it will and I get into UCLA with a full scholarship, it could happen. No, it *will* happen. It has to. One way or another, I'm climbing out of this hole. With any luck, one day I'll figure out a way to get Benny, Gabriel, Carlos, and Eddie out, too.

"Pay attention, mijo." My mom puts her hand over mine and pats it. Her palm is rough from too many years spent working nights, cleaning office buildings or waiting tables, after spending all day taking care of my sister and trying to get her T-shirt company off the ground. I look over at her, at the shadows rimming both eyes. She still looks young and pretty—if tired—all polished up like her special-occasion silverware. I hate that she works as hard as she does. My dad is no help. He's probably still lying on the sofa, alcohol oozing from every pore.

He was out cold in the living room when I got home last night, a giant Gatorade bottle lying empty next to him. I didn't need to sniff it to know he'd had more than blue Gatorade in it. Damn silly that he hides his vodka, but so is Mom's refusal to call him on it. He gets so creepy-still sometimes when he's drinking heavy like that. When I was little, I used to think he might die while we were asleep, so a couple of times a night I used to come out of my room and put my fingers under his nose and wait to feel the heat of his breath on my skin. Now sometimes I sort of hope he does stop breathing. I know Mom doesn't believe it, but we'd be better off without him.

Maria is next to Mom, her hair done up in braids with little pink silk ribbons, her head leaning on my mother's shoulder, her chubby little legs straight out in front of her. She's messing with the lace trim on her dress and humming the theme song to her favorite TV show. "Hey, sis," I whisper as I reach over and squeeze her hand. She gives me this silly grin before climbing over Mom to sit in my lap. Letting my three-year-old sister snuggle on me doesn't exactly jibe with my tough-guy cred, but whatever. I tug her braid and she giggles.

"Shh." Mom frowns at us, but she's not really mad.

Just as Father Diaz really gets going, Soldado and Rosie slip into mass, late as usual. Guy can't make a grand entrance any other way. He nods at me as they take a seat with Benny and his mom. Nearly everyone is staring at him, but he acts all chill, like he doesn't notice. As the newest leader of the Florencia Heights gang, a full-on Eme carnale, he's the toughest dude in the hood, but to look at him right now, dressed up in his Sunday best with his arm around Rosie, you'd never guess it. If not for the gang tattoos peeking out from under his shirt collar along the back of his neck, he could be a businessman working in advertising or something. Homes dresses sharp for mass. He turns and looks back at me, a question in his eyes. He wants to know if I got the car. I nod, and he half smiles before turning his attention back to Father Diaz.

After church we usually linger outside. This week is no different. Mom is talking to the priest, wiping the tears from her cheeks with Abuela's lacy handkerchief—the one she always brings to mass. It's old school, but Mom is way into the vintage. It's how she got the idea for her T-shirt business. She remakes these old images of East Los Angeles and Mexico and turns them into T-shirts. Sometimes she uses band logos, too. At first she sold them to tourist-type shops, but lately she's started branching out. If the hipster store likes this order we just filled, it might mean orders from more stores like it. Someday maybe she'll get her stuff on Melrose Avenue. Mom deserves it. She dropped out of school and put her life on hold when she had me, and now that she finally has a dream for herself, I want more than anything for her to achieve it. All we need is a minor-sized miracle. A tiny boost. That's probably what she's talking to Father Diaz about. That or my dad.

I look down at my sister, who is about a minute away from melting down. "Just a little bit longer and we'll go. Then lunchtime. What sounds good?"

She grins up at me. "McDonald's. I want a Happy Meal." She's been begging all week for one, ever since she saw the latest commercial plugging the toys.

"You got it," I say, and Mom gives me a disapproving look because she's got food all set at home. "Come on. I'll take her to get it. And whatever you made for lunch, I'll eat her share and mine. Nothing'll go to waste," I tell her. "Besides, the baby needs a new Littlest Pet Shop." She rolls her eyes and Father Diaz laughs.

"I not a baby." Maria frowns, and I laugh and chuck her under her chin.

"We ready for tomorrow?" Gabriel asks me, materializing out of nowhere and pulling me away from Maria and Mom. "You got the car?" He looks older today in the bright sunlight. Not quite twenty-three, he's already got these lines forming around his mouth and eyes. It makes him look sort of sick. Drawn somehow. It's probably the visit he made to Pelican Bay to see his father yesterday. Those trips always seem to mess him up, but that doesn't stop him from going.

"Yeah, parked it in the garage of the Madison Street house, like you told us to." Gabriel works construction during the week, remodeling foreclosures for an investor and getting a percentage of the sales. Provided the houses sell quick enough. Soldado hooked him up with that gig, too—a reward after the first job.

Besides, the houses make for great meeting spots for Soldado and his boys until they're ready to sell. Keeps his business dealings off the streets, where the cops might see.

"Eddie's got the keys already. Thought you'd be early to mass so we could go over the plans again. Why weren't you?" I'm taking a chance. It bugs Gabriel to be accountable to anyone, especially me. He's just as likely to smack me upside my head as to admit where he was, and homes can scramble your brains, but I want him to know that I *know* he's not keeping to his usual routine. Besides all his visits to the jail, he's been hanging out with the Florencia boys more and more. It has me worried. We all agreed—no one gets jumped in. We stay free agents. We do the jobs only because it helps our families. Once you get jumped in to FH, that's it. There's no leaving. Ever.

Gabriel's Adam's apple bobs in his throat as he swallows. There are little beads of sweat lining his forehead and chin. "Why're you so curious?" He wipes his upper lip when he sees me staring closely at his face, and he squints at me. "I don't need you checkin' up on me. Soldado had an errand for me, if you gotta know. Had to do with the next job after this one. This one's big, homes. Huge. Seriously. Like, game-changing."

Benny looks over to where Soldado is leaning on his car, with Rosie wrapped up in his arms. He's laughing and joking with his boys, but his eyes keep cutting over to where we are.

He won't come over. The less he's seen with us, the less likely someone will connect that we're all working together. Soldado nods like he can hear what Gabriel's telling us and then kisses

Rosie's neck until she squeals. A couple of the old ladies leaving the church give him a disapproving look—lips all pursed like they sucked on a lemon just now, but they hurry by without saying anything. Eddie joins our group.

"We meeting at eight?" I ask, changing the subject because I don't want to talk about future jobs when we have one tomorrow morning that we need to concentrate on. Truth? I'd love not to have to worry about future jobs, period.

Gabriel looks down at his phone and nods. "Usual time, usual way. The shipments come in at nine-thirty. The hopper gets out of the truck with the delivery almost on the dot. In and out in maybe five, tops. You figure that they probably start breakin' up and spreadin' out the bills right after; we need to hit it the moment the truck pulls out again. Nine-thirty-five."

"And if they got the money put away already?" I ask. "We walk without it, right? Right?"

"Yeah," Gabriel says with a shrug, his fingers jabbing his phone too hard. He's playing some kind of game on it. "Son of a—it got me. Look, about the next job. It's gonna be sick."

"How big?" Benny asks, suspicious. "I thought we agreed to do only small stuff, that big jobs are too risky. What about rule number three? Don't get greedy, remember?"

"Soldado's got good reasons for us to rethink that. Fifty million of 'em, to be exact," Gabriel says, his voice getting low as several churchgoers known for spreading gossip walk by. "Got the go-ahead from his higher-ups already, right? They think it's solid."

I work a finger under the collar of my dress shirt. The sun feels too hot on my back.

Eddie whistles. "That's insane, bro."

"Only if it isn't thought through. Soldado's already worked it out. He's got some concrete guys who are real good at drillin' and stuff. They'll tunnel under the vault and get us into the bank so we can do the interior work once the digging's done. These guys take care of getting us in, we get the money, no one even knows we were there."

"You don't think all that drilling's gonna attract some attention?" Eddie asks.

"LA's sittin' on a bunch of sandy ground that's mad easy to tunnel through, dude. We do the job once the vault's cracked. Then Soldado arranges the fence and the laundering. That's eight of us with a hand in. We get twenty-four million. That split is sick! Our families would be living large."

Eddie whistles again.

I wait for Benny to raise another objection so I don't have to. Gabriel will take it better from him, but Benny doesn't; he just stares at Gabriel, a slight look of awe on his face, and I know I'm losing him.

"We agreed. No jobs bigger than a hundred thousand." I shake my head. "Greed gets you caught. Your dad is proof, man." It's not cool of me to mention his dad this way, but I don't care. Homeboy is out of his mind.

Gabriel's dad, my uncle, has been doing a stretch for grand larceny ever since Gabriel was three, which is probably why the

Eme wanted Soldado to get Gabriel, and then us, for these jobs in the first place. They're convinced we've got some kind of natural robbing ability or trade secrets or something. Plus, Soldado's personally vouched for each of us. Gabriel's dad was good. But then he started hitting more banks, trying for bigger takes, and ended up on the FBI's radar. Agents dogged him down and took him in. The lesson I get from this? The key to surviving in a city that held the title Bank Robbery Capital of the World for more than a decade is to keep a low profile. With bank robberies happening all the time, the police have to cherry-pick who to focus on: robbers who score big and robbers who hurt people. And God help you if you shoot at a cop or something. You will get caught. And you will do a stretch in jail. Like Gabriel's dad. A long, long stretch. The gun charges alone will jack you up good. I know because I researched it.

I'll be a thief if I have to, but no way I'm going to be a stupid one. "We can't do it. Come on, you guys gotta see it. Fifty million? We'll have the LAPD *and* the FBI on our asses."

Benny nods thoughtfully. "Yeah, it's too big."

Eddie looks torn but ultimately nods. "You gotta tell Soldado we can't."

A look of pure rage flashes across Gabriel's face. "We've done six jobs so far. And what have we got to show for it? After the split, we've each cleared what? Two to six thousand apiece for each job? Max. This is a different deal. How can you not get that? Think of it as freedom money. You think the Eme'll ever let us stop if we keep doin' small-time jobs? But if we do one big

5

Lexi

I watch as the US Bank Tower comes into view, my face pressed to the car window even though the sun is shining right on me, heating me up and making me sweat. It's been a little more than twenty-four hours since the jump, and instead of going to school, we're headed back downtown, this time because my mother is dragging us to my father's bank, LL National, to talk to the people there about our accounts. When she went online to get money for Dad's bail, all of our funds were frozen.

We pass the spot where I landed. I half smile, remembering. Crashing on top of that van was nothing short of epic. The two guys inside were thoroughly freaked out. I wish I could bottle the rush of happiness I felt. I could use it this morning.

"There's no way it's all frozen. He can't have left us with nothing," Mom says, her voice on the edge of hysteria, her hands gripping the wheel so hard her knuckles are white.

She looks wild this morning, not her usual polished self. Little pieces of hair stick out around her temples, and her hastily-scraped-together bun is already coming undone at the nape of her neck. She put on makeup but somehow forgot eyeliner. I don't tell her, because she's already so upset. She never even knew we were gone Saturday night. I waited for her to ask me about it, but she was too preoccupied with this errand. A perk of having your father arrested, I guess, is that you don't get questioned about where you've been or why you were out so late.

Quinn is sprawled in the backseat, snoring away; sleep is his way of avoiding uncomfortable situations. I envy him. I can't shut down like that when things get weird. I get itchy and restless instead. If I could jump out of the car and run the rest of the way, I would.

"He can't have left us this way. He can't. He can't." She half laughs and her fingers flex, strangling the steering wheel the way she'd probably like to strangle my father. "How in the hell did I get here? This cannot be my life." A sob chokes off her laughter, and then she's crying in a way that's both violent and ugly and so full of rage that it scares me. "How did I get here?" she asks again, softer. She's not really talking to me or Quinn.

"If you already know the accounts are frozen, then why are we going to the bank?" I ask, my voice harder than it probably should be. I guess I should feel sorry for her, but I don't. I'm angry. She had to have known that he was doing something wrong, that this might be coming.

"Because I have to try something. And I want those bloodsuckers to see us face to face and understand what they've done."

"I thought Dad was the criminal," I say.

42

She looks over at me like I'm crazy, and I shrink back against the seat. My mother has the coldest eyes sometimes.

"Do you really think that *your* father could've pulled off a multimillion-dollar mortgage scam all on his own?" The way she says "*your* father" makes me think that she's hinting that *I* might be just as stupid as she thinks *he* is.

"How am I supposed to know? I only found out about this on Saturday. For all I know, you were in on it," I fire back, stung.

"At the very least there's one other person involved. Possibly Colin Freed, but I'd bet anything that the real mastermind here is Mitch Harrison."

Mr. Harrison. Dad's old college frat buddy. The guy who got him his job twenty years ago. I go to school with his daughter, Bianca, but we haven't been friends since sixth grade, when she morphed into a mean girl and I decided I had better things to do than make fun of people. Quinn lost his mind and dated Bianca for half a second last year, so he knows the family a little better, but I've only seen Harrison on and off over the years, mostly at parties or school functions, from a distance. He's a typical finance type, always in a suit, giving off an air of superiority. He doesn't look like a criminal, but then again, neither does my dad.

Within minutes we are out of the car and walking down Figueroa toward Dad's building. I haven't been here since I was ten and he brought me for some take-your-kid-to-work thing that I only wanted to do because it meant a whole day away from school. I passed the place last night, after I jumped, but I didn't stop and reminisce. Last night was about forgetting.

We walk through the glass doors that lead into the lobby. Mom's heels tap on the marble floor, making each step sound like a gunshot. She heads straight for the security desk.

"Hello, Luther," she says to the guard behind the desk, an older black man with salt-and-pepper hair and a solemn face. "I'm going up to twelve to see Mr. Harrison." She stares Luther down like she's daring him to tell her no. It's unnerving to watch her do it, even for me. I'd be intimidated for him except that I can see her hands trembling at her sides.

Luther looks over his glasses at her. "He knows you're coming?"

She busies herself with signing in on the little clipboard on the counter. "No, but he'll let me up," she says. "Go ahead. Call and ask him."

Luther stares at her a moment and then picks up the phone. I can hear a man's voice on the other end. Brisk and businesslike.

"Mr. Harrison's coming down to meet you," Luther says. "He said to give him five minutes."

My mother taps the pen she signed in with against the clipboard and hesitates. "We can't meet him upstairs? Where it's more . . . private?"

Luther shakes his head, and she purses her lips but doesn't argue. Quinn and I follow her as she stalks away from the security desk without another word. She heads straight for the ATM in the vestibule that separates the outside world from the lobby. Quinn and I hang back as she goes to use it.

When the machine spits her card out a moment later and there isn't any money accompanying it, I start to really worry. The account information was right. Of course it was. But I think all of us were hoping there was some sort of mix-up all the same. She bites her lip and tries again. And again.

"Mom, it's not going to work." Quinn grabs her shoulders and gently steers her away. All the bluster and confidence she mustered coming in here is disappearing. I can see it leaving her in a whoosh, like helium from a balloon. Her shoulders slump, and she sinks onto the marble planter behind her, dropping her purse at her feet.

"We have nothing. We have nothing. We have nothing," she says over and over, staring all the while at the ATM. "My god. What are we going to do?" If I wasn't scared before, I am now. Is she being dramatic or is this for real? We really have nothing we can touch? How are we supposed to live? How do we get groceries or pay bills or get gas or a hundred other things?

"Elizabeth," a man says.

We look up in time to see Harrison striding toward us. He's good-looking for an older dude. Sort of George Clooney–esque, but the air he gives off is not quite as charming. He straightens the cuffs of his bright white shirt.

"Mitch," my mother says, holding out her hand to him.

He shakes it firmly and gives her a sad, pitying little smile. "I'm sorry about what's happening. I know it must be hard on you and the kids." He looks up at Quinn and then at me. His eyes flicker over my body. I don't like being here, having him pity us. I can't even imagine what my mother wants from him. It isn't like he can unfreeze our accounts or anything. Right?

"Thank you," my mother says. "It is."

Harrison—I can't think of him as Mitch—scans the lobby and then pulls my mother over to an area that isn't so exposed to the comings and goings at the front door. "So why are you here, Elizabeth?" he asks.

She frowns. "I'm here because we need help. The bank's frozen our accounts. . . ."

"No, *the FBI* has frozen your accounts," he says, his voice soft, as if he's speaking to a small child.

"What are we supposed to do? How are we supposed to live? Warren worked here for over twenty years. Surely that counts for something."

Harrison stares at her. "He committed a crime. And he used the bank to do it. This scandal hurts us, too. Disparages our reputation. You can't seriously think we owe him?"

My mother grabs his arms, her fingers digging into his suit coat. "Please, Mitch. I don't work. I haven't worked in ten years. How am I supposed to find something in time to cover expenses and bail Warren out? We had all our money in those accounts. Now I have maybe fifty dollars to my name."

He takes a step back, shrugs out of her grip, and I can see the distaste, the revulsion in his eyes. I feel sick, like I might throw up. People are watching us now, stopping midstep to see what will happen next.

"Mom," Quinn says, and when she doesn't answer, a little louder: "Mom!"

She ignores him. "I need some money. And you're going to help me, Mitch. You can't pin everything on Warren and let us all twist in the wind while you walk away scot-free."

Harrison's face goes stony. "Elizabeth, that's enough. Accusing me isn't going to clear Warren, and you know it."

"You had to have been involved! Warren told me as much," my mother shouts, her voice ringing out in the cavernous space. "You let him take the fall, but you're the one. You're the one!" She's not exactly making sense anymore. Quinn and I look at each other. *What do we do?*

"Elizabeth, that's enough." Harrison's voice is low, almost a growl. "Luther." He looks over at the security guard, and Luther grabs his phone and starts talking into it. He's calling for backup.

"I am not asking you for a handout here. Even if I think you owe it to us. Call it a loan against what you know we already have in our accounts. We just need enough to get by until we sort this mess out." Obviously angry and way past caring, my mother is begging now. "I don't know what to do. Can't someone tell me what to do?" She looks around the lobby at each person in turn. They scatter, making beelines for the lobby door or the elevators, carefully avoiding eye contact with my mother, who is about as unglued as I've ever seen her. Her voice cracks and she dissolves into noisy tears.

Harrison shakes his head. "You're handling this poorly, Elizabeth. This isn't going to help Warren's case. And it won't help your children, either." He glances over at us, and something about his expression makes me want to punch him. Was he in on whatever it is that my father was doing? The idea that he might have been and is walking free while our entire life implodes, it's just . . . it's too much.

Three security guards enter the lobby and head straight for my mother. "Time to go now, miss," the tallest one says, a look of grim determination on his face. He puts a hand on my mother's elbow, but she jerks her arm away.

"Don't touch me!" she shouts. "How could you?" she says, this time to Mitch. "You and Warren were friends." The guard goes for her again and this time grabs hold and doesn't let go.

"You can't come back here, Elizabeth. It's not good for Warren or the bank, understand?" Mitch says as the security guards start dragging my mother toward the door. There is a thin layer of sweat along his forehead. As cool as he's trying to be, I think maybe my mother's managed to make him nervous. *And why should he be nervous unless he's got something to hide?*

"Let's go," Quinn says to me, glaring at Harrison. "Now."

He's trembling, actually shaking from head to toe, he's so angry. I watch him clench his fists together so tightly that I'm sure he's leaving nail marks in his palms. He heads for the lobby doors and doesn't look back.

I start to follow him until I notice that Mom's purse is still next to the planter, turned on its side, the contents spilling out onto the marble. I stoop down to gather them up, my face hot and uncomfortable.

"Let me help you." Harrison is back beside me. He crouches down, picks up my mother's compact, and hands it to me.

"Don't put yourself out," I snap.

He takes in a breath and then picks up a pen and the gum my mother always has in her purse and thrusts them toward me. "Look. I know you don't believe this, but I had nothing to do with what happened to your father."

I look into his eyes and he smiles sadly at me, and I start to think that maybe he really means it, that maybe he had no idea that my dad was doing something wrong and was caught off guard just as much as we were. *Can you tell if someone is guilty just by looking into his eyes?* Either I'm not experienced enough to know exactly what to look for or Harrison is a pretty good liar, because I can't tell. "Sorry. I just . . . Things are bad. Obviously we're just . . ."

"Scared," he says. He slips the last item into the purse and helps me up. He's so close to me that I can see the pores on his chin, the tiny black whiskers that are just under the surface. "I guess you would be. Listen. I can't officially help. But I was your father's friend. I do care about your family. Let me think about it. There might be something I can do. . . ." His hand is on my shoulder. I can feel the light pressure of his fingers through my shirt. His thumb rubs the ridge of my bra strap. At first I think he's doing it by accident, but then he keeps stroking that spot, and I get the oddest feeling that he's trying to hint at something. I look up, and when I see the way he's looking at me, it isn't hard to figure out. Oh my god. And ew, gross!

49

I back away, holding Mom's purse in front of me like a shield. *Mr. Harrison is hitting on me!* I think, so shocked that I can't quite believe that it's real. *Am I so upset that somehow I'm imagining it?* But I can still feel the lingering heat of his fingers on my shoulder, and my stomach turns.

"Lexi?" he says, his voice all surprise and confusion. I'm not fooled this time. The man is a snake. I don't bother answering him; I just turn tail and bolt out of the bank.

"My purse," my mother exclaims when I nearly bump into her and Quinn. The street is loud with morning traffic. It feels good to be outside, but I want to get away from the lobby windows. I feel like Harrison is watching me from inside. Leering.

"Well, so what now?" Quinn asks.

My mother pulls out her phone. "We find a good lawyer."

"Who?" I ask.

She rubs her temples. "Your father has someone he wants me to use."

"Okay, but then what?" Quinn says, a little more urgently. "We have no money."

"We need to get creative," Mom says. "First, we ransack the house. I usually have a little stashed in a purse or two. Then we call every friend and family member we have and ask for help. We pool our resources until your father's lawyer gives us some other ideas on what we can do. I'm not sure if we can sell anything without the FBI considering it an asset directly related to the crimes your father's accused of and trying to take it. And then . . . I don't know."

Quinn pulls out his wallet. "I have thirty dollars."

Mom looks at him, and her eyes go shiny with tears as she puts her palm to his cheek. "It's a start, thank you."

I dig my wallet out of my purse and grab the thin stack of tens inside. "I've got forty-two," I say, and then I notice the bright red card tucked between the bills. *My Bank of America card. My savings account for college. Quinn has one, too. Oh my god. There's thousands of dollars in those accounts. Can that money be seized, too?* There's a Bank of America building less than two blocks up the street. If the FBI isn't aware of those accounts . . .

"I'll be right back!" I yell as I take off running. It was Dad's idea for us to open our accounts at a bank other than his in our own names. *Was he worried even then that this would happen?* I don't want to believe it, because that would mean he's been keeping things from us, lying to us for a long time, but as I run, it makes more and more sense. As mad as I am about the lies, I'm also excited. We just might have a chance.

6

Christian

My alarm goes off at six, same as always. Except instead of going to school, I'm getting ready to rob a bank.

I slip out of bed and lock my door before I lift my mattress and box spring off my bed frame. I pry up the loose floorboards and fish around in the space beneath them for the garbage bag–covered package inside that has my disguise in it. Once it's out, I stuff it into my book bag and replace the boards, then put the bed back together. I make sure to arrange my Galaxy blanket so that the giant soccer ball across the right-hand side almost touches the floor.

"Christian, breakfast." Mom knocks on the door and then jiggles the knob. "I don't like you locking doors, mijo."

"Even if I'm naked in here?" I call out, and zip up my book bag in a hurry.

"You aren't, though, right?" she asks, laughing.

Privacy isn't in my family's vocabulary. I've managed to keep the jobs hidden, but it hasn't been easy. The key is to never, ever let my guard down.

"How long do I have, Dad?" Mom asks my abuelo as I duck into the kitchen to grab a banana. She's sipping her coffee and pouring Maria some cereal.

"Christian!" Maria crows at me as she picks up her spoon and dunks it into her Cheerios.

"Less than a week." Abuelo glances up from the stack of bills in front of him, at the wall clock, and then at me. "Christian, tuck in your shirt. You look like a cholo. Five minutes before the bus comes, mijo." He's mad serious about being on time. Never been a minute late to anything in his life, even Mom's wedding, which he was adamantly against.

Dad should be out here helping. Worrying about the bills, too, since it's his fault we got so far behind in the first place. I glare at the closed door.

"We'll talk about the bills later, okay? I can probably get the water guy to give us a few more days. Unless you'd like to call for me?" Mom gives Abuelo a pleading look. "I have to meet with those buyers in an hour, then I'll talk to my manager at the café. If he gives me my check a little early, we'll have the money."

"Okay, so we get more time on the water, but what about rent?" he asks.

Mom presses her fingers to the center of her forehead and closes her eyes. Breathes. "We'll get it; we always do."

"Hey, Gabriel's got me doing some tiling this week. And he owes me from last week. I should have something to put toward the bills tonight, too, if I can get him to pay me," I say, laying the

53

groundwork so that when I hand her some cash later, she doesn't wonder where it came from.

"I don't like you giving us your money," Mom says. "You need to save that for college. Speaking of, did you hear from UCLA yet?"

Truth is, I haven't checked my email all week. I might've gotten one about my application, but I'm half afraid to look. Not because I'm scared UCLA will reject me, but because the school might actually accept me. My transcripts are strong, and I've done lots of extracurriculars. Even made state for cross-country last year. It could happen. Which is why I can't bring myself to check email. It's one thing to be rejected, to not have a choice. It's another to know I can go. *If* money weren't an issue. *If* my dad weren't such a screw-up. *If* Mom's business were on solid ground already.

"Well, I know that you'll hear soon, mijo," Mom says, patting my arm before she turns to put away the milk.

"Yeah." I pull on my Saint Jude, the medal I wear around my neck—a coin-shaped piece of silver on a leather rope, just like the one Benny wears. We bought them together before our first job because Benny thought they would protect us.

"I gotta go," I say, and I kiss her cheek and Maria's and head for the door. Going to school today won't help pay the bills. Robbing this bank will.

"Órale!" Eddie yells out the Mary Kay van window the minute I round the corner, safely out of sight of the house.

The back door slides open, and I throw my backpack at Benny and hop in. He, Carlos, and Gabriel are all dressed in the black-hoodie-and-jeans combo we always wear for jobs. Eddie takes off before the door's shut all the way, but otherwise he drives slow and steady, making a point to stay under the speed limit.

"You catch the news last night?" Benny asks, excited.

I shake my head.

"They had a thing on about some group jumping off the US Bank Tower downtown." He gives me a pointed look.

The girl.

"They catch them?" I ask. I don't know this girl from Adam, but suddenly I'm hoping like crazy she got away.

He smiles. "Nope. The way they talked about it, it sounds like a bunch of adrenaline junkies. Apparently, they think it's this group that's been pulling stunts all over LA. Street racing. Bridge jumps. Lots of crazy stuff."

What is that like? Breaking the law just for kicks? I don't get it.

"Hurry up and get ready," Gabriel interrupts. "Who cares about all that. Focus."

Benny raises an eyebrow at me as Gabriel mutters in Spanish under his breath and pulls his mask over his face. I wish my mom and abuelo taught me Spanish. They thought they were helping me fit in, but at times like these I feel like an outsider.

I unzip my pack and fish out the garbage bag–wrapped package I took from under my bed. Ripping off the tape, I pull on my black hoodie and slip my zombie mask over my head. I slide on a pair of aviators and settle into the seat next to Benny. Gabriel opens one of the long black duffel bags at his feet and pulls out the Glocks we've used for every job. We stick them in the front pockets of our sweatshirts.

The van is quiet. We're all in our heads, picturing how it's supposed to go down. The clothes, the masks, the guns, the silence—they've become our routine. Keeping to it has started to feel crucial to the success of the take.

"Dude." Eddie looks over at Carlos. "Seriously?"

Carlos works at the wrapper on the giant frosted honeybun in his hand, his mask still up over his forehead. "What?"

"You got a serious sugar issue, vato." Eddie makes a turn. "Pretty soon we're gonna have to get all your gear in XXXL."

"Shut it," Carlos grumbles, biting into his honeybun. "It helps calm my nerves, okay?"

"Whatever, man, but just so you know, you get so large you can't run, we're leaving your fat ass."

"Yeah? Then I'll beat your skinny one." Carlos glares at him, and the rest of us crack up.

The freeway's jammed, so we sit awhile, a weird sort of lull that makes it hard to maintain the right level of adrenaline. But that changes as we pull onto Figueroa and the Bank of America comes into view. My pulse quickens. We slip on the last of our gear: black gloves fitted with countdown timers on the wrists—Benny's invention. We set the timers to zero, and then as Eddie pulls over in front of the bank, we start them in unison. My stomach gets that free-fall feeling, even though I'm sitting down, and then the van door opens and I straighten my mask one last time and we are running toward the bank, my vision tunneling down till all I can see is the glass front doors. I take out my gun.

"Get down! GET DOWN!" Gabriel hollers.

He barrels into the bank with us close on his heels. My mask is hot and humid against my mouth. I can't stop panting. People start to scream, but most of them fall to the floor immediately— the customers standing in line, the two security guys by the door. The tellers are the only ones who are still upright, staring at us with wide eyes, their mouths gaping.

We fan out across the lobby, guns aimed at the tellers, the customers, the open office doors. The Glock is alive in my hand, volatile the way I imagine a bomb must be, like it might go off if I so much as graze the trigger. I'm always careful to keep my fingers wrapped around the handle so it doesn't. Benny pulls the plastic zip ties out of his bag and starts to bind people's hands behind their backs, beginning with the security guards and bank-manager types, while Carlos keeps his gun trained on them. Gabriel goes to the teller counter, throwing his duffel bags ahead of him as he does.

I rush over to the offices lined up on one side of the lobby, all of them clearly visible through the glass walls that divide them from the rest of the bank. I check under desks and around the backs of the doors. They're all empty, all except one.

"Out here now!" I yell. The sound of my voice echoing in the space makes my stomach clench. I hate this part the most. Hurting people. Scaring the crap out of them. I grab the woman hiding behind her desk, my fingers digging into her arm as I yank her up. She has to place a hand on my chest to keep from toppling over. Panicked, she claws at my shirt, almost pulling off my mask. I push her hand away as I propel her toward the door.

I try to ignore the two framed pictures on her desk—one of a baby, the other a pigtailed toddler who looks a little like Maria, both smiling right at me. My gut is pure acid, burning. The woman hurries through the door, shrinking as far away from me as she can, her eyes never once meeting mine.

"Stay where you are and no one gets hurt." This time it's Carlos talking, his voice deeper and angrier-sounding than normal.

He grabs the lady I brought out of the office, and I can't help saying, "It'll be okay. Just do what we say and you'll be fine." The woman looks back at me once, distrust all over her face. "I mean it," I say, but it's pointless. I'm her worst nightmare. I let out a breath and vault over the teller counter to join Gabriel.

He's got his gun pressed to the back of a teller who's chalky white, her whole body quaking, but she isn't crying, not yet. He has her fill up one duffel bag with money from her drawer, discarding the money stacks with dye packs in them—*if it can't bend, it won't spend*—and makes her open the small backup safe underneath it. The other tellers are on the floor by his feet. One by one I get their keys and then use my own set of zip ties to bind their wrists. I don't look at them, not in the face. They are just wrists and hands. Body parts, not people. I can't see them any other way or it messes with my head. I start cleaning out the drawers and safes at each teller station.

"One minute," Carlos shouts. His chest is heaving, his foot tapping the floor.

Benny has the manager's keys. He locked the front door in case someone tries to walk in, and now he's swinging them around one finger. We have two minutes from start to finish before the cops might get here. Every second longer than that is a risk. Our haul will be only what's in the drawer, the reserve cash safes, and the night-deposit safe. Not a huge take, but on a Monday morning it should be at least sort of fat with weekend deposits from local stores and restaurants.

I open the night-deposit safe, and bags waterfall out onto the floor, piling one on top of another, each landing with a satisfying thud, feeling heavy in my hand when I throw them into my duffel. I'd never admit it out loud, but I get a high from being around the cash. My head practically buzzes with it. I used to think I'd be disgusted or nauseated, but you see all that cash and you can't help yourself. The smell alone makes you giddy. This might be our best job yet. *It isn't like we're stealing from these people directly,* I silently remind myself. The bank's insurance will cover what we take. I don't like scaring them, but it can't be helped, can it? In a few minutes it'll be over. They'll go home safe with a crazy story to tell.

"Okay, ladies, ten seconds," Carlos yells as Benny unlocks the front door. We run for it. My duffel bag bounces against my side as I cross the lobby. Behind us someone is probably hitting the silent alarm, but it's too late. We'll be long gone before the cops get here. I hit the front doors first and shove them open wide, heart in my throat, chest tight, totally unprepared for the wild-eyed blond girl running straight at me.

7

Lexi

I run up to the bank's front doors and they burst open. A group of men come careening out, all dressed in matching jeans and black hoodies. Their faces are weird . . . burned? Wait. They're masks—five men wearing identical zombie masks. *But what are they doing?* I can't make sense of anything. At first I think maybe they're part of a flash mob or something, about to break into some weird dance in the middle of Figueroa with a whole bunch of other zombies I somehow failed to notice before now. I strain to hear the opening beats of Michael Jackson's "Thriller." But then the one in the lead raises his hand like he's waving me out of the way, and I realize he has a gun . . . and I'm standing directly in his path.

My brain wants to turn and run, but my body is having a hard time doing it. *Go! Move!* I think. It's too late. Zombie Guy is right in my face, his body slamming into mine, and the gun is flying out to the side, landing a split second before we do. My head connects with the concrete and bounces. The world goes blurry, and I can't breathe. I gulp for air as my vision clears. For a moment all I can see is that mask and his dark eyes because his sunglasses slipped a bit in the fall. He blinks and we lock eyes. *What's happening?*

"Sorry," he says, breathing hard as he untangles himself from me. His voice is low, gruff, muffled by the mask. "You okay?"

I stare mutely at him, trying to focus, and then I manage a slow nod. I have this urge to reach up and take off his mask, to see his entire face, but my arms are pinned to my sides.

"Just stay down, okay?" he says, sounding concerned. "I'm not gonna hurt you . . . at least not again. Sorry." He pushes the sunglasses back up, and I see my reflection in them, my head still reeling, my mind slowly putting the pieces together. He had a gun. It's next to me now. He's a bank robber! My brain buzzes with a swarm of panicked thoughts. Did he use that gun inside? Kill someone? Am I next?

He stands quickly, grabs his gun, and catches up to the other guys with duffel bags on their shoulders, now running for a minivan parked at the end of the sidewalk. He looks back once and waves at me, a little wiggle of his gloved hand before he ducks inside the van. It's such a weirdly benign gesture that, without thinking, I wave back. On the driver's side door is a square sign with script lettering: MARY KAY CONSULTANT. I blink a couple of times to make sure I read it right.

That guy. And the others. They just robbed the bank with my account and Quinn's. Which means I won't be able to get my money now, at least not here. The police will be coming. This is a crime scene.

The van screeches out onto the road and disappears. I stare after it and try to make sense of the last few minutes.

"Oh my god, are you okay? I'm calling the police, honey— just stay put." A woman crouches down beside me, coffee in one hand, her cell phone in the other. "Hey, watch where that car goes! Those guys just robbed the bank!" she yells at anyone within earshot. A few guys start chasing after the van, but I'm sure it's already too far away to catch on foot. I start to get up while she dials one-handed, and then, unbelievably, she hands me her coffee to hold while she finishes up. My head's all cottony and achy. I manage to stand, but I'm off-balance. I stumble a little.

"I think I need to sit again." I sink down onto the curb. Quinn and my mother are by my side, finally having caught up.

"Oh my god! Lexi, are you all right?" Mom asks.

How can so many bad things happen in so little time? I open my mouth to say yes, that I'm okay, even though I am most definitely not, but nothing comes out. No words. Instead, I start to cry uncontrollably, like someone's pulled the zip cord on my emotions and now they're just billowing out of me.

8
Christian

"**That girl came out** of nowhere, right?" Benny stares at me, openmouthed. "You all right?"

I shrug, still stunned as the van careens away from Figueroa. I dropped my gun back there. Anything might've happened. My insides feel all shook up. I can't stop trembling. "She hit her head kinda hard." I shudder, remembering the sound it made. "I didn't mean to hurt her. She was just there and I couldn't move fast enough."

"She'll be all right," Carlos says. "She was sittin' up when we left."

He's right, but I wish I could go back and make sure.

"Homeboy waved at her. You see that? And she waved back!" Gabriel looks at me and cracks up. "Player still has game even when he's running for his life."

"Nah," I say, but I'd be lying if I said I hadn't noticed how cute she was. Even half crazy on panic and adrenaline, I couldn't *not* notice.

We ditch the van a couple of blocks down from a 7-Eleven

63

and walk the rest of the way. Gabriel sends Carlos inside to buy us Slurpees while we get our new ride. A light blue Chevy Impala was left in the store's parking lot half an hour ago by some of Soldado's guys, with the keys tucked inside a magnetic key box behind the driver's side front tire. In the movies dudes always torch their getaway cars, but in the real world that makes zero sense. It's like sending the police a smoke signal. Literally.

If we're lucky, the van won't catch anyone's eye for hours, and no one will have any idea how it got where it is or who was driving it, because Eddie doused the interior with bleach so strong I'll be smelling it on me for at least a week. The thing's completely ruined, but that's probably okay. Judging by how much ground-up crackers and crap were crushed into the carpet, I bet the lady who drives it will be relieved it's totaled. If she has insurance. Which she does. She has to. Living in that neighborhood. *Quit worrying about it,* I tell myself. *You had to have the car. It's not your fault she left the keys inside.*

Carlos trots over to the car with a cardboard drink carrier and slips into the passenger seat, unwrapping a Milky Way bar the second he's settled.

I sip at my Coke Slurpee and look out the window as Eddie drives us toward the freeway and the Madison Street house. He turns up the music and drums the steering wheel in time to the beat, rapping along. Loudly.

"Saint Jude got us through again," Benny says, taking out his necklace so he can kiss the medal.

I shake my head, smiling, and pull open my hoodie to do the same.

Nothing.

It's not there.

Heat surges through me, and my blood roars in my ears. I check the floor of the car and the seat under me, hands dipping into the crack between the seat cushions.

"What's up?" Benny asks, his eyes following my every move, one eyebrow quirked up.

"My Saint Jude's," I whisper, hoping that the other guys aren't listening. "It's gone."

Benny lets this sink in. "You think you left it in the van?"

"Left what in the van?" Gabriel asks, suddenly alert.

"He lost his medal," Benny says, outing me before I can tell him not to. It ticks me off, but I can't really say anything. They need to know. My whole body goes numb. We have to find the medal. My name's engraved on the back. It's a freaking billboard sign pointing at me with the word *guilty* lit up in neon. Where could it be? The possibilities make me want to puke.

Eddie jerks the car around in the middle of the road, tires squealing the whole time. The driver behind us honks long and loud, and Gabriel shoots him the bird.

We barrel back to the street the car's on. I get out alone, pulling my gloves back on, then dipping my hands into my pockets because who wears gloves this time of year? I move carefully to the van and open the side door. The bleach smell wrecks my lungs and makes my eyes tear up, so I put my shirt over my mouth and nose and do a quick pass of the backseats, ducking to look under them, then running my hand along the seat cracks here, too. I pull up more crackers and sticky, nasty kid mess, but no medal. I stumble out of the van, eyes weeping, coughing like mad, feeling like someone sandblasted my throat and lungs.

"Well?" Gabriel asks, turning in his seat so he can look at me as I slide into the backseat again and Eddie takes off fast.

"It's not there," I say. My voice is as shredded as I feel.

A string of curses pours out of his mouth. "If it's in the bank . . ."

"I know," I say.

"No, I don't think you do." He runs a hand through his hair and glares at me. "If they find it . . ."

"I get it!" I yell, more mad at myself than at him. I'm always careful. How could I have screwed up so badly? Gabriel slaps the back of my head, just hard enough to make it sting.

"Hey, cut it out. He's sorry, okay?" Benny leans between us so Gabriel won't hit me again. My head throbs, but I don't go after Gabriel. I deserved the slap. We could get caught. For the first time since we started doing jobs, I'm really freaking scared.

"Any idea where exactly you might've lost it?" Benny asks. "Think hard, bro."

I run through the whole job in my head—going through the door, past the lobby, to the offices.

The offices.

That lady grabbed my neck. Or it came off when I ran into the girl outside. I don't know . . . but the more I think about it, the more I'm sure it happened inside the bank.

"The woman I pulled out of the bank office. She grabbed my chest. She could've pulled it off," I say, surer with every word that this is what happened. Somewhere in that office the medal could be just lying there. Would it have gone under the desk? Or would it be in plain view—one giant, ridiculously good clue that will lead the police straight to us? I need to get back to that bank. It's all I can do not to jump out of the car and run all the way there now. But that would be stupid.

"Perfect. Just perfect," Gabriel mutters. "The police are all over that bank right now. No way we can go back for it," he says, reading my mind.

"So what do we do, then?" Benny asks, and all of them look at me. I lost the stupid thing, so it's up to me to figure out the next step.

"I go back tomorrow. The police'll be gone and it'll be business as usual. I'll find a way to get into that lady's office and look for it. And if they have it already and they come for me . . . they get only me. No way I'd give any of you up. You know that. Ever."

"Yeah, we know," Benny says.

We keep quiet, each of us imagining the heat that could right now be headed my way. Much as they trust me to keep them safe and not rat them out, they're already putting distance between us.

But that's okay. I've got bigger things to worry about right now. Once Soldado finds out, he'll have to let his carnales know. . . .

"Look, we don't gotta say anything to Soldado about this," Benny says out loud, like he's reading my thoughts.

Gabriel stares out the passenger side window.

"Gabriel, think about my mom and Maria. For their sakes, don't," I say, hating how desperate and scared I sound.

"You have to find it," Gabriel says. "Whatever you gotta do. Do it."

When the Madison Street house comes into view, my insides start to shake. Soldado's favorite car is in front of it—a tricked-out Dodge Charger that looks like something from one of those Fast and Furious movies. Not the typical wheels for him, way too small to be comfortable for someone his size. He's over 210 if he's a pound, and at least six feet tall. The dude benches a sick amount of weight, and his arms and chest are ripped. I think if his dad hadn't been in Florencia Heights when he was coming up and inspired his son to do the same, Soldado could have been a football player with a nickname like Bulldozer.

"Let's get this over with," Eddie says as he climbs out of the car and grabs a duffel bag. "I got plans later."

"Yeah, with who?" Benny asks.

"None of your business."

Benny laughs—it's a nervous sort of sound, half amused, but riding on a current of fear. "Yeah, that means he's got a booty call in with Theresa."

"So what if I do?" Eddie shrugs, but he won't look directly

at us. Theresa's a girl who lives down the street from him, and as skinny as he is, she's equally . . . uh . . . curvy. Carlos always ribs him about it, which makes no sense, given his own weight issues.

Carlos looks ready to launch into a Theresa-bashing comedy routine when the front door of the house opens and one of Soldado's guys appears in the doorway, and the moment gets serious.

We walk inside, nodding to Twitch, the dude in the doorway, nicknamed for his tic, this constant jerk of his head that happens every few minutes and makes him look perpetually nervous. He probably has Tourette's syndrome, but I would never ask him about it.

The house is hot and loud. It's the middle of the day, but there's a bunch of people hanging out, dancing, and drinking forties.

Soldado has set up camp in the master bedroom. He's got a couple of camping chairs around a card table on the concrete subfloor and is eating a foot-long Subway sandwich, his hand on another one like he's afraid it'll roll off the table before he can devour it, too.

"It go smooth?" Soldado asks right out of the gate, and I feel my balls shrink up. I don't dare look at the others or show any sign that something's up, not with him and all his boys watching. They miss nothing.

I wait for Gabriel to tell him about my medal. A month ago he wouldn't have, no matter what. We're family. That comes first. But now . . . after all the time he's spent with the Florencia boys and the way they seem to get tighter all the time . . . I'm almost sure he'll offer it up.

Benny clears his throat. "Way smooth."

Soldado takes a bite of sandwich. Tuna salad. Ugh. I hate the stuff. The smell. It makes me want to gag. "Well, what are you waiting for? Unpack the bills."

We unzip the duffel bags and start stacking the cash in front of him while he eats. The pile is impressive, and his eyes light up. "Oh yeah. Now, that's what I'm talkin' about." He puts down his sandwich and thumbs through a stack of cash. "Nice."

It takes him a while to count it and then count it again. Fifty thousand dollars. He stacks it into seven piles: one for each of us, one for him for arranging the getaway car and supplying the guns and equipment, and one for the Eme because any job done in their hood is subject to their tax, which amounts to half the take. Don't pay it and they find out? (And they always find out.) You and everyone you love gets a hit put on their heads. It's the cost of doing business. Simple as that. Still, it sucks to watch the Eme pile grow tall and see our skinny piles beside it. All that risk. All that work. And all we get is a little over four thousand dollars apiece. But I'd rather have four thousand and still be alive than more money and end up dead. Except now I have to worry about getting caught. It's not enough money to go to jail for, not by a long shot.

"You tell them about the next one?" he asks Gabriel.

"Yeah. I mentioned it."

What is he doing? I dropped my medal back there, and now we're talking about the next job? There can't be a next job. Today cinched that. Even if by some miracle I manage to get the medal back, we need to stop. Today was a warning. The medal. The girl. It's over. Besides, what's the rush? We never do a job this close on the heels of another. Soldado knows how bad an idea that is.

"I got my guys ready to start diggin' now," Soldado says. "You're gonna hit on Fourth of July weekend. Bank is closed. Plus, there's construction going on in the building. Makes it less likely anyone'll hear any noise or worry about vibrations from underground. Gives these guys plenty of time to make sure they can bust through the vault floor and gives you guys time to empty it, plus the deposit boxes. The only time we'll ever get the opportunity on this one. And this time you get it all. Every last cent. None of this petty smash-and-grab stuff anymore."

Before I can think better of it, I blurt out, "We didn't agree to do it."

"What's there to think about? You do this job and it goes well? You'll be rich." Soldado leans back in his chair and looks at us, smiling. "We'll take a break. Even if we wanted to do more jobs, the heat'll be too much." He's basically repeating what Gabriel told us yesterday. "Imagine that." He smiles again, wide enough that I can see all his teeth. "You got my word."

I look over at Benny, Carlos, and Eddie, all of them extra anxious to leave, like me. And then there's Gabriel, cracking jokes

71

9
Lexi

My alarm goes off, jarring me out of a nightmare about the bank robbery from yesterday morning. This time when the guy runs into me, he lifts his mask and it's Harrison. He points his gun at my chest and it goes off. I have this phantom ache right under my ribs, just below my heart, and also a very real, very large lump on the back of my head. *What is going on?* I feel like I somehow dropped out of regular life and landed in the middle of some alternate universe where I'm surrounded by criminals.

It's Tuesday morning and I get out of bed, shower, and start dressing for battle. Even if Leo, Elena, and Whitney hadn't been texting me constantly all day yesterday to give me the school gossip blow by blow, I'd be expecting the onslaught of whispering, pointing, and laughing that will rain down on Quinn and me. Scandal like the one our family is involved in doesn't get ignored, even if up until now we've both been pretty popular—maybe especially because of that.

I've got on my skinniest skinny jeans—the ones that are guaranteed to make guys stare at my legs and forget about what my father's done—stacked-heel boots, and a shirt that adheres to the dress code and flatters in all the right places. I look sexy and confident. Good. I'm going to need all the confidence I can muster.

It's our first day back at Westwood Prep since Dad's arrest. We missed yesterday to go with my mother to the bank and the lawyer's office, but neither of us can afford to miss any more time, and besides, home is the last place I want to be right now. I have to keep moving. Stop and I risk thinking about everything too much.

"You're going all in," Quinn says when he sees me, one eyebrow raised. He's got on his usual jeans, T-shirt, and Converse combination. Guys don't need the armor girls do.

The day is nice—hot, but clear and a little breezy. We slip into the garage and stare at our bikes. The minute I got my license, the first thing I did was beg our parents for a motorcycle. That they gave it to me without a fight shows how much they like to spoil us. And that the following month Quinn got one just goes to show how committed my brother is to not letting me do risky stuff without him. My bike looks like bright blue-and-black death, a rocket with wheels, which is exactly what made me want it. What makes me love it even more is that it can go five miles per hour faster than Quinn's bike.

We strap our book bags to the backs of our bikes and roll them to the garage door.

"You look to see if the press people arrived yet?" I ask Quinn.

"There's a couple, but it looked pretty quiet." When Dad was arrested and the reporters started to show up, I pictured them camping out in front of our house 24/7, but it turns out most of them take off sometime after eight o'clock at night and don't return until morning.

"Should we mess with them a little?" I grab my helmet and slip it over my head.

"Why not?" Quinn laughs as he does the same. It makes me feel good that I can always manage to cheer him up, even at the worst of times.

We let the garage door rumble to life before we start the bikes. I can't see or hear the people out on our sidewalk, but I can sense them scurrying into action, grabbing cameras so they can tape some footage of what they hope is my mother leaving the house looking disheveled and emotionally overwrought. A thrill goes through me. We'll give them a show, but not that kind. I rev my bike and lean forward. The door is halfway up. When it's at three-quarters, I glance over at Quinn and he nods and we both shoot from underneath it, bursting out of the garage like we're being shot from a cannon, tires squealing. I spin sideways to the left, leaving a smear of black on the driveway, and feint like I'm headed straight for the cameras. Laughing into my helmet as a reporter dives out of the way and face-plants into a patch of flowers, I correct my course and hurtle onto the street.

There's an unspoken dare in the way Quinn looks over at me and tilts his head once we leave the confines of our neighborhood. He wants to race—something we do often enough to earn us a ticket or two. Or four.

I lay on the throttle in reply, and we weave our way into traffic. School is a fifteen-minute drive, but we'll make it in ten. I'm laughing the whole way, mostly because I picture Quinn cracking up, too. We're competitive, but half the fun is in the race, not the finish. It's the feel of the wind on my face, the growl of my bike, and having Quinn right there next to me. Who needs coffee in the morning when you can have this to wake you up?

We pull into the parking lot with Quinn just a hairbreadth ahead of me. He guns his bike so it goes triumphantly up on one wheel, and even though he can't see it, I roll my eyes. *Show-off.* I might have lost, but I feel good as we cruise toward our designated parking spaces. My heart's pumping and my gut is a cage of butterflies after all the close calls we made to get ahead of the traffic. Which means there's no more room for nerves about what might happen at school.

Our friends are milling around our parking spots, waiting for us.

"I'm so glad you're back!" Elena says once I'm off the bike. She throws her arms around me and squeezes hard, as if we haven't seen each other in weeks. "So what happened yesterday? Quinn said you got mowed down by bank robbers or something. Is that true? 'Cause that robbery was on the news last night. They said the guys who did it have hit a bunch of banks. They're like pros or something."

"Yeah," I say, half embarrassed, though I don't know why. "I was standing in front of the bank, and one of them basically tackled me." I hesitate a second, remembering. "He was wearing a mask, but I did see his eyes." The exact shade is still crystal clear in my memory. Thinking about it now, it seems like we stared at each other for a long time, but it was maybe seconds. "They were really dark brown. Nearly black, actually. And maybe it was just the sun on his face, but they sort of glittered. You know how some people's eyes are like that? All lit up?" This sounds weird. I'm weird. *Stop obsessing about his eyes.*

I launch into an abbreviated explanation about why we were downtown in the first place, leaving out the part about our parents' accounts being frozen, because it's too embarrassing to confess even to my best friends. Instead, I say that I went to take some money out of my savings—which is the truth, just not all of it.

"He sounds cute," Whitney says.

"How do you get that from what I just said?" I ask, laughing. "He had a zombie mask on. I don't even know what he looks like."

"Come on, you described his eyes like you would a guy you're looking to date. And he's obviously dangerous. That's hot," she says, thoroughly convinced.

"Yeah, well, I don't date criminals," I say, and then when Whitney raises a brow at me because technically we're all criminals, too, I start to giggle. "Okay, not the dangerous kind, at least."

Quinn rolls his eyes and concentrates on getting something out of his backpack. I'm not sure what he's upset about until I realize that he's probably thinking about Dad. I'm making light of criminals and our dad's in jail. If the motorcycle race we just had made him forget for a second, this conversation reminded him all over again. *Smooth, Lexi, real smooth.*

"So how long before your dad's trial and stuff?" Leo asks.

"They set the start date for the end of summer. Both sides have to prepare their cases, I guess," I say, watching Quinn throw his backpack over one shoulder and stuff his hands in his pockets.

"Well, crap, that's forever," Whitney complains. "Does he have to stay in jail all that time?"

Quinn shakes his head. "No. The lawyer's helping us arrange bail, and then he'll be out until the trial's over. He only goes back to jail if he's convicted."

Elena hugs me again. "I'm so sorry this is happening to you guys. How long will the trial last?"

"It could take months. The lawyers haven't given us a set timetable yet," Quinn says.

"Months? How are you supposed to deal with not knowing if he'll do serious jail time for that long?"

I wince. She isn't trying to upset me, but her questions feel like daggers jabbing me in the gut. "We just will. Because we have to." Quinn's staring at me, his jaw clenched shut, hurt clear in his eyes. "Hey, can we just talk regular stuff?"

"Absolutely, my sister will stop with the inquisition this minute," Whitney says. "Whatever you want to do. We're here for you. And besides, I could stand to hear more about this robbery." Whitney gathers both me and Elena into another hug, so tight that my chin knocks against her collarbone and I get a noseful of her perfume, and then we're all walking together toward the front entrance of the school building, with Quinn and the boys bringing up the rear.

"I don't believe it. You're actually here?" Bianca, Harrison's daughter, is a few cars over, leaning against her black BMW convertible, her two besties gathered around her. She sips at a cup full of her usual morning cocktail of kale and other healthy stuff. She makes a clucking sound. "How brave of you two. My dad said you seemed so desperate when you came to the bank to beg for money that I thought for sure you wouldn't show up today. Good for you for proving me wrong."

"Ignore her," Leo warns me. "Come on, let's just get inside."

I want to listen to him, but I can't. I turn toward her, wanting to say or do something that will knock that stupid grin right off her face.

"Lexi. Don't." Quinn steps in front of me. "We don't need any more drama."

I glare at Bianca. She smirks, and her besties huddle tighter around her, prepping for me to go ballistic. I want to—badly— but Quinn's right. Getting in trouble will only make things worse.

"Have a nice day," Bianca singsongs, still baiting me. I let Quinn and the others lead me into school, but the whole time I picture running over Bianca's smug face with my bike, leaving tire tracks right down the center of her new nose job. It helps a little, but not much.

We don't get ten feet inside before Principal Weaver blocks our path. All six foot two inches of her.

"Alexandra and Quinn. Good morning." Her face puckers as if she's sucking on a handful of Sour Patch Kids. "We weren't expecting you back so soon. How are you?"

"We're fine," Quinn says. "Thanks for asking." He looks her right in the eye, and she fidgets. Obviously, something's up here.

"That's good, but really, you shouldn't feel like you have to return to school this quickly. Why not take a few more days to be with your family? I'm sure you could all use some time to process what's happened. We can have your friends bring you your assignments." She starts to corral us back outside.

"No, really, it's okay. We want to be back. Doing normal stuff will help the most," I say, walking around Weaver. She doesn't need to worry about us making a scene. Quinn and I are tougher than that. I can see other students stopping to stare at us, at Weaver, curious about what's going on.

Weaver licks her lips. "Well then . . . come with me to my office for a few minutes. There are some things we'll need to discuss. Please." She looks at Leo and the rest of our friends. "Go on to your classes. You can talk to Quinn and Alexandra later on." I hate when she uses my whole name like that. It makes me sound like I'm a hundred years old or something, but in all the years we've gone to Westwood, she's never once called me Lexi.

Quinn and I follow Weaver past the gawking kids in the hallway. I can hear them whispering as we pass by, but I don't try to make out what they're saying. I just hold my head up and concentrate on the Westwood Prep banner hanging overhead, mentally tracing over the white outline of the lion head on it.

The principal's office is large enough to have a sitting area, and that's where we end up, each of us tucked into a shallow navy-blue upholstered chair with stainless-steel armrests. The room is a calculated mix of sleek modern furniture, Chinese jar lamps, Persian rugs, and gleaming mahogany tables meant to impress the parents of future students.

Our school is the most prestigious one in Los Angeles, with a waiting list to get in, so the office is appropriately over the top, and Principal Weaver treats it like a museum. Nothing is out of place. She crosses her legs and tucks them under her chair before folding her hands neatly in her lap. Her hair is pulled back into a low bun, and she's wearing pearl earrings. The glasses perched on the end of her nose give her a librarian sort of vibe—very stiff and buttoned up, but sitting this close, I can easily see that she has a tattoo, a large one, its tip visible above the filmy collar of her shirt. It looks like it could be the raised ridge of a dragon. Rumor has it that on weekends she's into cosplay and going to science-fiction and fantasy conventions. I can't quite picture it. Her in a Black Widow costume.

"I know you are dealing with a lot right now. I really hate to add to it." She sighs. "I did try to call your mother several times but couldn't get an answer. Of course, I assumed that I'd have a few more days to try to reach you before you came back. . . ." She trails off.

"My mother isn't big on answering the phone right now,"

Quinn says. "We've been getting a lot of threatening phone calls."

This is true. Some from credit card companies and some from anonymous callers who are really angry with my father.

"Well, I'm very sorry to hear that," Principal Weaver says, looking as if she means it. She glances down at her hands. "I wish she had answered. It would have saved you the trip over here this morning. Given the nature of your father's crimes—"

"His *alleged* crimes," Quinn interrupts her. "He hasn't been convicted of anything."

"Yes, well, the school's trustees have decided that you will not be able to attend the last few weeks of school. It would create an unsafe environment, given the highly public nature of your father's crime." She lets out a relieved breath, like having to tell us this has weighed on her. *The poor thing.* "We've already collected your things from your lockers, so you won't have to do that in front of your classmates." Until now I hadn't noticed the two cardboard boxes half hidden behind her chair. I stare at them, feeling like somehow this has to be a joke. I expected gossip and rude comments, but being thrown out of school never even occurred to me.

"We don't want to cause you any further trauma. I know it's been hard." She leans over to pat my hand but stops when she notices the expression on my face.

"How exactly is the school in danger?" Quinn asks.

The pitying look on her face makes me want to punch her. I have to look away, focus on something, anything, that will

82

keep me from losing it. Above her desk are framed photos of Weaver with the various school board members. I shouldn't be surprised, even though I am, to see Harrison.

"Did the board make this decision, or did you?" I ask.

She stares at me. "I'm not sure what difference that makes," she says.

"Mitch Harrison is the difference. Did he help make this decision?" I ask, my voice slow and deliberate.

She avoids my gaze, and it's all the answer I need. Suddenly I'm sure that my father isn't lying about Harrison's involvement in the mortgage scheme just to make himself look better in our eyes. He's telling the truth. And now Harrison wants to distance himself from us as much as he can because he wants my dad to take the fall alone.

"What about finals? What happens to our grades?" Quinn roars as what she's said finally sinks in.

"I've emailed your mother some names of private instructors who are willing to proctor your finals. Pass them—I have no doubt you will—and your grades will not be affected at all. But I do need to be clear: all end-of-the-year activities—the upcoming Griffith Observatory field trip and the school's Summer Celebration Dance—neither of you will be allowed to attend." She stands up. "Look, I know this isn't easy. But it couldn't have come at a better time in terms of how far along we are in the school year. Try to see it as bonus summer vacation time."

"What about next school year? We'll be able to come back then, right?" Quinn asks. "For my senior year?"

She presses her lips together and begins massaging her temple. "I can't answer that right now, Quinn. The school's admissions committee and, of course, our board of trustees will have to readdress your enrollment at our July meeting." *Which is as good as saying no.* I think I might be sick.

"Whatever happened to innocent until proven guilty?" I say. "This isn't fair. None of this is our fault, and yet we keep getting treated like it is. We did nothing wrong!" I'm yelling now, and I don't care if the whole school hears me. This isn't right. We've gone to this school for eight years. Every friend we have in the world goes here. Quinn's wrestling team, my architecture and design club. Our whole lives are centered around this place. I can't wrap my head around the fact that we might not ever get to come back.

"Alexandra, calm down. Getting hysterical won't change things." Weaver hands me a tissue even though I'm not crying. "Why don't we stop by the counselor's office on the way out? Taking a little time to chat with Mr. Soto might help." She picks up her phone and looks relieved to have something to do. "Eugenia, ask Tom to come get the kids' boxes for them, and have Mr. Soto clear his morning schedule. The Scotts will be coming in to meet with him. Thank you."

"We're not meeting with Soto," I say loudly. "We don't need a counselor. What we need is some compassion, but apparently you're incapable of it."

Quinn gets up from his chair, his face a total blank, the way it always is when he's really upset. Where I blow up, he withdraws.

"This isn't the end. My father's lawyers will see to that," I say, hoping like crazy it's true.

That she doesn't look at all concerned rattles me. Without another word I storm past her. Quinn stumbles after me. The ladies in the office get hyperfocused on their paperwork as we go by, but outside the office a group of students has gathered, and they are staring in through the large front window at us like we're animals in a zoo exhibit.

I don't want to go out there, but then I spot Leo, Whitney, and Elena in the crowd. I take a deep breath and push the office doors open. It's quiet. Everyone in the hall is watching us.

"Lexi." Derek pushes past them. "Everything okay?"

He should be mad at me. I text-dumped him with barely an explanation. It was awful. *I* was awful. He's a nice guy. I had fun dating him. But then he started looking at me as though he really liked me. It sounds mental now, thinking it. I know it does, but his look felt like . . . a trap.

I couldn't feel the same about him. I didn't want to feel it back. I just wanted to be free. He should be furious, because he didn't deserve what happened.

"Lexi, are you okay?" he tries again. He goes to take my hand, but I wrench it away. I can't have him being nice right now. All I want is to get out of here. I have to stay mad. Mad is better than crying.

"I can't do this right now," I say, and then more softly, "I'm sorry. Really. But I can't."

He looks wounded and maybe a little bit angry. That's good.

I deserve that. Someday I'll try to talk to him about things. Right now, I'll just screw it up if I try. Note to self: no more dating for a long while. I need to figure out how to not suck at relationships.

"What's going on?" Leo calls, running to catch up with me and Quinn as we head for the parking lot. "Lexi! Wait."

I shake my head. I can't talk, not now, or I'll cry—and I won't do that in front of half the school. No way.

"I'll call you," I say over my shoulder, and am relieved that I sound calmer than I feel. The bell rings. I turn around and paste on a smile. "Better not be late to class or maybe they'll kick you out, too."

Leo's eyes go wide.

We don't wait for the custodian to bring our boxes out. Stupid Weaver. Where were we supposed to put them, anyway? We drive here on motorcycles every day; has she really never noticed?

We jump on our bikes, and I slam mine into gear and take off for the exit. I let out a scream. Harrison needs to pay for his part in all this. If my family is going down in flames, I will make it my mission to drag him down with us.

The one bright spot in this crap storm? Having no school means I can concentrate on getting my money and going after Harrison.

The Bank of America looks completely normal. No crime-scene tape or police blocking the front door. If I hadn't been here yesterday, it would be hard to believe a robbery happened at all.

Stooping down, I touch the spot on the concrete where I

fell and replay the moment in my mind. I try to imagine what it must've been like. To be him. Running out of the bank, racing against time, leaving with a whole lot of cash. There's something sexy about stealing that much money, especially knowing that no one was hurt. Besides, banks have insurance for this sort of thing. I envy the guy a bit. Today he has money. *Not sure I can say the same thing for myself,* I think, glancing at the ATM at the front of the building.

My phone vibrates against my hip. Quinn's just texted.

Where r u?

Had an errand 2 run. Nothing important. C U L8R.

I sneaked out almost as soon as we got back from school. Maybe I should've told him I was going, but I knew he'd want to tag along, and I needed some time alone. Also, I wanted to prove that coming here was no big deal. Get back on the horse and all that. I could've gone to another Bank of America—there's practically one on every street close to our house—but it felt important to do this. I won't let my father's arrest or getting kicked out of school *or* a freak run-in with a dangerous criminal do me in. I am determined to get back some control over my life, even if it's doing something as silly as revisiting this ATM.

I walk to the end of the line of people waiting to use the ATM, and I dig into my bag for my card. The sidewalk is crowded with tourists and shoppers headed for the Bloc mall. I don't pay much attention until one of them bumps my shoulder, hard enough that I drop my bag. My wallet and half a dozen other things tumble across the sidewalk.

"Thanks a lot," I call after the suit who knocked into me. He turns and shrugs a halfhearted "sorry" but keeps going.

Jerk.

"Need some help?" A boy about my age stoops down as I scramble to retrieve my lipstick. My wallet was unzipped, and half of my cards are strewn out beside it. A quarter rolls right under the boy's shoe. *Just perfect.*

"No thanks. I have it . . . ," I start to say. I look up and he's right next to me, his mouth twitching into a grin. Oh wow. I stare, taking in his short black hair and the scruff along his chin, accentuating his jawline. He has thick lashes over deep brown eyes that gleam softly every time he smiles. I suck in a breath. He looks at me, one eyebrow raised, his smile less certain all of a sudden. I'm full-on gawking at him like I've never seen a boy before. I laugh a little, feeling embarrassed. My head's obviously all screwed up. The past few days are starting to get to me. Here I am, going weak in the knees over some random stranger. That's not me. Whitney maybe, but definitely not me. I concentrate on retrieving my things.

"Yeah, I guess I could use some help."

He plucks up my wallet and begins to put the cards back inside it, his eyes going from it to me and back again. "Are you all right?" he asks.

Okay, Lex, shake it off. You've got work to do, I tell myself.

"Yes. I'm fine. Thanks." I stuff my lipstick, gum, and phone back into my purse.

He slips the last card into place and holds out my wallet. "Here you are."

I take it, and our fingers accidentally touch. A little fizz of energy passes from the spot where my fingers are brushing against his to the center of my stomach. His hand draws back quickly. I look up. He's staring at me, his eyebrows knit together in surprise or maybe confusion. There's something between us. Undeniable. *This boy.* Looking at him is like letting a hundred hummingbirds loose in my chest. I feel an irresistible urge to find out more about him. . . . It's sudden and unexpected and weird. Exciting, too. Disconcerting? Um, *yes.*

"I can manage," I say, busying myself with taking out my ATM card as I stand up. I need to focus. Breathe. He's hot. So what? A lot of guys in LA are.

"So," he says, chuckling a little under his breath. He rubs at his chin and looks sidelong at me, smiling and shaking his head. He's into me, too. I can tell. I can't help it—I flash him a smile. For a moment I feel like my old self.

"Thanks for helping me," I say as I get back into line by the ATM. I turn away, but I can still feel him there, watching. After a second, I turn around. "What?" I ask. I should ignore him and concentrate on getting my money . . . or I could flirt a little more. It would provide a nice distraction from the "Will there or won't there be money in my account?" question rolling around in my head, right?

"Nothing. You on vacation or something?" He has this slight East Los Angeles inflection that adds to the overall tough-guy impression he's working hard to maintain.

"No. Just running errands."

"You have a half day at school?" he asks, getting into line behind me. His weighted tone suggests that he probably thinks I'm ditching.

What does it matter?

"Maybe. Did you?"

"Maybe," he says, mimicking me, a smirk on his lips. The dimple in his right cheek deepens.

"And you picked the financial district as your ditch destination? Of every place you could've gone?" I tap my ATM card against the fingernails of my right hand impatiently. The line is moving at a snail's pace. There are still two people ahead of me. "Doesn't seem worth it."

"Actually, I accidentally left something here the other day, and if I don't get it back, I'm as good as dead," he says dramatically, leaning in so that it seems as if he's whispering it into my ear. I can feel him smiling. "What's one or two missed classes compared with that?"

"As good as dead, huh? What'd you leave behind? Military secrets?" I joke, giving in to the back-and-forth that's developing so easily between us.

"Worse. A family heirloom."

"That doesn't sound death-worthy."

"You don't know my family," he says, eyebrow raised flirtatiously, obviously enjoying himself.

"What kind of heirloom?"

"A medal on a leather rope."

"You mean a necklace?" I say.

"No. I mean a medal on a leather rope . . . that I happen to wear around my neck." He struggles to keep a straight face.

"Ah, okay. Man jewelry."

He groans. "No! That sounds even worse." We laugh. "It used to be my grandfather's. He says it gave him luck when he left Mexico for the United States. He gave it to me when I started applying for colleges." He seems embarrassed or something. All of the sudden he won't look me in the eye.

"Yeah, I can see where you'd catch some heat for losing that. Any idea where to start the search? Did you leave it by the ATM?"

"Actually, I have a pretty good idea about its exact location." He hesitates. "This is going to sound weird, but how would you feel about helping me? Get it back, I mean? Up for a little intrigue?"

The way he's asking is part plea, part dare. The line moves forward once more, and it's my turn. I step up to the ATM, and he backs up a respectable distance, giving me space while I punch in my PIN. It's been good talking to him. Standing here all this time, waiting by myself, I would've been stressed about whether the money was still there. I logged into my account several times this morning already. Every time, the balance indicated that the funds were there, but until the cash is in my hands, I feel as if the FBI might swoop in and seize it. I press my finger to the numbers and hold my breath. The machine begins to whir, and a stack of bills appears. *Thank god.* I exhale shakily and slip the money into the inside zippered pocket of my bag and hug it close. Relief washes through me.

The boy is watching me intently, his head cocked to one side, and I want to laugh. I must've looked crazy just then. Who stresses that hard about a withdrawal?

"So that's done," I say, patting my bag. "Now you. How can I help? What would I have to do?" I'm suddenly feeling generous. My money is all there. I took out enough to make it easier to breathe. By now Quinn's probably withdrawn some of his, too. We have enough to get groceries and stuff. At least for a little while.

"I think the medal is inside the bank. In the second office on the right."

I raise a brow. "Okaaay. So just go in and get it. Can't be that hard, right?"

"Normally? No. But the lady who works in that office is not too happy with me right now. I used to date her daughter."

"Used to?"

"Until I broke it off last week. It didn't, uh, go very well." He blushes, which makes him that much more adorable.

Bad breakups are something I understand intimately. I'm the queen of them.

"I dropped off some stuff here yesterday. You know, things my girlfriend gave me while we were dating that she wanted back. I was wearing the medal, but once I left, I realized it was gone. It has to be in the office. But I don't want to go in and see her mom again. She was less than cool about it. Besides, the bank was robbed yesterday. You knew that, right? She probably doesn't need to see me again, you know?"

I nod. "Yeah. I was here, actually. One of the robbers ran right into me."

His eyes widen.

"But let's not talk about that right now. Let's focus on your 'medal.'" For some reason I want to help this guy. Probably because it's no big deal. It's a problem with an easy solution, unlike the ones in my own life. And talking to him has been the first fun distraction I've had since I jumped off the Bank Tower on Saturday night. "You want me to go in and get it, right?"

"Right," he says. "Without her getting suspicious. Think you can make up some reason for going into her office?"

Not quite a BAM-worthy maneuver, but it has the same feel to it. How can I say no?

"I think I can manage," I say dryly, and he laughs, shaking his head like he thinks I'm a real piece of work.

This boy has no idea. *Piece of work* doesn't even begin to cover it.

10
Christian

I watch the girl walk into the bank and try to chill. That she actually decided to help me still has me shocked. I did my best to flirt, but truth is, I always feel like a giant tool putting on the charm. And with this girl, I'm not sure I pulled it off. I don't have half the game Benny claims I do. Gabriel's better at it. Girls practically throw their phone numbers at him the second he raises an eyebrow in their direction. But whatever I did must've been enough, because there she goes, past the teller counter and toward the offices. I close my eyes and breathe deeply as she disappears from view.

It'll be there. It has to be there. I can picture it in my head. A small silver disk lying on the floor, half under the desk. The more I think back, the more I'm positive that's where it is. It feels right. I don't let myself think too hard on the fact that the cops probably already have it and are on their way to my house right now to arrest me. Mom opening the door, the look on her face. I shake my head.

No.

My medal is inside. It has to be.

I try to picture where the girl is now. Maybe signing in at the little kiosk you have to go to first before someone helps you. Would she try to just walk into the office? Or worse—will she tell her she's here to pick up her daughter's ex-boyfriend's medal? I pace the sidewalk.

Calm the hell down, man, I tell myself as I move to the edge of the sidewalk near the curb. *She'll get it. It'll be there.* That she showed up this morning—that she's the one helping me—feels weirdly like fate, like maybe God is giving me a sign that he's going to let me get away again. I lit a candle at the church on my way home last night. Ducked in and struck a match, like one of the tías. Then I got here this morning and there she was, looking up at me, those blue-green eyes of hers, not exactly trusting but curious, and I just thought, *Okay, so here's the answer to my prayer.* The medal's in there, and she's going to get it for me.

I can't see much of the bank's lobby from here, just the guard, the same guy who was there yesterday, looking more alert than he did before, staring at every person coming through the door as if they're a threat. It's weird to see the victims afterward. It kind of feels like another violation or something, like I'm hurting them twice—him and the girl. I don't like it.

I look down at my phone. Five minutes. It's only been five lousy minutes since she went in. My skin feels like it's crawling off my bones. I can't stay still.

I reach into my pocket and take the girl's student ID out and stare at it. I swiped it when I helped her pick up her wallet. I didn't really plan to do it; I just saw it and wanted a better look. I shouldn't have, but I'm curious about who she is. Alexandra Scott. Sophomore class. Student number 5756439. Westwood Preparatory. Never heard of it, but obviously it's one of those rich-kid schools, probably in Orange County somewhere. Figures. She's got that rich-kid look. Nice clothes, the air of cool confidence that only comes from getting whatever you want, whenever you want. I must've totally flipped her out good yesterday. It had to be the first brush with crime this girl's ever had. *Maybe that's why she came back here this morning? To revisit the scene of the crime?* I've heard some people are into that, that they find it exciting or something. I laugh. Yeah, it's exciting all right. Until you get caught.

I wonder what she told the police afterward. Did she notice anything in particular about me? Something that could help them? My nerves are getting the better of me. I stare at the ID again and rub the corner with my thumb. *Please, please, please. Hurry.*

A few more minutes pass, and then she's coming out, scanning the street for me. I wave her over, feeling suddenly anxious about more than just whether she found my medal. She's tall, lean, and graceful as a dancer, walking like she's on a catwalk. Her blond hair bounces with every step, falling over her shoulders in perfect, loose waves. *Alexandra.* It fits her. Guys passing by turn back around for a second look, and I have to laugh because I'm ridiculous to think she'd want anything to do with me. I feel out of place standing next to her in my faded jeans and white T shirt.

"Did you find it?" I ask, running my hand nervously through my hair and trying not to stare into those deep-ocean eyes of hers.

She smiles and holds up one hand, and dangling from it is my Saint Jude's. *Holy crap. It was really there.*

I go to take it, but she pulls it out of reach and turns the medal over in her hands. "Christian Ruiz? Is that your name?"

Actually my last name is Sims, like my dad's, but I wanted Ruiz instead so it'd be the same last name as Benny's. I get a little closer and cover her hand with my own, trapping the medal between them. "Yeah," I say as I untangle the leather cord from her fingers. I let out a sigh of relief. I feel as if I haven't breathed since the medal went missing.

Her face is close to mine, and she's staring at me. "So do you go by Chris or . . ."

"Christian." I almost call her Alexandra but catch myself. "And you?"

"Mata Hari." She laughs. "No, it's Lexi." She tilts her head to one side and watches as I slip the medal around my neck.

"Thanks for getting this back for me, Lexi."

Our eyes meet. *Say goodbye. Turn around and get the hell out of here,* I tell myself. "Listen, I know this place down the block. Best doughnuts in the city. Let me buy you a couple. To say thanks properly," I say instead. *What am I doing?*

"Doughnuts?" She narrows her eyes, but her mouth turns up a little, a sexy half smile that makes my stomach turn a slow flip.

"Fresh out of the oven. The kind that sort of dissolve when you bite into them, they're so light." I don't know why I'm trying to sell the idea so hard. I can't actually get to know this girl. Besides, she's going to say no anyway. A girl like this agreeing to go somewhere with me, a guy she barely knows? No. Never gonna happen.

"Lead the way." She folds her arms over her chest, and that smile—it goes from playful to challenging. She knew I didn't expect her to say yes, and now she expects *me* to wuss out.

I clench my jaw tight to keep it from dropping open. "Cool," I say, forcing an easy *I'm totally up for this* grin, my heart suddenly jackhammering in my chest. *Way to go, genius. Now what?* I rack my brain for something to say.

"So. Who's the dude on the medal?" she asks, beating me to it.

"It's Saint Jude. The patron saint of lost causes," I say.

"Is that what you are? A lost cause?" Her smile gets wider.

"Nah, I just seem to get mixed up in them."

She takes this in, not saying anything, just giving me an appraising look as she slips her arm through mine and we step off the curb and into the street.

I walk her a couple of blocks over to my favorite place: Fried Dough. There's nothing fancy about it, but the doughnuts are ridiculous and, best of all, cheap. We're nearing the door when I start to smell them. She sniffs the air and closes her eyes.

"Oh wow."

"I know. They taste even better, trust me." Her fingers tighten on my arm, and I feel the stress of the past day—all that worry over my medal and whether the police discovered it—disappear. I'm okay. The job is over. I got the medal.

I look down at Lexi. I should order our doughnuts to go, but curiosity's got the best of me. I want to see if she'll tell me about yesterday. Her take on things. What it was like at the bank once we were gone.

The store is warm and thick with sugar. The air tastes sweet. I come here every time we start to case a job downtown. Something about the coziness of it is comforting, and it's central to at least a dozen banks. In fact, the first one we hit is almost directly across the street.

We order our doughnuts—a couple of chocolate-iced ones for me, a maple bacon one for her—and settle at a table near the front window, where we can watch people walk by.

"Hey, look. They've got games," she says, pointing to a basket near the door with a stack of old games inside. Chess. Scrabble. Sorry.

"Chess. Nice. You play?" I ask.

"Do you?" She looks at me all shocked.

"I've been known to play. When I'm not breaking hearts and stealing cars," I joke, an edge to my voice. To a girl like her, I must look a little street, but I'm no thug. To an actual thug, I'm laughably far from it. "My grandfather taught me. He's big into chess."

She looks down, color rising in both cheeks. "I didn't mean you didn't look like you played. Lots of guys I know don't. I barely do. I mean, I'm not horrible, but I don't exactly practice. . . ." She's talking fast, rambling because I've made her feel bad. Not how I pictured this going.

"No. My bad. I get defensive sometimes," I tell her. "You wanna play?"

She raises her eyebrows. "Sure."

I get the board and start setting out the pieces. "So I guess you want to be white?" I ask, taunting her now.

"Oh, whatever," she says, grabbing the black chess pieces from me and setting up her side. I laugh and she looks up, pretends to glare, but the smile tugging at her lips gives her away.

I make the first move. She takes a bite of her doughnut and makes a move of her own right away. It's bold. I'm not sure if she's just playing recklessly or if she's really good. I focus on the board.

"So you were really at the robbery yesterday?" I make my next move.

She looks up at me, startled, and I mentally curse myself for not being smooth.

Her eyes get a faraway look. "Yes. I still can't believe one of them ran into me." She countermoves. I try to determine what her strategy is, but so far, I'm not seeing it.

It's weird to hear her talking about me *to me* without her knowing that's what she's doing. Weird and kind of fascinating. I move my rook.

"He was coming out of the bank and I was about to go in and we just . . . crashed into each other." She moves.

"Were you scared?" I ask, really wanting to know. "Check," I say.

She studies the board and moves her king. "No. I was just taken off guard, that's all. She takes a bite of her doughnut, a surprisingly enthusiastic one. A bit of icing is stuck to her cheek. Without thinking, I reach out and brush it away. Her eyes jump to mine, and I freeze. I pull my hand away and quickly move again, taking one of her pawns this time. Lexi taps her finger on the bishop and considers the board.

"So what happened after? Did you have to hang out and talk to the police?" I feel like I'm balancing on a dangerous tightrope between seeming curious and nosy. I talked to her yesterday. Not a lot, but I did speak. If she's thinking about the robbery when she hears me talk, will something click inside her head? I watch her take my knight, and I consider my options. I move. She moves. The game feels like a dance.

"Yeah. They didn't keep me long, though. I didn't see much. Well, except the van they took off in. That I could describe pretty well." She rubs the back of her head. "I hit my head, and things got pretty scrambled. Like, for example, I couldn't remember exactly how many of them there were, but I know that I saw them all run past and pile into the van. See? I've got a lump back here the size of an egg, I hit the ground so hard." She grabs my hand and puts it to the back of her head.

All at once I'm leaning over the table, my face right up close to hers. I don't think she meant for us to be this close, so close that to anyone else, it must look like we're about to kiss. Suddenly this dawns on her, too.

"Um, TMI. Sorry," she says, surprising me by not giggling or blushing. How is she this chill when I'm about to go crazy being this close to her? The temptation to try to unsettle her the way she has me is just too much. I lean a little closer, tilting my head sideways like I'm making a move. She hesitates, her eyes going wide . . . until I move my queen and scoop up a pawn. I grin.

She laughs a little and looks at the chessboard, shaking her head. "Coward," she says. After a moment, she declares, "Checkmate." She moves her knight, and suddenly I see it. My king is trapped. She winks at me and I laugh out loud. This girl surprises me in the best way. If we'd met under any other circumstances, I'd ask her out for real, but I can't take this any further. Going for doughnuts was risky enough.

"Good game. So why come back to the bank this morning? I mean, Bank of Americas are everywhere. You coulda hit about a million other ATMs. Why return to the scene of the crime?" I ask. I start putting the chess pieces back in the box.

Her smile drops a little.

"I just figured why avoid the place? It's the safest it'll ever be, right? The day after a robbery? What thief would try to hit a bank that *just* got robbed? Kinda hard to get one over on someone twice in a row." Her face gets serious. I wait for her to tell me what she's thinking, but she goes quiet and then gets up from the table and brushes the doughnut crumbs off her jeans.

"I gotta go. Thanks for the doughnut and the game, Christian." She gives me a little wave. Before I can figure out a way to stall and ask her some more questions about yesterday, Lexi is out the door, pulling her hair back into a messy bun and weaving through the stream of people walking past the shop.

I clean up our trash and then leave the shop, too. As I turn up the block, she rolls out of a parking garage on a Ducati racing bike. She slips her helmet on as she waits for an opening in the traffic, and before I can remember to close my mouth, she gives me a nod and accelerates into the street fast enough that her tires squeal. And all I can think is that it's a good thing I won't see this girl again, because I really, *really* want to.

11
Lexi

"I want to spy on Harrison," I tell Quinn once I'm back home.

I plop onto his bed and lie back against the pillows, my hands over my stomach. I passed LL National after I left Christian at the doughnut shop on my way out of the financial district. Harrison happened to be out front, leaning against the building. Every good feeling lingering inside me dried up at the sight of him. For one irrational moment I thought about aiming my motorcycle at him and driving it right over his smug face. But then I realized that the best way to get back at him would be to expose him for who he is. And now it's all I can think about.

"Well, hello to you, too, Lex," Quinn says, his eyes never leaving his computer screen. "What do you think I've been doing? Been trying ever since yesterday." His fingers tap the keys furiously. "So far I'm batting zero. Either we got it all wrong and he's a saint, or he's some kind of criminal genius with formidable cover-up skills. I can't find so much as a damning email. He's squeaky clean."

"Maybe he's one of those old-school types. You know,

Internet-averse, still does everything on paper. Maybe the only way we're going to get anything on this guy is to search his office or his house or both."

The doorbell rings, an uptight sequence of *bing-bong*s that my mother loves and that makes me crazy.

"Lexi? Quinn? Up for some visitors?" my mother yells from the foyer. I peek over the banister to see Oliver, Leo, Whitney, and Elena huddled by the door. Elena's holding a pink-and-white box from Sugar High Cupcakes.

"I brought comfort food," she calls. Doughnuts and cupcakes in one day. I'm going to gain ten pounds overnight.

"Come on up," I say.

Our friends sprawl out around Quinn's room, Whitney and Elena across his bed with me, the boys on the floor. Oliver turns on the TV, and he and Leo start playing a video game.

"So how you guys holding up?" Elena asks, passing the cupcake box to Quinn.

"Weaver is a first-class idiot. I still can't believe she let the board muscle you guys out." Whitney stares at her phone, taps the keys. "The gossip is rampant, by the way. I'm handling it, but you should know that Bianca's been telling everyone that you got kicked out and that your dad's guilty."

"Girl's on a revenge trip, man. You shoulda never dated her," Oliver says to Quinn, his fingers flying over the controller in his hand. "Get my back; get my back. I need to reload," he says to Leo. Leo gives me a look, rolling his eyes, but he covers Oliver as his shooter reloads.

"Speaking of revenge and retribution, Lexi's on a trip of her own. She wants to spy on Bianca's dad." Quinn stops typing and swivels around in his chair. "So, sis, tell us. How do you propose to do it? He knows who we are. We get within a ten-foot radius of the man and he'll sic the bank's security on us. Even if we wanted to, we have no in. Bianca hates my guts since I dumped her, and yours by default because you're my sister. So using her to get dirt is out."

Everyone stares at me expectantly.

I haven't thought it all through. Quinn's right that we can't just waltz into Harrison's house or the bank. We need an excuse. Or help. I think about when I went into the bank for Christian to get his medal back. Except I can't exactly ask some random stranger to go into Harrison's office and ransack it. . . .

"What if I don't look like me?" I ask. An image of the robbers' masks pops into my head. "I could get a disguise and, I don't know, change my eye color. Hair. All that stuff. Ooh! I could apply for a job at the bank. . . . You could create a résumé or something for me, right?"

I'm getting carried away, but I can't stop myself. This is what happens when we begin planning a BAM; my brain starts going a hundred miles an hour. "If I get inside, we can figure out how to get access to his office. Bug it. Bug his phone. He's bound to slip up sometime. I work there until he does."

"Why you? Why not me? Why do you always need to be the one sticking your neck out?" asks Quinn. He gives me an exasperated look. "I'm older. I should be the one to do it. And

106

besides, it isn't that easy. How are you going to pass for a bank employee? Even if I can manage to hack into the system, the minute you're inside you'll give yourself away. Harrison's office'll be up with all the other VPs'. You don't think they'll notice that you don't belong?"

I flop back on his bed. "Oh, come on, you're older by one year, not ten. Besides, it'll be harder to disguise you. I mean, you dated his daughter. He knows you better. Anyway, I can figure out how to fake it. Admit it—I'm a brilliant actress. That BAM where we broke into the Staples Center during Katy Perry's concert proved that. Those security guards believed I was one of her posse."

"I could get her a wig," says Whitney, excited about the prospect of a good makeover. "Some colored contacts and different makeup, and *you* probably wouldn't recognize her."

Quinn leans back in his chair, balances it on two legs. "You can't pass for a twentysomething, Lex. Even with all that stuff. You look too young."

"Well, okay, then I pretend I'm on the cleaning crew or something. Emptying trash cans."

Quinn snorts at the thought of me as a janitor, but I can see his wheels turning.

"Oh, come on, Quinn. Let her try," Whitney says, winking at me.

"What have you got to lose? You guys are already out of school." Oliver looks up from the video game long enough that his guy dies. "You have to at least try."

Quinn rocks back and forth. "Let me check something." He starts typing again in earnest, his fingers flying over the keys, most of which don't have letters on them anymore. He's actually tapped them off. Not that it matters; he rarely looks at his hands when he types. "Here. This. This could be your in."

Elena, Whitney, and I peer at the screen. He's got it open to the bank's website, to a page about community involvement and education. At the bottom is a link to an internship program the bank is running with UCLA.

"You want me to enroll in UCLA so I can apply for this?" I ask. "That seems sort of overcomplicated, don't you think?"

"No. I want to use a UCLA student's records to get you into the program. Under someone else's name. It says the internship rotates through each department, so you'd get to be in the business offices, right where Harrison is."

"So what do we need to do?" I say. My blood starts humming through my veins. I want this to work. I *need* this to work. It'll give me something to do, something to control, so I'm not sitting here worrying about my family's future every minute.

I can do this. How hard could it be to pretend to be a college kid? I'm only two years away from being one now. Who knows? Maybe we'll get lucky and find a way to clear my dad's name completely. "Come on, spill," I say, ready to roll up my sleeves and do whatever it takes.

"*I* need to hack into the UCLA student records and find someone whose profile fits the usual intern applicant's. Then I make you a fake student ID, we forward your new records to the internship coordinator at the school, and I make sure it gets accepted." He glances up at me. "New interns start every three months, and it looks like the next session you could be a part of starts in . . . less than a week. Which is crazy soon." He stares at the computer some more. "Or there's another one in the fall."

"The first one. We can't wait three whole months to start!"

"You have no idea how much work is involved in this, do you?" he asks. "Same old Lexi, ready to jump at a moment's notice. Screw the details." He sighs.

I start karate chopping his shoulders the way I used to when I was little and thought that was how you gave a massage. But he's not laughing.

"I can't. There's no way."

"You can do it," I say. "Come on. Think of it as a challenge."

"I'd be super impressed if you pulled it off," Whitney says, coming up behind him. I move out of the way as she puts her arms around his neck and winks at me.

"Aw, come on. I'm not that easy," he says, but he's blushing and his fingers are already flying over the keyboard again.

12

Christian

I get home after four, same as any other school day, my backpack hooked over one shoulder, the Saint Jude medal on my neck, where it belongs. The house is quiet and dark, which is weird. Usually this time of day Abuelo's got the telenovelas on. He swears he watches them because it reminds him of my abuela, but that's not true. She told me once that *she* only watched them because *he* was hooked. The old man is a sucker for any story line with a pretty girl who's pregnant with her brother's friend's father's baby while also battling a rare form of blindness that a witch (the brother's father's wife) cursed her with. . . . Dun, dun, DUN. Every time I see him watching, I want to laugh, but I don't dare.

"Maria? Abuelo?" I don't bother with calling Mom because she's never home until after nine anyway. *Where could they be?* I round the corner and peer into the darkened kitchen.

"Surprise!" The lights flip on, and suddenly there are people everywhere. All my tias, my cousins, Eddie, Gabriel, Carlos, Benny. Maria. Abuelo. Mom. Dad's here, too, looking sober for once. Half the neighborhood's behind him.

"Mijo, congratulations!" Mom tackles me with kisses on both cheeks. *What is going on?*

"Uh, for what?" I ask.

Mom starts to laugh. "For *what*? What do you think? For getting into UCLA. With a full scholarship!" She yells the scholarship bit, jumping up and down as if she won the lottery. "They want you to start over the summer. Can you believe it? Some early program, the email said. But you'll know what that is, right? You got a full ride, baby! Mijo's going to be a college boy!" She is crying, literally bawling, her makeup running down her cheeks in black lines.

"Way to go, Christian!" Dad gives me an awkward slap on the back and wanders over to the refrigerator. I look away the minute he reaches for a beer.

She checked my email. Of course she did. Because I have no privacy. I am speechless. I look over at Benny and he shakes his head, his forehead creased with disappointment. I'd never let the boys know I applied. What was the point when I couldn't go anyway?

"Congratulations, white boy," Eddie says all over-cheery, punching my shoulder hard enough to sting before he pulls me into a hug. "What are you playing at, son?" he whispers in my ear. He probably thinks I'm trying to bail on him, on all of them somehow, that I'm really, seriously leaving. My chest feels loaded down with rocks.

"It isn't like that, man. I'm not going," I say a little too loud.

"Not going?" Mom stops midbounce and stares at me, fire

in her eyes. "You absolutely are going. Even if I have to drag you there by your ear every single day. Don't think you're so old I can't do that."

"Can we talk about this later?" I say quietly, willing her to just shut up about it.

"There's nothing to talk about. You're going," she says, and then to everyone, "He's going!"

A cheer goes up and someone turns on the music. The women start taking off plastic wrap and shoving serving spoons into steaming dishes of tamales and birria. The men gather around, paper plates at the ready. Except for my dad, who wanders into his bedroom with his beer. Five seconds of being happy for me seems to be his limit before he has to go get wasted.

The worst of it is when Abuelo says a prayer over the meal and then over me, thanking God for blessing the family. I can feel the guys staring daggers at me the whole time.

"Christian, make up a plate, come on. You have to go first. You're the guest of honor." Tia Iliana pushes me toward the food, and I halfheartedly take a scoop of everything, fully aware that all the ladies are watching to make sure I get some of whatever they made, but there's no way I can eat any of it. I got into UCLA. Full ride. It finally settles in, and it hurts way more than I expected it to. I can't go unless I can get out of the jobs, and yet I really, really want to. Why did she have to go through my email? I can barely breathe, I'm so disappointed.

I walk back to my room with my plate, and it isn't long before

112

the boys show up carrying plates of their own. Gabriel is last. He shuts the door behind him. "What's going on, Christian?"

"I just wanted to see if I'd get in. That's it. Curiosity. Plain and simple," I say.

"Except now your mom's out there makin' plans. Now you gotta tell her, because no way you're skipping out on this next job. When she finds out about how deep you're in, it's gonna kill her, vato."

"Soldado's gonna straight up lose it if he hears, and the Eme, man, if they find out ...," Carlos says around a mouthful of food. He wipes some cheese from his lips with the back of his hand.

"Except I'm not going!" I drop my plate onto my dresser and lean against the wall. "I was curious. That's it. How would I go? Leave my mom with my dad's debts and my sister to take care of? The bills? Nah, man. I ain't leaving. You know that. I'll figure out a way to get out of it without my mom finding out about the jobs," I say, my chest all tight so I can barely breathe. Up to now I realize I didn't really believe it. For a minute I can't speak. I can't go to school. Not yet. *I'm not leaving. I'm probably never leaving.*

"You sure?" Gabriel asks.

"Hundred percent," I lie.

The guys start going over yesterday's job, recounting it like it's already an old, funny story now that it looks like we aren't in danger of getting caught anymore. I try to join in but can't. I look out the window instead. The blinds remind me of prison bars.

113

13
Lexi

"We can get her close, maybe not exact, but close." Elena studies the picture Quinn printed out for her and puts her hand on my chin, moves my face right and then left.

"The bone structure's basically the same. Green eyes instead of blue. Their noses are nearly identical. That's a plus," Whitney murmurs. "Angela has black hair, but I have a wig. We can trim it to match her hairstyle. Her complexion is darker, but we can fix that with a good spray tan."

I'm sitting in the middle of her basement on a stool, everyone gathered around so they can study me under the overhead lighting. I feel like a lab rat. "Let me see her file again."

Quinn hands me the manila folder, and I open it up to the girl's profile to examine her picture for the hundredth time. Angela Dunbar, nineteen years old, five foot seven, 125 pounds. We look nothing alike, but I trust Elena and Whitney to make it happen. By the end of the night I will be Angela, and tomorrow morning I'll start the LL National internship program.

"She's studying abroad this semester. She'll never even know you used her identity to get into the bank," Quinn says. "I'll wipe the document trail in a few weeks, and it will be like the whole thing never even happened."

He is exceedingly pleased with himself, and it shows. He keeps throwing out little nuggets of information about what he did and how he's covering it all up—using as many big, technical terms as he can muster. Honestly, though, I am impressed. Somehow he managed to pull it off. Now it's the twins' turns. They have one night to make me into Angela.

"Okay, so tan first, then hair and makeup," Elena says as she pulls me from the stool and marches me into the next room. The entire basement is devoted to movie stuff: costumes, makeup, and hair. The twins' father directs for a living and constructed the basement so that he could basically make his home a permanent movie set. It's actually been in a dozen or so indies over the last decade. One of them with Channing Tatum.

We were about thirteen when their dad made that movie. I slept over on the weekend he was scheduled to film, because Whitney, Elena, and I had an enormous crush on Channing. We lurked around the set, trying to get a good look at him without her father finding out. When we couldn't, we actually stole one of his shirts on the last day, and we each took turns wearing it to school for a while, like it was a trophy or something. Thinking about it now, I realize that was a tipping point. Helping Whitney steal the shirt was such a high; it wasn't long after that when I got the idea for doing BAMs.

I spend the next thirty minutes at the far end of the basement in the makeup room, tucked inside a collapsible tent just big enough to fit me, entirely naked, while Elena and Whitney take turns spraying me down with tanning solution. To distract all of us, I tell them about Christian and the doughnut shop, but as fun as the story is, it's hard for any of us to concentrate on anything other than the fact that every millimeter of my body is on display. Plus, the tanning stuff is freezing. I'm all goose bumps and shivers by the time they're done.

"Well, we've reached a new level of bestie closeness," Whitney says soberly, her face at eye level with my, um, nether region, and we all crack up.

Whitney does my hair next, braiding it tight to my head and then running a cotton ball soaked in alcohol over my hairline.

"What's that for?" I ask.

"To get rid of the natural oils near your scalp so the wig adheres better." She walks over to the long, black-haired wig resting on a Styrofoam head and carefully lifts it off. "This is a full-lace, human-hair wig. Very expensive, okay? So be careful with it, because if my dad knows I lent it out, I am toast."

"I have no idea what 'full lace' means, but I will be. Promise."

She shows me how to apply the wig glue to get the wig on just right, and then Elena gives me a pair of colored contacts and gets to work on my makeup.

"Are you sure this is a good idea?" She stops dabbing foundation on me. "If Harrison is who you think he is, you could be in real danger. I mean, if he'd throw your dad under the bus and then be sleazy enough to hit on you two days later, don't you think he might be capable of much worse?"

"Gah," I moan dramatically. "I already went through this with Quinn. Since when do any of us run from a risk?"

"That's different and you know it." She sits on the makeup table. "This isn't a game."

"Yeah. I know," I say, sobering up. "But I need to do this."

How can I make her understand? I mean, *really* understand? I need someone to blame, and it's easier for me to hate Harrison because he never tucked me in at night or took me to breakfast on the beach Saturday mornings, just him and me, a bag of bagels and a coffee cup full of apple juice between us, our toes dug into the sand. Trying to figure out a way to expose Harrison is like a BAM, a way to distract myself from the fact that I have a father who *did* tuck me in but who lied to me about who he is, and a mother who's debating whether she wants to stick around and support the man she stopped loving a long time ago. I can't wait around to get blindsided anymore. I'm done with that. It's my turn to do the blindsiding.

"I give you Angela Dunbar, UCLA sophomore and bank intern." Elena walks me out to face our friends. Leo's mouth drops open. Oliver stops fiddling with his lighter. Weirdly, nailing her look has me nervous, as if it's making the whole thing too real all of a sudden. *Am I rushing into this too fast?* I want to spy on Harrison, but I'm scared about keeping up this new identity eight hours a day for several weeks.

I twirl around and Oliver starts to clap. "Great job, baby," he tells Elena as she drops down beside him. He kisses the top of her head, and she grabs his arm and wraps it around her shoulder.

"I know," she says. "My sister and I are makeover geniuses."

"And me. Don't forget me," Quinn says. "The guy who made it all possible. Slaving away for hours. Night and day. Without sleep. Without food. Or water. Or video games. Or company. All alone. Into the wee hours." He looks at Whitney and sighs loudly.

"There's no way we could forget you." Whitney laughs. She leans over to kiss him.

His face goes bright red, which is hilarious because he tries so hard to be cool about girls. Our little group is slowly pairing off: Elena and Oliver, Whitney and Quinn. Leo and I are the odd man and woman out, but that's okay. Leo doesn't mind, because he's already plotting his next conquest, and unless it's serious or if the guy hasn't come out yet—which has happened once or twice—he won't bring him around to meet us. Which leaves me. But I can be alone. I'm perfectly fine with that.

Still, I suddenly find myself thinking about Christian again and wishing I hadn't left so quickly the other day. I keep picturing his eyes. They felt so familiar. And then there was that moment when we almost kissed. Seeing him again would be nice, but I don't even know what school he goes to or where he lives. It shouldn't bother me. I don't want it to bother me, but somehow, frustratingly, it does.

14

Christian

When a car pulls up alongside me and slows, I know who it is. *Soldado*. I've been expecting him ever since I lost the medal and word got out about my scholarship. He's sitting in the backseat of an old car I don't recognize—beige and nondescript—but I can see the familiar outline of his head through the tinted windows.

"Hop in." Twitch is behind the wheel, but it's Psycho ordering me around. He's hanging out the window, his eyes so dark they look pupil-free, just two giant black holes staring, dead. It's hard not to feel intimidated. The dude is infamous. Youngest kid in the neighborhood to get jumped in to Florencia Heights. He's got a line of ink up one arm—a dozen skulls—one for every person he's killed.

I look up and down the street. There were a bunch of kids walking by a minute ago, but now the whole street is deserted. They probably took off the second Soldado's car rounded the corner.

"Where we goin'?" I ask, trying to buy some time. I can't miss another day of school.

The back window rolls down. "Just get in," Soldado says wearily. He looks up at me, his mouth set. He doesn't seem angry, but I know he's heard about the UCLA scholarship. Gossip spreads through this neighborhood like a disease.

I walk around to the other side of the car and slip into the back. I set my backpack between my feet. The second the door closes, Twitch jerks away from the curb and starts cruising down the street. I stare at the school as we drive past.

Soldado turns so that he's facing me, his leg propped up on the seat, his foot tapping up and down. "You know you're my boy," he says. "Straight up always have been."

I nod.

"And I take care of you, don't I? Protect you. Give you ways to keep your family outta trouble and pay back what they owe." He scratches the side of his nose and looks out the window as we pass a group of Florencia boys milling around the grocery store parking lot. They make thirteens with their fingers, showing allegiance to Florencia and the Eme at the same time. Soldado lowers the car window, lifts his chin in the air, and does the same.

Sometimes I think he's trying to pass himself off as a mexicano version of a Mafia don. He's smart the way the guys who run large syndicates and crime rings are. Not book-smart but street-smart. People-smart. He can look at a guy and know how to use him, how to work him over. He's done it to me before—when he offered the jobs to me and my boys—and I can feel him working up to it again now.

"I've been hearing things about you," Soldado says. He picks at a piece of string stuck to his jeans and tosses it to the floor. "Things that make me worry for you. I thought you and me were on the same page, cabrón. I thought you had my back. Now I hear you're getting sloppy. Leaving clues behind."

My stomach drops. Gabriel must've told him.

Twitch eyeballs me in the rearview mirror, and Psycho turns all the way around in his seat and cracks his neck. Somewhere outside, a baby's crying and someone's honking a car horn, and music's playing faintly, giving a festive rhythm to the way people amble down the street, but inside the car, the air is still, loaded. Soldado and I have always gotten along. Maybe we don't see eye to eye about everything, but we've been friends a long time. My mom took him in for a bit when he was nine and stuff at his house got really bad. And when I got jumped by a couple of gangbangers from a rival hood, he came to my rescue. Then there's my dad's debt. Soldado bought me the time to take care of it. The Eme wouldn't have given it to us if he hadn't stepped in. It's uncomfortable as hell right now, having his boys look at me like they have to teach me a lesson.

"Come on, bro. I got the medal back before anyone found it. And the whole college thing was just a stupid what-if. . . ."

"Forget the whole college thing. That's not what's bothering me. The medal, yeah, that's a concern, but what's really got me wondering is your attitude. You losing your enthusiasm for the work?"

Yes. "No."

"Don't lie," he says. "It wastes time."

"What do you want me to say?" I shake my head and stare out the window. "You want me to ask you to take me off this next job? We both know you can't."

The car slows at a light. We're headed toward my house.

"That's true. But we can't afford to have any mistakes on this one. I need your head straight." He shakes his head. "You know what your problem is?" he asks, leaning over so he's close enough that I can see the bloodred inside of his mouth. "You don't know how to be grateful for what you already got. You can't make peace with your fate, man, and until you do, you ain't gonna be satisfied, are you? Never mind that I hooked you up with the best gig goin'. You stand to make more than any of my Florencia boys on any job they've done—all of 'em—guys who pledged their lives to the gang, and you turn up your nose to it. You think college is gonna save your family? A degree don't mean jack where your family's safety is concerned, vato. You don't keep them protected and they won't live to see the day you can finally move them out of here."

We make a turn and we are on my street, driving straight for my house. I can see Maria sitting out front, behind the fence that separates our yard from the street, a coloring book across her lap, her fist around a crayon, running it back and forth over the paper. She's bent over her work, so she doesn't see us coming. Abuelo's supposed to be watching Maria, but he's not outside. She's alone. I look over at Soldado and then at Psycho. "Why are we here?" My heart starts hammering against my rib cage.

Twitch parks the car across the street, directly opposite her. The engine idles.

"You think what you do gets back to only me? The Eme has ears everywhere. In Florencia Heights and out. If they think you're flaking on this job and they get pissed off enough, I can't stop them green-lighting you or your family. Even if I want to," Soldado says. He nods at Psycho, who gets out of the car and starts across the street. "The most I can do is give you a heads-up that it's comin', cabrón." He folds his arms across his chest. "You want out? Tell me. But understand it's gonna come at a cost."

"What are you talking about?" I ask, nerves thrumming.

Psycho's reached the fence and is leaning over it, talking to my sister. She looks up, smiling at him, her hand still running her crayon over the coloring book. Psycho reaches around and lifts his shirt so I can see the gun tucked into his waistband. I nearly gag; the nausea is instantaneous.

"No. No, no, no!" I lunge for the car door. My hands are shaking so bad I can't grab hold of the door handle.

Soldado blocks my path with his bulk and shoves me back. "*She's* your cost," Soldado says quietly. "Got the word last night. I begged them, vato, *begged* them to reconsider, but the job is too big and the other guys can't handle it without you. The Eme's already got too much invested in it to start changing out players. You don't get back in the game, you don't give it your all, and she's green-lighted." He leans over. "Every homeboy in a twenty-block radius will be committed to taking her out."

As if he can hear Soldado, Psycho turns and looks into the car at me and grins.

"I can only do so much to help you, bro. Keep bein' stupid and this goes beyond my reach. I got your back, but I'm not prepared to die if it comes down to it. And we both know they'd still get her in the end—maybe your whole family and mine, too, if it comes to that. Just to prove a point."

I look past him as Psycho jumps the fence and moves behind my sister, his gun in his hand now and pointed at the back of her head. I feel like I'm sitting at the epicenter of an earthquake. My whole world's about to shake apart.

"I'll do it, I'll do it!" I scream.

Soldado lowers the window and signals to Psycho, who strokes my sister's hair in a way that makes my blood run cold before he puts the gun away and walks to a car parked just behind us. I hadn't noticed it until just now.

"They told me to threaten you, and now they see I did," Soldado says, tilting his head back toward the car. "And I did it without hurting anyone, which isn't the way they initially wanted me to approach things. See? I'm still trying to protect you, homes. Do me a favor and quit screwing around." He leans his head back on the seat and sighs. "Let's go over this one more time. The job happens in less than three weeks. Fourth of July weekend. My guys are already working on the tunnel you and your team will use to get inside. Now all we need is to figure out the vault layout. I want you to case the bank, cozy up to one of the tellers for intel—when the money gets delivered, security camera locations—what we need to know to get in and get out. Rosie's got the food truck out there already. You just gotta work with her awhile—starting today—and survey the joint while you work. Then you hit the vault when the time comes. Nothing you can't handle. Just do what you're told. Understand?"

I don't trust myself to answer. I still feel like I might throw up. I force a nod instead.

"Hey, cheer up, vato," Soldado says as I open my car door. "It'll all be good. One month from now you won't have a worry in the world."

I step out of the car and walk across the street to my yard and Maria. I can feel the guys in both cars watching me. I look back once, forcing my face into a blank expression, calm and decided, but inside I am one giant ball of panic, alarm screaming out of every pore. I scoop up Maria as soon as I'm inside the yard and hug her to my chest.

"I can't breathe," she complains, squirming to get away, but I don't let go. I kiss her forehead and both cheeks and try to calm down. She never saw the gun. She has no idea what just happened. She's okay. But I'm not. If anything had actually happened to her . . .

I could never live with it. This next job has to go off perfectly. Whatever it takes, I have to make sure. No screw-ups. No distractions. No thoughts about the future. The job is all that matters now. Everything and everyone I care about depend on it.

15

Lexi

My father's office building looms over me. Every window feels like an eye, staring. I run a hand over my head. My wig feels heavy and unnatural, but I'm glad it's there. Like armor. I don't recognize the girl I see in the building's glass front doors, and so I hope that no one else will, either, that I will walk inside and go upstairs to the orientation without being caught. I was confident before—when this was all planning and conjecture—but now, standing here, I'm terrified. *What if I get caught? What if I make things worse instead of better?*

"Going in?" A woman in a navy-blue suit with a coffee cup in one hand steps in front of my reflection and opens the door.

I turn the charm on, the schemer in me fully coming to life now that my audience has shown up. My nerves don't disappear so much as fade. I tuck them away at the back of my brain. "Yes, thank you," I say, aiming for a tone that sounds mature and confident.

"You must be one of the new interns, right? Welcome to LL National."

"I hate to bother you, but do you know which floor I need to go to? I forgot my orientation packet." I wring the handles of my purse and feign embarrassment.

"Sure, I'm going that way myself. I can take you." She holds out her hand. "Jackie Fuller. I work in the mortgage division here. You'll come visit my department at the tail end of your internship."

We sign in at the front desk. I have to concentrate as I sign *Angela Dunbar*. My hand wants to make an *L,* not an *A,* every muscle in my fingers seeming to resist me. I didn't really think about that, about the nearly reflexive need I would have to be Lexi even now. I can feel myself starting to sweat. Am I already giving myself away? The security guy checks my UCLA student ID and then hands me a temporary visitor's badge. I clip it to the suit Elena picked out for me, and together Jackie and I ride the elevator up to the twentieth floor. I look at her out of the corner of my eye. I think I've met her once before at one of my father's parties. She looks familiar. I wish I'd paid better attention, cared a little more back then. *Does she recognize me?*

"You said you work with mortgages?"

"That's right."

"So then I guess you're dealing with a lot of fallout right now. They arrested your VP, right?" It's risky to bring this up, but I can't help myself. I want to watch her face. Harrison might not be the only person I need to keep an eye on here. Besides, I'm curious. What does she think of my dad? Does anyone think he's innocent?

Jackie blinks. "They did."

"Did you work with that guy ... what's his name? Warren something? Did you work with him directly?"

Jackie licks her lips. "Look, I'm sure that they'll mention the case during orientation, but I'd rather not address it right now."

I nod, immediately regretting asking her about my father. I'm here to check Harrison out. Period. Whether my dad is really guilty doesn't have anything to do with that. *Focus on the goal, Lex,* I tell myself.

I rack my brain for something else to say, some small talk that might make this woman warm up to me. I'm not good at gaining people's confidences, probably because I'm horrible at confiding in people myself. What am I supposed to talk about with this woman who is probably at least twenty years older than me to put her at ease?

"I love the art deco feel of this place," I say after a few awkward seconds. My default with adults is to talk architecture and design. I founded the architecture club at school, and we spent tons of time last summer helping to make student-created houses for Habitat for Humanity in Orange County. It's something I love that grown-ups seem to have at least a passing interest in, too.

"Oh, I know. Beautiful, isn't it? One of the few buildings in LA with some real historical character. To think that until LL National came along and bought the building, it was in danger of being converted into lofts! Can you imagine? The bank made sure to keep all the original architecture. Even this new renovation happening on the upper floors has to follow a strict set of preservation standards so that the new work won't compromise the charm this place has. You'll get to tour the building while you're here, and really, it's one of the best parts of orientation. If you're into design, you'll love it."

I almost tell her that I want to be an architect someday when I catch myself. Angela is an econ major. She probably wouldn't dream of being an architect. Divulging even this much of my true self to this woman was a real risk. Even if the chances of her checking up on me are remote, if I don't want to get caught, I can't start offering up too much information.

When the elevator doors open, Jackie walks me to a conference room, where twelve other interns are seated. Two of them are also from UCLA but didn't have classes with Angela—Quinn checked to make sure. Still, there is a risk that someone will know her or of her and figure out right away that I'm a fraud. I slip into the seat nearest the door in case I need to run. My palms start to sweat, and I flatten them against my skirt, hoping the fabric will wick the dampness away.

"Hey. I'm Maddie," the girl next to me says. She's got a coffee in one hand and a pastry in the other. She's rail thin and rabbit twitchy.

"Angela. Nice to meet you."

"What school are you coming from?" she asks.

Automatically I think about Westwood Prep and my friends

who are, at this very minute, riding out the final few days of school. "UCLA, you?"

"Same!" She scoots a bit closer, and I brace for questions I can only guess the answers to. "Are you on campus? Maybe we could carpool in the mornings? I mean, for the next week, until they send us to separate banks for our in-branch training, at least. It would save us gas money."

"I live off campus—like, way, way off campus, so carpooling won't work, sorry." I stop myself from adding that I live with my family or lying and saying that I live in an apartment, because everything I say I have to keep track of. Running any scheme is like spinning several spiderwebs at once, every thread connecting to another. Spin too many and it becomes impossible to remember them all. I've learned that the hard way more times than I care to count. And now so has my dad.

"Good morning, LL National interns." The conference room door opens, and Mitch Harrison strides in. I freeze. I wanted to run into him, but not quite this soon. "Good morning. I'm Mitch Harrison, president of Strategic Initiatives. On behalf of the bank, I'd like to welcome you to our internship program. We hope you'll take full advantage of all that the next few weeks offer and consider applying for future employment with us after graduation. I reviewed each of your internship files personally and am very impressed with what I read. A group as creative, intelligent, and innovative as you has a very bright future here. I look forward to getting to know each of you better over the course of your time with us. For now, enjoy your breakfast."

There is a smattering of applause, and then he walks around the room, shaking hands with each intern. In a matter of a few seconds he'll get to me. I imagine chucking a tray of croissants at his head. He should be in jail, not smiling like he doesn't have a care in the world, like my father never even existed, like my family isn't suffering horribly right now. Nausea grips my stomach. I put my hand into my suit pocket and feel for the listening device Quinn and I bought online. I just need to figure out where his office is.

"Hello, Miss—?" he says, smiling down at me the way he did my mother the other day before she started yelling at him. He's good. Being a liar myself, it's almost impressive the amount of warmth and sincerity he manages to exude.

"Angela Dunbar." I wait for some flash of recognition to cross his face the longer he keeps staring at me, for him to figure out who I am in spite of the wig, contacts, and makeup, but he doesn't. "Business economics major, huh? At UCLA. My alma mater." I force myself to keep smiling. *Holy crap, I never thought to check on this.* "What do you think of Professor Hildebrand?"

He stares at me, waiting. I swallow. I have zero idea who he's talking about. *How do I even pretend that I do? Is it a man or a woman?* I could be done here before I even begin. I get this wrong and he'll probably pull my application again for closer review. "Um, well ... what do *you* think about Professor Hildebrand?" I ask, smiling in a way I hope is conspiratorial.

He throws his head back and laughs. "Ha! Smart. It's never

131

wise to burn bridges, is it? It just so happens that she's an old friend of mine."

I smile wider, relief rushing through my whole body. "Well, then I think she's brilliant."

He smiles widely. "Angela. Nice to meet you."

We shake hands and then he's on to the next person, and it's all I can do not to pass out. For every detail I did think about, there are ten more I didn't, and any one of them might expose me.

"He's a Clooney. Bet his wife is probably our age," Maddie says. "Lucky girl." I shudder and she laughs. "Not into older men, are you?"

Not when it's him, I think. Honestly, though, she's probably right. I don't get girls who are into guys their fathers' ages. It feels way too—I don't know—Oedipal to me.

We finish breakfast while one of the bank's managers goes over a PowerPoint presentation about the program and how the next few weeks will play out. We'll be at our assigned banks for the duration of our internship, starting next week. Quinn's working on hacking into the bank's computer system to make sure I get placed downstairs at the main branch so I can stay close to Harrison. With any luck I'll uncover something about him long before the internship is finished.

Our tour of the building comes next and turns out to be less a study in its architecture and more a snooze-worthy walk through floors of cubicles and conference rooms with more talk about investing and lending than is humanly possible to take unless you are Scrooge McDuck. The only remotely interesting thing that Trisha, our tour guide and the internship coordinator, brings up is that right before LL National bought the building from the bank that was here before, three major Hollywood movies used the basement vault as a film site.

"We won't be visiting the vault on this tour, but those of you who end up here at our main branch will get to see it during your training weeks. Fun fact: the film crews couldn't get their big equipment from the parking garage to the vault, so they built a dumbwaiter to lower the stuff down. Cool, right?" She leads us down one hallway and then another, past a series of cubicles, and then through a mini version of the main lobby near the elevators, with a security desk and a series of glass double doors that lead out to the parking garage.

"If you have a car, you can check in here with Reggie and he'll get you a parking pass and assign you a temporary spot. From now on please feel free to use this entrance into the building. But before you do, there's something really unique about the dumbwaiter that I have to show you guys." Next to the bank of elevators is what looks like another elevator door, only shorter and less shiny, more brushed metal. It has a keypad and a regular key lock. Trisha unlocks it, then punches in a series of numbers on the keypad, too fast for me to make them out. She presses another button, and the dumbwaiter door opens. Inside, it is just like a cargo elevator, nothing but a square box, totally utilitarian except for the signatures covering the walls. "The actors and crews on each movie signed the inside of the dumbwaiter. Right there is

Michael Keaton's signature, and next to his, Robert De Niro's." Tricia beams at us. "Only bank employees and interns get to see this." A smattering of *ooh*s and *aah*s rise up from the crowd.

The dumbwaiter *is* cool, but not any more impressive than, say, the handprints in front of Mann's Chinese Theatre. Sort of commonplace for those of us who grew up seeing these same people grab coffee at the local Starbucks, where their autographs are scrawled across the walls there, too. I wonder if the dumbwaiter goes to the floor that Harrison's office is on.

"So this still leads down to the vault? Isn't that a security risk?" Steve, one of the interns, asks. I snap a few pictures with my phone once I see some of the others do the same.

"The dumbwaiter can be accessed only from the outside, with the security code and key. So even if someone were to manage to get in here and ride it down, they wouldn't be able to get out without someone on the vault side letting them out. But for argument's sake, even if they could, the dumbwaiter opens up into the space before the actual vault. They'd still be faced with getting into the safe-deposit box area and then the actual vault itself." She smiles. "Breaking in there would require tools way too big to fit down this thing. But"—she glances down at her watch—"speaking of security and vaults, it's about time for us to head back for your next session."

Trisha corrals us onto the elevator. I text Quinn and Oliver the dumbwaiter photos and a summary of what she said. Even if it ends up that we can't use it, it's worth investigating further.

16
Christian

My eyes are on fire. Rosie's had me chopping an insane amount of onions and peppers all morning long. I wipe the back of my hand across them and slide open the window cut into the center of the truck, just above the long counter where we assemble the tacos, to get some fresh air. I look down the street to where a few people are walking into our next target, gripping paper bags with the words FRIED DOUGH printed in the shape of a doughnut on them. Lexi's face flashes through my brain, and I half smile as I remember the way it felt to lean in close to her, our faces nearly touching. I thought about trying to find her school so I could figure out a way to accidentally run into her somehow, maybe ask her out for real. But that was before I ended up in Soldado's car. Before Psycho put a gun to my baby sister's head. I turn away and go to the sink to start soaping up my hands. No point in daydreaming about this. I can't get mixed up with anybody right now, anyway. The job has to be my only focus.

"It'll be insane for about the next three hours," Rosie says, her head popping into view as she sets the large chalkboard menu out on the curb next to the truck. "I'll handle all the money and you take the orders. We have maybe five to ten minutes before people start showing up."

"Sure." I look at the space above the order window, where Rosie's hung these laminated food cards with a picture of each kind of taco she makes and what goes in it. The meats, sauces, veggies, and other stuff are basically prepped and ready to be assembled into Rosie's homemade tortillas. She actually uses our abuela's recipe and old iron tortilla press, even though the hinge that holds it together is almost broken off. It's sitting in a place of honor on the counter where the customers can see it. All I have to do is follow the cards and put together the orders as she makes them, which is good because half the stuff she has on the menu is a hybrid of Mexican, Korean, and Argentinean cuisine, and I don't have the first clue about the last two. For Rosie, the truck is more than a way to spy on future jobs; it's a passion. She's always wanted to own a restaurant, and while the taco truck isn't exactly that, it's a pretty good start. Soldado was way smooth giving it to her. Listening to Rosie talk, you'd think it's basically a love letter on wheels.

It's not quite eleven-thirty, the time Rosie says marks the beginning of the lunch rush, but we've already got the music going and the fan on inside the truck, blasting out toward the street so it spreads the scents of roasted meats and Rosie's signature freshly squeezed cilantro-lime-jalapeño lemonade to the people walking by. I've been steeped in it for the past two hours, so I can't even smell it anymore, but it has a definite effect on everyone else. It isn't long before we start to get customers. I size each one up, looking for teller name tags and employee badges to tell me who works at LL National. One or two customers seem promising. I make a note of their names in a little notebook.

I fill orders and Rosie works the money bit, and a comfortable rhythm develops between us right off the bat. We've always been close. Back when she was still in braids and Benny, Gabriel, and I were playing army commandos in the stairwell of their apartment building, she used to pretend to be a hostage we had to rescue, always hiding somewhere clever. We would race to see who could find her first. She always made sure it was me, and then the two of us would sneak up behind Benny and Gabriel and scare them half to death. Plus, she likes to read as much as I do. Of course, most of the time she has her nose in a cookbook, not a novel.

"Hey, wake up. What're you thinking about?" Rosie snaps her fingers in front of my face. The line's gone—for now—and she's leaning on the counter, staring at me.

"That it's good to hang out with you a little bit, cuz," I say. "It's been a while."

She smiles and pulls her ponytail up into a bun. "Yeah, I guess it has. You have school and I have the truck, and then there's Soldado. . . ." She smiles softly when she says his name.

"You think you guys'll get married?" I ask. Rosie's nearly twenty, and Soldado's twenty-four. They could. Everyone thinks they will.

"He's gotta leave Florencia Heights for me to give it serious thought." She smooths her apron out. "I'm not marrying a career gangbanger."

This will never happen. He can't leave. She knows this.

"So why'd you start dating him in the first place, then?" I ask. Rosie's always had plenty of choices when it comes to guys. She didn't have to settle on Soldado.

"Because he's the only guy who ever gave me the butterflies. And he's good to Mama and Benny." She hesitates, her eyes far away for a second. "And I have hope he'll get out. If I make a success of this truck, who knows? We could open a few more. Maybe rent out a space somewhere."

Soldado isn't leaving Florencia Heights. No way. I can't picture it. He loves the notoriety and the power. He's always wanted it. How can she not see that? But then I think about my own mom and dad. He's screwed up like crazy, and she's still taking him back. Sometimes people see what they want to and not what's true. Or they think being in love can change someone. But I don't think it can. I think a person's who they are all along. All love does is blind a person to that truth. Better to always have your eyes wide open.

More customers interrupt us and we stop talking. Just before noon an armored truck pulls up to LL National, and I watch as the guy in back gets out and makes the week's delivery. I mark the date and time in my notepad. A bank this large probably has two deliveries. It's Monday, so my guess is the next one might be on Friday, which would be perfect for this job. The take come Fourth of July weekend will be fatter for it.

Rosie watches me write while she takes a clean rag to the order counter to mop up some spilled salsa. "What about you? I know you didn't want to start doing the jobs. Benny didn't, either. But do you ever get off on the rush part? Running in and out, beating the clock? Benny's always so wound up after." Of all our family members, Rosie is the only one who knows we do the jobs. She doesn't like it, but she gets why we have to because she's involved, too.

I finish my notes and pause, thinking. "A little." I feel sort of ashamed admitting it, but the thing is, leaving a bank with a bag full of cash? It's like conquering the hardest level in Call of Duty or getting a home run or something. You against the bank. A series of obstacles and a ticking clock. Getting out alive? It's a high. I can't even try to pretend that it isn't. Leaving a bank with my blood pumping, my heart roaring in my chest, my brain and every nerve ending on alert. It's the most awake I'll ever be. Aware of everything. It's hard not to like that feeling— feeling bad for the tellers and witnesses doesn't make it go away. And the most screwed-up thing of all is even though I want out and to be as far away from the Eme as I can, a part of me will miss the jobs. Just one more example of how the Eme messed me up, messed us all up.

17
Lexi

"Can I help you?" Harrison's assistant peers at me from over the top of her computer screen, the light from it making her glasses reflect the Michael Kors handbag page she's obviously drooling over instead of doing whatever it is she does for Harrison.

"I wanted to stop in and see if Mr. Harrison was available to answer a question? I'm one of the new interns. He talked to us at breakfast, and I was so impressed by something he said. I mean, I know he's busy. I just figured I'd try." I smile innocently at her and lean over a bit so I can see her screen. "Isn't that one hot?" I say, pointing to the bag. If I weren't currently reduced to selling half my purse collection on eBay right now, I'd be all over it, too.

She minimizes the page and gives me a guilty smile. "Very."

"So can I pop my head in? I promise I'll be quick." I'm already walking toward his door, praying she won't head me off, when Harrison opens the door himself, cell phone to his ear, and nearly runs right into me.

"Angela—right?" He finishes up his call as I nod. "Orientation going okay?"

"Yes. Actually, we're breaking for lunch, but I wanted to see if you had a minute so I could get your advice about something."

"Well, I'm headed out right now. Tell you what. Walk with me and I'll try to help if I can, okay?" He taps his assistant's desk. "I'll be back in time for my one o'clock."

I look past him at his office, where I'd been hoping to go so I could slip the bug under his desk or a chair or something. But how am I going to get inside before he closes and locks the door? The bug's just a slim rectangular piece of plastic, barely wider than a penny. I can hide it easily. I just need an opportunity.

"Oh wow, that's really beautiful," I say, palming the bug as I make a beeline to the large ivory-inlaid box sitting on his desk. I turn around. "May I?"

Harrison lifts an eyebrow, but nods.

I will my hands not to shake as I pick it up and pretend to examine it, turning it over in my hands so that the lid falls off and lands on the carpet. "Oh my god! I'm so sorry!" I hurry to pick it up and then replace it—my back to the door, pressing the sticky side of the bug onto the bottom of the box as I do. I hold my breath as I set it down.

"Angela, I'm afraid we need to go if I'm going to get back in time," Harrison says, from closer behind me than I expected. I feel his hand touch my elbow, and I jump a little.

"Sorry! I guess I got distracted." *Did he see anything?* I can't be sure. I don't know when he came back into the room. I try not to imagine that his hand at my elbow is gripping me tighter than is normal, *but is it?*

"So what was it you wanted to talk to me about?" Harrison prompts, his eyes twinkling as we wait for the elevator doors to open.

"Actually, I was hoping to ask you about your time at UCLA. I've only just transferred there and have been a bit overwhelmed about deciding a minor. Do you mind if I ask what yours was?"

The elevator doors open as he starts talking, listing the courses he feels I should pay close attention to, what minors would be best if I hope to work somewhere like LL National. By the time we're walking through the lobby doors, I'm feeling calmer. I did it! The bug is in his office. And Quinn is parked somewhere near the building, listening.

"Where are you headed?" Harrison asks.

"I don't know. To wherever I can get a salad or something before we're due back from lunch."

He looks up the street. "There's a food truck up there. Probably more than one. Fast and usually amazing. I'm headed there myself. You're welcome to tag along if you'd like. Actually, you'd be doing me a favor. I've got a present on hold for my wife at the jewelry store around the corner. If you wouldn't mind, maybe I could show it to you and you can tell me if you think it's a good choice. A twenty-fifth anniversary present. So, you know, it's gotta wow." He winks at me. Ugh.

"Sure," I say, even though now all I want to do is get as far away from him as I can. This whole nice-guy routine he's working is unnerving.

We get closer to the truck, and the aroma of the food is ridiculous. Spicy and mouthwatering. Whatever they're making, I want five. Wow. "'Cocina de mi corazón.'" I read the words printed in graphic black letters on the side of the truck. The vehicle itself is bright red, with a series of colorful, elaborately designed hearts that remind me of the kind you see in Day of the Dead decorations or as part of a cool tattoo.

"'Kitchen of my heart,'" Harrison translates. "One of my favorites. It's this hybrid of Argentinean, Korean, and Mexican food. Absolutely amazing."

If I were with anyone else, this would be the perfect lunch stop.

"It's not parked in the area all the time. Lately it's been setting up out past the Bank of America building a few blocks down. We got lucky," Harrison says as his phone rings. "You go ahead. I'll get mine in a second." He directs me toward the counter, and I look over the wooden menu tent propped up next to the truck.

"Can I help you?" the guy behind the counter asks, and I look up. Christian is standing in front of me in a stained apron, with a basket of tacos in one hand. My heart nearly stops.

"Christian," I say, completely forgetting that I'm not Lexi right now—I'm Angela. I freeze. *Crap!*

He leans over. "I'm sorry . . . do we know each other?" His eyes take me in, from the top of my head to my heel-clad feet, and he smiles a little. "I feel like I'd remember you if we had . . ."

He narrows his eyes and looks harder at me. "Wait, there is something familiar. . . ."

It is all I can do not to panic and run. "Just give me some, uh, chips and a carnitas taco, please. And a Diet Coke." I hold out my debit card and pretend to be bored.

He takes it, still frowning at me, and turns toward the stove.

"Have you ordered?" Harrison asks, off the phone now.

"Yeah," I say. I need to get out of here. Now. But it would look weird if I didn't get my lunch first. *Please, please don't let him recognize me.*

All at once, there's a gust of wind, just enough to blow a stack of menu flyers from the counter to the sidewalk. *A total gift from God,* I can't help thinking as I turn and begin to chase them down. I'll take my time and with luck, Harrison will get my card and meal from Christian before I collect all the menus. I stoop over and start gathering the fluttering papers.

What I don't expect is for Christian to be outside the truck a second later, stooped down next to me, grabbing for flyers, too. His arm brushes mine as he leans closer.

"Lexi," he says quietly, and my heart goes straight into my throat, choking me.

How does he know? I thought the disguise was solid enough to fool anyone who didn't know me really well. We've only met once, and I didn't look anything like this. *How can he know it's me?*

"The card," he says, holding it up briefly so I can see my name, my real name. Oh my god, I'm an idiot.

"Why do you look like . . ." Christian starts.

"Angela?" Harrison holds out his hand to help me up. Christian's eyes flick from mine to him and back. He raises one eyebrow.

I stare at Christian for a second, take a deep breath, and stand up. After a beat, he does, too. I thrust the collected flyers into his hands, hoping beyond hope that somehow he'll pretend he doesn't know me.

"Here you go." I give him a pleading look.

"Thank you . . . Angela," he says purposefully, and I mouth the words "Thank *you*" right back at him. "Give me a sec to get back inside and I'll get your order."

Harrison peruses the bottles of hot sauce and grabs some napkins while I wait for Christian to come around to the window with my food.

When he does, he gives me a little smile that sends both panic and butterflies careening around my stomach. He holds out a bag, and his mouth twitches. "Your order, miss."

I feel my face heat up. "Thanks."

"You work at LL National?" the girl behind the counter asks. Her eyes focus on the employee badge hanging around my neck.

"I'm interning there, yeah."

She hands me some of the flyers. "Would it be weird if I asked you to put these in the lunchroom there? We'll be parking here every day over the summer. You do and I'll give you your next lunch free." She raises her eyebrows expectantly.

I can feel Christian watching me. "Sure. Sure," I tell the girl as I stuff the flyers and my debit card into my bag.

"Enjoy your lunch," Christian says. That he doesn't try to say anything else or throw me any weighted looks is a relief.

"Thanks," I say, meaning it in more ways than one.

"No problem." He leans over the counter and grins, and even though none of this is funny, I find myself grinning right back. Grateful. He's not going to expose me to Harrison, even if he has no idea what's going on. Well, I helped him out with his medal; one favor deserves another, I guess.

I join Harrison on a bench opposite the truck, and we dig into our meals. Talking about the kinds of inane things you talk about with people you barely know: the weather, the orientation, summer plans. I don't glance at the taco truck, not even once, but I swear I can still feel Christian watching me.

"So, should we get that anniversary gift?" I ask Harrison when I just can't stand it anymore.

Harrison wants to buy his wife a heart pendant with scrollwork and about a dozen diamonds in the center. It makes me think of something you might find around a medieval princess's neck— elaborate to the point of being tacky.

"Well, what do you think?" he asks.

"Perfect, really. If I were her, I'd love it." I'm lying, of course. If I were her, I'd hate it, but I've never been into jewelry like this. I like bling, but the heart shape makes this necklace feel cheesy. I liked the heart on the food truck better. *The food truck.* Just thinking about it makes my nerves jingle.

Harrison motions to the salesperson. "Okay. Wrap it up."

I watch her pull out pretty silver paper and a ribbon, and an unexpected lump forms in my throat. My father bought me a ring when I turned sixteen. I don't wear it every day because it's my birthstone—an opal—so it's a little too fragile for constant wear. Harrison will still get to buy his family jewelry. My dad may never get the chance again. It's so unfair that I can barely keep from screaming.

"I need to get back," I say. Suddenly, being with him for even one minute longer and acting like I think he's this amazing mentor-type person is unbearable.

"Oh yes. Well, thank you," he says absently as he signs his receipt.

I duck out of the store and begin the short walk back to the bank.

"Angela." And when I don't turn around right away, "Lexi." Christian's jogging from the food truck toward me. I wince and stop in my tracks, waiting for him to catch up.

"So. Nice hair. But I gotta tell you. I like you better blond." He folds his arms across his chest and grins.

I shake my head and look down at the sidewalk. What am I supposed to tell him about all this? Certainly not the truth, but then what? I grasp for some halfway-plausible explanation, but there's nothing. I've got nothing.

"So you want me to guess?" he asks. He paces back and forth in front of me. His jeans fit loose everywhere except his backside, and as panicked as I am, I'm also human. I can't help noticing how sexy it is. "You're a spy stealing bank secrets?"

When I roll my eyes, he says, "You just became part of the witness protection program? Or you're just, um, really into older, married banker-type dudes and don't want your friends to know?" He reaches out like he wants to touch my hair, but at the last minute he decides not to. "Tell me it's not that last one."

"Ew, no," I say immediately. "Let's go with the spy theory. Close enough. But no bank secrets involved." I step closer to him so that our shoulders touch, and I look furtively to my left and right before standing on tiptoe so that my lips are close to his neck, grazing his earlobe. "If you must know, I'm trying to infiltrate an elderly band of white-collar criminals stealing mass quantities of paper clips from office supply closets." I'm flirting. It's only to try to distract him. And it helps me feel like I'm gaining back some control. If I can't get him to stop asking questions, I'm in real trouble here. This guy gets too nosy and it could mess up everything.

Christian laughs, and the sound of it—warm and low—nearly makes me forget to keep my guard up. "Okay."

"So you work there?" I ask, pointing at the truck, eager to change the subject. "What about school? Am I going to have to start investigating you, too?" I tease. At the risk of sounding conceited, I'm a master flirt. And it's paying off right now. His eyes are alive, lit up inside, and his gaze keeps drifting to my mouth. He wants to kiss me. And in the name of protecting my agenda, I might let him. A girl's gotta be willing to do what it takes to get the job done, right?

He grins. "That depends. Does your investigation involve a thorough pat-down?"

I roll my eyes again and he laughs. "School's over in a few days, and my cousin really needed me. I'll be doing this all summer anyway, so why not get a head start snagging some cash, right? But you don't really want to know about all that. Seriously, what's going on, Lexi?" Dang it. I thought I had him.

"That's classified. Top secret. You know, spy stuff. I could tell you, but then . . ."

He groans, "Yeah, yeah, but then you'd have to kill me. Right. But . . ." He waits, frowning.

I stop smiling. "Look. Can't you just forget you ever saw me? Please?"

He considers it. "Nah, sorry, but you're impossible to forget."

I shake my head. This is too much. "I can't do this right now. I'm sorry." I look back at the jewelry store and see Harrison walking out with his phone to his ear.

"Okay, fine, but I need some kind of explanation if I'm going to keep covering for you. Meet me tomorrow afternoon," Christian says. "Right here. Four o'clock."

I can't tell if he's being flirty or if he's threatening me. Like if I don't show up, he'll somehow expose me to Harrison. I decide to call his bluff.

"I don't get off until five. And no," I say.

"Please. I'm not looking to hurt you. You helped me. Maybe

149

I can help you." There's something in his eyes that makes me want to give in.

I glance at my watch; orientation resumes in less than five minutes. "Look. Thanks for before, but I don't owe you an explanation." I hurry back toward the bank before he can argue, heart in my throat, hoping that he won't even try.

Leo's beach house is alive with lights, music, and people when Quinn and I pull up. It feels chaotic after the hushed atmosphere of the bank. I would normally be excited, but my brain is full to bursting with inane banking information, and after cozying up to that snake Harrison all day, I just want to go back home and take a long, hot shower, think through what to do about Christian if he doesn't let our little meet-up at the food truck go, and go to bed. But this is Leo's last big party of the school year, his "Night Before the Last Day" blowout. He'd be crushed if I didn't show up.

I get off my bike and stretch, relishing the freedom of not being in my work disguise. I take off my helmet and run a hand through my hair and sigh. The air is a thousand times cooler without that awful wig on my head. It's not quite dark, but the sky is close to succumbing to night, the last tendrils of sunset pinks and oranges fading on the horizon. Quinn and I walk up the steep driveway past familiar cars, but as normal as it all seems, I feel different, like I don't belong. We don't go to Westwood Prep anymore. I wonder if this is what it feels like once you graduate, like some invisible curtain has suddenly dropped between the life you had and the one you're headed toward. All I know is that it sucks, this abrupt separation I'm feeling.

We let ourselves into the house and weave our way through the tightly packed crowds of people holding red Solo cups, laughing at the kind of stories and jokes you'd have to be there while it was happening to understand. A few people wave; several more glance at us and then away, whispering behind their hands as if we can't see them, as if we don't know that they're talking about us.

"Quinn! Lexi!" Whitney jostles her way over to us, barefoot and casual in a floaty little sundress, her hair pulled back in a loose braid. I can feel Quinn take it all in: the golden glow of her skin, the way her teeth look extra white by comparison, the fact that her wide smile is mostly meant for him. The one good thing about our leaving school is that it seems to have shifted something between them. They aren't officially exclusive, but you can tell they're close. Tonight could be the tipping point.

"How was your day, dear?" Whitney asks me, half laughing. "Did you play nice at the office?" She leans into me and puts her mouth up to my ear. "Did they buy the disguise?"

Everyone except Christian. But how do I say this right here? Right now? Quinn will panic. Someone might overhear. Besides, I want time to think, to form a plan so that when I do tell them, I'll have a way to fix things.

"Went exactly as planned. We'll talk later. You see Leo yet?"

Whitney shakes her head. "No, but knowing him, he's hiding out in his darkroom."

Leo throws parties all the time, something his parents not only endorse but engineer. His playboy, high-rolling image has been carefully cultivated by his mother practically since he was born and she dressed him in a onesie that had BALLER on it. She'll call the effort a success if and when he and his two brothers achieve Kardashian-type fame and she gets to be on their reality show. Leo goes along with it, but inevitably he spends half of every party holed up developing photographs the old-fashioned way in his basement, so that's where I head now.

"Lex, how's it goin'?" Amanda Blake, a friend of Bianca's and one of the mean-girl trio, is one floor above me, leaning over the circular glass-enclosed staircase that leads from the house's third floor to the basement. Her straight red hair hangs over her face. "We miss you *so* much, hon." A total lie. With me gone, she's next in line to the It Girl throne—not a title I was all that eager to have or keep, mind you, but one she's coveted since we started high school. She teeters a bit on the stair, and Derek, my text ex, steadies her elbow, looks pointedly at me, and nuzzles her ear. I guess he thinks I'm going to be jealous . . . and maybe that's what that sinking feeling is in my stomach, but whatever, I'll live. I have bigger things to worry about than high school drama.

I make my way down the last few steps to the bottom floor. The entire back wall of the house is floor-to-ceiling windows meant to take advantage of the ocean view, but with the lights on, all I can see is my own reflection—a girl with long blond hair, not-so-pale skin thanks to my recent spray tan—gliding across the dark world beyond the glass like a ghost. I make my way to Leo's darkroom. The door has a sign on it telling me to KNOCK FIRST OR DIE. I rap on it a few times.

"It's me."

Leo opens the door a few seconds later, squinting. "Lex!" He pulls me inside and puts his arm around my shoulders. "How's my little spy doing?"

"Not so peachy," I say. "I have a problem I need you to help me brainstorm. Can you spare a few minutes and come hang with me?" I don't want Quinn to know about Christian yet. I know my brother too well. He'll decide that it's too dangerous for me to stay at the bank and refuse to let me go back, maybe withdraw me from the program with a couple of keystrokes. Leo, on the other hand, knows me well enough to realize when he can't talk me out of something, and he can keep a secret better than anyone I know. He's the perfect person to confide in and hit up for advice.

"I was just finishing up the last of the photos I took during the jump. Give me two more minutes and I'm game," Leo says, leaning up against the countertop. "So what's going on?"

"After you're done," I say. "It can wait."

I go down the clothesline strung from wall to wall, examine the still-drying pictures clipped to it of Quinn and the others hovering over the street. They are beautiful. Everyone's a study in shadow and light, their parachute canopies making them look almost angelic, like they have wings. I reach the one that I decide is my favorite, the one of me landing on that van's hood in a crouch, my parachute like a drifting cloud behind me. It's taken from far enough away that you can see the city in the background looking Gotham-esque. I look like a superhero, or maybe a villain, but tough either way, my boots shiny in the glare of the streetlights.

"Can I have a copy of this one?" I ask.

I could use a reminder of how strong I can be sometimes, how in control. Especially after what happened earlier today. I managed to do what I set out to do: get some security information that might help us and bug Harrison's office, but the run-in with Christian and the few slipups I made at the bank and with my debit card really threw me. In theory this little scheme seemed so much easier. Now I'm not sure how to fix things. Do I meet with Christian? He knows I'm not Angela. All he has to do is tell someone at the bank. Tell Harrison. It's obvious that I'm up to something sketchy.

"Ha! I knew you'd want that one, so I already made you a copy. It's drying over there. I got a better one of the guys in the van, too. You're gonna laugh when you see it. Their faces when you landed? In a word: *awesome*." Leo strides over to the other side of the room.

I grin and follow him. I could use a laugh. I lean over and take a closer look. The driver ... it takes a second, but then there's no mistaking him, and my whole body goes cold. *What the hell? Christian*. Again. My stomach turns into a hundred butterflies beating at the sides of a too-small cage, swirling up inside my chest. He was there that night? *How? Why? Everywhere I've been lately, he's been there, too. Now I'm thoroughly freaked out.*

Leo laughs. "Two dudes in a minivan looking scared crapless and you all Black Widow–tough on the hood. It's almost too amazing to keep hidden in the BAM book. The passenger is my favorite—he's so shocked, it's adorable." Leo touches the photo gently with one finger and smiles. "Don't you think?"

"Sure, adorable," I echo.

The car. Something about it is so familiar. I take the photo down and examine it close up. A gray minivan. I look at the next photo—it captures the side of the van with me running, blurry in the background. There's a sign on the van's door. I inch closer, squinting to make out the words: MARY KAY CONSULTANT.

I suck in a breath. The bank robbery. The getaway car was gray and had a sign just like it. No, *exactly* like it. Christian's driving the getaway car. Which means . . . Oh my god, he's one of them. That's why he's been at all the same places. He's the robber who ran me over. I can't prove it, but suddenly I know it's true. Those eyes, how did I not see it before? That's why he was at the Bank of America. He was asking me to get that necklace because he needed it. It was evidence. *He used me to get rid of it.*

I turn my back on the photo and half sit on the counter. The cute boy who flirted with me and took me out for doughnuts is a criminal. A bank robber, for crap's sake! It doesn't seem possible. He seemed so sweet . . . but when he asked me to get his medal, he had to know I was the one he knocked over in front of the bank. It's messed up, flirting with me like that. Playing me. Part of me can't help but be impressed. Oh, he's good, but I'm also ticked off. How dare he use me like that?

"Hey, what is it? You look freaked out." Leo's frowning, watching me.

"Can you make me a copy of this picture? And this one? Two copies?" I yank down the ones I want and hand them to him. I am so angry I'm shaking.

"Sure, but what's going on?"

"Too much to tell you right now. Just make the pictures, please. And can I use your laptop?"

"Okaaay," he says, confused.

I hug him hard, thankful that there are at least a few guys left in my life I can actually trust, and rush up the stairs. I need to find out everything I can about Christian before he comes looking for me tomorrow. Now that he knows I'm interning at the bank . . . it will only be a matter of time before he does. And when he does, I want to be ready to play him right back.

156

18

Christian

"**You've been skipping school.** A lot, according to the office. What's going on, mijo?" Mom is waiting at the door for me to show up, her arms folded, foot tapping. *Not good.*

I leave my backpack by the door and try to walk past her, hoping like mad that she'll drop it so I can go to my room and figure out what's up with this Lexi girl and her repeated appearances at banks I've either robbed or am planning to rob. But Mom is like a dog nipping at my heels, raining questions down on me. I'm not up for this discussion. My brain's still reeling from my run-in with Lexi. Half of me is psyched to have a probable "in" to exploit at the bank, but the other half is still caught up in those eyes of hers and the way her bottom lip curves and how it would feel to kiss her.

"Did you think they wouldn't call to tell us? A full scholarship, and what do you do? Skip school. I don't get it. Why would you jeopardize your whole future like this?"

The truth is, I've had too much to worry about, and the possibility that the school would call wasn't high on my list of priorities. Besides, Gabriel's little sister just started working in the front office. He promised me she'd take my name off the absentee list before the automated phone calls to my house went out. Which he obviously didn't do. Pendejo. I walk past Mom and into the family room, where Maria is parked in front of the television, glued to *Curious George*. She laughs as George falls off a chair into a bucket of water. Every time I look at her I remember Psycho pointing his gun at the back of her head. I shiver.

"Where were you?" Abuelo asks before I can answer Mom's first round of questions.

"Well?" Mom leans against the wall, her lips pressed tight together like she's trying hard not to totally lose it.

"I was helping Rosie at the food truck. She's swamped during the lunch rush downtown. She can't keep handling it alone, and if Benny misses any more school, he'll have to repeat this year. If I don't help her, she loses all that business, and you know she and Benny need all the money they can get. Tia Jeanne's treatments and all." I take a long drink of water and look out the window so I won't have to look either of them in the eye. "Besides, she's paying me. If you want me to go to college, we're gonna need some money saved up, right? To make sure you guys can carry the bills? I thought it would be smarter to help the family out while I can and take advantage of making a little extra for you than to show up at school. Come on, it's the last week before the seniors are done. It's basically a waste to show up anyway. I already took my finals. My grades are in. It's not like I'm risking not graduating or something. Look, I know I should've told you and called the school about it. I'm sorry. I just forgot." I hate myself a little for using my aunt's cancer and our financial stuff as my cover, for the awful pride that's suddenly radiating from Mom's face because now she thinks my skipping is somehow noble, but it's the only lie that will keep her off my back. Especially after I told her I was going to wait to start college in the fall.

"You are such a good boy," Mom says, putting her hands on either side of my head and then kissing both my cheeks. "You make me so proud, mijo." Her eyes are glassy with tears. I feel slimy. "But you shouldn't miss your last few days. You only graduate high school once. You should be having fun with your friends."

Yeah, that's what we do. Have fun. Robbing banks is a freaking party. "It's cool. I've got plenty of time for that."

"S'up?" Benny pokes his head around the door at just the right moment.

"Hi, Benny, how's mi hermana feeling today?"

Benny's smile slips a little bit. "Tired. The chemo's wiping her out."

"I'll come over tonight after work to see her. You staying for dinner? It's just leftovers, but you're welcome to it. And make up a plate to take to Rosie before you leave if I'm not here." Mom ruffles first Benny's hair and then mine.

No matter how old my cousin gets, he always reverts to about ten when my mom starts asking him questions. "Gracias, Tia." Benny puts on his best angel face.

"I was gonna work out. You game?" I ask him. I need to

burn off all this stress and guilt I'm carrying or I won't make it to the end of this job. Lifting for an hour will help clear my head.

"Man, why else d'you think I'm wearing these shorts?" Benny's got this thing with shorts. He hates them. Dude never wears anything but jeans even on the hottest day unless he's working out. He'd never admit it, but I think it's because as big as his chest is, his legs are like twigs. He'll probably spend the next hour doing weighted calf raises and lunges to build them up.

"How's it goin' downtown? You score any good intel yet?" Benny asks.

I look back down the hall to see if anyone's listening.

"Maybe. Give me a day or two and I'll let you know."

We head for the bench and weights out in the garage. They used to be my dad's, but since he barely comes out of my parents' room when he's here, they're mine now.

Mom calls down the hall. "Want anything? Water? A snack?" Leave it to Mom to keep pressing food on us. Only she would think eating is a good idea in the middle of a workout.

I roll my eyes at Benny. "We're good."

I put on some music, my usual routine when we hit the weights.

"So I never asked you where the medal was or how you ended up getting it out of there," Benny says as soon as we're both sure no one's eavesdropping on the other side of the door. "Man, I was too relieved that you had it back. That night after the job I could barely sleep a wink."

"It was in one of the offices. Under a desk."

"And you what? Just walked in there, looked around, and snatched it up?"

"Nah, man. I met this girl outside the bank, and I got her to go in and look for me."

"What girl?"

"Just some random girl. I don't know. She told me her name, but I can't remember it." I avoid looking at him. Benny's got this way of reading me. If he thinks I'm holding back, he'll press me for details. I don't want him knowing much about Lexi just yet, not until I figure out what she's doing at the bank and how I can use it to help us.

I grab a set of dumbbells and start curling them. *What am I going to do about her?* She's obviously doing something shady, but what? *Could we have some competition on this job?* I still have her ID, and later, once I have a little time to myself, I'll start sifting through whatever pops up when I Google her. I want to do it now, but if I try to rush Benny out, he'll wonder what's up.

"Hey, dipwads. Got room for three more?" someone shouts from the hall.

Gabriel, Carlos, and Eddie step into the garage. Is it my imagination or do all three of them look a little guilty? One of them told Soldado about the medal. I thought it was Gabriel, but could they all have gone to Soldado—or, worse, straight to the Eme to tell them about my slipup? Gabriel's been so weird lately. I think about Maria and Psycho, and my temper boils over. "You ratted me out to Soldado. Do you have any idea what you started?" I rush toward the door, and Gabriel throws his hands up.

"Whoa, whoa! Take it easy."

Everything that happened outside my house with Maria comes pouring out of me. I tell him the whole story. The accusation is clear.

"I didn't tell him. None of us did," Gabriel says, looking me right in the eye. "I swear."

"Then how'd he know?" I growl, careful to keep my voice low enough that Mom doesn't come out here to see what's up.

"How should I know? Guy's got eyes and ears all over. I just know it wasn't me. I would never do anything to put the family in danger. Maria especially. Come on, you know that." His face is pure emotion, tears swimming in his eyes, shining under the garage's overhead light. "He could've had you followed or something. After we dropped off the take, he called and asked me what was up with you. Why you seemed all jumpy. All's I told him was that you were getting tired of the jobs and, yeah, I did mention the school thing, but I didn't think that would put him over the edge. I told him you weren't gonna go. Man, I'm sorry. For real. I woulda never said that if . . ."

I think about the last few days. Could I have been followed? It seems paranoid, but then . . . Soldado can be crazy, so maybe it's true. A creeping sense of dread inches up my spine, and my mouth dries up.

"Yeah. I know," I say. As suspicious as Gabriel's behavior's been lately, seeing him now, all torn up, I know he didn't screw me over. "I feel you. We're good." He grabs me and pulls me in for a quick back pat/hug combo.

He clears his throat and sniffs. "We'll get this job done, and Maria will be safe. No matter what. We're in this together, right?"

"Right." I hand Gabriel a set of forties so he can do biceps curls, and Eddie heads for the pull-up bar. He's got on his dad's old steel-toed work boots and a pair of jeans with drywall crusted on them, so he must've come straight here from work. He takes off his shirt and starts doing pull-ups. I remember when we came out here the first time, all of us skinny like Eddie back then. All Gabriel could curl was a five-pounder. He was basically a stick bug, all arms and legs. Really, we all were. We started the weight training to survive. You don't get tough, you don't make it. Sometimes not even if you are tough.

Benny lies back on the bench and lifts the already stacked bar off the stand and down to his chest. He presses it five quick times, his cheeks puffing out by the end, making him look like his face might explode. The weights are set for me, not him. It's too much weight and he knows it, but it never stops him from trying anyway, every freaking time we come out here. I swear it's his goal in life to best me at least once.

"So. Did Christian tell you exactly how he got his medal back?" Benny says.

I punch his arm, but he keeps going.

"He got some chica to go in and get it for him. Homes is legit," Benny jokes. "Some girl he doesn't even know, and she gets it and doesn't even think twice."

"So she gets your medal and what? You go your separate ways? That doesn't sound like you, bro," Gabriel says, exhaling hard as he starts another set. He looks over at the mirror on the far wall so he can watch his form. I have a rep for dating my fair share of girls, but I'm nowhere near the ladies' man these pendejos are trying to make me out to be. So far the jobs and school have taken up most of my attention. Plus, the second I date a girl more than once or twice, Mom sits us both down for a talk about the dangers of teenage sex. She had me when she was seventeen, and while she swears up and down I was one of the two best things to ever happen to her (Maria being the second), she also has a very long list of all the ways her life imploded because she got pregnant. It's usually enough to put an end to things for me and whatever girl I might be with.

"Yeah. Kind of. I mean, I took her for a couple doughnuts to, you know, say thank you, but that was it," I tell Gabriel. I don't mention playing chess. They'd have a field day with that.

Benny breaks into a crazy grin. "Doughnuts? Ha! I knew there was more to this story than you were letting on. Where's this girl from?"

I set down my weights and shake out my arms. I forgot to count my reps while we were talking, and now my biceps are quivering. "Who knows? Dude, it's not a thing. She was going into the bank, and I made up some story and asked her to get the medal, and she did. So I felt like I should thank her. End of story."

The guys start to laugh, and then Carlos goes into a detailed explanation of what he'd do to thank her, like he has any experience at all and isn't just riffing off stuff he's only seen in online porn.

"She was hot, right?" Eddie stares at me hopefully, one eyebrow sort of arched. He tries to do a chin-up with just one arm, but he can't quite isolate the right muscles to do it. I can't help it—I crack up because the guy looks like he's having a seizure when he does that.

"Yeah, okay. She was hot," I say. *More like drop-dead gorgeous.* They would lose it if they actually saw her.

"Knew it." Benny laughs. "You ask her out for real after the doughnuts?"

I hesitate.

"Ah, she turned him down!" Carlos punches my arm— lightly for him, but it still stings.

It's nearly eleven when the guys take off. We decimated last night's leftovers and then watched the game, and they just lingered, especially Gabriel. He hates going home. His mom has a new boyfriend, and he and Gabriel don't exactly get along. Old as he is, I think sometimes Gabriel's still hoping his parents will get back together once his dad gets out of jail, like deep inside he's still a little boy or something. He tries to drive away any guy his mother hooks up with . . . only this time, it hasn't worked.

I turn off all the lights except the one over the kitchen table, and then I pull out my laptop and open a browser window. I start out simple and just Google Lexi's full name. I find her Instagram account, which is full of pictures of her friends doing everything from water-skiing to drag racing. *This girl just gets cooler and cooler,* I think. An hour goes by before I finally abandon the stacks of vacation photos (all in crazy exotic locations) and the more surprising pictures of abandoned buildings and long steel bridges— these lonely-looking places that she always tags the same way: *#inspiration.* They fascinate me. I don't get it, but I want to.

I check her Twitter and then her Facebook, which is old and hasn't been updated all that much since last year, but it does give me her parents' names. I decide to do an address search. If I can't find out anything that tells me why she's hanging around LL National in disguise, I can follow her and eventually figure it out.

Instead of an address, I find news articles and videos, all of them about her dad. I read each one, then watch the videos. It's basically the same footage over and over: Lexi's father being yanked toward a police car in handcuffs, Lexi and her mom and brother trailing after as a reporter does a voice-over about the charges her dad is facing. And that's when things start to make sense. Her dad worked for LL National. Our target bank. Supposedly, he committed some kind of fraud involving risky mortgages. I read the articles, making notes to myself. Is she trying to clear his name? Get revenge?

I lean back in my chair, balance on the back two legs. Whatever it is, she's in disguise because she doesn't want employees at the bank to recognize her. Now the only questions I have are, how badly does she want to keep her secret, and can I put aside my feelings for her to exploit it?

19

Christian

"Delivery for Angela Dunbar," I tell the security guard. I shake the paper bag with the COCINA DE MI CORAZÓN logo on it in front of his face. He sizes me up. I open the bag so he can see that the only things inside are two foil-wrapped tacos. With a sigh, he picks up the phone.

"You can leave it here. I'll make sure she gets it," he says, dismissing me while he waits for whoever's on the other end of the phone to answer.

"She still has to pay for it, though," I say.

"Have Angela Dunbar come to reception, please. Delivery from, uh, co-keen-a dee me core-aye-zonn." His pronunciation makes me wince.

I put some distance between me and the security desk and lean against the wall to wait. Elevator music is playing, some instrumental version of a Pitbull song, which is so messed up that I want to crack up. I stare at the floor, keeping my face down so it isn't turned toward the security camera near the ceiling. I adjust my COCINA DE MI CORAZÓN baseball cap lower on my head.

I should've waited to catch her outside somewhere, but showing up at the bank felt more effective. It's a jerk move, but I don't get to be a gentleman right now. Not after what happened with Maria. Still, I'm having trouble being chill. I just want this over with.

Play the part, pendejo. She has to think I'll really do it, I tell myself.

"Christian?" She doesn't look surprised to see me, even though she didn't order lunch from the taco truck. Actually, she looks almost pleased. *Huh?* It doesn't make sense, but I don't have time to puzzle it out. I just need to get through this quickly.

"Got your lunch delivery here . . . *Angela,*" I say with a smirk, really emphasizing her fake name, once again holding up the paper bag.

She narrows her eyes at me and then walks over and takes the bag from my hands, her fingers deliberately brushing mine. She gives me this sexy little smile.

"I forgot to bring cash. I'll walk you out and get some from the ATM," she says loudly enough for the security creep to overhear. She seems utterly chill, and it's freaking me out.

As soon as we're outside, she leads me to a quiet little courtyard between LL National and another building and leans against the wall. Lexi considers me the same way she looked at her chess pieces that day we played. "So? Are you going to tell me why you're here, or do I have to guess?" She folds her arms across her chest so that the side of her bra is visible through the silky fabric of her blouse, and of course I look, because how could I not? Now it's her turn to raise an eyebrow, and I'm so taken off guard that I start to laugh. I pictured her getting all scared and upset. But this? I have no idea how to react.

"I need your help with something," I say once I've gotten hold of myself, cutting to the chase.

"Yeah? With what exactly?"

"You're not going to like what I'm about to say." I try to think about how to word this. "So . . . sorry." *What am I doing?* Rule number one of blackmailing someone has got to be not apologizing for the blackmail. I shake my head and try again. "Here's the thing: I need some information about the bank. Security information. And you're going to get it for me."

"Why? Why do you need information about the bank?" she asks, but she doesn't seem shocked or even all that curious. It's unsettling how calm she is.

I stare at her a second. Has she already put two and two together and realized I'm the one who ran into her at the Bank of America robbery? "I just need it." There. That's better. Tougher. Even if she has figured it out, what does it matter? I still have the upper hand either way.

"You 'just need it.'" She walks around me, arms folded, head down, thinking. Her heels click on the concrete, and I can't help looking down at the curve of her bare calf. There's something on it. I lean over and suck in a breath. She has a tattoo on her ankle. A goldfish. That night we stole the car. She's the one who dropped onto the hood. She's the BASE jumper. I blink, staring at it in disbelief.

"What?" she asks, looking down at her leg. "I like goldfish."

She makes a face and walks a circle around me. "And what happens if I say no? What if I don't want to help you?"

"I think you know what happens," I say, my voice coming out all wrong—not forceful enough, like a deflating balloon. I'm not dealing with some regular girl here. Pulling off a BASE jump from the top of one of LA's most well-known buildings without getting caught means this girl is no run-of-the-mill high school kid. I can feel my advantage slipping away.

"I want you to spell it out," she says, calmly watching me puzzle out what's happening, why she isn't rattled. "Go on. Say it." She closes her mouth, and I find myself staring at her lips, at the little dip at the center of the bottom one.

I shake my head and take a breath. "Or I'll have to tell them who you really are, *Lexi*. I know you're Alexandra Scott, Warren Scott's daughter. He's the guy who's been in the paper for mortgage fraud, right? You're up to something at the bank, and obviously you don't want to be exposed."

She gives me an amused smile. "So what kind of security information could you possibly need, exactly?" She's not upset; if anything, she's enjoying this. I have the checkmate right now—all the leverage—and yet she seems to be the one setting me up for something. It's both terrifying and fascinating.

"Building plans, standard positions of every security officer, and who works what shift. That would be a good start."

"Planning on robbing the place?"

It makes sense that she'd come to this conclusion after hearing what I want, so I'm not surprised. "What I plan to do isn't really your concern," I say, grinning. I can't help it. She is freaking impressive.

"And what if I go upstairs and quit right now? Then what?" She bites her lip and gazes up at me with a look that makes me want to pull her into my arms and kiss her.

I shrug and lean against the wall, throw her some badass attitude of my own. I don't want her to see how much she's messing me up. "I don't think you'll do that."

"No?" She stares at me, her eyes twinkling.

I stare right back. "No."

"So how is it that you think I'm going to be able to get you this stuff? You know I'm only interning here, right? I'm not, like, head of security or something. The building plans aren't exactly lying around, readily available to anyone who wants them. I can't just walk up to security and say 'Hey, by the way, you guys mind giving me the location and codes for all of your alarms?'"

Lexi gets closer, invading my space, mocking me with her eyes. I don't get it. If she knows I'm planning to rob the bank, why isn't she freaked out? I would've expected her to be trembling in her heels and crying. I was feeling guilty about blackmailing her, scaring her, but here we are, and the only one trembling seems to be me.

"Draw me the areas you do have access to. Create a map of the bank's layout. Give me the basics—where the cameras are in the bank downstairs, when the money deliveries come in and how they get processed. How much is in them on average. Where the vault is located exactly. The safe combinations at the tellers' desks for their individual safes. That'll be a good start. It's not my problem how you get the information. I'm not the one being blackmailed here." I lay on my best boy-from-the-hood, East LA accent, narrowing my eyes and folding my arms across my chest.

"And when you rob the place and the police realize that you know too much and they start looking for insider accomplices, then what? Huh? You don't think they'll figure out that I had something to do with it? Eventually?" she says, pacing.

"Like I said, not my problem. If you weren't looking for trouble, you wouldn't be wearing a wig and carrying a false ID around."

She stops pacing and looks at me, one eyebrow quirking up. "Touché."

"Just get me the info. By the end of the week." I am Soldado in this moment, or at least doing a pretty good impersonation of him. It is both awful and somehow thrilling. "I'm gonna make this crystal clear. I can take this info up to that guy's office—the one you were with when I saw you. Harrison? That's his name, right?" For the first time she looks surprised and maybe even a little impressed by me, too. She probably assumed I wouldn't be smart enough to check out the LL National website's employee directory. A guy like me can't be all that clever, right? I'm used to being underestimated, but it ticks me off anyway. I get right up close to her and hold up her student ID. "Won't look good. Warren Scott's daughter sneaking around the bank building. What do you think that'll do to his case?" I pull out my phone and flip through the pictures I took of her leaving her house this morning. She's in her Angela disguise already, but the house address is clear in the background as she gets on her motorcycle. There's no denying she's at the Scott residence.

I felt like a total creeper taking the photos, but having insurance in this case is essential. It was fascinating to see where she lives. The house is huge—but based on what's happened to her dad and the haunted air the house gives off, she probably won't be living there much longer. Makes me feel sort of sorry for her. I've never had money, not like that, but it has to be pretty damn traumatizing to be used to having it and then lose it overnight.

She stares at me, lips parted, stunned silent. She hesitates for half a minute and then she agrees. "Fine."

"Good," I fire back, trying to keep my head. Being this close to her is a recipe for disaster, because some part of me is still maddeningly desperate to not have her hate me. "Bring me what you got Saturday. Five o'clock. Griffith Park. Meet me by the abandoned zoo. Do you know it?" It's a dramatic choice for this meeting because the place can be downright eerie. But I want her unsettled and uncomfortable. It'll be easier to get her to do what I need her to. It's messed up, and I'm not pumped about having to play the jerk, but I need to pull this job off perfectly, and the only way to do that is to get her to cooperate. Besides, it's far from the bank and Soldado's prying eyes and anyone else who might be watching in the hood. I know I have to use Lexi to get what I need, but I don't want the Eme to find out about her. I'm only pretending to be threatening—I wouldn't actually hurt her to get what I need, but they would.

Lexi nods. "I can figure out how to get there. Are we done here?" She glances at her phone, probably checking the time.

I nod. "For now."

She turns to walk off, then stops and swings around. Her eyes glitter, and once again I get the distinct impression that I'm missing something. "You sure you want to go through with this?" It's a surprising question, one that almost sounds like a dare or a threat. Truth is, I'm sure I *don't* want to go through with it. I just don't have any other choice, but I can't admit that. She needs to think I don't care about her, about anything but the job. Otherwise she won't take me seriously.

"Absolutely," I say.

20
Lexi

My meeting with Christian went better than I'd hoped. Still, I'm strangely disappointed. I guess part of me was hoping he'd have a change of heart and let me off the hook, but hello, he's a criminal, so of course he didn't, and now here we are. He thinks he's blackmailing me, and I'm biding my time until I decide how best to return the favor.

I have pictures of my own, don't I? I'm not entirely sure when the best time will be to leverage them, but I have faith that I'll figure it out.

What I need now is more information. I hung out at Leo's until late last night, doing Internet searches on every bank robbery in the area over the last few years. I found his group pretty quickly. The Romero Robbers, named after the famous horror director George Romero, who made the classic zombie movie *Night of the Living Dead*. Apparently, the detectives who work these cases give all their bank robbers nicknames that reference something about the case, like the zombie masks Christian's group wears. I found a handful of articles about them, as well as some security footage, but you can't tell who's who. Only one guy stands out. He must be well over two hundred pounds, but the others all look like identical zombie clones, with their dark clothes, masks, glasses, and black hoodies.

But other than the pictures I have of Christian in the stolen getaway car, I have very little else to go on. You can't exactly Google *Christian Ruiz* and not expect a bazillion hits. I even looked up the food truck, but other than some reviews raving about the Korean bulgogi tacos, there wasn't much. No website. No details. So I'll play along for now, using each meeting with Christian to glean information about him and the Romero Robbers.

I make my way back upstairs, barely paying attention to where I'm going. I'm too preoccupied with all that's happened and whether I should let Quinn and the others in on my blackmail situation. I think I have to. Quinn is going to freak out, but the pictures of Christian should calm him back down. Besides, I can't just go meet Christian at the abandoned zoo alone. I'm all for risks, but I'm not stupid. It's too remote, the perfect place for the rest of the Romero Robbers to hide and ambush me.

Quinn will tell me to just quit. But I want this too bad now, and if I can manage to somehow get my brother and the others to help me, this could be the biggest BAM yet—we could bring down not one criminal but six.

Almost as if the universe itself is rooting for me, it turns out that our last orientation session is with the bank security team and two police officers. Maybe I can squeeze some information about Christian and his group from them. They have to know about the Bank of America heist.

There are two people standing at the front of the conference room—a man and a woman in plainclothes who appear to be in a good mood, joking and talking with Trisha while they wait for us to file in and settle into our chairs. I'm excited to listen to them . . . that is, until I get a good look at the guy. He's the one who questioned me outside the Bank of America the other day. Detective Martin. Even as shook up as I was, there is no way I could ever forget him. He's got this military air about him and eyes so intense they're practically giving off an electric current that makes my arm hairs stand on end. He's got a bristly gray crew cut, and his shoes are so shiny I can make out the blurry image of the overhead fluorescent lighting in them. This is a man who prides himself on details. I almost walk back out the door, but then it's too late. He glances over and sees me, and I can't run out without looking obvious.

I don't recognize the woman. She is a lot younger than Martin is and most likely pregnant, because there's a little swell below her belt. It's small enough that I would be afraid to congratulate her, though. There are dark circles beneath her eyes, and her hair is too wild to do much with except pull it back.

I feel conspicuous even though this guy saw me only once and my face was red and swollen from crying at the time. Has he seen through my disguise? He looked right past me like he'd never seen me before.

I read somewhere that people have tells that make it obvious when they're covering something up or lying. I wish I knew his. And then I have a horrible thought. *What about me? Am I giving off some kind of liar alarm only the police officers can detect?* I should leave; I can't take this chance. I start to get up from my chair, but Trisha shuts the door.

"Okay, this is Detective Martin and Detective Hobbs. They're part of a new program the theft department has initiated to help train LL National's employees in the event that we are held up. This is a routine part of orientation. Every one of our employees takes this training. Even those of us who don't work directly with customers. They have some very practical ways to help you identify a possible robber before he makes his move and to deter him from following through. Pay close attention. But I don't want you to be nervous. In all the years we've had interns in our banks, we've never had a robbery occur while one of them was present. Detectives." Tricia sits down in the last available chair at the conference room table, and we give our full attention to Martin and Hobbs.

For a second all I can think of is Calvin and Hobbes—the cartoon characters from my father's old desk calendar—something my grandfather got him every year at Christmas, before he died. My father still has the last one on his desk at home, even though it's from almost ten years ago. It helps calm me down now to try to picture Detective Martin as a fifty-something version of Calvin. Detective Hobbs looks nothing like the tiger Hobbes, so I try to imagine her in a tiger suit, belly pooch and all. I can't help smiling a little. When she catches me, she smiles back.

"Thank you, Ms. Bryant." Detective Martin paces as he talks, as if staying still isn't something he can do. I keep my head down, pen in hand like I'm eager to take notes.

"We're here to talk to you about Effective Capture, the new program the LAPD has been implementing with the FBI throughout the Los Angeles area to great success. Bank robberies are down across the board since we began our training. We're on track for less than half the robberies we had just last year."

There is a smattering of applause.

He goes on to tell stories about a few robbers they've caught recently. The clues they leave! They're so obvious that I can barely believe they're for real. One guy wrote his stickup note on the back of an electric bill with his name and address on it. Another guy didn't check for dye packs and got a face full of bright red dye mixed with pepper spray as soon as he stepped out of the bank.

"Most robbers will try to carry a note to one teller, passing the note to her alone and asking for the money in her drawer. They may or may not have a gun, and in most cases they don't plan on using it if they do."

Christian had a gun. He dropped it next to me that day, I think. I'd nearly forgotten, but remembering it now makes him seem more dangerous ... and earlier I was taunting him. *Smart, Lexi. Real smart.*

"While you are here, it is your job to keep yourself and the other employees and the customers safe. Even if the odds of a robber using a weapon are remote, statistically speaking, you should never challenge a robber once he or she passes you a note. Comply as fast as you can with the goal of getting the robber out of the bank as quickly as possible."

I was feeling smug walking in here, but between recognizing Martin and the training itself, I'm starting to freak out. Most robbers are desperate and careless, but Christian's group has robbed at least three banks without getting caught. They aren't a typical heist team. Suddenly, messing with them doesn't feel like such a good idea, but then I don't seem to have a choice. Christian knows who I am. He took pictures of me at my house. But then, thinking about the few times we've talked . . . he doesn't seem like a dangerous criminal. I can't make myself believe he's bad. Which is ridiculous, given the overwhelming evidence.

And then I think about all the things I've done. The BAMs. Some—okay, most—have been illegal in some way. If I were found out, I wouldn't look so good, either. True, I've never done anything involving a gun. But in all the robberies Christian's helped commit, the guns were always waved around but never used. Maybe they're just for show. When he crashed into me that day, he never pointed the gun at me, not once. And he seemed worried that he'd hurt me. I remember it, the concern in his eyes.

Detective Martin stops in front of me. "It seems counterintuitive, doesn't it?" he asks, ripping me out of my thoughts. He's studying me the way he probably studies everything—like he remembers every detail. He doesn't just size me up; he catalogs me and files me away for future reference. Under his gaze I have the intense urge to run screaming and puke simultaneously. Instead, I paste what I hope is an unassuming smile on my face and hope for the best.

"But every bank robbery has the potential of going bad, and when it does, it endangers every single person in the bank. What's your name?" he asks me.

I swallow. "Angela Dunbar."

He refers to the papers he has stacked on the table. "UCLA, huh? How've your first couple of days here been?"

"Fine. Enlightening . . . and carb-heavy," I say, gesturing to the stack of bagels still on the side table. The other interns laugh. I'm not sure if cracking jokes is appropriate, but when I'm nervous, it's what I do.

He gives me a fatherly smile, meant to put me at ease. It doesn't. "The most important thing you'll learn here today is that most bank robberies occur without anyone being harmed, and that's a good thing. That's what we want. Because the chances of the robbers walking out that front door and being able to spend the money they take before we catch them are next to zero. We will get them. It's just a matter of time."

"But what about the ones who have evaded capture?" I ask. "The Romero Robbers, for instance. If you haven't caught them by now, what makes you so sure you will?" It's a bold question, and his eyes narrow.

"Because all robbers eventually get greedy and break from their routine to try and up the take. Plus, based on where they've hit in the past, we can predict what banks are most likely their next targets. We are alert to every possible threat."

And maybe he's right, but then again, I'm sitting here in front of him with a false ID, fake contacts, and a wig on my head, and he seems to have no idea.

Martin taps the table in front of me and goes back to the front of the room.

"Now, just because we're asking you to comply with the robbery once it's in progress does not mean we don't want you to take steps to prevent one. Many would-be robbers give off subtle and not-so-subtle clues about their intentions *before* they act. We're here today to go over the most common ones and what your response to them should be."

He explains that we're supposed to pay attention to people as they enter the bank. If we get the sense that there's something off about them, we should speak to them before they can speak to us, pretending that we're just overeager to help a customer. Something about being overly friendly can throw robbers off and convince them that something's up. Hobbs says it's because they've been noticed before they're ready, and the job starts to feel wrong. It can make them rethink the robbery and leave. But this technique doesn't work for all cases, especially if the person doing the robbing becomes aware of it.

I raise my hand. Sometimes a BAM can be as simple as asking a risky question.

"Angela?"

"But what about the robberies where there's more than one person and they come in with guns pointed at you, yelling for everyone to get down?

"What you're talking about is a takeover. In those cases there is nothing you can do except comply and work to get the robbers out of the bank as soon as possible. These robberies have the most potential for violence and, in most cases—not all, but most—the perpetrators are experienced criminals. The only thing you can do to aid us with these investigations is to remember as many details about them as you can. Any conversation that they have, the time they entered the bank, their approximate height, distinguishing physical features that you might notice, clothing, tattoos, that type of thing. Even experienced thieves leave clues. The more information we have from tellers and other witnesses in the bank, the easier it is to track them down."

Detective Hobbs puts a hand on my shoulder. "Most tellers never encounter that type of robbery. The note jobs are the most common and usually happen so quietly and quickly that only the targeted teller is aware that a robbery is taking place at all." She turns to Trisha. "When you worked downstairs, did you ever experience a takeover?"

Trisha shakes her head.

"See? Even though the Romero Robbers hit the Bank of America just down the street, the odds of them targeting LL National while you're here are slim to none. There's too much heat this close to the last target. Every employee here has security pictures of them and is watching for men matching their description."

"I can say unequivocally that we'll get 'em no matter where they show up," Detective Martin says, his blue eyes like frozen fire. "Because I won't give up till we do."

21

Christian

Rosie drops me off at the Madison Street house after work. She keeps trying to lure me into a conversation—has been all afternoon. I'm not biting. I haven't been able to focus since my meeting with Lexi.

I keep going over it in my head, looking for some way to make sense of how she acted—that and replaying the moment when she dropped out of the sky and onto the car that first night. More and more she fits the Bond girl profile: mysterious, bold, and up to something. She's one very sexy puzzle, and all I want to do is put the pieces together. Except I can't. Not yet. Soldado's called a meeting. He's never done this before. Usually all his communication is done through Gabriel. The less we're all together in one place before a job, the better. I don't like it. Everything feels out of my control and risky as hell.

The house is dark, the windows papered over so you can't see inside, but there is a weak arc of light bleeding into the back-yard, barely visible from the food truck. There are a handful of cars scattered along the street. I spot Soldado's and Gabriel's right off. And then there's the one that Twitch was driving the other day. I don't recognize the fourth car.

"I'm not going in," Rosie says as she idles at the curb. "Gabriel's driving Benny home. You can hitch a ride with him."

"You don't want to say hi to your boyfriend?"

She shakes her head. "Not here." Her face tightens as she gazes up at the house, but she doesn't say anything else. Lips pursed, she taps the steering wheel impatiently.

I slip out of the car. The minute my door's shut, she pulls out onto the road again. *Breathe and focus, bro,* I tell myself as I walk up the driveway with a confidence I don't feel, and knock on the front door. Twitch opens it almost immediately, a forty in his hand. He tips it to his mouth and drinks deep. "S'up, vato?" He motions me in and saunters to the back of the house. It's quiet. No music. No talking. Unsettling as all get-out.

I round the corner into the main living space, where Soldado, Gabriel, Carlos, Eddie, and Benny are all sitting on camping chairs. Everybody but Benny's got a forty, too. Benny's like me. Neither of us drinks much. At all, really. Alcohol withdrawal is no joke. I have memories of my dad going through it that I can't ever get rid of. I can barely smell the stuff without my stomach turning. Benny doesn't drink because he says he hates being out of control.

I take a seat on the low wall that separates the kitchen from the living room.

"Christian." Soldado tips his beer in my direction. "Okay, now that we're all here, let's get to it."

Twitch disappears into the other room and brings out a stack of maps and blueprints that he spreads across the floor. No telling who Soldado had to bribe to get them.

"This one here shows the pipe system beneath the financial district," Soldado explains. "LL National is here." He points to a Sharpied-in black rectangle right above a section of pipes and access tunnels. "My dig crew's breached this tunnel here and is digging a path from there right under LL National. We got maybe another two weeks of digging before they're underneath it. That's about five days before you go in to do the job. I need the exact location of the vault way before then so we don't waste time we don't have digging in the wrong spot.

"Christian, you have until the end of this week to get the interior layout of the bank's lower level. Gabriel, you ask your old man to give you the name of his phone company connection. We need him to reroute the alarm calls that come in from the bank to one of our guys from now until you leave the bank. So that way when we dig right up under the vault itself and the alarm goes off, our guy'll be the one interceptin' those calls. Already got the cops managed. Paid off two to make sure they work that part of the city exclusively and can make an appearance at the bank to check things out so the bank managers don't get suspicious. Benny and Eddie, you two run down to San Diego and snag the supplies your crew's gonna need once you're in. Here's the dude's contact number. The meeting's already set. They got you tools to jimmy the safe-deposit boxes open. Ammo. Extra guns. Camping lanterns. You'll have at least one full day inside the vault—that

Sunday—to empty it. Take everything not nailed down. The only thing we leave is the night deposit and the ATM."

Soldado looks up at us. "You enter the tunnels early Sunday morning. You gotta walk to here." He stabs a finger at the map. "We'll have four ATVs gassed up and waiting in this side tunnel. You ride 'em to the tunnel under the bank. My guys blow the vault floor. You climb up. You get it all before sunrise Monday morning and then you load up the ATVs and drive the haul out. There's an abandoned warehouse a mile from the entrance to this access tunnel. Ditch the ATVs there. Twitch will take care of them. Then you get into the getaway car and come straight here. We split the take same as always. Launder it a little at a time. Use the usual places."

"And then we retire?" I ask. "We just walk. The Eme lets us go."

Soldado stares at me. "That's what I said, right? The heat from this one's gonna be intense. They'll be looking for you. When this heist is done, consider yourselves free, but don't be stupid. You got my word this is it long as you pull it off right." Soldado looks me right in the eye and smiles. "Go to college if you want. Hell, whatever. Sky's the limit."

I'll get to go to UCLA. I'd be excited except for the one giant, glaring catch: first I have to help pull off the biggest heist this city's seen in decades. As organized and easy as Soldado's made it sound, there are about a million things that could go wrong, nearly half of them out of our control. More than a few with Lexi's name on them.

"So where you at with getting the bank information we need?" Soldado asks, obviously eager to get back to the planning.

"I'll have it by Saturday night," I say. "Middle of next week at the latest."

Soldado leans back in his chair, and the whole thing creaks in protest. "No kidding? Well, well, looks like you rediscovered your enthusiasm. You gettin' it from the girl?"

I stiffen. "What girl?"

"You think Rosie and I don't talk? The girl interning at LL National. Angela. Rosie said she's some college intern gringa." He whistles appreciatively. "Cute, too. I underestimated you, son."

"Absolutely you did," I say. Better he thinks I'm just charming her into getting what I need. I don't want him to know it's blackmail.

"And you're sure she's not suspicious?" Soldado asks, his eyes sharp.

"I told her I'm trying to be a writer and that I have this story idea about a bank heist I need her help with," I lie. "Said I'd name a character after her if she did. Besides, she's hot for me, so I'm takin' her out this Saturday. A couple of dates, she won't care what I'm up to, trust me." I sound like a first-class jerk.

"You're brainy enough to pull that off, no doubt," Gabriel says, half impressed, half resentful.

"Dude, hell yeah!" Carlos laughs, coming in for dap I only halfheartedly return.

"All right. So we're square for now. Gabriel's got the map.

He'll be my go-between with you guys after today, same as always. Do your jobs. Just because I ain't meeting with you after this doesn't mean I don't got my eyes on you twenty-four/seven. Eme's orders." Soldado tosses his beer can in an empty box and walks out without looking back, Twitch trailing after him. Suddenly Psycho knocks on the sliding glass door leading into the room we're sitting in. He puts his face right up to the glass and grins. Soldado must've had him walking the perimeter. Anger, lava-hot and explosive, courses through me. I don't care that he was following orders; he didn't have to hold that gun to Maria's head. I would've gotten the point. I don't like that he's here. Soldado should have never let him get jumped in to Florencia Heights. He likes the threats and violence too much.

I make a move toward the sliding glass doors, breathing hard, my hands balling up into fists.

Psycho watches, smirking. I kick the door, rattling the glass, and he doesn't even flinch.

"Ease up, man. You don't want to start something with him, 'cause he'll finish it," Benny says, grabbing my arms, holding me back. "He's packing right this minute and you're not. What're you gonna do? Shoot him with your finger?"

Psycho pats the glass one time and then turns around and disappears into the shadows. I can hear faint laughter and then a car horn from out front. Even if Soldado's got faith in us, it's obvious the Eme's got Psycho keeping an extra eye out. And he's just dying for me to screw up.

22

Lexi

"You're not going back. It's over." Quinn is practically yelling at me as he paces around the bonfire. We're in Leo's backyard, which just so happens to be the beach, the whole crew gathered on bright red Adirondack chairs, our feet in the sand. I had everyone meet me here after I finished up at LL National so I could tell them about Christian and the Romero Robbers. And it's going exactly how I thought it would. Badly.

"But I haven't gotten anything on Harrison yet!" I yell back, frustrated.

"Because there isn't anything to get. I've been listening in on him nonstop, Lex. I hacked his home computer last week. I've been reading through every single file, and nothing. Nothing. Oliver and I even went to his house and looked through his home office the other night just in case he's so generationally handicapped that he still keeps paper files. Still nothing. We had to con our way in with a dozen heart balloons and a story about wanting to put them in Bianca's room to convince her to date me again. Ask me how much fun that was."

"Better have been no fun at all," Whitney says, arms folded.

Quinn stops behind her and puts his arms around her neck. "You have nothing to worry about," he says, nuzzling her.

I feel like someone hit the fast-forward button on their relationship. Two days ago they were teetering on exclusive; now they're all in. It makes me feel weird to have been absent for the transition. It's one thing to feel removed from the kids at school, but I couldn't handle it if that happened with my friends.

"Look," I say, "I'm not planning on meeting him without you guys there to back me up. And I'll let him know right away that I have my own evidence—the pictures of him in the van—and that I've got copies that I've arranged to be sent directly to the cops if he tries anything. Also, I've been doing some thinking. We need money, Quinn. So why not blackmail him to give us some of the take? I get the security information he needs, and in return he gives us a cut. We get the money but assume practically none of the risk."

"Yeah? And how do we manage to explain the sudden windfall to Mom and Dad?" Quinn asks.

"We don't. We use the money a little at a time, so gradually that no one notices. It won't be all that much anyway, just enough to keep us afloat. I sat in on a seminar today with the LAPD, and they talked about Christian's robberies. By the time his team splits the take after a job, they don't even clear ten thousand dollars each."

"So then it's hardly worth it," Quinn argues. "Why do it?"

"Uh, have you forgotten that we have a cash-flow problem?

Something beats nothing every day of the week. Think of it as a creative method of withdrawing some of the money Mom and Dad had in their accounts at LL National. The bank doesn't care about what happens to us. Why should we care about the bank? It's as good a way as any to get a little revenge, don't you think? I still want to go after Harrison. This is just a little bonus."

"And what if Christian's group gets caught this time? What then?" Quinn asks.

"We make sure that we get rid of any evidence that might connect us to the crime, like those pictures he has on his phone. And if that proves impossible, I could say that Christian heard about us through the newspapers and that he blackmailed me into infiltrating the bank to get him insider information. It would be my word against his. You can wipe your computer so there's no way to refute it. In the face of a total lack of evidence, who in their right mind is going to believe him over me?" Admittedly, I would feel bad if it went down like this and I was forced to lie, but given the Romero Robbers' track record, it seems unlikely it will. Still, my gut starts churning. I shouldn't feel bad for him. But somehow, inexplicably, I do.

"Now that that's settled, let's get back to Harrison. What else can we do to investigate?"

"What we really need is his computer password at the office so we can log on as him and go through his files and emails there. It's the only place we haven't been able to check out," Leo says.

Quinn shakes his head. "I've tried to remote hack the bank's system. So far no luck. Server security is tight. We need a way to access his computer in person."

"I have a question about the robbery thing. How are you going to get this guy to give up the details of the job? Seems like we should know when they plan to hit the bank and how many of them there are, that sort of thing." Elena chews on her lip as she mulls it over.

"We need to get Christian's phone so I can get the pictures he has. When we do, we look for texts between him and the other robbers. Quinn, Leo, and Oliver could take turns following him over the next couple of days. Find out where he goes. Who he meets up with. Where he lives."

"The dude is a bank robber, Lex. And you want to break into his place to get his phone? No way. That's suicidal." Elena traces a circle in the sand with her toe and thinks. "Unless . . . unless we make positively sure he's not home. I mean, really make sure. And we get in and out fast. Leave zero evidence we were there."

Quinn rubs his chin with one hand and breathes heavy. "So we get what we need from Christian and we work on Harrison. That's two breaking-and-entering-type maneuvers we have to plan in a short period of time. Before your meeting with Christian. So three days."

Leo sits back in his chair and stares at the sky. "We've never pulled anything off in that short a time period. Risky. Definitely risky." Then he smiles. "But if we manage it, it'll be the most epic series of BAMs we've ever done."

Quinn rubs his chin and clears his throat. "About the office break-in. Maybe we could pose as a cleaning crew. We would need a back way into the building, something unexpected. And some uniforms." I want to do a little dance because he's already working things out. He's 100 percent on board even if he hasn't come right out and said it. "The security cameras pose a problem. We either have to get into the security room where the footage is reviewed—which will be impossible because it's monitored by security guards at all times—or figure out a way to cover up the camera near Harrison's office just long enough to get what we need and get out."

"Hey, you guys ever watch *Ocean's Eleven*? Remember how they used the balloons to block the camera? Can we riff off that somehow? Pose as delivery people or something and then slip upstairs?" Whitney asks.

"Hold on," Oliver says, barely loud enough to be heard over the crashing waves. He leans closer to the fire and fiddles with his lighter. "Oh my god, it's freaking perfect. LL National is under renovation, right?"

"Right," Quinn says.

"And my dad's running that job, right?"

"Well, are you going to tell us what you're thinking?" Elena stops making toe circles in the sand.

Oliver looks at each of us, considering. "Yeah, definitely, but first—how well can you guys climb?"

23

Christian

After seeing Psycho at the house, I want to check out for myself these diggers Soldado's got lined up. With Maria's life threatened, I'm not taking any chances with this job. I want to personally make sure that everything's going according to plan and that there aren't things going on that my boys and I don't know about. I had Gabriel give me a copy of the drainage-system map right after we left the meeting. I was going to wait until morning to go underground, but Gabriel said the men work all night and rest during the day, when the noise might attract suspicion, so I ask him to take me there directly from the house.

Gabriel, Carlos, and Eddie all have work in the morning, and if they're too tired to show, it might look suspicious, so Benny is the only one going with me. Together we make our way to the exit point Soldado marked on the map for us. Using his directions, we move back toward the tunnels and the bank, where the dig site should be.

I switch on my flashlight. Benny does the same.

"It's full-on creepy in here," Benny whispers.

"Haunted house creepy," I agree.

The tunnel winds forward, disappearing into black where our flashlight beams can't reach. Water drip-drops somewhere up ahead. There are other sounds, too. Scurrying, foraging-type sounds. The scrabble of claws as something tries to get out of our way. We walk slowly, flashlights bouncing. We focus them on the floor, then the ceiling, then the floor again. I half expect bats to be hanging above us. Or vampires.

"The dig site's at least a mile or two in," Benny says, examining the map. "We got about half an hour before we're there, at this pace." I don't want us to jog it because I'm not sure if we'll run into anyone. We need to make as little noise as possible.

We walk in silence most of the way. Who knows how far our voices might carry into the tunnel. I listen, ears straining, for some hint that people are coming toward us from deep inside the tunnel or are sneaking in behind us. The echo is tricky in here. Twice it makes me think someone is coming when they're not. There are these little alcoves here and there that we can duck into if we need to, but they're shallow enough that we still might be seen.

"So how are things going with your connection at the bank? How'd you manage to get her to agree to give you the security stuff we need? You weren't lying, right? She's really going to get them?"

I point my flashlight toward my feet so he can't see my face. Benny has a way of reading into my expressions.

"She's going to help. That's straight-up fact. I meet her Saturday."

"What's she like? This girl?" Benny is watching me in the dark, I can feel it.

"I don't know. Nice, I guess."

"Nice, huh? Like the girl you met outside the Bank of America, the one who got your medal? That kind of nice?"

He can't know Angela and Lexi are the same person. But the fact that he's bringing up Lexi right now has me wondering if somehow he knows just the same. "Why would it matter?"

"It doesn't. You just seem ... I don't know, to be sort of guarded, like you're not giving us the whole story."

"What are you getting at?" I ask. "Spit it out already."

Benny goes quiet a second, as if he's chewing over what to say. "I just think that the whole writer story doesn't add up. You got something on her. That's why she's helping, right?"

"What? You don't think my charm alone could convince her?"

Benny laughs. "Possibly, but in this case? Uh. No."

"How would you know?" I say.

"Just a feeling." Here's the thing about Benny. We're tight enough that it's hard for me to keep secrets from him. Turns out I want to tell him about Lexi. I need to tell him. If only so he can tell me what I already know. I have to blackmail her. There's no other option.

"Okay, the truth is that this girl from the bank is the same girl who showed up at the Bank of America, the one I clobbered that day."

"Doughnut girl."

"Yeah. Except now she's in disguise: wig, colored contacts, tanned skin, the whole nine yards . . . and suddenly working for LL National."

Benny stops walking. *"What?"*

"I don't have all of it figured out, but the LL National thing is about her dad. He used to work there. Before he got arrested—something to do with bad mortgages and shady lending. My best guess? She's trying to find something to help clear him. Or maybe she's planning to rob the place out of revenge. She is feisty. I'll give her that."

"Okay, but either way you're afraid she could cause a problem for us, right? I mean, if she figures out who you are. You think there's any way she might already know?"

I shrug. "I've thought about it. Maybe, but I don't see how she can prove it."

Benny nods. "So when you get the information we need, then what?"

"I let her go. She doesn't talk; I don't, either."

"Do you like this girl?" Benny asks.

"What?" I feel blindsided. I don't see why it matters.

"You heard me. Do. You. Like. This. Girl?"

I snort. "She's hot, but do I like her, like her? No. I don't really know her."

"I don't believe you," he says, smiling. "I can tell. The way you've not talked about her? You've got it bad."

I don't want to talk about this anymore, and besides, I'm

starting to hear noises, faint ones, but noises that aren't of the scurrying or dripping variety. "Shh," I say.

We start walking softer, straining to hear. We go another quarter mile and the noises get deceptively loud, like I can't tell if they're coming from around the corner or from where I think they should be coming from based on the map.

I motion to Benny that we should shut off our lights. I don't want to, but we have to if we want to stay hidden. I click off my flashlight, and with a sigh, Benny clicks off his. The world goes away. All that's left is a velvet-black void. My heart squeezes, panicked. My lungs tighten. I feel buried alive, but then my other senses take over and I can feel the open space around us again, can smell the air—dank, for sure, but also full-bodied somehow, like I can actually sense that the oxygen level's good. Benny's to my right. I can't see him, but I feel him there, the slight displacement of energy in the air around me.

"Use the wall to guide you," I whisper. "It's a straight shot to the dig site after we turn this corner."

The going's slow as we feel our way along. I trip a couple of times on stuff I can't make out. Hopefully, not some rat. I keep my teeth clenched in case I do step on something that moves. I'm not sure I can keep from screaming. Not macho, losing it over a rodent, but I am not into rats. At all. It's weird, because in a darkness this thick, your mind plays tricks on you. I keep thinking stuff is brushing up against my legs. I feel someone's breath on the back of my neck.

All at once there is a high-pitched metallic shrieking that

knocks me out of my own thoughts and has both Benny and me hugging the tunnel wall. It's so loud I can't believe no one up above on the street hears it.

We inch forward and my feet hit . . . something. I test it with the tip of my shoe. Dirt. It's a huge pile of dirt. Very carefully we navigate around it only to find another pile and then another. Light. There is light up ahead, faint but there, to the right, glowing, flickering. I can see a bit better now. I look at Benny and can't help grinning. His eyes are huge in the dark, and his skin is covered in dust. He blinks at me and grins back—crazy wide. Teeth so white against the grime they glow. I must be just as dusty as he is, judging from how hard he's laughing. I couldn't see it before, but now, riding on the ambient light, there's this storm cloud of cement dust and dirt.

We peek around the corner at the tunnel to our right. About halfway down there's a hole in the concrete wall, the left side. The light's coming from it. Bright light. So bright I'm squinting trying to look at it. Shadows flicker, the looming shapes of people, dancing across the tunnel wall. I can hear laughter and voices, men speaking Spanish.

We wait a few minutes, and when no one's head pops through the hole in the wall, we hurry toward it, flank both sides. I peek in. There is a chamber beyond the hole, roughly dug, but a near-perfect square with arches made from thick wooden beams every few feet or so. There are battery-operated lanterns hanging on thick nails hammered into the arches. I can't see anyone in here, but they're close.

Do we risk going in?

I look at Benny and he shakes his head.

I hesitate a second, then climb into the chamber anyway, edging my way to the far end. It's about ten feet long, narrow, but tall enough that I don't have to crouch. I'm about halfway to the arch when the metallic shrieking starts up again and I nearly jump clean out of my skin. It is unbearably loud. I clap my hands over my ears, but it barely helps. If someone's coming, no way I'm gonna hear them.

The chamber I'm in ends. The next arched opening in front of me is covered by a comforter—to muffle the noise, I guess. Fail. There's nothing that can muffle that god-awful screeching. It's some kind of saw brought down here to cut the beams needed for the tunnel arches. Very, very carefully I lift the blanket a half inch. There's another chamber, this one bigger, big enough that they had to use some of the wood beams as columns at the center of the room and run crossbeams perpendicular to the arches. The whole place feels like a mine. No one's in this chamber, either. But there are stacks and stacks of equipment. Beams, saws, tool belts, shovels, and two very large wheelbarrows piled high with dirt. None of this concerns me. What does are the three crates tucked into the far right-hand corner of the room with what looks like TNT in them. Why do they need that? No way they can set that mess off anywhere near here without risking a tunnel collapse.

Wait . . . unless . . .

Do they want a tunnel collapse? Is that how Soldado's gonna

cover our tracks? Blow up the tunnel after we haul the cash out? It makes sense, but I don't like that he didn't tell us this part of the plan.

I look toward the opposite side of the chamber, where there's another comforter hung up in that archway, too, light bleeding out from under it. The voices are crystal clear now, as if the guys are within a few feet of us. Unfortunately, most of what they're saying I can't understand. Just snatches. My Spanish amounts to a handful of words and a few choice phrases. That's it. Damn. I make a pact with myself to take a Spanish course at UCLA next year.

I watch Benny listen in. He and Rosie speak Spanish almost exclusively at home with Tia Jeanne, so I know he's getting most of what's being said. From the pained look on his face, it's obvious something's wrong. I give him a questioning look, but there's no way he can translate right here.

The saw starts up again. It's time to move. I don't want to risk being here too long, even if I still have little to no idea what's going on. On a whim, I take out my phone and start snapping pictures of the site so I can show them to the other guys later. Benny watches me silently. He looks sick, and my pulse starts to race. What exactly did he hear?

24

Lexi

"This is the only chance we have to get inside while no one's home, so let's do it like we planned. Quick and by the numbers," Leo says. "Christian's whole family is at his graduation right now. From what I've seen, it is one of the rare times that the house is empty. And there was some cyberbullying at the school. An incident. Student cell phones are banned from graduation."

We're in one of the craft-services trucks from the latest film the twins' dad is working on. It's a nondescript white cargo van with no windows in the back and no seats, either. We didn't exactly get permission to take it. It was more like Whitney called in a favor. The guy who drives the van owes her for not telling her dad that he took some on-set pictures of the two leads and sold them to *Star* magazine.

Elena's riding shotgun, and Leo, Quinn, and I are tucked in between boxes of fruit and Smartwater, trying to keep upright. Oliver had to pass on our little Christian recon adventure because he's busy setting up for our bank break-in tonight.

"I'll go in and get the phone," Quinn tells me for the

hundredth time as he stares at his phone. He and Leo are busy monitoring Christian's Facebook, Instagram, and Twitter.

"We've been over this. I'm going in. Just me. I'm smaller, and the window's not big enough for you to fit through," I say. "And if for some reason everything goes wrong, he won't hurt me because he needs me. You he doesn't even know. You'll get shot. Besides, if all of us get out of the van and head into the house, the neighbors will likely notice, right? How long before they call 9-1-1?"

"Children, please, can we get through one car trip in peace?" Leo says, eyes closed, head resting on a stack of tablecloths. "No ice cream for either of you."

Quinn rolls his eyes and starts back in again. The boy is relentless when it comes to protecting me. But I'm just as relentless about getting my own way.

"We're here," Elena says, bouncing in her seat, her GPS announcing our arrival in the sexy male Brit voice she programmed it to use. "Yep, yep. This is it."

The house is small—a stucco box with a handful of windows, all of them covered with wrought-iron bars. There's a rectangular patch of front yard bordered by a chain link fence and a set of stairs that lead down to the sidewalk. Covering the entire length of the chain link are brightly colored streamers and a homemade sign that reads CONGRATULATIONS, CHRISTIAN! It's kind of messed up—breaking into his house the day he graduates from high school. But then, if we're careful, he won't know we've done it.

His family has set up for a party, so it shouldn't be too hard to use the quick-release handle on the window—there to make sure the people inside the house can get out in case of fire—to unlock the iron bars and slip out unnoticed. (Christian's room faces the side of the house where there is a thick clump of trees.) It's a gutsy plan, but given the time frame we have, we need to be bold.

We pull around to the alley behind Christian's house. It's deserted, but that doesn't put me at ease. Everywhere I look there are gang tags, but there are these wonderful, colorful murals, too, most of them of Mary Magdalene or Jesus, and a few of assorted saints.

"Let's get you inside," Quinn says, eyeballing the back of the house.

"But once we're in, you leave," I say.

"Yeah, I get it," Quinn grouses.

Together we slip out of the van and scale the back fence as quietly as we can. Every time the chain link rattles, I grit my teeth and pray no one's looking out a window at us right now. I'd wanted to do this at night after the family went to bed, but once we found out Christian was graduating and that the ceremony was today, it was the perfect opportunity, so we changed the plan. The neighborhood feels quiet. There is only the sound of a bee droning around the flowers near the fence and the far-away hum of a helicopter overhead. We drop to the ground at the same time and hurry across the backyard. The windows and the back door are covered in wrought iron, too. All except one smallish window that looks to be in the kitchen, possibly over the sink.

"Hoist me up," I tell Quinn. He does a squat stance, and I step up onto his thighs so that my head is at eye level with the window. I try opening it, but it's locked. "Hand me the glass cutter," I say.

Quinn rocks a bit as he shifts position in order to reach the pack he brought with him. "Here."

I run the cutter around the perimeter of the window, cleanly removing the glass pane from the frame. I let it down slowly, and Quinn sets it on the grass. My heart is jackhammering as I pull myself through the window. The space is narrow, but I manage, sliding forward onto the kitchen counter.

The room smells wonderful—rich and spicy. There are half a dozen aluminum pans covered in foil spread out across the kitchen table and countertop. Something delicious is simmering inside the Crock-Pot beside the sink. I wriggle all the way inside and then slide off the counter and onto the floor. I know the house is empty, and yet I can't stop flinching at every sound. The tick of the refrigerator nearly sends me back outside.

"You okay?" Quinn asks, peering through the window. "I'm going to put the window glass back in. Once I'm done, I have to head back to the van, and you're on your own in there."

"Yeah. I'm going to take a look around. Text me if something's up." I try to sound confident so he won't rethink this, but it's hard. I'm so on edge I'm trembling.

I have my phone set to vibrate in my back pocket. The house

is basically one big square divided into a series of tiny rooms. There's the kitchen and the narrow living room directly across from it, as well as three small bedrooms and a bathroom. The whole place is neat and meticulously tidy. Pieces of lace cover most of the end tables and the sideboard near the kitchen table. Scattered around are prayer candles, and in one corner of the living room is a stack of cardboard boxes filled with cool vintage-looking T-shirts. As modest as the place is, there is something really warm about it. Pictures of the family hang on the walls in nearly every room. There is Christian as a little boy, and there he is at eleven or twelve, gangly and grinning, his hair stuck up in a dozen different directions. It's hard to look at them and still picture Christian as a dangerous criminal. I touch the edge of one frame.

"Lex, hurry up," Quinn says from the window.

I work my way back to what has to be Christian's bedroom. There's a Galaxy blanket across his bed (he must be into soccer), a UCLA poster and assorted soccer paraphernalia papering one wall, a scratched-up dresser, and a small bookshelf crammed full of books with titles that surprise me: *Watership Down, Fahrenheit 451,* and *Lord of the Flies.* Just above the bookshelf there's a picture tacked to the wall of Christian and a little girl with braids. Other than that, the room reminds me of a monk's quarters. It's sparse and as neat as the rest of the house. Looking around, I know I have very little chance of finding anything useful.

Still, I open the closet and start going through his clothes. The tiny space smells like him, like cologne and boy, and both smells are better than the food ones in the kitchen. He has a few pairs of jeans and a handful of T-shirts, as well as two button-down dress shirts and a pair of black pants. There's a tie or two and a few pairs of shoes lined up beneath the clothes. I check his pants pockets, the back wall of the closet, and the shallow shelf above it. Nothing. I try his dresser next, moving quickly through the underwear drawer. He's a boxers kind of guy. Nice. Then the other two drawers. Nothing. The bookshelf is also disappointing. The only place left to look is under the bed. I jump as my butt starts to vibrate.

They r home!

Christian's back from graduation. Suddenly I can hear them, voices by the front door. There is the unmistakable sound of a key sliding into a lock. I slip under the bed and scoot as close to the wall as possible. I was expecting it to be dusty, but surprisingly, it isn't. I lay my palms flat on the floor and wait.

"I'll be out to help in a minute. I just need to change real quick." Christian strides into the room. I can see his shoes from where I'm lying. He drops something onto the bed and then walks over to the dresser. I breathe as shallowly as I can, but every inhale sounds ridiculously loud. I close my eyes and pray it's just my imagination getting the better of me.

"Everyone will be here in fifteen minutes. Hurry up, mijo," Christian's mom calls out from the kitchen. I wait for her to say something about the window, to notice something's up with it, but there is only the clatter of dishes and the sound of hurried footsteps.

Christian lets out a breath and kicks off his shoes. Then his shirt and pants drop to the floor and I can see his bare legs. I have a sudden and overwhelming urge to giggle. This has to be one of the most absurd things I've ever done. I watch as he pads around the room in his socks, quietly humming something. He pulls on a pair of jeans and a shirt. I can't see it all, but I can hear the rustle of fabric. His hand appears as he scoops up his discarded clothes. I hear something thud on top of the bookshelf—his phone, maybe? The rebel took it to graduation anyway. Christian is striding over to the closet. I can hear him put his clothes away, and then the closet door creaks shut. Suddenly the bed moves, and the space around me narrows as he sits on the edge to put on his shoes. I hold my breath and get perfectly still.

"Mijo, please. We need you." I can hear them, a crowd of voices, each talking over the other, getting louder.

"Christian, come on!" A little girl rushes into the room, small enough that I can see most of her. "Play with me."

"I can't, Maria. Mom needs me to help her out in the kitchen. But tell you what. I promise right after that we'll play."

Maria lets out a disappointed sigh. "Oh, okay."

Suddenly Christian's scooping her up and tickling her. I can feel her feet kick the bed and I can't help smiling. She must be the girl from the picture. It's cute, this little tickle session. And totally unexpected. He's a big brother. Yet another thing about him that further confuses and fascinates me.

"Stop!" Maria squeals, but it's obvious she doesn't mean it.

"Come on, big girl. Let's get out there before Mom has a meltdown."

They both get off the bed and leave the room. I wait for five minutes. Listening. There are at least four people, from what I can hear in the kitchen: two girls—Maria and Christian's mother—and two guys—his grandfather, from the sound of it, and his father?

"I'm going to lie down a little," one of the men says. There is the clink of ice in a glass, and then whoever it is walks toward the bedrooms. I get a brief glimpse of a man carrying a bottle of vodka and a glass of ice, and then there is the soft snick of a door shutting. Christian's dad? He's pale white, with thinning brown hair and a sleeve of tattoos on one arm, and he's staggering in such a way that I'm pretty sure that bottle isn't his first of the day. The defeat in the way his shoulders hunch reminds me of my own dad.

I stay still a minute longer.

When I am sure I am alone, I slip out from under the bed and head straight for the bookshelf. Yes! Christian's phone is there, lying screen up. I grab it and then pull out the little container of baby powder I brought with me and very carefully sprinkle it onto the screen. Fingerprints begin to appear in the powder. I have ten tries to get this before his phone locks up. I try one combination. Wrong. I try another. Wrong. The third try? Wrong, too. *Well, crap!*

People are starting to arrive at the house. I've gone back

under the bed to get out of sight, and I'm starting to feel suffocated. I have to get out of here. Quinn and the others will be frantic. I take out the phone and stare at the powdery prints, trying to predict the right order. I try my next guess. Wrong. Sweat forms on my back and neck. With shaky fingers I try again. This time it works! I don't waste any more time. I navigate straight to his photo album and begin looking through what's there, starting with the most recent history. It takes all of about two seconds to find what I'm looking for. "Oh, bingo!" I murmur before I delete them all and wipe the phone off with my sleeve before inching out from under the bed.

The hallway is really small. Anyone could come this way at any moment and I would never have enough time to duck back under the bed. I need to open the window and release the bars over it quickly. Spotting the release handle is easy, but getting it to work is not. I tug and tug, my heart in my throat, my whole body humming with panic. When it finally lets go, I nearly cry out with relief. I keep turning around to check the doorway, sure that Christian will be standing there, but he isn't. In the kitchen there is music playing, laughter, and loud, excited talk.

I slide the windowpane up and climb outside. I can't replace the bars, but I close the window. With luck, he won't notice right away. There are people in the front yard, and they nearly see me before I'm able to crouch behind the trees beside the window. Men clinking bottles of beer together in a toast. I take one last look, and then I turn and quickly scale the chain link fence, drop to the other side, and run for the van.

I don't breathe until I'm safely inside.

"Well?" Leo asks.

"I deleted the pictures on his phone. But I couldn't find any-thing else," I say.

"The pictures were the main thing. The rest we can get. When you see him Saturday and he knows you have those pictures of him in the van, I'm pretty sure he'll spill the heist details," Quinn says, smiling, obviously relieved to have me back safe.

"Yeah, sure," I say, but after what I just saw, I'm not totally convinced I'll be able to blackmail him back.

25

Lexi

LL National looks different at night. Mysterious, even though I know it's just a building. Four sides with lots of glass and row upon row of cubicles inside.

We're in the back, on the top level of the parking garage. The whole crew, Oliver leading the way, a lunatic grin on his face, happier than I've ever seen him. Two opportunities in less than a month to mess with his dad's work sites. He's in heaven.

I, on the other hand, am having trouble keeping it together. Breaking into Christian's house this afternoon really messed with me. I don't know what I was expecting it to be like, exactly, but what I found was a total surprise. He's this regular guy with a family who love him and a dad who seems to be just as messed up as mine. And seeing it all, I can't believe he's a coldhearted criminal. It doesn't add up. But then, I believed my dad was a good guy, too, and it turned out that everything I believed to be true was a lie. I'm not sure I know how to tell anymore. What's real and what's not.

"You ready for this?" Oliver asks as we make our way toward

the giant trash bin positioned beside the building. The Left Coast Construction logo is everywhere. Even the long white trash chute hanging from the eleventh floor is covered in the logo.

"I got it all prepared this afternoon. We're set to go. Used my dad's security pass. Even wore his glasses. I don't know whether to be proud of myself or skeeved out because I looked enough like him that no one asked to see my ID." His grin slips a little when he mentions his dad, and I wonder if things at home have gotten rough again. Usually when they do, he comes to our house and bunks in Quinn's room, but lately our place isn't much better.

He hoists himself up into the trash container, a giant rusted-metal rectangle almost full with layers of old insulation, warped pieces of metal, crumpled-up McDonald's bags. He lifts the end of the trash chute and points it at us. Lolling out of it like a tongue is a thick, knotted rope. "This is gonna be fun," he says, his dark black hair bobbing as he balances on top of the trash.

"You want us to climb?" Whitney stares at the rope and then puts her hands on her hips. "All the way up there?"

Oliver nods.

"But that'll take us forever. And I'll get calluses," she complains.

"No. Not forever. I timed it. The first person takes the longest. Thirty minutes. But then once I get the winch working up top, it'll be like three minutes apiece, and if two of you go up at the same time, it won't even be ten minutes total for the five of you. Just grip tight, okay, because falling back down that many floors would be a bad idea." He ducks under the trash chute, lets it swallow him up. "I'll go first. See you losers at the top."

We watch the chute vibrate and wiggle as he works his way up. It looks alive, like a giant tapeworm or something, burrowing into the trash bin.

We sit in the shadows by one of the cranes and wait.

Almost precisely thirty minutes goes by, and then Quinn's phone starts vibrating.

"Who's next?" Oliver's voice floats out of the phone, making him seem farther away than just eleven floors.

I opt to go second to last. Quinn chooses last. Whitney and Elena are first and second. Leo shrugs his way into third. We line up like we're at the playground waiting to go down the slide—or, in this case, up. There's a swishing, nylon-rubbing-nylon sort of sound, and a knotted rope drops out of the bottom of the chute, and then a second, unknotted one. Whitney corrals them to her chest.

"He says you should attach yourselves to the first rope and use the other one to help climb so the winch doesn't get overloaded," Quinn tells her and Elena, holding the chute above her head for just a moment so he can kiss her. She touches his cheek with her fingers, then waits as Elena secures a belt-type thing around her waist and clips it to the knotted rope, just above one of the knots, before she does the same. Quinn lets the chute drop over both of their heads, and I can hear them start to move upward, the winch attached to the knotted rope doing most of the work, so the chute barely ripples this time.

"You think we'll really find anything up there?" Quinn asks once Leo starts up and it's just me and him on the ground.

"We need to," I say.

"But will it really make much difference? In the end, I mean. Dad'll still go to jail. Even if Harrison was in on it. There's no denying he's guilty, Lex. You get that, right?"

I don't want to believe it, but after eavesdropping on a few of the late-night phone conversations my mom's had with my aunt, the evidence is overwhelming.

"I want him caught, Quinn. If our family goes down, shouldn't his? Shouldn't every single person involved hurt the same way we are?" We're losing everything. My dad can't come home because we couldn't make bail. We've had to liquidate what we could to help pay for Dad's defense and for our expenses, but we're losing our house and maybe our motorcycles. Definitely Dad's Mercedes. Mom had to let our housekeeper, Anh, go—the one person in the family besides Quinn who really looks out for me. Now she's with another family, and I'll probably never see her again. Then there's our college savings accounts. I thought that money would carry us for a while, but the truth is, it probably won't last the summer. I gave up the one thing I really cared about, and it won't save us. Mom is selling all her jewelry and staring at the classifieds every morning, brooding over them. I can't think about it for long without wanting to cry.

And then there's Harrison, still on top, buying fancy necklaces for his wife and walking around the financial district like he doesn't have a care in the world. It'll make me crazy if we can't figure out how to expose him for what he is.

The rope sails down again, and this time Quinn and I crawl into the chute. It's dark—not pitch, but close. I tug on the rope to let Oliver know we're ready, and then up we go. It's a weird sort of slow-motion thrill ride, the reverse of our BASE jump.

The eleventh floor is wide open. No interior walls, a scratched-up concrete floor, the ceiling a maze of wires above my head. There is plastic tarp covering the open outer walls where the glass has been removed so the crane can bring supplies straight up. It makes this sucking flapping noise as the wind hits it. A creepy, desolate sort of sound. I take a cleaning-crew cap and uniform from the pile Oliver got for us. It's a one-piece jumpsuit kind of thing, so I slip it on right over my clothes.

We'll all go up to the twenty-first floor together, but only Quinn, Leo, and I will hit Harrison's office. Elena, Whitney, and Oliver will pretend to clean the cubicles and other offices, keeping watch for the real cleaning crew.

"Okay, picture time," Leo says, waving his hand at us to gather closer together.

"Didn't you get enough of us coming up the chute?" Quinn asks, sighing.

"Not of us all together. Come on, you'll thank me later." Leo sets the camera on a stack of drywall, checks the timer, and runs over to join us.

"Weirdest BAM photo ever," Oliver says, shaking his head, and by the time the flash goes off, we're all cracking up.

We take the stairwell the whole way up. Ten floors. The elevator's too risky because we can't be sure where the real cleaning crew is. My legs are burning by the time we reach the twenty-first floor. I make a mental note to up my cardio workouts. Every sound we make echoes down the stairwell. Quinn takes point, easing open the door leading out to the offices inch by inch.

"Clear," he whispers.

We have two bright yellow cleaning carts waiting beside us on the landing. Oliver was impressively thorough in arranging it all. There are mops and brooms corralled in each, next to identical trash containers with cleaning products hooked onto the sides. We haul them out of the stairwell and start making our way through the maze of hallways and cubicles to Harrison's office. I can feel the security cameras watching even if I can't see all of them. We keep our heads down and our caps low over our faces.

"Be fast," Elena whispers when we reach the split in the hallway. Whitney and Oliver follow her into the first set of cubicles to their right and start emptying the trash cans.

Quinn and Leo follow me to Harrison's door. It's locked. *Keys. Crap.* One detail Oliver couldn't cover. I was hoping that since the offices get cleaned every night, they'd be unlocked. Custodial probably has a set—which doesn't help us any. We can't exactly call down and ask them to bring the keys up.

"Would his assistant keep a key?" Quinn asks.

Leo gets busy dusting the office doorframe, effectively blocking Quinn and me from the security camera's view. There's only one in the hallway outside, pointed at Harrison's office and the office next to his.

I hurry over to the assistant's desk and start opening drawers. There's just paperwork, gum, a couple of Post-its with random phone numbers scrawled on them, some makeup, and female supplies in the first two drawers, but in the third there is a set of shiny silver keys strung onto a Coach key chain. I hurry to Harrison's door. The fifth key is the right one.

Leo scoots the cart closer to the door, positioning it with the mops and brooms smack in the center, taller than him so they take up the top half of the door. Then he empties the assistant's trash can and sets it on the cart so that it blocks the middle part of the open door. The cart covers the rest, and we are effectively out of sight.

We rush into Harrison's office. It's different at night. Not creepy, exactly, but the picture of Harrison that is hanging on the wall puts me on edge. It's like he's watching us.

Quinn pulls out the baby powder, makeup brush, and little condiment dish he brought. He pours some powder into the dish and then gathers the tiniest bit of powder onto the makeup brush and dabs it onto Harrison's computer keyboard. We hold our breath and watch the powder settle onto the keys. The problem is that most of the keys have been heavily used. There are fingerprints everywhere. Quinn paces the room, thinking. He consults his phone, where he's keeping a running list of all the things he knows about Harrison. He tries Harrison's birth date first, then his wedding anniversary date. No good. The birth dates of his kids. The birth dates of each of his parents. "He's too smart to use something easy," Quinn murmurs. He stares at the computer for a long time, and I start to fidget. We need to hurry.

"The elevator just went up to nineteen," Leo calls from the outer-office doorway. "Elena thinks we might have ten minutes before we need to go."

"What is it?" Quinn chews on the inside of his cheek. "Hey, go look through his assistant's desk again."

"Why?"

"He might've given her the password. Maybe. I don't know. Maybe not. But I don't know what else to try."

I rush back over to the desk and look for anything that might resemble a password. I'm about to give up when I lift up her keyboard and discover a whole list of passwords taped to the underside. Some or all of them are probably hers, but . . .

Quinn goes down the list, trying them. It's there—the third one down. We're in.

I help Quinn sift through emails on conferences and meetings, entire files detailing bank procedurals, but there's nothing that might help us.

"We're done here, Lex." Quinn leans back in the chair and rubs his face with his hands. "He has some personal banking records here, sure, but with no unusual deposits, no email trails that I can see right off the bat that hint at anything. Even his work files are clean. Too clean. He's got to be hiding something, simply because everything is too tidy, know what I mean?"

I lean against the wall and start knocking my head against

221

the plaster. There's nothing in his home office, nothing here. Where is he hiding everything?

"You're out of time and we're at a dead end here. If we had months to monitor him, maybe, but days? It's a lost cause."

This can't be it. I can't—*we* can't—have gone through all this effort and in the end have nothing to show for it.

26
Lexi

I walk into the bank's main branch for the second part of my orientation, my purse clutched tightly to my side. What am I even doing here? Last night proved that whatever slim trail of evidence that exists to link Harrison to my dad and the mortgage scam won't be discovered here. I'm wasting my time. And yet I couldn't stay away. I can't give up, even if the whole thing's hopeless. And then there's the thing with Christian. I'm supposed to get him the security information he needs. I don't have to, but the more I think about it, the more I want to. Stealing from the bank isn't going to hurt Harrison, but it's something to hold on to. Elena thinks I just want an excuse to see Christian again, but that's not it . . . at least not entirely.

"Angela?" Approaching me with her hand extended is a woman with hair the color of raven feathers and lipstick so red that it almost glows. I shake her hand and muster up a smile. "I'm Stella, the lead teller this morning. You'll be with me today, okay?"

She shows me to the break room, where I put my purse

into a locker, before she leads me back out to the teller counter, and together we go behind it. Half a dozen people are lined up in front of computers, fingers flying over the keys or flipping through money, their lips moving a bit as they count. "Every teller is assigned a station," Stella explains, her voice low, her mouth close to my ear. *So the customers don't hear?* I wonder.

"Each station has a cash drawer and its own small key and a combination safe with backup funds." Being here, behind the counter, watching the tellers counting out money and handling transactions, is sort of exciting. Maybe I'm imagining it, but the air almost smells like the green stuff, like paper and ink and chemicals. The bills coming out of one girl's drawer are crisp enough that they make this snapping noise as she counts, setting bill after bill onto the counter as the customer in front of her watches, both of them making sure that the amount is correct.

"Okay, so basically our tellers take deposits, cash checks, help with money orders, that sort of thing. Margo?" She walks me up to a stubby red-haired woman with a blizzard of freckles on her arms and chest, a middle-aged, frumpy Lohan type with a set of lines in her forehead so deep that they make her look like she's got the number eleven branded between her eyebrows. "This is Angela, our intern. She's going to sit with you. Talk her through your transactions, and when you think she's got it, feel free to let her handle a few herself."

"Nice to meet you," Margo says, but those frown lines of hers make it hard to believe the sincerity or cheer in her voice. I'm mentally scheduling her a Botox session when our next customer walks up. "Good morning, sir." Margo takes the man's deposit slip and a stack of checks and begins to bring up his account on the computer. Margo processes the guy's deposit and hands him a receipt, and then there's another customer and another. After an hour, I learn something important: after the initial *Oh my god, look at all the money changing hands,* the teller's job is totally boring. I mean, an utter snoozefest. Mainly it's a lot of counting and computer inputting and "Hi, may I help you" and "Have a nice day." Lather, rinse, repeat. There are a few interesting insider secrets, but they only come in little bursts. Stuff like how much is in the teller drawers (less than five thousand dollars at any given time); where the money with the dye packs is (in Margo's drawer, it's in the center slot) and what it feels like (it makes the stack stiff so it doesn't bend); where the button that activates the silent alarm is (every counter has one, but the bank manager also has a remote one on his person); and the intel on the safes (the teller and the head teller or bank manager have two distinct codes that have to be input to open them). The whole time I can feel the overhead security cameras watching, their black lenses taking in every person's every move in high-def. I see why Christian wanted me to get him as much security information as I could. I can't imagine walking in here cold.

"Angela!" I look up, startled, straight at Harrison's smug face. After last night, it's disorienting seeing him like this. He's on the other side of the counter, side by side with a girl who looks to be in her twenties. She has these little-girl doe eyes that she's emphasized with eyeliner so that she looks like one of those retro Barbie dolls, and her brown hair is pulled up into a high ponytail, making the resemblance even stronger. The only thing that doesn't jibe with her overall appearance is the bruised-looking spot along her collarbone that I'm pretty sure isn't a bruise at all but a hickey. *Ew.*

"Mr. Harrison," I say, feigning enthusiasm when all I really want to do is spit in his face. "What brings you downstairs?"

"This young woman and I got to talking in the lobby. She used to go to my daughter's school, if you can believe it."

I look at her. No, she didn't. I would know her if she did. *Weird.*

"Small world. Anyway, she wants to open a safe-deposit box and, well, I thought I'd offer to accompany her so I could check up on my favorite intern." He winks at me and I want to puke. The man is habitually pervy. Not so much that I can be sure it's intentional, but enough that my skin crawls every time he looks at me.

Stella walks over to us. "Mr. Harrison. Nice to see you down here, sir. You know Angela?"

"She goes to my alma mater. Sharp, this one. We'll be fortunate to nab her if she decides that banking is in her future. Stella, this is Stephanie Crawford. Stephanie, Stella. She'll get your deposit box squared away for you."

"Hey." Stephanie holds out a hand to Stella, then to me. It's all limp and clammy. *Ugh.* I hate when people don't commit and dead-fish shake.

"Look, I've got to get back upstairs. You're in good hands

with these ladies," Harrison says. He pats Stephanie's arm. I stare at the Rolex around his wrist and the soft, manicured look of his fingers. Everything about him reeks of ease and wealth and untouchability. Stephanie gives him this confused little frown as he starts to walk away.

"It was nice to see you again. I'll have my daughter call you," he says as he heads for the lobby, a little too loudly. Several tellers look up from their counting.

Stella calls over a woman in an emerald silk shirt and heels so high I'm surprised she can walk. She's probably five four without them, but right now we're almost standing eye to eye. "Brynn, the young lady would like to open a safe-deposit box, and our intern, Angela, will be watching the process."

Brynn motions us over to her desk. She has Stephanie sit across from her, and me to her right, so I can see the computer as she pulls up the screen.

It is a pretty straightforward process in the end. Stephanie fills out the paperwork and gives Brynn her license and account information. Then it's just a matter of collecting the year's rent for the box, which Stephanie hands her, all in cash, and then Brynn's handing the girl her keys.

"Clint, can you walk down with us to the vault?" Brynn leans back in her chair, her phone balanced in the crook of her neck. "Yes, now. Thank you."

Stephanie leans down to grab her purse, and a necklace slips out of her shirt. A necklace with a pendant on it. It's unusual in an ugly kind of way. A heart with some diamonds layered on top of . . . wait. My breath hitches. It's the one Harrison bought the other day. The one he said was for his wife.

"Nice necklace," I say, leaning in so I can get a closer look. *Yep, it's the one.*

Stephanie looks down, her cheeks reddening, and quickly drops it back under her blouse. "A gift from a friend," she says.

"A male friend, right? And not your garden-variety college boy, either. Are those diamonds real?"

She nods and I whistle. "Wow. Lucky you." Actually, unlucky her. She had to let Harrison suck on her neck—probably worse.

Clint appears, and there's no time to ask Stephanie any more questions. We follow Clint down the stairs to the vault where the safe-deposit boxes are kept.

"This way," Brynn says, motioning us down the hall, all of our shoes clicking on the marble floor. It's an impressive space, a throwback to the art deco era. I run a hand along the wall admiringly. No wonder they shot films down here.

"Okay, here we are." Brynn walks up to the thick steel door at the end of the hallway. There are two key-code pads, and she and Clint each stand in front of one, then punch in a set of numbers simultaneously. "Angela, all the vault access doors have two keypads. To get in, we need both of the employees with codes to enter them at the same time. In this branch it's the head teller, the bank managers, and a few of the loan officers who have the codes. The codes themselves change often and are not shared between employees. For example, Clint would never know my code and I can't know his. This ensures the security of the vault.

Well, that and the security cameras." I look up at the cameras hanging at various points along the hall, at the one right above us, trained on the door. I try to imagine who might be watching us through them right now.

"Is someone inside the bank watching the camera feeds all the time?" I ask.

"At this bank, yes. Our security division is upstairs, but at our other satellite branches, no. Their camera footage feeds directly here and is housed on our security systems upstairs and is only reviewed when there is a security breach." Brynn opens the door and we walk into the safe-deposit-box room, a sort of antechamber to the actual vault, which is behind another huge steel door more imposing and impenetrable than the first. The walls are lined with boxes, all of them numbered and each with two locks. Brynn leads us to number 1539, down at the end of the left-hand wall, close to the main vault door.

"Ms. Crawford, every time you come to view the contents of your box, you'll need your key. I have the bank's master to release the box from its location, but the box won't actually open without your key. If you were to lose it, we would have to force open the box at your expense, so you're going to want to keep it safe." Double safety measures on everything. The vault is a fortress.

Brynn slips her key into one lock and then waits while Stephanie does the same. The box slides out, a long narrow shoe box–looking thing. Brynn carries it back down the hall and then veers into another, smaller hallway, where there are a series of cubby-sized rooms. I can't help thinking that they look like the person-sized version of the box Stephanie's holding.

"You can view your box inside this room. Once you're done, flip the switch on the wall and the light outside the door will come on, alerting us that you're ready to put the box back."

Being down here, with all the cameras, key codes, and steel doors—not to mention the millions housed mere feet from where we are—is enough to leave me speechless. Christian and the Romero Robbers have never hit a vault during one of their jobs. But he wants the layout and location from me. *Are they going to attempt it here?* It seems like a suicide mission.

Brynn sets the box on the small desklike shelf inside the room, and we back up to allow Stephanie inside. What is she planning on keeping in the box? The necklace? Something else? Something of Harrison's? He brought her in to get the box. And he's not hiding anything anywhere else. I think about my own bank account, how the FBI seized my father's accounts, but not mine and Quinn's because they were in our names. There was no way to put a freeze on accounts where there was no evidence of a direct tie to the crime. Like my dad, Harrison made money off those mortgages. Stephanie has to have the money or something that could lead us to it. It makes perfect sense.

"Coming, Angela?" Brynn asks as Stephanie ducks into the room and shuts the door. I stare at it for a second or two, wish like mad for X-ray vision.

"Coming." I sigh and we walk back to the end of the hall to

wait. The only way I'll get into that box is if I break into it. But that's impossible. "So are there cameras inside those rooms?" I ask when it occurs to me that there might be.

"No. What people put in their boxes is considered private."

"But if you suspect someone of having something bad in them? Like . . . I don't know . . . a murder weapon or something."

"A warrant to search it can be issued," Brynn says. "But it's not something that happens all that often. *I've* certainly never had to open one for the police. It's fun to wonder what people put in them, though." She laughs. "One of our managers said that this older lady came in once and asked if she could store her dead dog in hers. She'd had him stuffed and wanted to keep him safe. Weird, right?" I nod. Right now the only thing I wonder is what Stephanie's storing for Harrison. It's important, whatever it is—I can feel it. This is the thing we've been looking for. Just beyond that door. I'm so close. *So* close.

The light outside Stephanie's room goes on, and we let her out and reverse the process we used to get down here, relocking the vault door. "Tonight, remind me to have you come down to watch us set the timer. At the end of every night we set the vault door to stay locked until the morning. This means that even if someone with the codes tried to open the vault, they couldn't until the appropriate hour. Same for weekends, so, basically, the vault is impregnable even by bank employees when the bank isn't open," Brynn says.

We climb back up the stairwell, Brynn and Clint leading the

way, followed by Stephanie and me. Frantically, I try to think of something to say, anything that might help me wheedle out some clue about what's in the box. I have nothing. Think, Lex, *think!*

All at once it's too late. She's leaving the bank, her phone up to her ear. I ask to go use the bathroom and run to get my purse. Once I'm safely locked inside the handicapped stall at the back of the bathroom, I text Quinn, briefly explaining what I saw.

Check Harrison's phone convos from today.

I pace the stall and wait for him to reply.

Got something. Meeting you for lunch.

I nearly cheer and then type:

Fine. Anywhere but the taco truck.

I can picture Quinn reading this and laughing. It makes me laugh just thinking about it. Our little mission here isn't dead after all.

We settle on sushi at this little out-of-the-way restaurant over a block from the bank, two blocks away from the taco truck and Christian.

"So?" I slide into the booth and wait for Quinn to spill the details about what the bug in Harrison's office picked up.

"So he talked with someone named Stephanie twice today. Actually, he talked to her a couple of times over the past twenty-four hours, but the calls were so short and vague they didn't set off any bells. He had her on speaker. Here. I typed out the conversation. Not much to go on, until you get to the second page."

I flip through. At first it's just:

Harrison: We should meet soon.
Stephanie: We should. But I'm busy with finals. Can it wait?
Harrison: Come on. Just a quick dinner. Tonight? That
    restaurant on Sunset you like? I can pick you up at
    seven. Two hours. I need to see you.
Stephanie: (*giggles*) Okay, sure.
Harrison: I have something of yours.
Stephanie: Really?
Harrison: Well, it isn't yours yet, but it will be.

I look at Quinn and make a gagging noise. I skim until I reach the second page.

Harrison: I want it done. It's risky. Waiting.
Stephanie: Will you go with me?
Harrison: That's not a good idea.
Stephanie: But I'm nervous. What if I mess up?

Harrison: You'll be fine. I have faith in you. Let's talk about this face to face, okay? That way I can help make you feel better about things.

Stephanie: You're sure I have to go in?

Harrison: Yes. We can talk about the process more in person.

Stephanie: Fine, but I want something major in return. You can afford it now, can't you?

Harrison: (*cuts her off*) Sure, sure, anything you want. Look, I gotta go. Take care, Ms. Crawford.

Stephanie: (*giggles*) Yeah, you too . . . *Mr.* Harrison.

"So he's given her some sort of financial statements. That's what I'm thinking. Probably offshore-account information. We can't know for sure, but I'd bet you anything that's what she put into the safe-deposit box. If we can find a way in, we might have all we need to expose him to the police . . . or . . ." Quinn messes with the empty teacup in front of him, turns it end over end.

"Or?"

"Well, I was just thinking. About what you said about robbing the bank before? If we manage to get the account information . . ."

"Are you asking me if we should transfer whatever we find in his accounts to us?" I ask.

"Well, hopefully, he has several accounts, so not exactly. I'm saying let's transfer some and then turn the rest in to the FBI. I have a feeling *that* haul could be worth our while." My brother, usually the cautious one in our family, who does the BAMs only because I do, wants to break into a safe-deposit box and take Harrison's money. I'm not exactly proud, but then in a weird way I am. He would've been such an uptight dude if I hadn't come along. Taking money that's already been stolen. The idea has a certain sense of poetry to it. And it feels less wrong than stealing directly from the vault. Is stealing really stealing if you're taking the money from a criminal?

"I think it's a great idea except for one thing, big brother. How are we going to break into the box without getting caught? This isn't like sneaking into Harrison's office. I watched the whole process this morning. It's way elaborate. You need two sets of keys—one of which stays with the person renting out the box. And there are cameras everywhere."

The waitress comes and we order. A spicy tuna roll for me, tempura vegetables for Quinn.

"I've been turning it over in my head, all the way here. And on our own, there's no way we can manage. We don't have the expertise. It would take a professional bank robber to do it right."

"You mean Christian. The Romero Robbers." The scope of what he's trying to tell me finally becomes clear.

"I don't have all the details straight yet, but what if we used what you have on him to blackmail him into getting what's in the box? You said yourself that they're already planning on robbing LL National. We just need him to get what we need while he's in there. It's just paperwork. As long as we don't tell him what kind, what does he care?"

This makes perfect sense; in fact, it's sort of brilliant. We could nail Harrison and secure enough money so we won't have to worry about the future. A heist within a heist. All I have to do is blackmail Christian the way he tried to blackmail me. It's not like he doesn't get something out of it. His team still gets the money they planned to take in the first place.

"So you really think we should do this?" I ask.

He presses his lips together and nods.

"But there's only one issue. If I come right out and tell him what we're planning, he might try to figure out a way to double-cross us."

Right now I'm pretty sure Christian sees me as a girl he can manipulate. What if we use that to our advantage? The more I work it out, the more I like it. I meet with Christian and pretend to cooperate: give him the security information his crew needs, tempt him with the idea that I can help them get an even bigger take. I could flirt some more, get closer to him so I can find out exactly when he's planning on hitting the bank . . . and then find a way to take the box. Everyone will just assume the missing stuff in Stephanie's safe-deposit box was part of the heist. The Romero Robbers get blamed and we walk away. Send the evidence we gather to the FBI anonymously and keep enough money to set ourselves up. It could work. It *will* work.

27

Christian

The parking lot closest to the old zoo is jammed, so I have to park Gabriel's car in the lot near the merry-go-round. There's the typical Saturday crowd of families. I watch the kids line up beneath the red-and-white-striped roof of the carousel. The music is bright and cheerful and nerve-jangling. I'm too on edge for this kind of chaos—ever since Benny and I left the tunnel and he told me what Soldado's men were saying.

"Soldado's gonna show up during the job with his Florencia Heights boys. They plan to take the money and then collapse the tunnel. We'll be trapped inside the vault until the bank employees come in and unlock it the next morning." Benny was bug-eyed as he told me.

"He's going to sacrifice us to the police? Man, seriously? That doesn't make any sense. We could just rat him out. Make a deal with the cops." But then I remembered Psycho standing behind Maria with his gun.

"How could he do that?" Benny was still trying to wrap his mind around it. "I know the gang comes first, but he's always looked out for us. He's like family. I mean, he's with my sister. . . ."

"The Eme probably wanted it done. We never committed to Florencia. The way they see it, they don't owe us a thing."

It still hurts to think about it. We do this job and we go to jail. We don't do this job, people we love get killed. I can't see a way out no matter how hard I try. My heart's been racing in my chest the past three days.

I've been looking forward to and dreading this meeting with Lexi. Now that I know what Soldado's planning, I don't want to do anything to help the job along. But if I don't bring him the intel I promised, he'll know something's up and I'll lose any chance I have to get us out of the job somehow.

I trudge up the path that leads to the old animal cages, hands in my pockets, deep in thought. My stomach feels full of acid, burning and turning in my gut.

"Christian."

She's here. Early. We weren't supposed to meet until five. She comes toward me, all traces of Angela gone, gold hair blowing back, away from her sun-flushed face, a leather tote bag hanging from one shoulder. She's in shorts and a T-shirt. She looks younger now that she's Lexi again. Maybe it's that she barely has any makeup on, or the way her hair is loose around her shoulders. Maybe it's the way she hesitates as she gets closer, eyeing me.

"Lexi." I start to smile on reflex. She's beautiful.

She stops a few feet from me. "So I'm here. And I have the items you wanted." She pats her tote.

I look around to see if anyone's watching us. There are dozens of families milling around, but all of them seem preoccupied with each other. There's no sign of Soldado's boys. I picked Griffith Park precisely for this reason. This isn't a place those dudes would hang out. Still . . .

"Let's talk by the animal cages," I say. "Up there."

We walk silently toward the picnic area that marks the start of the zoo. The tables are tucked into a graffiti-covered stone exhibit that doesn't have any bars. A long time ago lions probably stalked this place. I can almost imagine them here, pacing the enclosure, roaring deep. Intimidating zoo visitors. I wish I could channel their strength and power. I'm gonna need it in the next couple of weeks.

I lean against the wall, arms over my chest, muscles flexing, trying to make myself big and imposing. I still have to play the game even if I don't want to. "Let's have it, then."

She stares at me, considering. Sighs. "Fine. But first we need to talk about something."

"Talk about what?" I ask, surprised.

"I know who you are." She sits on one of the picnic tables and leans back on her arms, all casual and calm, like she's not scared.

I narrow my eyes. "Really?"

"You're one of the Romero Robbers."

239

Smart girl. She waits, her eyes never leaving mine. I know she's wondering if I'll deny it.

"What makes you think so?" I ask instead.

"Don't play dumb. You ran into me that day at the Bank of America. I know it was you."

"I thought those guys wore masks. How can you be so sure?"

"Your eyes. That, combined with the medal you wanted me to get, and this information you asked me for. Doesn't take a genius, now, does it?"

I'm blown away. She thinks I'm a bank robber, and yet here she is, meeting me and telling me she's got it all figured out.

"Let's say that were true. Why show up here today? If I'm a bank robber, I'm probably dangerous, right?" I take a step toward her.

"You won't hurt me," she says with complete confidence.

How can she be so sure? She barely knows me. It catches me off guard the way she sees right through me. Suddenly, I don't have one clever thing to say.

"You should know that I didn't come alone, but even if I had, I wouldn't be scared of you." She points up at Bee Rock. I can't see anything, just the fence surrounding the top. But then a guy's head pops up, and then another and another, just enough so I know she's not bluffing. And I'm not even mad. If anything, it makes me like her more.

"I asked them to hang back so we could talk," Lexi says.

"Look. I'm going to give you what you want. We aren't here to stop you or turn you in or anything."

"Because you know if you do, I send those pictures I have of you to your bank buddy."

She makes a face. "He's not my bank buddy, and no. Not because of that. I think if you look at your phone's photo album, you'll see that the pictures are gone."

She found a way to erase the pictures? How in the—? I double-check and sure enough . . . She's smug, watching me. I can see her smirking out of the corner of my eye, and, man, I can't help being impressed. When did she get my phone?

"Well, that'd be checkmate for sure . . . if I hadn't made physical copies," I say, smiling at her. "You think I wouldn't take precautions? You got me pegged as a Romero Robber. Those boys haven't been caught yet, now, have they? Probably because they are all about precautions, don't you think?" I pull out the Target-printed photos I brought with me—not because I actually thought this would happen. I didn't. Totally underestimated this girl, I'll admit it. But because holding and touching actual photos somehow still feels more legit than swiping through a set on someone's phone.

"Well. That's . . . surprising." She gives me a once-over like she's really seeing me for the first time. "And maybe those would be checkmate," she says, imitating me, "if I didn't have photos of my own."

She digs into her tote and whips out a thin stack of

black-and-white photographs. She drops them on the picnic table so they slide apart, revealing four separate shots of Benny and me in the Mary Kay van with a time and date stamp at the bottom. I'm shocked.

"How did you—? You were skydiving. You didn't have a camera."

"You knew that was me?" It's her turn to look impressed.

"Your tattoo. It gave you away that day at the truck. But what I can't figure out is how you took these."

"Well, I wasn't alone then, either. I've got my own posse, thank you very much." She grins, obviously proud of herself. "Looks like we might have a stalemate, huh? You've got dirt on me. I've got dirt on you. We can either call it even and walk away and ignore each other ... or we can figure out a way to help each other first, *then* walk away." She stretches out her long, tanned legs and crosses them at the ankle. I kept wondering why she didn't seem afraid of me and now I think I know. She's not afraid of anything. This girl jumps off skyscrapers for fun. She's successfully infiltrated the bank and managed to break into my phone without my knowing. She's a force of nature. Forget the lions. I want to channel some of what she has.

"What do you have in mind, exactly?" I ask, sitting close enough beside her that our legs are touching. Like every other time we've touched, a jolt of adrenaline shoots through me and I feel energized. Weirdly happy.

Lexi gets this almost shy smile on her face, like she feels it, too, and then leans away from me so she can look me in the eye. "Okay, so you obviously know who I am and who my dad is, right? Here's the thing. His boss—the guy I was with at the taco truck—is the one who's really behind the mortgage fraud my dad was arrested for. I mean, they're both guilty, but my dad's taking the fall while Harrison gets off scot-free." She brushes some dust off her knee and I'm staring at her legs, at the line of her thigh muscle, wondering if all that skin is as soft as it looks.

"Where was I?" She swallows nervously as I look up from her legs and into her eyes.

"Your dad's boss," I murmur.

"Oh yeah. So he's got this secret safe-deposit box where he's stashed the documents that tie him to the fraud. Understand? Well, yeah, of course you do, sorry. You're college bound, right? UCLA?"

"You broke into my house. That's how you got my phone." The bars that go over my bedroom window somehow came off on graduation day. It was her. She was in my room. I should be mad, but thinking about her in my bedroom makes me anything but.

"I had my phone in my pants that day," I say, remembering out loud. "How did you . . . ?"

"You changed clothes, remember? Nice calves by the way. Sexy." She raises an eyebrow and I bust out laughing.

"You are something else," I say, and for a moment we lock eyes and then I'm leaning in without thinking, my hand coming up to cup her face.

My lips are hovering a millimeter away from hers when

suddenly she slides along the picnic table, putting distance between us.

"Is that really such a good idea? How do I know you're not playing me?"

"Because *you're* playing *me* and doing a much better job than I ever could," I say. I came here nearly out of my head about the job, and somehow she's managed to make me forget for a few minutes all about Soldado and what he's planning. She's got the upper hand here, no question.

"I think it's better if we keep this strictly professional," she says.

I laugh. "Baby, there is nothing professional about what we're doing."

Her mouth quirks up. "Okay, so we keep it strictly criminal, then."

I still want to kiss her. Bad. But she has a point. Getting involved with me would not be a good idea. She's got a dad who's in jail; does she really want a boyfriend who might end up there, too?

"So can we get back to the job?" she asks.

"You want me to get you the contents of Bank Guy's safe-deposit box," I say.

"Yes."

"And then give it to you after the job? I hate to break it to you, but those boxes are in the vault. And we never touch vaults. They're hard to get into and even harder to get out of without getting caught."

"I've been down to the LL National vault. I think I have a pretty good idea of how elaborate the security is. But that's why you wanted me to get all this stuff, isn't it? This time you're going for it, and you need to figure out the best way in and out."

The best way in and out. This sentence rattles around in my brain, and I get this feeling in my gut. *The best way in and out.* There's something there, something important. I lean over and put my head in my hands. What? What is it?

"Oh my god! That's it!" I yell, jumping off the picnic table because suddenly I need to move. Soldado wants the plans so he can locate the exact right spot to dig into the vault. He doesn't care about getting out because he wants us to get caught. And I only asked her for the extra intel to keep her from figuring out about the tunneling. But maybe . . . Lexi knows the inside of the bank. The way the security works.

"That information of yours—is there anything in there about how the vault opens up?"

"Well, yeah. A couple of pages. The only way in is to get the codes the bank managers and security have. They change all the time, so you'd have to force the manager and the lead security officer to go down to the vault with you and open it."

The boys and I couldn't do that from inside the vault, but she could do it. From the outside. I get her the safe-deposit box in exchange for her letting us out. I'll have to come clean about how the heist is being planned, but as long as she knows she's getting what she needs, it shouldn't make a difference how the robbery goes down. We get out of the vault. She gets to expose this Harrison guy. There are still some things to sort out—like how to keep Soldado and the Eme from green-lighting us the minute they realize what we've done. And then there's the money. I'm not risking everything to come out empty-handed.

"I'll get you what you want. But I've got some conditions of my own," I say. "You and your posse up there agree to help us with the job."

For the first time she's the one who looks unsettled. "Help how? We've done some stuff, but we're not bank robbers."

"You want what's in that box? You're going to have to become one."

She looks up at the spot above us where her friends are. "I don't think we . . ."

So I tell her about the tunnel and Soldado and what Benny overheard, as well as my idea to salvage the job, and when I'm done, she goes silent for a while as it sinks in. I'm in league with one of the most dangerous gangs in LA and the Mexican Mafia. This isn't a chess game we're playing. This is real life, and there are real consequences if we make a wrong move. But on the other hand, the only way to get what she needs is to enter the bank with her group the way my boys and I usually do. Pretend to be us and get the vault open so we can all leave the bank through the front door. The decision should be easy. This guy at the bank isn't worth risking everything for. I should tell her this, but if I do, then I'm back to square one, and my boys and I don't get out of the vault. Do I turn noble and save her from herself or go the selfish route and take care of Benny, Carlos, Eddie, Gabriel, and me? The fact that I can't do both really sucks.

"But if he takes all the money and collapses the tunnel, you leave with nothing, and he'll probably still come after you. And eventually . . ." She looks up again. "Us."

"Well, I still have a few things to figure out. . . ."

She leans back on the heels of her hands and chews on her bottom lip. "You could collapse the tunnel before he does. Wait for him to get underground and then rig it to blow before he reaches the vault."

"You're suggesting I bury him alive?" It's a clever plan, but there's no way. As awful as Soldado is for double-crossing us, I can't kill him in cold blood. That's not me. If I did that, I'd be as bad as the Eme. *Does she really think it's an option?*

"No! I would never. What I'm saying is I think we could figure out a way to collapse a *section* of the tunnel without the whole thing coming down. We could trap them inside so that you have enough time to get out of the bank." She half laughs. "You could even work it so they have some of the vault money with them. Make it look like they were the ones inside the vault. You tip off the cops and they dig them out."

And then they would be the ones to go to jail. It's brilliant. "You're brilliant," I say, and I'm tempted all over again to kiss her.

"I have to talk to my friends about this before we can commit to anything," she says. "*If* we decide to, we'll have to get everything ironed out before the day of the job. And I want to know every single detail. If I think you're holding anything back, it's off."

"Understood."

"Call me once you talk to your boys and let them know about all this." She leans over, grabs my phone, and punches in my security code before she accesses my contacts.

"Note to self: change security code," I say dryly.

"I wouldn't bother," she fires back. "I'll only figure it out, too."

She adds her phone number and puts *Angela* in the name box, then uses my phone to call hers so she has my number, too. She opens her bag and hands me the packet of papers she brought with her. "Here's what I have so far."

"There's one more thing," I say. Heat creeps up my neck. My face feels like it's catching fire. "Soldado knows I have a contact at the bank, and his girlfriend, Rosie—she works the taco truck with me—knows it's you."

She frowns. "And?"

"Well, I wanted to keep you safe before, and really, I still need to, so I told him that I got you to give me the information because you have the hots for me."

She raises an eyebrow. "You did?"

I shrug and concentrate on my shoes. *Oh hell, this is humiliating.* "Pretty much. So if we're going to keep meeting up . . . it would be better . . . I mean . . . it would help if . . ."

"If I acted like I have the hots for you when we're together. In case they're watching."

"I've been followed a couple of times lately, and chances are I might be again. It would help convince them that we aren't up to anything."

"Except fooling around." I still can't look at her, but I can hear the amusement in her voice.

"Just when we're out in public anywhere. Can you do that? Make like we're dating? Fake it until the job?" Now I do look at her, straight into her eyes. I'd be lying if I said I'm not hoping she'll say yes.

"So much for keeping it strictly criminal," she says.

28

Lexi

"Okay, you way undersold that boy. He is off-the-charts hot," Elena whispers to Whitney and me as we walk toward the car. Quinn, Leo, and Oliver are up ahead, deep in conversation about the prospect of our joining the Romero Robbers' next heist.

"And a criminal," I say, "who's basically trying to recruit us." I can't think about how hot he is. Or how I nearly let him kiss me back there. I have bigger things to worry about. Like figuring out exactly how we're going to go from risk takers to bank robbers by the Fourth of July.

"Is it bad that it kinda makes him hotter?" Elena asks.

Whitney laughs. "It shouldn't, but you're right. Somehow it does."

"Maybe because in spite of that he still seems like a nice guy," I say. And there I go, thinking about him again, giving myself reasons why it's okay to be into him. This is why faking that I like him whenever we're together is a bad idea. There won't be much pretending involved.

"It's an act. Gotta be. Those guys are good at cons, right? Otherwise he'd be in jail right now," Elena reasons.

She's probably right. I think back to my conversations with Christian so far. Am I letting whatever chemistry we seem to have blind me into thinking he's being honest? What do I really know about this boy?

The carousel is in full swing as we approach the parking lot. I watch the little kids wave from their horses, all smiles. Quinn and I came here with our housekeeper a lot when I was small. I stop for a second and stare as the horses blur by, try to pick out the one I used to love to ride the most. I remember it was a light tan color with a blue jewel near its hindquarters and a long white tail that nearly grazed the carousel's platform.

"Remember when we used to ride that?" Quinn asks, coming up to stand beside me.

"I remember that you let me pick my horse first, and you'd always get the one beside me so we could ride together."

"Anh would stand over there and watch us." Quinn points at the little space by the ticket booth, and I can almost see Anh there now, squinting up at the carousel, bouncing up and down because when she waved at us, she did it with her whole body. Of all the things we've had to give up or give away, letting her go has been the hardest. I would never think of telling my parents what we're up to, but I would consider telling Anh. She would know whether Christian can be trusted. But she's not here, and so I have to rely on Quinn and myself.

"Do you think we can trust him?" I ask.

"Not even a little bit," he says, shaking his head.

"Well, then let's make sure we don't need to," I say.

"I still don't like it. But I also know you won't stop until we get what's in Harrison's safe-deposit box, so fine. Whatever we have to do, let's do it."

I nudge Quinn with one shoulder and he nudges me back. I'm lucky to have a brother like him—still letting me choose the horse and riding alongside me to make sure I don't fall.

29

Christian

I pull out of Griffith Park and head toward the interstate, the Five, and home, my head swirling with all that's happened. I get my phone out and call Benny, fill him in. Once he realizes I've got a plan in place to keep us from getting stuck in the bank, he laughs for, like, a full five minutes. "So, college boy, how'd it feel not to be the smartest person in the room for once? I think I like this girl."

I think about Lexi sitting in the early-evening sunlight, tucking her hair behind her ear as she entered her number into my phone. "It feels pretty good," I admit. And it does. An hour with her and suddenly I have hope that we can get out of this job without our lives imploding. And I'm going to make sure she and her friends do, too. If we figure out how to collapse the tunnel the way she said, and I work with them on how to enter the bank and effectively manage the place once they're in, there's no reason why we can't all get out safely.

"So what happens next?" Benny asks.

"We gather the boys and let them know what's up."

Benny's end of the line goes quiet for a few seconds. "You think Gabriel will believe it? He and Soldado seem to be pretty tight lately."

"Speaking of, I need to stop over at the Madison Street house first to drop off Gabriel's car and give him the information Lexi gave me, so he can pass it on to Soldado. You think we should wait to tell him?" I exit the freeway and head for Madison Street. "You don't think he's in on it? That's not what you're saying, right?" As much as I've doubted Gabriel lately, he's still our cousin, and blood comes first. I know he believes it, same as me.

"No. You're right. He's still one of us." Except Benny doesn't sound like he believes it.

"We'll talk about it when I get there," I say before I hang up. I rest my head on the back of my seat and try not to worry. If Gabriel is suddenly more loyal to Soldado than us, I'm putting Lexi in real danger if I let him know about her or the new plan we worked out.

Once I'm about a block out and sitting at a traffic light, I use my phone to take pictures of the building plans and the security information. I want to make sure I have my own copies. An ambulance screams by, startling me so I drop my phone on the car floor. I lean over to dig it out as a fire truck whizzes past, both vehicles driving on the grass on the right-hand side of the road, close enough to Gabriel's car that it rocks in their wake. I lower my window and poke my head out, try to see where the accident is up ahead. I watch them turn right and round the corner, heading in the same direction I am.

But it isn't until I near the Madison Street house that I really start to panic. The ambulance and the fire truck are parked in front of it, along with a handful of landscaping trucks and a backhoe. There's a crowd of people, too—guys from Gabriel's crew, people who must live nearby—all of them staring at something in the yard that I can't see. I park the car a couple of houses down and run for the crowd, push my way in.

Someone's lying in the yard, his face too bloody to recognize, but I know who it is anyway. Gabriel. He's lying at a weird angle, head cocked back and oddly misshapen, his right arm broken badly enough that a piece of bone pokes out of his forearm. My stomach lurches, and I grit my teeth to keep from gagging.

"What happened?" I ask the man next to me. Mateo. The landscaping guy Gabriel uses to sod the houses before they go up for sale.

"The backhoe ran over him," Mateo says, not looking at me.

"The backhoe?"

"That's what I said, yeah." Mateo shoots me a warning look and then cuts his eyes to the other dudes around us. In other words: don't ask anything else. I take a closer look at the crowd and see a few Florencia Heights gangbangers lingering at the back. This isn't an accident, no way. I curse under my breath. What happened? Of all of us, Gabriel's been the tightest with Soldado's crew and the Eme. I watch the EMTs work on his body. He looks dead already. Too bloody and ruined to be okay. I edge closer so I can hear what they're saying, but none of it makes sense. It's just a jumble of words: *intact distal movement* and *weak radial pulse.* They get him on a longboard before they very gently slide-move him to the stretcher waiting nearby. He groans faintly as they pass me and I let out a breath. He's alive. I don't understand what could've gotten him in enough hot water that he got jumped this close to the biggest job we've ever done. It doesn't make any sense. The EMTs load Gabriel into the ambulance, and then the doors shut and the siren starts to wind up again.

I jump back into the car and call Benny.

"Something happened to Gabriel. It's bad. I'm coming to pick you up." I don't wait for him to ask questions. I just hang up and speed toward his house with my heart in my throat.

30
Christian

I don't like hospitals. Not since my abuela died. I know most
people come here to get better, but to me, the place reeks of
death. I never seem to acclimate to it, even after we've been in
the waiting room for hours while Gabriel goes through surgery.
He really was run over by the backhoe . . . but only after he was
beaten down to the ground. The cops came early on, and we
heard them talking to the nurse about his injuries and how they
needed to talk to him once he stabilized. Benny and I made
ourselves scarce and hid out in the hospital cafeteria until after
they left.

We don't ask permission to go see Gabriel once he's placed
in a recovery room. We wait until the nurses are busy with their
paperwork and we slip in on our own. The room is dim and cool
and filled with noise: the rhythmic beep of the machine he's
hooked up to, the faint echo of footsteps in the hall outside, the
soft in-and-out sound of Gabriel's breathing. Benny and I work
our way to his bedside, both of us going slow, reluctant to look
too closely.

He's a mess. There's no other way to describe him—flat on his back in the hospital bed, IV snaking from one arm, a cast encasing the other. His face has the look of a bruised and rotting banana.

"Gabe?" Benny calls softly, resting a hand on the bed beside Gabriel's leg.

Gabriel groans, licks his lips. "Hey." His voice is nothing more than a whisper and tight with pain.

"Man, what happened?"

Gabriel takes a long, shaky breath and blinks at us. His eyes are swollen to slits, the skin around them a violent smear of purples, reds, and blues. He grabs at my shirt to pull me closer and misses. His arm flops down at his side and he winces. "Listen to me. I found out something I shouldn't have." He tries to sit up, winces, and then falls back against his hospital pillow. "The job is a death sentence."

A chill runs up my spine even though I've known there was trouble from the minute I saw him lying on the Madison Street house lawn. "Why?"

"He was never planning to let us go. It is the last job, but we aren't meant to walk away. Dad overheard some of the Eme talking. Soldado's been bragging about the job to some of the brothers, the carnales, at the prison. He keeps telling us that they're the ones who want us to keep doing all these heists, when really it's him. Soldado is going to let us"—he swallows—"I mean, you guys get the dough, and then they ambush you in the tunnel and open fire. No one's supposed to make it out alive.

258

They shoot you and take the cash and then collapse the tunnel. He gets to keep the whole take for himself—minus what he owes the Eme." Gabriel coughs, and Benny grabs the cup of water on his nightstand and helps him get a drink.

So the tunnel guys have it wrong. Soldado isn't going to strand us in the vault so we get caught. I believed it because I never thought he would go this far, not with us. He's been in our homes. Hung out with our families. He *was* family. I thought jail was the worst thing that could happen, but this? This is so much worse. My whole body goes numb. "So what are we supposed to do?"

Gabriel stares at me. "You have to find a way to trick him somehow. You run, and he'll kill you and your families for walking out on the job." He sucks in a breath and hisses, holding a hand to his ribs. "Psycho did it. He found out that I knew. He told me if I said anything to you guys, he'd kill my dad. And my mom . . ." Tears roll down his cheeks. "They'll kill her, too, but not before they . . . um . . . they . . . uh . . ." He can't finish the sentence. I close my eyes and try to steady myself. The room feels like it's spinning.

Benny walks over to the window. He's breathing hard, folded over like someone's punched him. He leans against the windowsill and looks out. There's not much to see. Just another wing of the hospital building, floor after floor of windows and brick wall.

So this is it. We can't go to the police—we have no proof. Our word against Soldado's, that's it. And considering that he's got a handful of cops on the payroll, he'd know the minute we walked into the precinct. If we want to keep Gabriel safe, we have to pretend he didn't tell us anything. Either we walk into the job knowing we're going to die and accepting it to save our families, or we figure out a way to save ourselves. But how? I want to rage. Smash the windows out. Yell at the top of my lungs. Find Psycho, Twitch, and Soldado and obliterate them.

"So this is how it ends?" Benny asks, his voice ghost-hollow.

I put my head in my hands and close my eyes. My temples are throbbing so hard my face feels hot and full of blood. "No." I think about Lexi and the plan. It could still work. We just have to make Soldado believe that we don't know what's really going on.

"We can still make it out of this," I tell Benny and Gabriel. "All of us. We'll do whatever it takes."

31

Lexi

It's nearly noon on Sunday. Quinn is in his room playing video games with Oliver, and I'm in my room with Leo, Whitney, and Elena, the four of us sprawled out on my bed watching heist movies because, after our meeting at the zoo yesterday, Whitney insisted that we get together to watch *Ocean's Eleven* and *The Thomas Crown Affair*. Neither has anything to do with bank robberies—they're about more glamorous casino and art heists—but according to Whitney, they're both required watching anyway.

I think she just wants an excuse to eat popcorn and deconstruct why both movies continue to be popular with people so long after their releases. If she doesn't follow in her dad's footsteps someday and become a director, I'll be shocked. When the phone rings, we're forty-five minutes into *The Thomas Crown Affair*, and the twins have convinced themselves that Christian is my Thomas Crown and I'm his Catherine Banning—the younger, considerably less refined versions, anyway. It's ridiculous. I'm not in love with Christian. In another world, *maybe* I'd let myself be in serious lust with him, but love? No way. I don't do love. In that way, Catherine Banning and I have a lot in common, except unlike her, I intend to stick to my guns.

I stare at the caller ID, at Christian's name in bold block letters, and debate answering.

I shake my head and turn away from the screen. I press talk and put the phone up to my ear. *Great.* Thanks to the movie, now I'm picturing Christian and me dirty dancing. *So much for sticking to my no-lust guns. Nice willpower, Catherine. . . .* I get up off the bed to go talk in the bathroom, where I might be able to hear him better over the TV and so no one notices that I'm blushing.

"You ready to start your training?" he asks. His voice is gravelly, like he just woke up. I picture him lying on his bed now, the phone to his ear, his hair sleep-twisted, the hand not holding the phone resting on his bare chest.

"If you're ready, I'm ready," I say, blushing harder.

Behind me, Whitney and Elena start to giggle.

"You should bring your friends along. I'll bring one of my boys, too. There is a lot to go over between now and the job. What do you say we meet somewhere near you? Somewhere we can talk and not worry about being overheard?"

I cover the phone's speaker.

"What does he want?" Elena whispers, a handful of popcorn halfway to her lips.

"To start training us to rob the bank," I say. "Where do you want to meet him?"

"The beach house would probably be best," Leo says. "My parents will be with their friends at the club all day. And my brothers are away on some surf overnight thing. We'd have the whole place to ourselves."

"You sure you want him to know where you live?"

"Why not? He obviously knows where *you* live, which means he could find out on his own easily enough. And it *is* our usual spot for plotting mischief."

"So?" Christian asks. "You have a place yet?"

I give him Leo's address.

"See you in an hour, okay?" Christian asks. There is a click and a sudden flood of silence as he hangs up before I can answer. After yesterday I'd expected him to flirt more, but this morning he's all business. Good. Fine. *Excellent.* The job is the priority. I walk over and turn off the movie.

Less than an hour later we're sitting out on Leo's deck, waiting for Christian and his friend to show up. Leo's gone all Martha Stewart and prepared a couple of pitchers of lemonade and some chocolate chip cookies. They're smack in the center of the table, artfully arranged on a wicker tray. I keep staring at them and cracking up. Only my bestie would bring snacks to a heist-plotting session.

When the doorbell finally rings, I leap out of my chair and run to get it.

"Nice place," Christian says, his gaze drifting over the entry hall. He steps inside. "This is my cousin Benny." It's the guy from the Mary Kay van. Benny is shorter than Christian, but it's easy to see that they're related. They both have the same cleft chin and thick dark eyelashes.

Benny slips inside and shakes my hand as he gives me an appraising look. "It's good to finally meet you." His eyes cut over to Christian as he presses his lips together to keep from smiling. Obviously they've had a conversation or two about me. Cue the roller-coaster plummet sensation in my stomach.

I lead them straight out to the deck and introduce them to everybody. Whitney and Elena nearly explode out of their chairs to shake Christian's hand. "Hey there, Thomas," Whitney says, looking sidelong at me.

Christian looks down at his hand, which is still firmly in Whitney's grip. "No. Christian."

The girls dissolve into giggles.

"What's so funny?" Christian asks, frowning.

"She's referencing an old movie," I explain. "About a thief." I don't elaborate, because the whole plot of the film is basically a seduction and Christian might get the wrong idea.

"Okay, a couple of things right up front." Christian settles into a chair. "My team goes in to start the job two weeks from yesterday. Between now and then we need to familiarize you with how my boys and I rob a bank, get you identical disguises and equipment, and steal your getaway car and ours. We need to do all of it without leaving any kind of trail for the cops to follow."

"That's all? And here I thought this was going to be hard," Quinn jokes.

Christian's expression is granite—hard and unyielding. "This isn't like the stunts you guys usually do. We get caught and we do serious time. If you're going to treat it as a joke, you shouldn't be a part of it."

There's something up with him. I didn't notice at first, but now I see it—the shadowed hollows around his eyes, the way he and Benny keep exchanging glances. At the zoo he was almost playful, but now he's all business.

"Be careful," Quinn warns him.

There is a tense moment, and then Leo clears his throat. "So do we start with getting the disguises or . . ."

Christian rubs the back of his neck. "That would be a good idea, since we have to track down a place that carries our particular brand of mask."

"Wait, we have to steal the masks, too? How many robberies are we going to commit here?" Oliver asks.

"If you buy the masks online or in a store, the cops can track you. All they have to do is figure out which stores carry them, go through every receipt created around the time of the bank robbery for sales of that particular mask, and then check up on the customers who bought them. Even if you use cash, they can go back through the security-camera feed to the time the sale occurred, and get a visual image of you."

I stare at him openmouthed. The boy has definitely done his homework.

"What do the masks look like?" Whitney asks. "Do they have a specific name?"

"Radioactive zombie," Benny says.

"Okay, cool." She whips out her phone and starts tapping it.

"There's a good chance that at least one of the costume-supply warehouses my dad uses has them. The inventory in those things is so huge, it's pretty likely we could sneak some out and then put them right back after the heist without anyone even realizing they're gone." She swipes the screen and squints. "This it?"

Christian and Benny get closer so they can peer at the screen.

"That's it," Christian says. "How secure are these warehouses?"

"They have cameras and security guards—an alarm system for sure. Looks like they have over . . . fifty. Must've been used in a zombie horde scene or something. So it's perfect, right?"

"I can hack the system," Quinn tells him. "Wipe out the alarm and intercept the camera feed."

"So can I leave the planning to you?" Christian asks.

Quinn nods. "Whitney, give me the address on that warehouse." Quinn and Oliver hunch over Quinn's laptop and scroll through the warehouse's website.

Down on the beach someone squeals, and Christian jumps as if he's just heard a gunshot. He and Benny stand up, eyeballing the door. I don't like how jittery they are.

"Hey. Can I steal you for a walk down there?" I ask him, gesturing toward the long stretch of sand that constitutes Leo's backyard. "We have a couple more things to discuss."

He shrugs, which I decide is a yes. I grab hold of his hand and pull him down the weatherworn stairway.

"What's up?" I ask.

"Nothing's up."

"You're acting weird. Why?" I lead him to the wet sand, where it'll be easier to walk and wait for him to answer me. Shining nearly directly above us, the sun is unrelenting, beating on my head and back until I feel like I'm igniting. I edge closer to the water and walk through the surf, stooping briefly to cup some and pour it over the back of my neck.

He watches me silently, the serious expression on his face unchanged and worrisome.

"Come on, what is it?"

He avoids looking at me and starts walking down the beach, kicking up clumps of wet sand. His shirt ripples in the breeze, crackles like a sail. "Nothing I want to talk about."

He walks and I keep pace, neither of us speaking. It's a strangely somber moment, given all the banter we've exchanged back and forth the past few times we've met. I don't know what to do or say, but I feel like he's waiting for me to say something, to find the perfect combination of words that might get him to release whatever he's bottled up inside. Except unlike BAMs or bank robberies, this isn't a challenge I feel confident I can tackle, so I do what I do best: ignore and deflect.

"I want to see the tunnels under the bank."

He snorts. "No."

"I'm not asking permission," I say. "If we're going to do this job with you, I want to see what your half of the plan looks like. For example: how are you going to collapse the tunnels?"

He whirls on me. "I said no! This isn't a game, all right? You aren't getting anywhere near the tunnels. They're dangerous.

And besides, what does it matter? They won't be a viable way out for any of us after the job. We leave the bank through the front door. The only thing you have to concern yourself with is getting us out of the vault. You don't trust me. Good. You shouldn't. But the tunnels aren't your concern."

I glare at him, blood roaring in my ears, my heart beating hard. "Every part of this job is my concern. You don't get to tell me what I can and can't do. We're in a stalemate, remember? Equally compromised."

He laughs bitterly. "No. We aren't. You're looking to expose Harrison and get some thrills. Things don't work out and all of us get caught, you're not looking at life in jail once all the charges come down. They'll probably cut you a deal if you testify against my team. You fail and you lose *stuff*. I fail and not only do I go to jail, I lose *people* I care about. The men I do the jobs for kill my family. Benny's family. Carlos's, Eddie's, Gabriel's." His nostrils flare. "So don't tell me we're the same. You have zero idea of what you're talking about."

He turns abruptly and takes off down the beach without a backward glance, and I'm so shocked by his outburst that I don't know what to do or say. So I stand, my feet swallowed up in wet sand, hands fisted at my sides, and watch him go.

32

Christian

I stomp on the gas pedal and roar away from the beach house—and Lexi. My skin feels coated in ants, crawling and uncomfortable. I can't sit still.

"What the hell happened back there?" Benny asks, turned halfway around in his seat so he can stare at me.

"Nothing. It's just . . . how are we supposed to rely on them to help us? You see that house? They aren't invested in this like we are. They walk away now and what happens? Nothing much. Lexi's dad stays in jail and his boss doesn't get exposed, but so what? They survive. Maybe with less money, but people like that find a way to get it back. They have choices here. We don't."

I grip the steering wheel hard enough that my fingers ache. I knew Lexi was rich. I saw her house that day I took the pictures of her. But seeing her with her friends just now, all of them lounging around that deck in designer clothes and radiating privilege, while Gabriel's laid up in the hospital and Benny, Carlos, Eddie, and me are facing the same, I couldn't deny how different our situations are. And I definitely couldn't listen to her stupid brother make patronizing comments and pretend like it was cool.

"We can make this work, bro," Benny says quietly. "But only if you get your head straight. We need them to get us out of the vault. Period. So we have to make sure we keep them committed. That means dealing with their jokes, promising to get them that safe-deposit box, and putting up with them."

I stare at the stream of cars in front of us and force myself to breathe. He's right. I know he's right. I shouldn't get so worked up, but standing on the beach with Lexi while she asked me what was wrong, all the swagger she normally has gone—for a minute I felt like she cared about me, and I couldn't . . . I don't know. I just felt the weight of everything that's happening crash down on me.

"And you're wrong that they don't have a lot to lose. If Soldado were to find out about what we've got planned, he'd go after them, too. They just don't realize the stakes, vato."

And that's really what's gnawing at my gut, if I'm being honest with myself. I'm putting Lexi and her friends in danger. Deciding to put my boys' and families' lives ahead of theirs. It's a terrible choice to make, and being near her, looking into her eyes and pretending that I'm not, is only making it harder. I don't think I will be able to live with myself if this job goes bad and something happens to her.

"We gotta pull it off, that's all," Benny says. "We pull it off and everybody lives happily ever after. You can't think about it going bad. It won't. The closer you get to that girl, the better the chances that we come out okay. What's that saying? The means justify the ends? Something like that?" He lowers the window and lets in a blast of hot summer air. "The more this girl likes you and thinks she has a chance at getting what she wants, the safer we'll all be. So man up and play the game, bro. It's the only way to keep her safe in the end."

"Yeah, you're right," I say. I have to get Lexi and her friends to see the job through. I'm not really putting them in danger or hurting her if I make sure nothing goes wrong . . . right?

33

Lexi

It's the last full week of June, and the temperature has spiked to one hundred degrees, record heat this early in the summer. I walk out of the air-conditioned cool of the bank to go grab some lunch, dreading the wall of humid, breath-stealing air.

Three days have passed since Christian stormed out of the beach house without an explanation, and I haven't heard from him since. Everything suddenly feels tentative: the job, exposing Harrison. We can't do the job without Christian. It would take too long to break into the safe-deposit box on the morning of the robbery. The tellers and employees show up just before opening. That leaves us minutes to storm the bank, get inside the vault, and pry open a box so secure we'd have to take a crowbar to it just to get it out. How long could that take? More than five or ten minutes, for sure. The bank wouldn't open on time, and the cops would show up before we could get anywhere.

I cross the street and walk the block to where the food truck is parked, careful to keep enough distance so I won't be spotted.

The girl, Rosie, is there, but Christian's not. I take out my phone and try calling him again. I've left four messages so far.

"Hi, it's me," I say.

"Hi, me."

I whirl around and there he is, standing right next to me, his COCINA DE MI CORAZÓN cap pulled low over his eyes, making them look even darker.

"Where have you been?" I say, hating how upset I sound. *He needs you just as much as you need him,* I remind myself. "Give me one good reason why I shouldn't call this whole thing off." *There. That's better.*

"I will, I swear, but not here." He glances over at the taco truck. "I know you're mad, but give me a chance to explain. You're on break, right? Listen to what I have to say, and lunch is on me." He grabs my hand in his and pulls me closer. "Come on, please." Eyes flashing with mischief, he begins walking backward, leading me.

"Okay, fine. But I'm getting my lunch to go, so talk fast." I give in, but only because we can't afford to keep wasting time. There's too much to do.

"I'm sorry for Sunday. I was dealing with some stuff, and I shouldn't have taken it out on you. One of my guys, my cousin Gabriel, got hurt over the weekend. He does construction and there was an accident." He looks straight ahead. "He was crushed under a backhoe. He'll make it, but for a while we weren't sure. . . ."

"Oh my god, I'm so sorry. But why didn't you tell me on

273

Sunday?" No wonder he was so shook up. Now I feel like a huge jerk for being so flippant a second ago.

"Because we agreed not to get too close, right? I didn't want to get into it. I was too upset. And because he was supposed to be on the job and I knew it complicated things. I didn't want to talk about it until I was sure he'd be okay and that we could move forward without him."

He takes me into a little sandwich shop with a movie star–inspired menu. I order the Meryl Streep's Complication, which is a croque monsieur (basically the French version of a grilled ham-and-cheese sandwich), a nod to one of her movies, *It's Complicated*. It's a fitting choice, considering the movie title perfectly sums up this whole heist and Christian. I feel like I'm constantly scrambling to stay one step ahead, and the last few days have made me feel as if I've failed.

He pays and we find a place off to the side to wait for our order.

"So, you still a go?" he asks.

I was planning on making him sweat it a little, but given his explanation, I don't want to. Playing games now feels cruel. "Yeah. We're in."

We don't talk again until we're back outside. "We've been working on the masks. We can hit the costume warehouse this weekend. Quinn's almost got the security stuff worked out, and there'll only be one guard on duty."

"I'd like to come with," Christian says. "That way I can make sure we get the right ones."

I am just about to argue with him when all at once he pulls me inside the office building we happen to be passing. "We have a problem," he says quietly, pulling me over to one corner, away from the windows.

The guy at the security desk eyeballs us. "Can I help you?"

"No, sir. My girlfriend got overheated, so we came in so she could cool off. We won't stay more than a minute."

The guy mulls it over, tapping his fingers on the counter. "One minute."

Christian turns back to me. "Listen. The guy I told you about, the one who organizes our jobs?"

"Soldado," I say, nodding.

"Right. Some of his guys are out there. Most likely checking to see that I'm doing what I said I would."

"Seducing me for information," I say.

He stares past me to the street. "Yeah. When we walk out of here, I need you to . . ."

"I get it. You need me to act like I like you," I say with a smile.

"I need you to act like you *want* me," he corrects. "And to play along. Follow my lead. Can you do that?"

I'm a little insulted. He doesn't think I can believably pretend to have the hots for him? The boy has no idea who he's dealing with.

"Watch me," I say. I grab his hand and pull his arm over my shoulders, then put my arm around his waist, letting my hand drift downward until it's resting on his butt as we push through the exit doors. He sucks in a breath the minute my hand touches him. I give him a playful squeeze, barely holding back laughter as he tenses.

Soldado's guys are right outside, sauntering down the sidewalk, their arms sleeved in tattoos, their close-cropped hair glistening with sweat.

"Yo, man. Qué pasa?" They're talking to him but looking at me, giving me a slow once-over. "Who's this?"

Christian bumps fists with both of them and introduces me. "This is Angela. Angela, this is Twitch and . . . I mean, Eli and Jesus."

They nod at me and I paste on a smile. I don't like either of them. Not just because of what Christian's told me about Soldado and the kinds of guys who work for him, but because they have these flat vulture eyes. I feel as if they're circling us, trying to decide if we'd make a good meal. "Nice to meet you both," I say in a voice that's higher-pitched than my real one, one I hope gives off a certain gullibility.

Christian kisses the top of my head. "What's up? You guys headed to the truck to see Rosie?"

The taller of the two, Jesus, nods. "Soldado sent us to get some lunch for him."

"Her food is delicious!" I exclaim enthusiastically. "I love that truck. Of course, that's where we met, so . . ." I look up at Christian adoringly, and out of the corner of my eye I can see them grin meaningfully at Christian.

"We heard about Gabriel. Bad luck, bro. But it's good he's gonna get better, right?" Eli asks, his eyes boring into Christian.

Christian tenses a little. "Doctors say he'll be okay. It'll be a while before he can work, but he'll live."

"That's good. Does he remember what happened? From what I hear it was brutal, dude. The backhoe went right over him. Can you imagine? Your bones slowly crushing like that?" Eli whistles. "Pain like that would make you wish you were dead."

I can feel the anger in Christian, humming just beneath his skin. His whole body is coiled tight like a spring. These guys are baiting him somehow. I have a gut feeling that if I don't get him out of here soon, he might explode.

"Hey, I hate to do this, but my lunch break is up. Christian, can you walk me back to the bank?" There is a beat of silence before Christian nods.

"Say hi to your mom and sister for me," Jesus says, still staring at Christian, a slow smile spreading across his face as he and Eli turn to go.

I lead Christian toward the bank, my arm around his waist. "Are they still watching us?" I ask.

"Probably," he says tightly. "Thanks for that."

"For what?"

"For getting us outta there before I ripped their heads off."

"What was that about, exactly?" I ask.

He exhales heavily. "It's nothing. They're just reminding me that doing this job isn't a choice."

"You don't rob banks because you want to?"

He looks startled, like he hadn't realized he just said what he did out loud. "It doesn't matter."

Except now I'm curious. "How is the job not a choice?" If he isn't robbing banks because he wants to, this changes who I thought that he was. I think about being inside his house, about the way he was with his sister. At the time, I found it hard to see him as both this criminal and this boy with college posters on his wall and a bookshelf filled with literary classics. But if somehow he was being blackmailed . . . "When he mentioned your family . . . are they threatening them somehow to keep you committing robberies?"

Christian slips from my grasp and takes a step away from me, putting distance between us. "Just leave it alone, please. We agreed on boundaries and this is one of mine. I'll call you later, okay?"

He gives me a half smile and then, as if remembering that Eli and Jesus might be watching, pulls me close. "I wouldn't do this if it weren't necessary. Sorry," he says in a rush, and then he moves a hand to my face and leans in and kisses me.

I'm so unprepared that I stiffen on reflex, but then his lips move against mine and I can taste him and he's so close to me, filling up the space, stealing my air, my ability to think straight, and I forget my surprise and kiss him back. Now it's his turn to stiffen, but instead of pulling away, he crushes me to him. His lips move more urgently. Caught up, I lift my hand to his face and trace the length of his jaw. The way he kisses! I've kissed guys who knew what they were doing, and those kisses were good, but this one is immeasurably better. Whatever this is between us is different. My whole body responds. I can feel a ribbon of nerves and excitement flutter through my insides, and every inch of my skin is aware of the feel of him against me. I could kiss him for hours. Days. Weeks. I want him. Really want him. And the minute I realize this, fear as bracing as a bucket of ice-cold water washes over me and I go rigid in his arms.

He pulls away, his expression serious, searching. "I'm sorry. That was probably overkill, right?" He licks his lips as if he's testing to see if he can still taste me. I take a shaky breath and put some distance between us. The moment gets awkward, and the world rushes back in—the heat, the harried sounds of traffic and people.

"I should . . . I gotta go." He shoves his hands into his jeans pockets and hurries off, back hunched against the sun and maybe me, never once looking back.

I put my fingers to my lips, the feel of him still lingering there and on my skin where his hands gripped my back and waist. *He kissed me because he had to,* I tell myself. I say it over and over in my mind as I walk the rest of the way back to the bank, my skin still tingling, my heart beating faster than it should. After the way that kiss made me feel, I need the reminder. Nothing can happen between Christian and me. I don't do vulnerable, and especially not with a boy I can't possibly trust and who definitely can't trust me.

34
Christian

I haven't seen Lexi since Wednesday, when I kissed her. Every time I attempt to, she has an excuse why we can't meet up. I've tried waiting for her outside the bank, but she's managed to slip away, probably using one of the back exits to the building, where I can't go without attracting attention.

That kiss completely freaked her out; that much is obvious. And the stupid thing is, I wouldn't have kissed her except that Twitch and Psycho were watching, angry after I introduced them by their real names. I'd needed to shut her up. I couldn't answer her questions about why I'm doing the jobs. If she realizes how much I have to lose, she might also realize I'd do anything to keep it from happening, including—if things go very wrong— letting her and her friends take the fall for this job.

I'd meant the kiss to be quick, but the minute she started to kiss me back . . . I lost control and things got carried away. I hadn't expected it to feel like that—like a jolt of pure lightning going through me. She felt it, too. I could tell when I pulled back. She sucked her bottom lip and stared at me, her eyes liquid heat, all shimmer and want and fear. I knew right then that I took things too far. Still, it was all I could do to turn away.

Now I wonder what it will be like to be close to her again. We've spent a couple of days arranging tonight's zombie mask smash-and-grab over a series of texts. The span of days was supposed to make this meeting easier for her and, I guess, me. But now, standing here along the weedy edge of the lot beside the warehouse waiting for her to show, I'm not so sure it will.

"How long before they're here?" Eddie asks, lounging on a broken piece of curbing. "It's muy caliente out here, bro." He grabs the giant Gatorade he brought and guzzles half of it in one gulp.

Carlos and Benny are at the far end of the lot, scoping out the back of the warehouse.

I'm glad they're all here. It'll be easier to keep some clarity. And I like the idea that my boys will be keeping watch, too, not just her crew.

Twin beams of light dance across the lot, momentarily exposing us before they snap off and an Escalade eases to a stop at the curb. Lexi jumps out, dressed head to toe in formfitting black: T-shirt, pants, knee-high flat-soled boots. Her hair is slicked back into a high ponytail that swishes as she moves. She looks a little like she did that first night I saw her, so much prettier and more herself than she is with that stupid brown wig she has to wear when she's at the bank. If kissing her when she was Angela nearly made me lose control, what would it be like to kiss her now, looking like that? The thought is enough to rattle me, so I turn away and busy myself with picking up the pack full of gear I brought: metal cutters, a flashlight, a can of glow-in-the-dark spray paint, some putty, and a few firecrackers.

Lexi's team trails out of the van, each of them dressed similarly to Lexi. They look like some kind of movie-inspired band of military recruits. I shake my head and chuckle. She glances in my direction, but the minute our eyes meet, she looks away.

"Seriously?" Carlos says, gawking at them. "What is this? *Mission: Impossible*?"

Benny and Eddie crack up.

"Oh, whatever! We're more invisible than you guys are. We could see you nearly a block down the road," one of the twin girls—I think Lexi called her Whitney—says, arms folded, posing with one hip jutted out, her expression fierce. She could be Beyoncé's younger sister, she looks that much like her. Her sister, too, although she doesn't have the same fire as this girl.

My boys edge closer to her crew, their eyes narrowed.

"This is Quinn, Oliver, Leo, Whitney, and Elena. And I'm Lexi," Lexi says to Carlos and Eddie. It's so awkward standing here all together like this, with Lexi looking everywhere but at me. It's painful. The distrust on both sides is hanging over the lot like a cloud.

"Carlos and Eddie," I say. "Benny and me you already know."

"So what? We supposed to shake hands? Or can we get on with this?" Carlos asks. He's not thrilled to have to work with

Lexi's crew, but after what happened to Gabriel and finding out from us what's supposed to go down during the job, he's come around.

"Everybody knows where to go?" Quinn asks. "The security tape is on a loop so the guard won't see you inside. I'll keep tabs on the manual alarm from out here. If it goes off, I'll text you and give you an ETA on the cops. I'll be listening to their secure channel, so once I hear the call go out and who's being sent to answer it, I can estimate the arrival time."

I gotta admit, Lexi's brother is damn impressive. We could've used him on the jobs. Would've made it a lot easier, that's for sure. "Cool. Carlos and Eddie got watch over the field and the street. Benny'll go in with me."

"Whitney will stay in the car with Quinn and drive over a block so they aren't too close by. Oliver, Leo, Elena, and I will go inside with you and Benny. We split into groups of two once we get through the back door. Elena and Oliver keep tabs on the guard's station. Leo and I take the right side of the warehouse, you and Benny the left. There is a mix of costumes and props inside. We couldn't get an exact location for the masks, but they should be housed on the first floor."

"Fine," I say. "Let's just get on with it."

The warehouse looms at the edge of the lot, surrounded by a chain link fence. We crouch-run around the perimeter until we come to a place where the fence touches a small copse of trees. I kneel down, take the metal cutters from my pack, and snip the links until we have a hole big enough for a person. One by one we slip through. There are cameras mounted along the roof line, but thanks to Quinn, we shouldn't need to worry about them. We sprint across the parking lot anyway, though, since out in the open there's always the chance that someone in the surrounding buildings or houses might see us.

There is a metal door halfway around the back of the warehouse at the top of a low staircase, and we aim for it, running in a straight line, shoulders grazing the concrete wall. The door is flat, windowless, smooth except for the lock and handle. Next to the door is an intercom system. Press the speaker button and it alerts someone inside that there is a person waiting to be let in. Directly above us is another camera.

Benny takes out the tension wrench and pick he brought and goes to work on the lock. Three minutes later the pins line up and the lock disengages. Leo opens the door very slowly and peeks inside before giving us a thumbs-up.

The interior of the warehouse is morgue-silent and shadowy, filled with massive shelving systems, boxes, and crates. I slip some of the putty I brought into the doorjamb to keep the door from automatically relocking, so when we come back to return the masks after the job, it'll be easier to get in.

"The guard station should be straight ahead," Lexi whispers, and Elena and Oliver take off. She turns toward me and our eyes lock. She presses her lips together like she's got something to say and is holding it in, but then there's a shift in her eyes and she refocuses on the job. "Time to split up. Of course, you guys could wait here. Leo and I can cover this."

"You think you'll find it first, that it? You think you guys can beat us?" I say. If there's one thing I'm beginning to get about this girl, it's that she cannot resist a dare.

She shrugs, and then all at once she's smiling. "Absolutely."

"She's bowing up on us, bro," Benny says, looking both surprised and impressed.

"If we're about to place bets, understand you're gonna lose," I say, looking directly in her eyes. A rush of adrenaline shoots through me because I can feel things between us realigning.

"Wait. Are we really doing this?" Leo asks, looking from Lexi to me and back again.

"Absolutely," we both say in unison. I raise an eyebrow at her and she laughs quietly. I'd thought it would be awkward until we discussed the kiss, but now that we've devised this game to play, she's acting like it never happened. I'm kinda grateful for that.

"On your mark . . . ," she begins.

"Go," I say, and she takes off. Leo scrambles to keep up, nearly wiping out as he rounds the corner of a shelving system.

I nod, and Benny and I bolt down another row. The place is full of one fantastic object after another. There's an ornate horse-drawn carriage, glowing gold and silver under the security lights, and a giant Buddha that looks to be made out of stone but turns out to be hollow. I could spend hours exploring in here if we weren't trying to steal something. Every few feet I stop just long enough to spray a small dot of paint so we can remember the way back.

"This is crazy," Benny murmurs, staring up at a replica of the Trojan horse, big enough to fit a car inside it.

My phone buzzes in my pocket. Elena.

Guard is at station.

She and Oliver have reached their position. So far everything seems to be going according to plan. *Good.* I run a little faster, anxious to get to the costume rows ahead of Lexi. We round corner after corner, and finally I start to see racks of uniforms, street clothes, and evening gowns.

"Up there," Benny whispers, panting, his rubber soles squeaking as he cuts across the aisle.

There is a wall of masks straight in front of us. Row after row of eyeless faces. We pick up the pace, skidding to a stop in front of a row of clown heads. The wall is long, taking up nearly the length of one of the warehouse walls. Down at the other end I see Leo and Lexi emerge.

She skids to a stop. She looks at me. I look at her.

Benny is panting hard-core next to me, struggling to catch his breath, like he might have a heart attack or something.

"Ready?" I murmur.

"When"—*gasp*—"you"—*gasp*—"are," he says, wiping one hand across his forehead.

"Now," I murmur.

Benny breaks right, checking the small section there, and I go left, heading for Lexi and Leo, scanning the wall as I go. There must be thousands of masks.

"There!" Lexi says to Leo, just loud enough for me to catch it, and then I spot the masks, twenty feet ahead. I'm closer. If I hurry, I'll beat her there.

I run flat out, and so does she. I'm not actually looking at the masks; I'm looking at her, that ponytail flying out behind her, and her arms and legs pumping. She's laughing, and as I watch her I start to feel so good I laugh, too.

We make it to the masks at the exact same time and nearly collide. I catch her in my arms and then whirl her out of the way as I reach up to grab the masks.

"Hey!" She launches herself onto my back and snatches the mask in my hand.

I'm just about to go after it when a beam of light bounces over the top of the shelving unit to our left.

"Who's in here?"

At nearly the same time my phone starts to vibrate.

I don't have time to check the text, but there's no need. It's the security guard. Somehow he figured out we were here. The light is close, flicking over the props and costumes one aisle over. We have mere seconds to either move or be seen. But we still don't have all the masks. I lunge forward and grab up the remaining five masks with one hand, yanking the bar they were hanging on clean off the wall. It clatters to the floor, and the sound is metallic and echoing. God-awful. I grab Lexi's arm with my free hand and drag her down the aisle. Benny and Leo will have to make their own way back.

"Hey!" the guard hollers.

We run, taking the first turn we get to and then the next, purposely following a roundabout route to the back of the warehouse to throw him off course.

"He's right behind us," Lexi breathes as the flashlight beam swings down our aisle.

"Stop right there!" the guard shouts.

We dart down another aisle and head in the opposite direction—or at least I think it is. This place is starting to feel like a giant maze. I'm not so sure we'll ever find our way out. And the guard is getting closer. Too close. When I feel like we've put enough distance between us and him, I pull Lexi into a shadowy area behind one of those giant red phone booths—the kind they have over in Europe. England, maybe? Right now I can't remember. I'm breathing hard and my head is pounding. We crouch together behind it, our shoulders and knees touching. I shove all the masks in my pack and then take out the fireworks I brought.

"What are you going to do?" Lexi mouths.

Instead of answering, I take out a lighter, ignite the fuse on one, and toss it over the top of some boxes into the next aisle over.

Lexi stares at me, and then her eyes go wide.

"Come on," I say, grabbing her hand. Our fingers lace together and she holds tight. I pull her along and try to focus on where the exit might be from here.

There's a loud bang, and the guard makes a surprised noise before taking off, feet pounding, in the direction of the sound.

We run to the end of the aisle and round the corner. Lexi's grip on my hand gets tighter. By some miracle the door is up ahead. We're almost there.

Suddenly Benny and Leo appear, practically leaping out at us from around an enormous fake pine tree. The branches rattle as Leo trips over the tree base. He slams into it as he fights to stay upright. The tree rocks violently back and forth.

"Go! Go! Go!" I whisper-yell.

We leap forward and the tree topples behind us, crashing to the floor with a concussive boom. A pinecone rolls past my feet, and then we are at the door, through it, and out in the parking lot. I don't look back. The hole we cut in the fence is there, two yards to the right. We adjust our course and dive through it one by one. My back scrapes against the snipped metal ends of the fence, and my skin burns, but I keep going, fully expecting the guard to grab my shoulder and haul me backward. But when I turn around, the parking lot is empty. Dark. Silent.

"What about Elena and Oliver?" Leo says breathlessly. "Think they're still inside?"

We stare at the warehouse.

"We can't leave them in there," Lexi says, panic in her voice.

Our phones go off again and I dig mine out. It's a text from Elena.

We r ok

She's added a smiley face emoji and, inexplicably, a party hat. Lexi takes out her own phone and texts her back.

R u outside?

The answer comes in a split second.

Now we r.

I scroll up to see the text they sent us when the guard nearly caught us.

Leave now!

I shove my phone back into my pocket. They had one job and they pretty much flubbed it.

I almost laugh, but it's not actually funny. These are the people I'm counting on to get us out of the bank? I thought I could get them ready fast, but now I'm thinking we'll need more time. Lots more time. Time we don't actually have. I could kick myself for letting Lexi avoid me for the past few days. I should've insisted we start holding nightly drills. I will now, that's for sure. One week. That's all we have to get this right.

"Well, not perfect, but a success," Lexi says. "We got the masks."

"Barely," I say. "You guys need to clear your schedules. 'Cause we got a whole lotta work to do."

35

Lexi

There are LAPD patrol cars parked in front of the bank when I show up. It's Thursday morning—my last day as an intern and the final workday before the bank closes for the long Fourth of July weekend. Do I go in? No way this is about the masks. . . . It can't be, can it?

"Angela. Angela. Angela!" Someone taps me on the shoulder. I turn around and Harrison is standing there. "I've been calling to you for the better part of a block." He looks at me funny.

I try to swallow the panic welling up inside me. I didn't turn around because I forgot for a minute that I'm supposed to answer to Angela. I'm so tired I can barely see straight. After our near-capture at the costume warehouse, Christian had us spend the last four nights rehearsing for the heist at Leo's beach house, where we could draw a rough layout of the bank's main floor in the sand. Over and over and over again. It's gotten so that I'm hearing "Everybody get down on the floor!" on a loop in my head.

I blink at him. "Sorry. Late night last night."

"Hot date?" He grins his pervy, leering, toothy smile that makes me want to barf.

"Actually? Yes," I say. Which is a lie. There's been nothing datelike about the last four nights. Christian's been all business since that kiss on the street. He seems keyed up and worried about how the job will go, which has *me* keyed up, too. As much as I want to nail Harrison, I don't want to go to jail myself in the process. But I have to admit, it's been a relief to have the distance there between us. I thought I could play like I liked him, but it turns out that I'm not really playing. And that is more terrifying than the looming bank job. Turns out the vault I've built around my heart isn't as impregnable as I thought.

"The alarm went off last night. Five times." Harrison blows on his cup of coffee and takes a sip. "Must've gone off again this morning."

"Did someone try to break in?" I ask as casually as I can, but my heart is racing. So *that's* why the cops are here. Christian's tunnels. The guys must be digging right now, just under our feet. The thought gives me chills. We are four days away from Monday's heist.

"No. False alarms. Started about four. Poor Leslie, the bank manager, had to get out of bed twice and come all the way down here. Each time the bank was totally secure. It's probably the construction. The alarms on the vault are so sensitive that all the banging inside the building, coupled with the digging for the parking-garage extension, knocked it out of whack."

He walks me to the bank door and flashes his security badge to the guard standing just inside. The bank's not officially open just yet, so the door is still locked. Once he lets us in, I see Detective Martin near the customer counter, chatting with Leslie and some of the tellers.

"Leslie, how are you holding up?" Harrison says. He seems to know every woman in the building, but the guard at the door? He barely acknowledged him.

"I've had better nights." She sighs.

"Mitch," Detective Martin says, and there's something in the tone of his voice. He's not rude, exactly, but I don't think he likes Harrison much. I knew this guy was smart. "And . . ."

"Angela Dunbar. I was at the presentation you gave. For the interns. I'm an intern." I'm babbling. *Stop talking now, Lexi.*

"That's it. Nice to see you again, Angela." He turns back to Leslie. "What time can the vault be opened?"

She consults her watch. "In about ten minutes. I hate to make you wait, but . . ."

"No, no. That's why we're here." Detective Martin leans against the counter and stares at Harrison. "How are things upstairs?"

Harrison sips his coffee, shrugs. "Good, good. Same. Looking forward to the weekend. The wife's planned a little getaway. A couple of days in Vegas. She's on a mission to see that Beatles show. I forget the name. And I'm happy to take her so long as I can steal a few minutes at the blackjack tables."

"So you're a gambler, then?" Martin asks, only half listening, his eyes scanning the teller counters.

Harrison keeps blathering on, and like Martin, I only half hear it all. *What is he doing down here anyway? And why does he seem all keyed up?*

"Okay, ready to go downstairs?" Leslie asks Martin.

"Mind if Angela and I tag along? I think she might find this interesting. Have you seen the inside of the vault yet?" Harrison asks me.

"I saw the safe-deposit boxes," I say. "The day I saw you last. Inside the bank. I helped that girl, the one who went to your daughter's school, get a box." I look mildly at Harrison, as if I'm just making conversation. He pales instantly, and a little thrill of satisfaction goes through me. Four days from now I'll have what I need. He's going down and he has no idea. *Have fun on that Vegas trip because it'll be your last,* I think.

Leslie nods. "Why not."

"You'll have to wait behind me until I can clear it," Martin says, frowning.

"Oh, she will. But really, Detective Martin, I'm sure it's a false alarm. We've had a handful of them on and off since they started renovating the building."

The detective nods, but I can tell he's not convinced.

Leslie and one of the tellers whose name I can't remember lead the way through the safe-deposit room to the vault door. They each take their turn inputting their individual codes precisely at eight-thirty. I can hear the lock disengage, and then Martin is right there, hand resting on his sidearm as the door swings open. I don't know exactly what I expected the vault to look like—on some level I had these visions of stacked gold bars and whole pallets full of cash—but it is disappointingly straightforward. There's nothing blingy about it. It's just a gray-walled square room with industrial-style shelves. There is cash in shrink-wrapped bundles and a cart with all of the teller trays on it—more cash, but it lacks the same punch as, say, the vault in the Bellagio in *Ocean's Eleven*.

Martin walks around the vault, peering at corners and staring down at his feet. The whole room is solid, quiet, tomblike. I stamp my foot and it barely makes a sound. *Did they hear that down below in the tunnel?*

"The floors are reinforced steel on top of concrete," Leslie explains. "It really absorbs the sound, doesn't it?"

I nod. Harrison didn't come into the vault at all. I step out to see where he went. I find him almost immediately, staring at a row of safe-deposit boxes. So that's why he wanted to come down. He was nervous that there actually might've been a break-in. He needed to check on his stuff.

"So what did you think of the vault?" he asks, still staring at the numbered boxes.

"I thought it wasn't nearly as exciting as this room."

He looks at me.

"You know, anything could be in here. Every box hides a secret, right? Jewelry. Important documents. Family photos. Rare coins. Doesn't it make you curious?" I run a hand along a row of boxes, the one Stephanie's is on. He flinches when my fingers land on it, but it's a blink-and-you'll-miss-it thing.

"I never actually thought much about it," he says.

"Everything appears to be fine." Detective Martin walks out of the vault with Leslie. "Seems as if it might be the construction, but if it keeps happening, I'd like to put someone down here in a surveillance capacity. Maybe beef up security upstairs."

"Do you think it could be something more sinister?" Harrison asks.

"Call it a hunch, but yeah, I think it's possible." Martin looks back at the vault and frowns.

"Do you get those often? The hunches, I mean?" I ask. I clasp my hands together to keep them still. Suddenly I'm all shaky. If he suspects, what's to keep him from catching us? A guy like this? I feel certain that he could.

"I don't know. Often enough," he says.

"And are they always right?" I ask. *Please say no,* I think at him.

He looks down at the ground a minute before training his laser blue eyes on me. "Almost every single time."

36

Christian

"Well, this place couldn't be any creepier," Lexi says, her nose wrinkling up at the dank smell.

"You were the one who insisted on coming down here," I tell her.

The tunnel work is done. Benny found out from Soldado earlier today. They finished later than expected, but the diggers have finally packed up, so it's the perfect time to investigate. Until now someone's been underground 24/7. Doesn't leave me much time to figure out how to trap Soldado underground without burying his ass. Not that I'm not tempted, after what he had done to Gabriel.

"I'm here because you need me. Like I said, part of what my club did was build houses for charity. It's not the same as constructing tunnels, but I'm very sure I have a handle on the concept of load-bearing beams. I can show you exactly where to compromise the support system."

God help me, I'm putting this job in the hands of an

architect-club president. This is screwed up. Except she's right. She *is* my only hope.

We make it to the spot where the dig site is, but at first it's hard to tell, because the entrance has been blocked off with a concrete-covered board meant to mimic the tunnel wall. The concrete is still wet, and so it's darker than the surrounding tunnel wall, easy to pick out under the flashlight beam, but unless you needed to come down this tunnel and were shining a light on the whole thing, you would probably miss it. I muscle the board out of the way and set it aside. The dig tunnel is completely dark. Quiet. Empty. I knew it would be, and yet I've got this creeping feeling that there are Florencia thugs inside, crouched in the dark, guarding the place. I take a breath to calm down and shine my light into the first chamber. No one's here. I duck inside. Lexi follows.

"This is amazing," she says, awed. She runs a hand along the wooden beams at the entryway.

We walk all the way to the end, to the last chamber. There is some serious equipment inside. A concrete saw up on a platform, an empty wheelbarrow, and a long row of shovels and pickaxes, as well as the boxes of explosives I saw the last time I was here. Some of it must be for the vault floor. Seeing it all somehow makes the job more real. My heart starts accelerating in my chest, hammering hard core. I want to be on the other side of this. I want to know it turns out okay. I look over at Lexi and watch as she runs her hands over the dirt walls like she can determine where the tunnel is weakest by feeling it.

"You should attach the rope here," she says, pointing to one corner of the beamed entrance to the space. "Tie it around this beam. Then we can bury the rope inside the dirt. You'll have to wait down here for Soldado to show during the job. Hide behind this wall. When he does come, you and Benny pull the beam out as fast as you can, and all this dirt will come crashing down. My team hides in the tunnel system here. Once Soldado passes by and once we hear the collapse on your end, we'll bury the front end of this thing and he'll be trapped. The tunnel should remain intact at the center, so he'll have plenty of oxygen until the cops discover him. Less if he has anyone with him."

I want to tell her that she and her team can't do this part of the job. It's way too dangerous. But I can't. There's no one else. Thinking about her down here, watching Soldado walk by, being close enough to him that he might discover her . . . it makes my gut clench.

Very carefully I dig around the beam where she pointed and slip the rope around the thick wood. Together we bury the rest just above the beam, packing the dirt in tight.

"So how exactly did Soldado get you to do the bank jobs?"

I throw her a look, and she holds up her hands surrender-style. "You don't have to tell me, but what does it hurt if you do? You read classic lit and have a full scholarship to UCLA."

How does she know? I frown at her and she laughs.

"I have a hacker for a brother, remember? If it's online some-where, he'll find it. You graduated with a four-point-one GPA. Impressive. That smart, and the only way any of the jobs you've done makes sense is if you were forced."

I shouldn't tell her, but standing here in front of her, so close together, I want to. I want her to know the real me. And I can't seem to stop myself from confessing.

"How much do you know about gangs?"

"Only what I've seen on TV. And from seeing them on the streets. I guess the first things that come to mind are graffiti, tattoos, and drive-bys."

"Okay, so next to nothing. Basically, every inch of LA is counted as some gang's territory, right? All of them vary in terms of power and connections. Some are upstarts trying to make a name for themselves. Some are offshoots of larger powerful gangs, and even though they have their own lead dude, usually if they're connected, that lead dude answers to other higher, more powerful dudes. That's how it is with Soldado. He's Florencia Heights, and so he is under the Eme. The Mexican Mafia. The Eme is ruled from jail, but they have emissaries on the streets. Soldado is one. He runs our neighborhood, collects taxes from all the businesses for the Eme, and supervises drug dealings for his territory. If someone owes money to the Eme, he collects. Forcibly. Soldado was supposed to do that with my dad when he gambled away the money the Eme loaned him. But because Soldado and me were tight"—I nearly choke on the word—"he offered me a way to make good on the debt and keep my family safe."

She stares at me wide-eyed, as if she's really seeing me for the first time.

I don't know what to say, so I walk toward the front of the tunnel and get busy rigging the beams there, too.

After a moment she comes up behind me and puts her hand on my back. The heat from her palm warms up my shoulder blade and sends a tremor through my chest.

"All those jobs. You did them for your dad?"

"I did them for my family. Mainly my mom and Maria. My dad is a screw-up. If it were only him? I don't know. I wonder sometimes if I still would've done the jobs."

"You would've," she says, her voice full of certainty.

"Let's get out of here," I say, because the conversation's gotten too serious, and this close to the job, I don't want to think about all of this.

When we come out of the tunnel, I can hear fireworks, the familiar thumps, booms, and whistling sounds ripping through the sky. It's only July 3, but because the Fourth lands on a weekend, there are lots of fireworks displays. It's nice. Leaving the darkness of the tunnel and finding this. I take in a few deep breaths, glad for the fresh air, and look up at the sky. We're surrounded by buildings, so all I see is a narrow patch of sky and the tail end of a red-and-blue explosion. "Come on." I grab Lexi's hand, and before she can protest, I lead her to the fire escape on the building opposite us. I pull down the ladder and we climb, floor after floor, until we reach the top. It's an old warehouse with a sign draped across one side, just beneath the roofline, advertising new condos coming soon. Suddenly the sky opens up. Breathless, we walk out into the middle of the roof. To our right, giant flowers of neon blue, red, pink, and green light bloom before drifting over our heads and fading. I can see tiny remnants of them—dark black bits of ash—rain down around us.

"What is it about fireworks, anyway? They're just explosions—lights—and yet every time I see them it feels like magic." Lexi lies down on the roof, arms pillowing her head, legs sprawled out. God, but she's beautiful under the neon glow. I stare at her a minute, and then I lie down next to her so that our shoulders are touching.

"The last time I really watched them I was about five years old," I say. That was maybe the last time I remember Dad being completely sober. I could feel bad about it, depressed or whatever, but with Lexi next to me, the whole memory is far away, so distant it barely stings to think about it.

A red planet made of sparkles and ringed in white appears over our heads, and the momentary quiet is ripped apart by a thunderous boom I can feel in my chest.

"I'd forgotten how amazing this is." Lexi turns on her side to face me. Her eyes are lit up like the sky, and her lips parted the slightest bit. I want to take her hand and hold it in mine, to trace the lines along the center of her palm with my finger and kiss the inside of her wrist. I want to sink a hand in her hair, pull her close, and kiss her again, this time when no one's watching, when there isn't an ulterior motive behind it.

"What?" I ask, half mesmerized by how close she is, by the beachy coconut scent of her skin.

"Why did your parents stop bringing you to the fireworks?" She rests her cheek on her arm and watches me.

I turn my face toward the sky again because it's easier to keep it together if I'm not looking at her. Coming up here was impulsive and a mistake. We can't complicate things less than twenty-four hours before the job, no matter how much I might want to.

"Dad started to gamble . . . and drink." I hesitate. "Can we not talk about this right now?" I ask.

"We have a lot in common, you and I," Lexi says softly. "Both our dads are screw-ups, and we're on a mission to save our families, whatever it takes." The fireworks finale finishes up with a deafening onslaught of explosions, each one more grand than the next, until the whole sky fogs up with smoke and the ghosts of the fireworks themselves.

In the darkness that follows, she tells me about her dad and how he was arrested and why. I'm surprised at how little anger she seems to have toward him. It's like she's taken all her hurt and anger and directed it at this Harrison guy to distract herself from dealing with her dad. I know this game. Hell, I've played it myself. Avoidance for the win.

"Do you want to keep talking about this?" I ask.

She rests both hands on the flat plane of her stomach, and I can't help noticing that her shirt's ridden up slightly so that a narrow line of skin shows just above the top of her shorts.

"No, I don't want to talk about it. Or anything right now." When she looks at me now, there is that same want in her eyes from before, that day we kissed.

"So what do you want to do?" I ask, getting closer.

"I want you to kiss me," she whispers, her voice soft as she reaches up to touch my cheek with the backs of her fingers.

So that's exactly what I do.

37
Lexi

"I need an intervention," I say to Whitney and Elena as we enter the parking garage near the Bloc outdoor shopping plaza. I glance at the little booth farther down, where the sole security guard is housed, to make sure he's still looking down at his cell phone. He is. We're doing just fine so far. Our mission is to snag a decent getaway car for Monday. Cue the *Mission: Impossible* music. Except the only thing set to destruct around here is me. The closer we get to the job, the more I can feel myself starting to panic.

"For what?" Elena asks.

"I've gone and kissed him. Twice." I don't have to say who *him* is. They both know.

"Ah ha ha, I knew you would! Go get it, Catherine!" she says, nearly clapping her hands. "How was it? Is he Thomas Crown–worthy?"

"Dangerous," I say. "And, yeah, he's definitely Crown-worthy." I can feel myself blushing, so I get busy pulling on my gloves and double-checking my pack to make sure I brought everything we'll need.

The twins do a silent squeal and quietly high-five each other.

"Don't celebrate. This is screwed up," I say. "How am I supposed to like a guy I can't trust? Who says he won't try to pin it on us? I'd do it to him. I won't jeopardize us for a guy."

"Cut the crap—you won't double cross him," Elena says.

"I would," I insist.

We walk past the elevators and go deeper into the garage. There's a shadowy area toward the far corner with a couple of cars that look promising.

Whitney grabs my arm and spins me around. "Hey. I know you. You try hard to put up this front like you're coldhearted, like no guy can get close to you, but that's a lie. Can you trust Christian? I don't know. Risk is always involved, Lex. But what's the alternative? Never fall in love?"

And this is maybe the best thing about having friends like Whitney and Elena. They push me to face my fears. Still, I can't shake this free-fall feeling in my gut. I've had it ever since that first kiss out on the sidewalk by the bank. And it terrifies me because the thing about falling is that sooner or later you are going to hit the ground.

"So which one?" Whitney asks, deliberately changing the subject because she must realize how tense I am.

Both girls eyeball me like I have some kind of sixth sense about what car we should try to take. I don't. They all look the same to me, which is to say they look locked and intimidating, nestled in their parking spots, their windows dark and their engines quiet, like mousetraps set to snap at the slightest touch, taking fingers when they do.

Whitney pulls out her phone and consults the website she already has queued up, the one that gives a step-by-step guide to breaking into cars. Christian gave us a tutorial back at the beach house, but I like having the information at the ready just in case. God bless YouTube. The only way it could be better is if the information downloaded directly to your brain *Matrix*-style. "First we need to check for hidden keys—on tires, tucked into magnetized boxes stuck to the underside of the cars. Oh, and don't forget to just try opening them."

We trot in between the cars, stopping to look for keys, try doors, peer in windows. Row after row and no keys, no unlocked doors. Either we're in a particularly cynical neighborhood or that information is mostly wishful thinking. Maybe it's even a trap to catch amateurs. I glance around the parking garage, nervous now, feeling watched. Of course, we could be. I didn't see any security cameras, and we picked this lot specifically because there aren't supposed to be any, but that doesn't mean they aren't there.

"The kit, gimme the kit," I say to Elena as calmly as I can, but my heart is a pogo stick in my chest, leaping up and down against my ribs.

I take the tow kit from her and start pulling out the tools: a wedge to jimmy the door open and a sticklike thing to unlock the lock once I do. We've been practicing at home on our own cars, all three of us, timing ourselves to see how quickly we could get in. After more than fifty tries, we're down to less than a minute each. It only occurs to me now that we didn't rotate around and practice on each other's cars, not just our own. Basically, unless I spot my parents' BMW sedan in one of the rows, I might be in trouble here.

We walk up and down the rows once more, this time looking for a car similar to the ones we practiced on and when that fails, one that's old enough not to seem intimidating. After discussing a few, we settle on a nondescript white Toyota Corolla with a set of multicolored bead necklaces hanging from the rearview mirror and a bumper sticker that reads SOMETIMES I WRESTLE WITH MY DEMONS. SOMETIMES WE JUST SNUGGLE. It's the perfect combination of ordinary and old.

"Okay, this one, then," I say as I examine the passenger side door for the best spot to place the wedge.

"Wait. Why do you get to do it?" Elena asks.

"Because . . ." I can't think of a good reason.

"If we're doing the driving, we're doing the breaking in—or at least I am." Elena holds out her hand for the wedge.

"You brought us on to help, so let us help," Whitney says.

I hesitate, not because they don't make sense, but because I'm not ashamed to admit that I like to be in control. I'm less nervous that way.

"Give it up, Lex," Elena says. "God, it's so insulting when you hesitate, like you're the only person capable of taking care of things."

"Fine. Here." I hand her the tools. Now all I want to do is get out of here. "Just hurry."

"Hey, *fast* is my middle name, okay?" Elena says, then freezes. "Wait, that came out so wrong."

Whitney and I crack up, and Elena smiles. "Cut it out or I won't be able to do this." She gets to work, placing the wedge and then working it back and forth until the doorframe is warped. She slides the tool that unlocks the lock into the space the wedge created. I watch it wobble through the car's interior, down to the armrest on the door. It takes her multiple tries to get the thing positioned directly above the button that unlocks the car. One, two, three, four times she misses. Five excruciating minutes later, she finally lines everything up and presses the button. There's a clicking sound as the tool hits the button dead center. All the doors unlock, and then she's opening the driver's side door and slipping into the seat.

I look down the length of the garage to make sure we're still clear, my ears straining to hear the slightest noise, my skin tingling with the effort. It's dim, and every shadowy patch has me concerned. Could someone be watching us? I walk to the end of the row and peek over at the elevator. No one's there, nothing's changed. So far we're okay. Still, when a tractor-trailer truck whizzes past the garage, I can't help startling. The sooner we're out of here and on the freeway, the better. The whole plan could fall apart right here.

"Hey, wake up, Lex. Hand me the computer thingy." Elena leans out of the car to get my attention. The wedge that's been lying on the seat beside her falls out of the car and lands on the concrete with a clang so loud it makes my ears ring. The resulting echo seems to go on forever. I stiffen, and so do the twins, each of us staring at the others, horrified. The security guard up front—there's no way he couldn't have heard that.

"We should forget this and go," Whitney says as she swipes the wedge from the ground and starts stuffing it into my backpack.

"No, get in the car and get down!" Elena hisses. Whitney and I dive into the backseat at the same time, nearly smacking heads in the process. She lies across the seat, and I stuff myself into the narrow floor space. Elena shuts the front door and ducks under the steering wheel. We stay as still as we can, breathe in short, quick breaths, and try to make as little noise as possible. In the garage we can hear the echo of footsteps coming from the elevators and getting closer. I watch the window, fully expecting to see the security guard's head appear at any moment. I have this overwhelming urge to sit up and get it over with. Wondering when he'll confront us is excruciating. I see the arc of a flashlight beam travel over our car and the ones beside us, illuminating the insides for a few seconds but not stopping. A moment later the footsteps move away, fading. To be safe, we stay put for ten more minutes anyway, until both of my feet have fallen asleep and my neck is cramped. Just to be sure.

"Okay, let's finish this." I hand Elena the drill and she sticks it into the ignition to drill out the pins inside. Even though the sound isn't loud, it's enough to jangle my nerves.

"Come on, come on," Whitney murmurs.

"Crap!" Elena fiddles with the drill. "Okay, you two, out. I can't get this with you both breathing on me from back there. Your nerves are tweaking my nerves."

I set the screwdriver on the seat next to Elena so she can insert it into the ignition once the pins are all drilled out. Whitney and I crawl out of the car. Then we each walk the garage in separate directions to keep a lookout. It's taking too long. Any minute I expect someone to walk through the garage: the owner of this car or another. It's so late it's not likely, but with every minute that passes I become more convinced that someone will show up. By the time we get back, the car is running and Elena is leaning on the side of it, arms crossed over her chest, looking mighty pleased with herself.

"Say it," she whispers, looking from me to Whitney and back again.

"No, no way," Whitney whispers back.

"Say it!" Elena demands.

Whitney rolls her eyes and exhales heavily. "Fine. You're a rock star."

"And a goddess, don't forget that bit." Elena grins.

"And a goddess. You are such a pain in the butt when you're gloating, you know it? Can we go now?" Whitney opens the passenger door, banging it into the car next to the Toyota, and suddenly the entire garage is alive with the blaring howl of the other car's alarm.

"Crap!" I say.

We all dive back into the car. Elena throws it into gear before we've even managed to shut our doors and peels out of the parking space and down the ramp, the tires screeching almost as loudly as the alarm. She stomps on the accelerator and we literally launch out of the garage, all four tires off the ground for a half second before the car slams down and connects with the road again. We barrel down the street, all of us screaming our heads off.

We stop screaming somewhere between the next two intersections and the freeway, but we don't talk for a while, each of us too stunned to think of anything to say. I watch the road behind us from the backseat, hoping not to see a row of police lights trailing us, but feeling like it's a distinct possibility that they'll appear at any minute. We're accelerating up the freeway on-ramp before I finally let out the breath I've been holding. We did it. Holy freaking crap, we did it!

I slump back against the cloth seats that reek of cigarette smoke and floral perfume and try to get my heart to stop convulsing. Soon we will be helping the Romero Robbers rob LL National. This is really happening.

Up front, Whitney and Elena are still silent, recovering.

"Well, that could've gone better," I say after a while.

Elena dissolves into hysterical giggles. "Whitney, when you

hit that other car with the door . . . Your face!" She struggles to breathe. "Wait until the guys hear."

"No. We aren't telling them! I don't want them to think we couldn't handle this one job on our own."

"We won't," I say, relief making me want to laugh hysterically, too. "What happens in the parking garage stays in the parking garage."

38

Christian

I wanted to make sure she was okay. That's why I followed Lexi and her friends to the parking garage. Plus, I wanted to see her one last time before the job. After that kiss on the roof, I haven't been able to stop thinking about her. The way she felt in my arms. The way I felt having her there. I thought something shifted between us—like maybe she was finally letting her guard down a little, letting me in. Thinking I could be with her had me convinced that my luck had finally changed. Yeah, Soldado was a problem still, but I had her and we had a plan. Looking into her eyes on the roof, I felt like it could all work out.

Lexi's words echo in my head, tear at my gut. "Who says he won't try to pin it on us? I'd do it to him. I won't jeopardize us for a guy." I slip out from behind the elevator where I've been hiding. She won't trust me, so I can't trust her. This job has to happen, and I need her to help me pull it off. All this other stuff, whatever I thought was happening between us, is just a distraction. Benny, Eddie, Carlos, and I can't collapse both sides of the tunnel, and she has to let us out of the vault. We need her team.

I wait a beat and follow the girls. The way they're moving through the garage . . . it's too unsure. They look suspicious. Part of me hopes they get caught, but mad as I am, I can't let that happen, so I get as close as I dare and keep watch over the front of the garage. I can still make out the guard station. As long as he stays put, they should be all right.

It takes them forever to settle on a car, but once they do, I'm relieved to see that it's an old Corolla. Smart. I'm almost impressed—until they drop their tools. I check on the security guard. He's on the move. Headed this way. He'll catch them for sure. Cursing, I scramble down the row of cars to my left and head for the opposite corner of the garage. I take out my tow kit (I wanted to have it in case they needed help) and reach for the crowbar.

Smash!

I knock out the driver's side window of the car next to me. The sound is explosive, but just to ensure that the guard comes after me and not them, I smash another window. Then I can hear him, feet slapping as he runs this way. I vault over the low wall beyond the car and hang for a moment. We're up one level from the street on this side of the garage, but not high enough that I can't drop to the ground from here. I let go, land on my feet, and take off.

I double back as soon as I'm sure the guard didn't see me.

Somewhere inside the garage, a car alarm is screaming. It has to be because of them. I jog toward the entrance to the garage, ears ringing, my heart in my throat. What do I do about the guard? They get caught and we're all screwed. But suddenly I see them launching out of the garage like they're in *The Fast and the Furious*.

They got away. But can they on Monday? Not after what I just heard. Not if it comes down to us or them.

Last time I was in these tunnels I was with Lexi. I can vividly remember the sweet mint of her lip balm on my mouth when we kissed. But whatever, I don't even like that flavor. I might've thought I did, but it was just the fireworks—they messed with my head. Trapping Soldado and getting all my boys out of this bank safely is my only focus from here on out.

Our ATVs speed through the main tunnel, kicking up stagnant water so my jeans are wet up to the knees. Even after several trips down here, all of the side tunnels and turns still look the same. I have to pay attention so I don't take the wrong one.

"Turn's up here," Benny calls out. He's half sitting, half standing as he rides the ATV with the stack of duffel bags we're using bundled neatly on the rack behind him. He bounces over a seam and manages to get a little air, his front wheels going up off the ground for a second before slamming back down and releasing a giant spray of water that Eddie has to swerve to avoid.

"You get that nasty water on my face and you're toast, bro," Eddie hollers. He's beyond jacked up because he's never been on the job with us; he's always been outside waiting in the car. The only reason that changed was because Soldado insisted he be a part of this job.

"It's too big for just the three of you. You'll need the extra hands to carry out the loot," he said.

He just wanted us all in one place so it would be easier to take us out.

We navigate the tunnels smooth and easy, arriving at the mouth to our bank tunnel right on schedule. I park my ATV next to Eddie's. I can hear voices. Soldado's diggers are back to finish the job. I stick my gun in the back of my waistband. I've never shot at someone for real. Today I might have to if it comes down to protecting everyone. Can I do it? Pull the trigger? I hope so, but I don't want to have to. I touch my Saint Jude's and say a little prayer. *Please, please don't let it come to that.*

We work our way through the tunnel. With the guys filling up the space, it feels closer than last time. I keep brushing up against the walls. Dirt falls in my hair and face. I try not to look at the spot where Lexi and I buried the rope, because the piece of it we had to wrap around the beam is visible, even though it's nearly the same color as the beam. Anyone who looked closely enough could see it.

"I don't know, man. I can't breathe in here. I got claustrophobia for real. No, no, no, no," Eddie says, gasping. He stops midtunnel and looks back at the entrance. "I gotta go. I can't. There's no way. . . ." He's backed out nearly a dozen times since Gabriel got hurt. But he can't back out for real and he knows it. Being down here with us is his best shot at surviving.

"You have to. Just focus on me, okay? Don't think about it."
Carlos grabs hold of Eddie's shirt and pulls him forward. Usually it's Gabriel who does that sort of stuff. It's weird without him. Unlucky. Off. I wait until they get a little ways ahead before I start walking again. I look back at the tunnel entrance one last time. The last job. This is where it really begins.

We walk the final bit in silence and enter the chamber directly under the vault. Soldado's men are covered in so much cement dust that they look like ghosts. In the middle of the ceiling is the hole they've been cutting into the vault floor this morning. In my head it looked totally different. I imagined it as this neat square, big enough to get all of us into the vault at once, but in reality it's a series of smooth circles that make this clover shape, just big enough to fit one guy at a time. Soldado's guys have a rig-mounted drill positioned right under the hole and are cutting out the last of the concrete. The dust they're kicking up creates a cloud in the room, and we slip on the masks we brought so we can breathe. The room is hot. Like deep-in-the-jungle hot. Unfortunately, the mask doesn't block out the smell of the sweat and general funk.

"How much longer?" I yell so they can hear. They talk in rapid Spanish, and then one guy holds up ten fingers and opens and closes them twice. Twenty minutes. Eddie plops down in the dirt and puts his head between his knees. The tunnel's really getting to him.

Once the concrete's gone, the guys attack the steel vault

floor. The noise is muted by a drill silencer, but it's still loud enough to make me edgy.

Fifteen minutes in and Benny's phone starts ringing. Twitch. He's watching the outside of the bank so he can let us know if the vault alarm's gone off again. It's gone off dozens of times while the guys dug. Each time the cops investigate the vault, it's locked tight. Lexi said that they were blaming the malfunction on the renovation upstairs. Which is good. Exactly what we hoped for.

"Yeah?" He listens for a second, then waves at the diggers. "Bank manager's comin' in with two cops."

The men stop the drill and we go still. Wait.

Ten minutes more go by. We barely breathe, even though there's no way they can hear us this far down. The phone goes off again and Benny jumps, answers it. "They're leaving again. All clear."

"How many times did the alarm go off this morning?" Benny asks the digger closest to him, a guy whose hairline's so low it almost rests on his eyebrows.

He shrugs. "Four. They check the vault and go. That's it." He gets the drill going again and then it's just a few minutes more and they break through.

We start going in as soon as the hole's big enough to fit one of us. I'm up first. I let the boys help boost me up. It's nothing like taking the bank through the front door, the way we usually do. I'm more nervous, for one thing. The guys have to feel me shaking. It's quiet up here. Eerie and pitch-dark. I turn on my head lamp. Benny hands me the duffel with the lanterns, food, and water in it, and I start setting the lights out around the room. Cash is everywhere! Whole stacks of it on movable carts, bundled and shrink-wrapped. So much cash that I can't take it all in. Talking about fifty million dollars and actually seeing it are two totally different things. I didn't realize it'd take up so much space. We might not have the manpower or the duffel bags to get it all out. Some of it will end up down in the hole with Soldado when we trap him, but the rest? The rest is coming with us. We'll need it to keep our families safe until Soldado's in jail and things start to die down.

"Call Twitch. Tell him we need more bags, dude. Like, a lot more bags," I tell Benny, and then Carlos is popping up like some kind of mole from that arcade game, the one where you whack them with a mallet. Only he's a tight squeeze because his gut's so big.

"Ho-ly . . ." He stares, openmouthed.

Eddie's up next, and after we've all done our share of gaping, we get busy. At first we're throwing money into the duffels at top speed, like we're still on a two-minute clock or something. But slowly it dawns on me that we have all day and night before the bank opens again Monday morning. Hours and hours. It feels weird.

I slow down. There's a lot of work, and if we don't pace ourselves, we'll get tired too quickly. Burn out. We're going to need to save some energy for when Soldado shows up. He told us to have the cash ready to move by four in the morning so we could transport it out with plenty of time to get away before the bank opens at eight and the robbery is discovered. Nearly twenty-seven hours from now. That gives us twenty-three to do our work here.

"Dudes, take it easy, we got time," I remind the others. "Let's drill through to the safe-deposit vault. Get the stuff there first, since it'll take the longest, then bag the rest of the cash." I reach into my pocket and fish out the note with Harrison's safe-deposit box number on it that Lexi gave me. Benny makes a hole big enough to set a charge inside and blow the door but not mess up the tunnel or the two vaults.

"Fire in the hole," he says, and we cover our ears and duck in the far corner of the vault. The door sparks, then bows and warps as the charge goes off and the room fills with smoke. I keep expecting to hear the phone ring, for Twitch to let us know that the alarm's gone off again and this time half the LAPD is on the way in. So when he does, I'm not surprised. We sit in the center of the vault, barely breathing, waiting once again for the all clear. At this moment the cops could be less than twenty feet away, separated from us by the steel door and that's it. The only thing that keeps me calm is knowing that the vault can't be opened once it's time-locked.

"Let's go," Eddie says, and he's the first through the door with a crowbar dangling from one hand.

The boys start jimmying open boxes, ruining four for every one they manage to pry out at first because the frame the boxes sit in warps when you pry a box out. I knew it would take time to get them all opened, but I had no idea. It's a good twenty minutes for each box. If we were planning to hit all five hundred, the way Soldado wanted us to, it would take us forever to accomplish it at this pace. I hit Harrison's first. It's the only one I care about.

"Check this out!" Benny holds up a necklace so heavy with diamonds that it's hard to believe it's real. "Think it belongs to some movie star or somethin'?"

"Probably not," I say.

Carlos chuffs. "Man, what does it matter? It's ours now."

"No. We don't take any of this stuff, remember? It's sentimental stuff. Irreplaceable. You really want to do that to someone? This stuff is personal, bro. Family heirlooms. Special gifts."

Carlos sighs. "Yeah, yeah, I get it. The point is to scatter it around, bury a few with Soldado and the boys."

"That way the police can recover it when they get them."

"I know!" he says, not really ticked off but disappointed. I get it. There is a lot of money represented in this room. Maybe more than Soldado estimated. A whole lot more.

I sit down on the floor with Harrison's deposit box. It has a series of files in it and a thumb drive. I flip through the files, but there's no way I can check the drive from in here. The paperwork is nothing special. Receipts for jewelry and hotel rooms. Probably proof he's having an affair, but nothing that'll get him locked up. I pocket the drive. It's what Lexi has to be looking for. Whether it has what she needs is a mystery, but in the end it doesn't even matter. For now it has the potential to be the key to getting Harrison, and so it's valuable enough that it makes a perfect bargaining chip. She won't be leaving us behind in here.

We open box after box and scatter the contents on the ground. Some of the stuff we pack into one of the duffels we'll pass down to Soldado. I stare at the piles and shake my head. What I don't get is the point in having something so valuable that you have to lock it up instead of enjoying it. The stocks and stuff are one thing, but the artwork and the jewels? Why buy them in the first place?

The vaults are ventilated, and normally (according to Lexi's intel) the temperature is a coolish seventy degrees, but with all of us in here working, it's getting hot. I wipe at my forehead and go down to the tunnel to get some water. It's nearly empty. There are just a few more pieces of equipment to be removed. I watch as the diggers pack it into wheelbarrows.

"You outta here?" I ask.

"Sí," the guy closest to me says, his arms slick with sweat and grime. "It's all you now, cabrón."

I glance at my phone. We've been working for hours non-stop. I thought it would feel slow, working for this long, but the time is flying past. I can feel it running out. Soon Lexi and her crew will be down here, getting into position, and Soldado, Twitch, and Psycho will be headed our way, guns drawn, ready to take us out once they have the loot. Just because we have a plan to stop them doesn't mean I'm not panicked.

We finish going through the boxes just after one on Monday morning. The contents of the main vault take only one hour more. Two hours (or less) until Soldado could show up.

"Can we really pull this off?" Eddie asks, his voice quavery. I've just shown them where the two ropes are and explained what will happen when we pull the one on our side of the tunnel. "What if the beam doesn't budge? Or it does, but the ceiling doesn't cave?"

"It'll work," I say with a confidence I don't actually feel. The closer we get, the more I have the feeling that nothing will go according to plan. We could die. I don't want to think about it, but somehow it's *all* I can think about.

We bring a stack of the duffels down and place them in the tunnel, just beyond the chamber beneath the vault, where they will get trapped along with Soldado and the other guys. All we need to do now is wait for them to get this far in and pull out the doorway supports.

We sit just beneath the vault and wait. No one talks. I listen until my ears start to ring. I'm sweating and shivering at the same time. My fingers ache from gripping my gun. Every noise, every rustle of wind and we all startle. It's getting so the tension is driving me stark raving crazy. Sitting here is torture.

And then I hear them. Soldado's voice traveling through the tunnel.

We exchange looks. Benny, Eddie, and Carlos look terrified. I must, too. I feel it. My whole body is on high alert.

"Hey, dumbasses! You up there?" Soldado shouts, cocky as hell because so far everything's gone down exactly as planned.

"Yeah. We're bringing out the bags now. Got some of them in the tunnel already," I yell, and my chest constricts. I don't sound normal. My voice is too tight. He's going to figure it out. Sense it. I look at Benny to see if he heard it, but he's staring at the ground, rocking. Of all of us, he's been the most betrayed by Soldado. He's not hearing me or him or anything, I can tell. He seems ready to throw up.

I can hear footsteps and low laughter—Twitch and Psycho. Probably gloating because they're in on Soldado's plan. Getting some share of the take once they kill us.

"Up there," Twitch says. Psycho whistles. They're all the way in, standing in the section of tunnel where the bags are.

"Now," I mouth to the boys, and together we pull on the rope. It sticks and I nearly scream, but then the beam shifts. We pull harder. It shifts more.

"You guys comin' down or what?" Soldado asks, and there is the unmistakable sound of a gun cocking.

We pull until I think the blood vessels in my temple might explode, and the beam doesn't just shift this time—it flies out of place, slamming to the ground with a vibrating *boom!*

The dirt above it comes crashing down like a curtain. Dust clouds explode into the air, and I have to squish my eyes shut to keep from going blind. It worked! But then, once I see that the dirt is still falling, that it's coming down too hard, I start to panic.

"Get up inside the vault. Now!" We scramble to make it. We boost Carlos up first, and then he helps pull the rest of us up. The chamber is filling up the way an hourglass does, dirt rising like tidewater.

We lie against the steel floor, coughing, dust puffing off our clothes.

"You think we killed them?" Benny gasps, coughing violently.

"It just looked bad. They're okay," I say. The way the dirt was falling, most of it seemed to be collapsing in our direction. Even if some of the ceiling in the tunnel collapsed, there's a good chance that they got out of the way. Now the only unknown is whether Lexi and her friends were able to take care of their end.

I pick up my phone and text her.

The wait to hear back is agonizing. What if Soldado got out? What if he found Lexi's crew? The way he came into the tunnel, I wouldn't think so, but . . . the thought of her hurt or worse . . . my whole body goes cold.

My phone vibrates and I let out my breath in a rush.

We did it. Phase two is on.

I text her back, my fingers shaking so badly I can barely type.

Tunnel down here. See u soon.

39
Lexi

Quinn, Oliver, Leo, and I race for the turnoff where we hid our motorcycles and jump on. I'm buzzing, my whole body whirring like a helicopter, ready to fly. The plan played out perfectly! Our side of the tunnel went down just the way I predicted, the dirt avalanching like something out of a movie. Based on the way the supports were placed, I knew it would work. Still, it was crazy to watch it. Leo, Quinn, and Oliver take off, and I roar after them, leaning into the bike, picking up speed.

"So he's okay?" Leo shouts.

"Yeah. They all are," I shout back.

There is daylight up ahead. I weave past the boys and aim for it. We burst out of the tunnel one by one and take off down the street, cutting off a few early commuters. The city spreads out around us, the buildings shimmering because it's already hot. LL National is right there, partially obscured by haze. The bank is ours. We've done everything according to plan. Now all we have to do is take it.

— — —

Whitney pulls up to the front of the bank at precisely five minutes to eight.

"You guys all set?" Elena asks.

"Set." Oliver slips on his gloves and places his gun in his lap. It's fake. A prop. Just one more thing we borrowed from the twins' dad. It appears real enough, though. Looking at it makes my heart beat faster.

"Okay. Guns out. Masks on. Gloves on. Hoodies up." Elena goes down the list, and I mentally check off each item.

"They're starting to congregate outside," Elena murmurs, gesturing to the handful of bank employees sipping from Starbucks cups.

"Four minutes." Whitney taps the wheel.

"Any sign of cops anywhere?" I ask, leaning up into the front seat.

"All clear." Elena turns in her seat, her face pinched like she might cry. "Be careful. All of you."

"Three minutes." Leo holds up his phone, the countdown timer gobbling up numbers.

The employees in front of the bank—the manager, Stella, two tellers, and a security guard—edge toward the door. Stella takes out her keys.

"Two minutes." Leo again, his voice getting smothered up by his mask.

I slip my own mask into place. Oliver and Quinn do the same.

I feel like I'm burning up, like I might spontaneously combust.

Every inch of my skin is on fire from the heat or nerves. Maybe both.

"They're going in," Whitney squeaks.

"Now!" Quinn gives the order, and like a racehorse reacting to the starting gun, I bolt out of the car, legs panic-nimble, ears roaring, my fake gun smacking against my side as I pump my arms.

Time seems split in two. Some things happen very fast, while others feel suspended. The run seems to take seconds, but the woman walking down the sidewalk toward us doesn't seem to make any progress at all. My breath is fast inside my mask. Chugging like a train. It's all I can hear.

Quinn reaches the door just as Stella opens it. He crashes into her and they careen inside. Oliver goes for the guard, jabbing his gun into the man's back. I take one teller. Leo takes the other. I grip her arm with my gloved hand and move her into the bank. Her mouth is open. Is she screaming? I can't tell. There's just my own breathing, the awful gasping.

The door to the bank closes. With the blinds down, the interior is dusky. Filtered sunlight sends flickering shadows across the back wall and the carpet. I glance over at the stairs to the vault. Christian is down there, waiting.

"Make sure it's locked," Quinn orders Stella before he follows her to the alarm system keypad and has her enter her code to disable it.

"Everyone else, on the ground. Now!" Leo hollers.

Tears stream down the tellers' faces. They fall to the floor. I wince as their knees hit first and they collapse onto their faces.

I zip-tie their hands together.

"Please don't hurt us," Stella says, her voice calm but her bottom lip trembling. She twists her wedding ring around and around on her finger. "Please."

We are monsters. That's how she sees us. Even if we are doing this to get Harrison, she'll never know that. I've crossed a line now; there's no going back. Much as I hate Harrison, how am I any better? Look what we're doing.

I knew what to expect, and yet nothing feels like I thought it would. Robbing this bank isn't a BAM. We're hurting people, but I can't take it back. Say I'm sorry. It's too late for that. The only thing to do is move forward.

"I didn't know," I murmur.

"Focus!" Quinn snaps his fingers in front of my face. "We need to get them into the bathroom. Now."

We walk the two tellers to the ladies' room and zip-tie each of them to the pipes behind the toilets so they can't escape.

"Stay here. You're safe," Leo says. "We aren't going to hurt you."

We keep Stella and the security guy with us. We'll need them to open the vault.

"Five minutes," Leo says.

"You won't be able to rob the vault before the cops show up," the guard says calmly as he enters his access code. "If you're smart, you'll leave right now. You have a chance if you do. Stay and it's over."

"Shut it, dude," Oliver barks, jamming his gun into the man's back even harder.

The minute the lock disengages, Quinn and Oliver drag Stella and the guard back upstairs to the bathrooms. We don't open the vault door until they are out of sight.

I lean against the wall, dizzy. I was hyperventilating. Now I might pass out. Leo pulls the vault door open, and a rush of earthy air escapes.

Christian, Benny, Carlos, and Eddie spill out, their zombie masks collared around their necks, each of them gripping over-sized duffel bags.

"'Bout time you guys showed up," Eddie says, his face ashen, covered in a layer of sand and dirt.

I look at Christian and have this inexplicable urge to cry. I want him to gather me up in his arms and tell me it'll be okay. But that can't happen. The only thing that's important right now is getting out.

40

Christian

"**The bank is already** supposed to be open. We have to hurry," Lexi says. Her voice sounds strained. Frantically pushing her mask off her face, she stares into my eyes like there's something she wants to say or do. I expected her to come at me with her usual swagger, all flirt and confidence. Ready to con me into handing over the flash drive and then somehow trap us down here. Instead, she's ghost-pale. After what I overheard in the parking garage, I was ready to handle the usual Lexi. And best her. But this version has me wondering if underneath it all she's just a girl who's suddenly found herself in way over her head.

Welcome to my world, I think, smiling tentatively at her. I've felt in over *my* head since I started doing jobs. Carlos, Eddie, and Benny rush out of the vault like the place is cursed. It feels cursed. Every minute we spent locked inside with Soldado, Twitch, and Psycho buried less than fifty feet away felt like an eternity. I kept imagining them digging out and coming for us. I haul out two of the four money bags we managed to keep, and Benny and Carlos tote out the others. There are more than twenty more underground with Soldado—not that he'll ever get to spend it. It should be enough to satisfy the cops and keep them from looking too hard for the rest. I'm guessing we've got maybe four million total with us. Still the best haul we've had, and more than enough to get all of us and our families a safe distance from the Florencia Heights and the Eme. We leave behind our guns, wiped clean of fingerprints. While we were waiting for Lexi to come, we stood at the edge of the hole in the vault floor and tossed them down. It felt sort of momentous, like the first step toward a new life.

We shut the vault's outer door. I can hear the lock automatically engage again. I exhale. We're out. Now all that's left to do is leave.

From here the plan is supposed to be simple: we go out through the bank doors that lead to the building's lobby, avoiding the street exit altogether. Both getaway cars are now parked on the bottom level of the garage behind the building. The security guard stationed in the lobby will see us go and call the police, but he won't know what cars we drive away in, not until they check the garage's cameras much later, and by then we'll have ditched the cars and will be long gone. The hardest part of the heist is behind us; there's just the short walk outside now. Five more minutes and my bank-robbing days are over.

Lexi moves so she's blocking our path. "We had a deal. I got you out; now it's your turn to give us Harrison's stuff."

"Once we're outside," I say.

"No, now." She holds out a hand, and her friends gather close. Carlos and Eddie laugh in disbelief. They can't possibly be prepared to physically stop us. *This is going to waste time that we don't have.*

I sigh and drop my duffel, unzip it, and dig out Harrison's papers.

She and Quinn huddle together quickly.

"This isn't it," Quinn says, swallowing hard enough that I can see his throat working.

"That's all there was?" she asks, eyes narrowed.

"We need to go," Leo says, leading us toward the stairway. "We've been here almost fifteen minutes. Much too long. We can't deal with this here."

Fifteen minutes!

"We have to go right now!" I scoop up my duffel bag and grab Lexi's hand. She struggles.

"You want to separate? Trust me to meet you upstairs?" I ask.

She bites her lip and lets me pull her toward the stairs, her hand tightening on mine. I want her close.

We're nearly halfway there when we hear the sounds of shattering glass.

We freeze.

The bank's security alarm shrieks to life, but we can still hear stuff happening. More glass breaking, then pounding feet. The police. Has to be.

Without a word, we turn and run back down the stairs—to where, I have no idea. There's only the vault and the collapsed tunnel. We're trapped. We were so close and it was all for nothing.

I'm going to jail.

We all are.

People say in times like these your life flashes before your eyes, but it isn't true. There is only the sickening, sinking feeling of being caught and the kind of adrenaline spike that prey animals must feel when they're being hunted. They're running with all they've got, but deep down they know it's not good enough. In the end they were always meant to be eaten.

"Oh god, oh god, oh god, oh god," Carlos whispers.

"Shh," Lexi hisses. She jabs a finger toward the end of the hallway before she pushes past everyone to take the lead. I'm not sure if I'm imagining it, but I think I hear people coming down the steps now, the squeak of rubber on marble.

She pulls at a door I didn't notice before, probably because it's the same color as the hallway and the handle is near the floor and opens upward, not out. Hiding might buy us a minute or two, but what's the point? Except when I get closer, I can see that it's a cargo elevator with graffiti-covered walls. I have no idea where it goes or what we'll do when we get there. I just crowd inside with everyone else and wait, panicked and silent, as Lexi shuts the outer door and presses the up button. A second, inner door slides shut, and the thing shudders to life. I can't hear what's happening outside the elevator anymore; there is only the mechanical grind of the lift and the sounds of our breathing.

"How did they know?" Eddie says, his voice high and tight.

"One of the tellers might've gotten loose," Leo suggests.

"I secured the bank people. Oversecured them. There's no way," Quinn growls.

"What does it matter? We have exactly twenty seconds before this elevator opens up on the fourth floor, okay? We can access the parking garage from the exit up there. We'll only be a few levels from the getaway cars. There is one security guy who mans that door. We get past him and we can take the garage stairs to the first floor. The cars will be right there."

"We can manage one guard," I say, more to convince myself than them.

The elevator slows, stops. The door slides open. Lexi pokes her head out. "Clear," she says, and everyone files out of the elevator. The door closes again, and I can hear it start moving down, back the way we just came. Whoever's in the basement below has called it back down. We have a minute—two, tops—before they are right behind us.

41
Lexi

As we hurry toward the fourth-floor exit, I try not to think about how little time we have or about what we might have to do to get past the guard. I just move. Out of the elevator and down the hall. Quinn nearly collides with a woman when we round the corner. She drops the paperwork she had cradled in her arms and screams.

"Get away," Quinn yells at her. *"Move!"*

She takes off in the opposite direction, her feet wobbling as she tries to run full tilt in high heels.

We head for the exit. I can see it now, the glass double doors, the guard, his back to us, a phone cradled to his ear ... and a set of flashing police lights outside. The cop car's just pulled up. The two cops inside haven't seen us, but there is no way we can go out there now.

"The stairs," I say. "This way." I take the lead, turning down the hallway that branches off to the right. The stairs are at the very end. We hurtle toward it. I hit the door, open it. Up or down? Which way do we go? I listen for noise in the stairwell.

If we go down, the only way out of the building is through the lobby, so that's out. Up it is. I start to climb and the others follow. I am leading us now, and it sucks because I don't know what to do. The fourth-floor entrance is the only other one besides the one in the lobby. The most I'm doing is buying us time. Is there a place we can hide? Wait it out? *Think, Lexi, think.* Most of the floors are exactly like this one, filled with LL National employees. People will see us. Even if we could find an empty office to hide out in, the cops will know we're still in the building. Detective Martin will know. I think about those eyes of his, those determined, obsessive eyes. He will scour every inch of this building to find us. There is nowhere we can hide, no hope of escape. My foot slips on the step and I nearly fall. How could I be this stupid? Why did I ever think this would work? Harrison might have screwed my family to save himself, but I've screwed over my friends trying to get revenge. I'm no better than he is. Tears run down my face, tickle my chin.

"Guys, I'm sorry. I don't know. I mean, I'm not sure what to do now." I turn around so I can face them. Oliver is directly behind me. He's still got his mask on, but his aviators are pushed up onto the top of his head. The way his hair sticks up reminds me of the night we jumped off the Bank Tower building, less than two blocks from here. *We jumped.* And all at once I have an idea.

42

Christian

There is a moment when I think that our little trip up the stairway was an exercise in futility, but then Lexi lights up like the fireworks we saw the other night, and suddenly she's not just climbing but bounding up the stairs.

"Where are we going?" Carlos asks, panting heavily. Bet he's regretting all the honeybuns about now.

"Oliver, can we use the trash chute?" Lexi asks. "It's still there. Please say it's still there."

"At the construction site. Yeah. We could. But if the crew's already working . . ."

"We have to take our chances. Or . . . the fire alarm. Can we make the fire alarm go off? Then they'll have to clear the building, right? Crew. Everyone." She's out of breath; we all are. The money bag I'm carrying is making me slower than usual. I look at Benny, Carlos, and Eddie. They're feeling it, too. Twenty extra pounds each we're toting, and there's no good way to distribute it so that it isn't awkward to carry.

"The chute leads down to the bottom level of the garage. Other than that, there's only the elevator that leads from in here to there. You know they have the elevators manned inside the building, so it makes sense they wouldn't have cops in that part of the garage. We lose the zombie gear and the sweatshirts and go out on foot."

"So all we need is to set off a fire alarm, right?" Benny asks, his face slick with sweat. He shifts his duffel bag from one shoulder to the other.

"Basically, yeah. We just need someone to trip the system." Lexi keeps climbing. We must be near the tenth floor by now.

"On it," Oliver says, and he takes the steps two at a time to the next floor. He whips off his mask and hoodie, hands it to Quinn, and heads for the door with this fancy-looking stainless-steel lighter in one hand.

"The construction starts on the next floor up," Lexi says. "We need to get there before the alarm goes off and the stairwell gets crowded with people."

We run full out, not bothering to be quiet anymore and barely make it to the door before the alarm trips. We erupt out of the stairwell. The eleventh floor is stripped down to the building's reinforced-steel frame and concrete floor. There are pallets of building materials and some tools scattered around, but mostly it is an empty shell. Even half the windows are missing, so the floor opens up to the outside. It is crazy hot. July hot.

"Take off your clothes," Lexi orders.

"You picked a helluva time to start flirting," I say, because even panicked and on the run, I can't help it. She left herself wide-open.

Lexi pulls off her hoodie and rolls her eyes, but her lips twitch like she's fighting a smile. "No, I mean all your zombie gear. Hurry."

Oliver's back a few seconds later. "We need to go. Like now. The building's emptying out. It'll be that much easier to find us." He walks toward the far end of the floor to the group of pallets we changed behind last week and rummages around. "It's not here."

"What's not?" I ask, getting closer. I don't like feeling so out of control. I'm depending on Lexi and her crew to get me and the boys out, and I'm still not entirely sure we can trust them to, especially now when leaving us might buy them time to get away.

"The winch. It's not here." He runs a hand through his hair. "I had a rope and winch to get us down the chute. Otherwise . . ."

"Otherwise . . ." I lean forward. "Otherwise what?"

"We have to slide down the chute."

"Okay. And?" Lexi asks.

Oliver messes with his lighter, flips it open and shut. "And it's eleven floors up. That's a long way to go. We go down too fast and the impact at the bottom is gonna suck. We can't exactly flee the scene if we've all got broken bones. We need something to slow us down."

"We're at a construction site and there's no rope? No. No way. There has to be something." I start walking around, moving stuff.

"Electrical wire. There's a whole roll right there. Help me get it over to the chute." Quinn grabs hold of the wire spool and starts to drag it toward the chute. I grab the bottom of the spool and we go faster. There is noise coming from the stairwell. Voices. People from the upper floors evacuating the building. Most likely the construction crew, since, according to Oliver, they're working several floors up. But also office workers. Possibly even police.

Oliver examines the wire. It's narrow and coated in rubber. There's not much to grab on to.

"There's not enough time for us to go one at a time, but I have no idea how much weight this can hold," Oliver says.

"We either take our chances or go downstairs and turn ourselves in right now," Lexi says.

I think about what it would be like to do it. Just walk up to the police and confess the way I would at church. Excuse me, sir, but I have sinned. . . . With Soldado caught, it doesn't seem like that bad an idea. I'm so tired of doing jobs and covering my tracks. Coming clean might be a relief. But then I look at Benny. His mom is dying. If he goes to jail, he may never see her again. Carlos and Eddie will just end up caving to the Eme to survive and becoming carnales—sworn brothers, in for life. We've managed to avoid getting jumped in all this time. It wipes away any temptation I have to come clean.

We wedge the wire spool between a set of steel columns and start unwinding it, feeding it down the dark mouth of the chute. The wire snakes inside. I can hear it bouncing around.

"We have to go down at least two at a time, maybe three." The spooled wire runs out, and Quinn takes a nail gun and shoots at least a dozen into the end of the wire, securing it to the spool.

"I'll go first," Oliver says. "To make sure it's safe."

"Why should you be first? I'm the heaviest; it should be me." Carlos puts his duffel bag straps over his shoulder and heads for the chute, but right away it's obvious that both he and the bag won't fit inside together like that.

"You're going to have to send the money down separate," Lexi says.

"No way I'm leaving this up here with you all. No offense," he says, looking at me for backup.

"I'll go last. Make sure the money makes it down to you," I say.

"We alternate. One from your crew, one from ours." Lexi's eyes meet mine. "We'll both stay."

Carlos thinks it over and then reluctantly squeezes himself into the chute and lowers himself until he's hanging from his hands. He grabs hold of the wire and makes the sign of the cross on his forehead, since he can't exactly do it on his chest. "Here goes nothing." We peer in. It's narrow enough that he can prop his back against it and walk his feet down the other side. At first it looks easy, but as he lowers himself deeper, the chute gets steep, and I can hear his shoes slipping. His biceps flex as he struggles to hold on. Little by little he disappears from sight. I check my watch. Slowest getaway ever. No way we're getting out of here at this pace.

"Someone else needs to go." I look pointedly at Oliver.

He queues up. I hear a helicopter outside somewhere, the rhythmic sound of its blades slicing through the air. I can't see it, but it must be nearly directly overhead. "It is armpit-humid in here," Oliver complains, scrunching his face in disgust before he disappears by degrees, first his chest, then his chin, then his nose. We stare at the end of the wire, at the many nails holding it to the spool, and at the spool itself, snugly wedged against the steel columns. I can see the wire move when he moves, the gap that's starting to form at some of the nail points.

"Should we try one more?" Eddie waits for me to tell him what to do.

I glance at my watch and jog over to the side of the building that faces Figueroa. The sidewalks are packed with police, police vehicles, and curious bystanders. Officers are still heading into the building, and several others are looking up, examining the outside. I finally catch a glimpse of the helicopter, *LAPD* in bold lettering on the side. "I don't think we have a choice." Lexi comes to stand by me.

"There are a lot of people down there. It's perfect." She grins, and then when I look at her like she's nuts—because clearly she is if she thinks a whole departmentful of cops below us and crawling through the building is perfect—she adds, "We can blend in with the crowd. Especially once we split up. After you give me whatever it is you've got of Harrison's. I know there weren't just papers in that box."

I'm not surprised that she knows, only that she's waited this long to bring it up again.

The wire strains against the nails as Eddie goes in. By now Carlos should be at the bottom, or close to it.

"Okay, Lex, I want you to go—" Quinn doesn't get to finish his sentence because there's more noise in the stairwell. He looks at me, eyes wide. He's standing next to the chute, the money bags at his feet. He lunges for the tarp that's covering a pallet full of tiles and covers up the bags as the noise gets closer, louder. It's people talking. Cops? Construction crew? The noise stops, and the door shakes as someone leans up against it. The handle moves.

Quinn looks around frantically for somewhere to hide, but he's stuck. The door is between him and most of the eleventh floor. He gives Lexi and me one last look and jumps feetfirst into the tunnel, catching hold of the cord with both hands, and half slides, half lowers himself out of sight. Leo and Benny take off for the other side of the floor, the part that's blocked off by plastic sheeting. They duck under it and disappear.

There's a tarp-covered pallet behind Lexi. I drive her to it, and together we slip underneath and lie side by side so my mouth is right next to her neck. I slip my arms around her because there's nowhere else to put them—the space is too tight—wincing as the tarp rattles. The door opens a breath later. We go still.

"Just let me grab my water, man. I'll be quick." A guy walks

346

out of the stairwell. I can't see him, but I can hear him. Lexi presses herself even closer to me. Now my lips are touching her neck. She shivers when my breath hits her skin. I can't help myself. I run my lips down to the collar of her T-shirt, just once before I go still again. She inhales, and I can feel her arm break out in goose bumps against my arm. Every part of me is aware of her, the way her body rises and falls as she breathes, the way her shoulder fits into the crook of my arm. We're on the run from the LAPD and about to escape LL National through a construction-site trash chute and I still can't ignore the way she makes me feel.

"Hurry up!" someone else says, farther back, still in the stairwell maybe? "We're supposed to be outside."

The first dude rummages around. I study the edge of the tarp and watch a pair of construction boots flash past. I'm not nervous he'll find us, exactly, but I can't help tensing when the tip of one boot moves the edge of the tarp. "Got it."

I wait for him to notice the spool or the wire leading into the debris chute, but he doesn't say anything.

"Come on!" Stairwell Guy says, and the guy standing near us takes off toward him.

"Hold your horses, I'm comin'!" The two men continue to talk, but it becomes muffled because the stairwell door closes.

We wait, ears straining to see if we can hear anyone. One minute becomes two.

"I kinda wish he'd stuck around a little longer," I say, my voice low so only she can hear.

"Me too," she says almost shyly.

That's it, I can't stand it. I might never see her again, and there's just all this time that we've wasted playing games and dancing around whatever it is that's between us. I'm not wasting this one last moment. I shift so I can turn her to me. I stroke the side of her cheek, sink my hand into her hair and kiss her. She grabs my arm and presses herself to me. Her mouth opens and the kiss deepens. I make a noise low in my throat because I don't want it to end, but we're out of time.

"You can come out," Leo says in a stage whisper. I lift up the tarp and he's right there, Benny next to him, grinning like an idiot. He winks at Lexi and she blushes. Benny just shakes his head and gets back to it.

He leans into the chute. "We should do the bags next." He uncovers them and puts one into the chute. I start to object, because if Quinn or anyone else is still in the chute, they're about to get a twenty-pound cash torpedo to the head, but it's already sliding down, and then he's sending the next one down and the next and the next. Four bags in, like, four seconds.

"I guess it's me now, right?" Leo sits on the ledge, his camera pointed down, taking an up-close selfie of his feet. He slips the camera around his neck and gets into position.

"Quinn's going to be furious that I didn't go next," Lexi says as Leo disappears. She straightens her T-shirt and puts one hand on the back of her neck like she's still thinking about me kissing it. She won't look at me, though. She knows I'm still holding on to something Harrison-related.

Benny clears his throat. "Okay, so my turn, then." He climbs into the chute and grabs the wire. I look back at the spool where the end of the wire is nailed and notice that it's coming apart at the end. Several of the nails have caused it to split into two and come loose. There are maybe seven nails still holding it in place, but it's only a matter of time before the wire frays past them. "Benny, the wire," I warn.

"I know. I know," he mutters as he starts to lower himself.

"'So it is down to you and it is down to me,'" Lexi says in this dramatic voice.

"Huh?"

"*The Princess Bride.* You know . . . 'Inconceivable!'"

She's babbling. Nervous now that it's just us two again.

"The movie. Tell me you've seen it. Come *on*. Best. Movie. Ever."

"Never heard of it."

"Well, okay, it *is* pretty old, but it's on TV all the time."

"So you're surprised that I haven't seen a decades-old movie about a princess and a wedding?" I raise an eyebrow. "Because I look like the kind of guy who's into that sort of thing?"

"Well, the fact that you like chess is surprising. And you read Shakespeare and Cormac McCarthy."

"*No Country for Old Men* is a gangsta book, know what I'm sayin'?" I joke.

She grins. "I wouldn't know. I've never read it."

The helicopter we heard earlier is back, hovering over the bank, reminding me that as much as I don't want it to be, this is goodbye. At least until the heat dies down from this job. If it dies down. It's my last chance to just come clean and give her the thumb drive. She held up her end of the deal, just like she said she would, but I still can't bring myself to do it.

"So it's your turn." I hold out my hand so I can help her in.

She takes it and starts to climb in but then stops, looks at me. "If we'd met some other way, do you think . . . do you think things would've been different between us?"

I look into her eyes and really consider it. "Absolutely." I tuck a piece of her hair behind her ear and let my fingers trail her cheek. "Definitely."

Every girl I've ever been with has had to go up on tiptoe to kiss me, but Lexi and I are pretty much evenly matched, eye to eye, so all she has to do is lean in. Her lips are soft on mine, sweet. I pull her closer, hook one finger into the belt loop of her jeans, and she reaches around and sticks her hands in my back pockets. At first I am too distracted by the kiss to know why my brain starts sounding an alarm, but then I remember the thumb drive. Too late.

"Hey, that's—"

"Mine," she says, depositing it in her pocket. "You think I'd go to this much trouble to get into that deposit box if I wasn't absolutely sure about what was in it?" She slips into the debris chute. "Goodbye, Christian."

I watch her start down the chute, and I can't think of one thing to say to explain why I kept the flash drive as long as I did. I'm watching her leave, the same way I did that night when she jumped on my car, and like then, I have this overwhelming feeling that I shouldn't let her go. I make a move to head into the chute after her when something slaps the back of my leg and disappears into the chute.

Oh my god! The wire!

43

Lexi

The farther I get away from the top of the chute and Christian, the more my heart hurts. I don't want this to be goodbye. For the first time ever, I don't want to walk away, and ironically, for the first time ever, I don't have a choice. There was no other way for this to play out. I blink back tears. I can't cry. Not here. Not yet.

I am halfway down when the wire goes from taut to suddenly slack. Panicked, I quickly try to wedge my feet and hands to the sides of the chute, but it's too narrow for me to get a good hold. I have a slow-motion moment when I realize I'm screwed, and then suddenly I am falling, my body ricocheting off the chute walls. I tuck my arms tight to my sides as I pick up speed, trying to minimize any possible injuries. My head smacks into a ridge in the tunnel, and my vision blurs for a second. Then there is just pain and the horrible gut-clenching free fall that makes my stomach feel like it's lodged in my throat. The chute curves a little, coming up under me more like a slide. My shoulders and hips ram the sides, and then everything evens out and I'm going down on my back and dropping out of the end of the chute. I nearly land on my feet, but then my foot slips on some construction debris, my ankle twists painfully, and I end up on my hands and knees.

"Are you okay? Nothing broken?" Quinn helps me out of the Dumpster and dusts me off.

He's talking about the ride down, and while it hurt, finding Harrison's thumb drive in Christian's pocket hurt worse. I mean, I knew he had to have it, but knowing and seeing aren't quite the same things. Seeing means you can't rationalize something away. He kept the drive for one of two reasons: as insurance or so he could sweeten his already large take. Maybe both. Probably both. After all his talk about not wanting to rob banks, it turns out he's a natural at it. Knowing it was a mistake, I let him get too close, and now the only part of me that's broken is my heart.

I test my ankle. I can put my weight on it, but it feels tight.

"Think you can run if you need to?" Quinn asks.

"Yeah," I say, and hope I'm right.

Shake it off, Lexi, I tell myself. *You have what you came for. Your friends are okay.* Today was a victory.

"The wire came down with you. How's he goin' to get down?" Benny asks, the frayed end of the wire in his hand, his face tilted up as he stares at the chute.

Well, it was a victory for *my* team, anyway.

44
Christian

When the wire snaps off the spool and goes careening into the chute, I go cold. Lexi's been inside less than a minute; she's still too far up, the fall too steep. I lean into the chute's mouth and call her name. I can hear movement, can feel the sudden vibrations in the chute, and I know she's being bounced around inside, but she doesn't call out, not once.

I stand up, pace. What if she's really hurt? How do I get down there to find out?

I need more wire. But there isn't any.

Come on!

There has to be something. I race around, lifting up tarps, inspecting pallets.

Wait.

The tarps.

I pull the one off the spot where less than ten minutes ago I kissed Lexi, and I drag it over to the tarp that we used to cover the duffel bags. I start to tie the ends together, but it's slow going. My hands are shaking hard-core. I take a breath and will myself to calm down. Finally I have a workable knot. The tarps are long—probably not long enough to get me all the way down the chute, but maybe close enough that I don't bust myself up.

I take the nail gun and nail the tarps to the spool, using a sick amount of nails, knowing full well that under my weight, the tarps will probably start tearing away the minute I head into the chute.

There is noise coming from the stairwell again. The rhythmic sound of many feet. I'm out of time. I grab the end of the tarp and make a run for the chute. The stairwell door starts to open. I shove the tarp inside the chute and jump in after it, sliding a bit before I'm able to get a good grip on the tarp. I peer over the edge of the chute in time to see the stairwell door swing open and LAPD's finest crowd through the opening, guns drawn.

"Don't do it!" the cop leading the way yells, peering into the chute, trying to get a good look at me, his eyes flashing, his gun raised. I have time to think that he has the whitest hair and the bluest eyes I've ever seen, and then I scramble down the chute, hand over hand, feet slipping.

I'm feeling good, moving fast, when the tarp begins to shake and I feel myself being pulled back up. I keep climbing down, but I'm not making the same progress. And then suddenly I'm out of tarp and there's nothing else to do but fall.

From there it is a manic jumble of hits and hurts as I bounce my way through the chute, pinballing back and forth, falling,

falling, falling. It is both a long and incredibly short trip, and the only thing going through my head is *I don't want to die. I don't want to die. I don't want to die.*

I hit the curve in the slide and it slows me down a little, especially when my elbow impacts and gets stuck, wrenching my shoulder, maybe dislocating it. I cry out in pain because if I don't scream, I'll throw up. I rocket out of the end of the chute like a torpedo and slam into the Dumpster. The sound is a thundering *boom* that echoes through the parking garage.

I scramble out of the Dumpster. My shoulder is screaming, but I can move it, so it's probably only sprained.

"Cops. They're up there. We have to go. Now. *Now!*" Lexi's crew, my crew, all of them are staring at me, horrified. *"Go!"* I yell, and this finally snaps them out of it and they jump to. Quinn, Leo, Benny, and Carlos shoulder the money bags.

We run for the far wall, where there is an exit door. Up above us I can hear the screech of tires, a police siren, the sounds of people coming. I think about how much Carlos, Benny, Gabriel, and Eddie like that *Heat* movie and am really scared—for real this time—that we're about to go out the way they always imagined. Hail of bullets, money exploding out of the duffel bags, falling through the air like snow.

The money's going to slow us down. We don't have minutes before they're here—we have seconds. And how far are we going to get with giant black duffel bags this close to a bank?

"We have to dump the cash," I yell.

"No, bro, there's gotta be . . . we can't . . ." Eddie looks ready to lose it.

I get it. I can barely stomach the idea. All this work, all this risk, and we don't get anything to show for it?

"Would you rather go to jail?" I say, and then as if to drive this idea home, I see police lights reflecting on the wall behind us.

"Do it!" I shout, and everyone drops the bags.

I can see the top of the police car now, coming down the ramp. I take one last look at the bags, at all that money, and go.

I can't tell if I'm about to laugh or cry.

We explode out of the garage and into sunlight so bright it's blinding. We're in an alley behind the garage. Miraculously, it's empty, but it won't be for long. We need to get as far from the bank as we can, as quickly as we can, without attracting attention.

"We have to split up. A group of eight people running down the street attracts too much attention," I say, panting because I can't seem to catch my breath. My head is pounding after the beating I took in the chute, and my whole body is racked with pain. Lexi seems okay. She's limping, and there's a long friction burn on her right arm, but that's it. We share a look. I don't think she expected me to leave the cash. There's a lot to say, but I'm not going to get the chance to say it. This is goodbye. I'm losing everything I want in the space of a minute.

"We come out the end of this alley and we disperse in twos," Quinn says, taking charge because I've let myself get distracted by Lexi and the money.

"It's been real, gentlemen," Leo says. "Oliver."

"Good luck to all of us," Oliver says, and then he and Leo take off down the alley and disappear.

Carlos and Eddie go next. Then it's just Quinn and Lexi, Benny and me.

"Our turn," Lexi says. "Sorry about the money. Good luck, Christian." She looks ready to say more, but Quinn throws her arm over his shoulders, and with his help, she runs.

"It was all for nothing," Benny says, staring at the pavement like he's still seeing the duffel bags back in the garage.

Except it wasn't. Soldado, Twitch, and Psycho are still under the bank, and now that the money will all be recovered, there's nothing linking us to this job. There is the Eme to worry about (maybe—unless Soldado exaggerated their involvement) and the rest of Soldado's boys, but given the heat that's surrounding this whole thing, chances are good no one will come after us. At least not right away.

"Let's go," I say.

Benny and I take off, running from the bank as fast as we can. And the funny thing is, as sad as I am about saying goodbye to Lexi, I'm excited, too, because for the first time in a long time, I have no idea what comes next.

45
Lexi

Most of the time when I leave a guy, I get a sense of release, but not this time. Running away from Christian makes me feel more tied up into knots instead of less. I think about the last moments we were alone together, the way his lips felt, the way *I* felt kissing him. It was like jumping off the bank building times a hundred, simultaneously peaceful and violently exciting. It's that feeling of knowing for certain that something is so right it actually takes your breath away.

Quinn and I run only as long as we are safely hidden in the narrow alley, and then we force ourselves to walk, to amble like we don't have a care in the world. And we don't. We have the thumb drive, and I know, I *know* that the evidence we need has to be on it. Harrison's private offshore accounts—given how much money was lost during the mortgage crisis and knowing that less than a quarter of it was traced back to my dad—he has to have them. All that's left to do now is transfer the funds, which is a whole lot easier and less conspicuous than toting giant black bags from a vault.

I'd gloat except I don't feel like it. Christian left the cash. He ended up with nothing. And he didn't try to take back the thumb drive. I got it all wrong. I'm the one who couldn't be trusted. Christian had no choice but to leave the bags and walk away. I'm the one with all the choices, and I'm starting to realize that all I want to do now is make the right ones.

46
Lexi

After the excitement of the heist, watching Quinn transfer some of Harrison's funds into the account he created was anticlimactic. A few taps of the computer keys, and according to cyberspace and the Central Bank of the Bahamas, we are fifty million dollars richer—sort of. We've decided most of it should go to the victims of the mortgage scam. I want to right what few wrongs I can.

Getting Harrison into trouble, however, was much, much more satisfying. The thumb drive contained not only all his off-shore account information but a trail of complicated bank records that linked the mortgage program to a well-known vacation-club operator. Turns out lots of the mortgages my dad and Harrison were approving were for time-shares in that vacation club. Harrison was getting a kickback from the club's owner, as well as bonuses and profit off the mortgages themselves. We didn't even wait twenty-four hours before we put the thumb drive into an envelope and anonymously mailed it to the FBI. It wasn't twenty-four hours more before he was being dragged out of his house the way my dad had been dragged out of mine. And because the records make it clear Harrison was the one who had orchestrated the fraud, my dad got offered a plea deal to testify against him. Dad will still get jail time, but nowhere near as much. Harrison, however, is another story.

As for the bank, the police found the tunnel and managed to dig out Soldado, Twitch, and Psycho before they suffocated. They went straight to jail, which probably wouldn't have been that big a deal for Soldado—after all, he'd already sworn allegiance to the Mexican Mafia, so going to prison would almost be like getting a transfer to headquarters—except apparently they found out he'd been fudging the numbers on all the jobs Christian and his crew did for him so he didn't have to pay all the gang taxes his "brothers" required. He was dead in his holding cell before the sun came up the next day. Then a week later, Twitch and Psycho, too. It wasn't on most of the news programs, but there was this tiny piece in the *Los Angeles Times,* most of it about the perils of gang life and the Eme's reach. I wonder all the time whether Christian feels bad that Soldado and the others didn't make it, considering how much trouble we went to in order to keep them alive in the tunnel, or whether he's just too relieved to care that much. With all three of them gone and all the stolen money accounted for, it looks as if Christian and his boys will be 100 percent free—as long as all of them remain legit.

So what this means is that the LL National job doesn't appear to be a job at all. There was no money missing, no safe-deposit box items gone except for most of what was in Harrison's lover's deposit box, and it isn't like either of them will ever speak up about it. The FBI might figure it out, but by the time they do, the account we transferred it to in Angela's name will be closed and the real Angela won't know anything about it. As for Detective Martin, he watched Christian and his crew for the better part of the summer. After investigating Soldado, he had a hunch they were the Romero team. But two days ago there was a bank robbery on the outskirts of LA. The robbers hit as the tellers showed up for work and cleaned the place out and then shot and killed three of the five tellers. I'm guessing Martin reprioritized his cases.

Life is slowly returning to normal. Quinn and I start our new school next week. Principal Weaver tried to get us reinstated, but in the end, the board and most of the parents didn't want us—or, more precisely, Dad's scandal—tainting things. Bianca had to leave, too. Mean as she is, I feel sorry for her. Her friends didn't stick by her the way Elena, Whitney, Leo, and Oliver did for Quinn and me. I think about going to see her. Maybe sometime soon I will.

Now there are only a few loose ends to tie up: getting money to the mortgage victims without giving ourselves away—a BAM-worthy feat—and to Christian.

I sit in the car, watching his house, waiting for him to walk with his family to church. I haven't talked to him since the day of the heist, and he hasn't tried to talk to me. Not that I thought he would. With Martin watching him so closely, revealing any sort of connection between the two of us would have been a bad idea. Now that so much time has gone by, I'll admit I don't know what's better for him: to try to see him and tell him I still care or to just let him go. But I do know what I want.

And there he is. I watch Christian open the front door of his house and walk outside with his little sister on his back. He does a giddyup and she squeals and grabs hold of his neck. His mother and grandfather are behind them. I don't see his dad, but then again, he doesn't go to mass. He's probably passed out inside the house like every other Sunday when I've driven by and thought about breaking in.

Seeing Christian is like poking at a wound. I shouldn't do it. It'll never heal if I keep this up, but I can't seem to stop. His hair is still wet from the shower, and his dress shirt is tight across the shoulders and chest so that I can see the outline of his muscles. I'm too far away to see his eyes, but I can still remember them clearly, the deep brown shot through with bits of gold. I watch as he rounds the street corner and then he's gone.

I get out of the car, shoulder my backpack, and head for the house. I walk around to Christian's bedroom window, where the iron bars I dismantled are still leaning against the side of the house. I can't leave what I brought in the mailbox or by the door, so I use tools to jimmy the window and slip inside. The whole house smells spicy and warm because Christian's mother has already prepped the afternoon meal. I listen for his dad, but there is nothing, no sound other than the hum of the refrigerator.

Christian's room is exactly the way it was last time. Everything in its place. I wrestle the box from my backpack and stare at it for a minute before I set it on his pillow. On my way out I notice his stack of books, a nearly complete collection of Cormac McCarthy and some random others: *Lord of the Flies, The Catcher in the Rye.* And then I notice it: tucked among them is *The Princess Bride.*

47
Christian

Someone was in the house. The moment I come in my room I can feel it, even before I notice the box on the bed. The air inside feels disrupted somehow. Off. And besides, the window's cracked open. I close it and then shut and lock my bedroom door. Sitting on the edge of the bed, I stare at the box for a second. It's from her. Somehow I know, and for some reason I can't quite bring myself to open it. Probably because it feels sort of formal. Final. But then, if I don't open it, I'm just going to obsess about what might be in it. It's heavy. I tear the top off and dump the contents.

Three thick stacks of plastic-wrapped one-hundred-dollar bills fall out, along with a letter addressed to me.

Christian,

Your cut of the real take from the thumb drive. One million dollars in unmarked, clean bills. Buy yourself a whole lot of doughnuts. Maybe someday you'll get a maple bacon one and think of me. —Lexi

I stare at the money and the note. I don't know what to feel. It's more than enough to start over. I didn't know what was on the thumb drive, but I suspected. What I didn't expect was for her to share it.

Someone starts pounding on the door. I take the money and shove it back in the box and then tuck the whole thing under my bed. "Yeah?"

"It's us. Open the door," Eddie calls, and knocks nonstop until I do.

"Dude. Calm down," I say as he barges past—Benny, Carlos, and Gabriel hot on his heels.

"Did you get any mail today?" Gabriel asks, his eyes brighter than I've seen them in years.

I stare at him. "Yeah. You too?" Five million dollars. One mil for each of us. I can't wrap my head around it.

"So what do we do now?" Carlos asks, dumbfounded.

"Anything we want!" Eddie grabs Carlos by his enormous shoulders and laughs. "Anything we want."

Benny walks over to my bookshelf and picks up the book lying on top. I hadn't noticed it before, but it's out of place. I always put my books back underneath, on the shelves, spines out.

"*The Princess Bride*?" He raises an eyebrow and grins at me. "Getting in touch with your feminine side?"

I take the book. Some of the pages are bent, tucked in so that the book falls open. Circled in black is one sentence: "Her heart was a secret garden and the walls were very high." Beside it, Lexi has written in the margin: *I wish you would scale them.*

48

Lexi

We haven't done a BAM since the heist. Not that Leo and the others haven't brought it up. It's just that I haven't felt like it. I don't want to forget about what happened with Christian: the kisses we shared on the roof and during the heist, the doughnuts and chess—even that day at the Griffith Park zoo. I thought I was immune to all this sappy sort of stuff, but all I want to do is hide in the house with a container of Ben & Jerry's and binge-watch chick flicks. Somewhere along the way, I went from total badass to total mess.

But today, after weeks of listening to them beg and plead, I finally let Quinn, Leo, Oliver, Elena, and Whitney drag me out of the house for a maneuver they've planned without me. They're calling it a celebration, but I don't feel much like celebrating. Christian and his crew have their money. We have ours. The only thing I don't have is him. He read my note and maybe found what I wrote in the book, but he hasn't come around or called, and so it is officially and totally over. Now all I need to do is figure out a way to move on. It used to be so easy to do, but I think I've forgotten how.

I went into this whole thing to steal back my family's life, and for the most part I did, but what I never counted on was that along the way I'd have something stolen from me. My heart. God, it sounds melodramatic, but there it is. Christian stole my heart even if he didn't mean to.

"So what are we doing?" I ask.

"You'll see when we get there," Leo says. He puts an arm around me, and I rest my head on his shoulder.

Elena and Oliver are up front. Quinn decided to take his motorcycle. I watch him drive by with Whitney behind him, her arms wrapped tightly around his waist. It's almost twilight outside and the sky is filled with pastel light. We drive out of the city and toward the canyons. Oliver's playing some audiobook on learning Japanese, and he and Elena are laughing and repeating the Japanese words for *cup* and *fish* and *hello*. Now that Oliver's got the money to leave, he's decided to actually do it. In a few weeks he is going to Japan to live with his mom. Since he's nearly eighteen, he won't have to worry about his dad making him come back. He says if he likes it he might stay for good. Elena is planning to visit over the winter holidays from school. Our group is gradually going to start drifting away. Oliver now; Quinn after this school year, when he heads off to college. Leo, Elena, Whitney, and I will graduate the year after, and then we'll be off to college, too. Tonight might be the very last BAM we do together.

We park down the road from an extreme-sports place that does tree obstacle courses and zip-lining. It's closed up for the night, but after bank robbery, it is no big thing for us to scale the fence. And tame as it is to break into this place, after all we've done, the thrill level feels just right. We put on the head lamps Quinn brought, but we don't turn them on until we are next to the obstacle course. I shine mine up at the trees and the rope course.

"Got room for one more?" Christian comes up behind me in the dark. My heart squeezes. I don't have to shine my light in his direction to know it's him; I'd know his voice anywhere. I slip the head lamp off my head and shakily set it on the ground.

"I didn't know you were into this sort of thing," I say, trying to play it cool, but in the end I can't. A big, silly grin spreads across my face. *He's here.* After so many weeks it almost feels as if we're meeting for the first time.

"In scaling things? You could say I'm a recent convert." He holds out his hand. "I'm Christian, by the way. I don't think we've met." Obviously, seeing me again is strange for him, too.

I laugh because this is silly and I feel silly, but I also feel wonderful. He wants to start over. Can we? After everything that's happened? After all the things we did, or almost did, to each other?

I wouldn't have left him the note if I didn't believe it.

"I'm Lexi." I hold out my hand.

We shake, and then he brings my hand up to his lips. My friends make noises behind us, cheers and gagging sounds.

"A little privacy, please?" I pretend to glare at them and they busy themselves with climbing, all except Leo, who holds up his camera and snaps a picture just as Christian scoops me up and spins me around.

The way he looks at me—for a moment I can feel that old familiar panic, the animal-like instinct to run because it is too much, I feel too much, but then he takes my face in his hands and leans in to kiss me.

The night we met I jumped off the US Bank Tower downtown. As exhilarating as it was, it was no match for this moment, this kiss. I'm hanging off the edge without a parachute, trusting him to catch me before I hit the ground. Given what I've known about love and all the ways it can go wrong, it seems like a reckless and crazy thing to do, but suddenly I can't seem to stop myself. I close my eyes and let go.

Acknowledgments

Many thanks are due to the incredible Random House Children's Books team. I am lucky to work with such creative, dedicated people. It takes a village to make a book, and I am so very happy you are mine.

To my editor, Chelsea Eberly, who is always just a phone call away. Thank you for all the patience, care, and attention you've given to this book and to me. I enjoy working with you more than I can express!

To Caroline Abbey, who gamely took the time to nudge me in the right direction early on.

To Elizabeth Tardiff for the brilliant cover. You captured the essence of Lexi perfectly!

To Barbara Bakowski for your genius copyediting. I'd still be lost in the revision stage if not for you.

Much love to my agent, Lucienne Diver, who is my own personal superhero. Thank you for believing in me and having my back. You are more than an agent. You are a very dear friend.

To Stefanie Marks and Shann Keckler for helping me work

on the bank-related bits. Every technical thing I got right is thanks to the two of you.

To the YA Chicks: Vivi Barnes and Christina Farley. One of the best things that has come out of this whole writing thing is meeting you both. Here's to many more years of crazy adventures!

Shout-outs to my GFA girls: Michele, Ruth, Amy, Lori, Corinne, Kim, Natalie, Gemma, Deborah, and Stephanie. I'm honored to be sharing the journey with you all.

Enormous gratitude to my early readers: Tara Gallina, Stefanie Marks, and Jennifer Baker. You waded through a messy draft and inspired me to dig deeper.

To my parents; Tom, Erika, Lauren, Kiersten; and my in-laws. Your love and support mean the world to me.

And finally, to my husband, Jay, and my two daughters, Samantha and Riley. You have given me the ability to pursue this dream of mine, and I love you all to the moon and back and back and back.

About the Author

AMY CHRISTINE PARKER is the author of *Gated* and *Astray*. She writes full-time from her home near Tampa, Florida, where she lives with her husband, their two daughters, and one ridiculously fat cat. Visit Amy online at amychristineparker.com and follow her on Twitter at @amychristinepar.